Caught up in You

Wartime Druid Saga, Volume 2

Shawn McGee

Published by Assetstor, 2023.

CAUGHT UP IN YOU

First edition. June 5, 2023.

Copyright © 2023 Shawn McGee.

ISBN: 979-8215530115

Written by Shawn McGee.

Chapter 1—The Patio

RACHEL SQUIRTED ME with the hose. The neighborhood dogs jumped around and played in the water flow. Most would be mad being wet in forty-five-degree temperature in late November, but I was barefoot and stood on Earth. Being a druid, Earth Power flowed through me and kept my body temperature fine.

We washed my competition orange Mustang, maroon F800GT, and Rachel's loud blue GSXR on my front lawn. A quick leap over her bike let me tackle her. I wouldn't do this with most girls, but she was as strong as I, and trained me in martial arts. She and I were like peas and carrots. Our therapist called us codependent with abandonment issues. I didn't know about that; it's just we couldn't really function without each other.

I stuck the hose into the side of her bathing suit, and she screamed in laughter. The dozen dogs jumped onto and round us, barking in the joy. Even some of the neighborhood cats jumped around.

She pushed me off. "I'm freezing. You need to make a circle now!" Her laughter kept going as she ran to turn off the water, while I drew a circle.

Like I was the Druid of the Spring Fey Court, she was the Bard of the Spring Fey Court. She could use my circles without initiating them. I'd made thousands of circles before Old Donnie let me use one for real and I could knock one out in seconds. After I popped my trunk, I grabbed a spare honeysuckle twig. If I were to make a circle in my font yard, it might as well be usable by me in emergencies. I drew a six-foot diameter circle and a six-foot six-inch circle from the same center point.

I'd been at this house too many days this week and the grass was green and the southern elderberries trees were blooming three months early. This new circle was next to a small flower garden with the annuals beginning to bloom. When I cleaned today, the front yard would be even prettier. The circle stayed hidden in the grass, though, so there was one benefit to a lush lawn.

I used to think circles were useless until I initiated them. Rachel used my uninitiated circles when she became a bard. My circle powered, and the ground became warm. The warm ground and the sunny sky made it feel like Spring.

Rachel grinned. She'd been practicing using her minor powers without making faces or moving her hands.

Rachel and I were Realized. This means out of the billions on the planet, we were not only part of the small number that had the spark, we actually used our power that normal people called magical. She was a specialist and a bard. She could learn a few things better than any human could, but she was incompetent in most other areas. The caveat to this was our co-dependence. If she had been around me recently, she was like a high schooler. Without me around, she was like a fifth grader. I became smarter with her around, but not that much.

We both dried off, and I cast *Local Nature* from my Earth Domain on the front lawn to remove the soap and other impurities from our washing. The minor spell removed all non-natural items from plants in a small area and made it easier to use druidic magic.

Rebecca's car pulled into the driveway while we enjoyed the warmth. She drove her red convertible with the top up on a sunny day. What a waste. I'd have my top down today.

Three women exited the car. Rebecca was the beautiful blonde woman who dumped me a few months ago. Her blonde hair flung around with her practiced head turn, which highlighted her face with the golden hair. "Parking cars on grass. You really are high class." She teased me with a huge smile. I wasn't high class, but she was from high falutin' Old Virginia money.

Madison got out after her. She'd become even less of a free spirit this week with her red hair cut traditionally and no more 'bohemian' clothes. I chalked up these changes to issues since we rescued her from a demon last week.

Lastly, Nicole strode around the car. She and I dated for a hot minute, last week, and I screwed it up in record time. She's Rachel's sister and Rachel wanted us to try again.

Rebecca got a look at us around the cars. "What are you two doing?" exclaimed Rebecca. She laughed because Rachel and I acted like goofy kids despite our twenty-four years of age.

"Sis, did you forget to tell Corey we're taking over his bedroom for a girl's only meeting?" Nicole laughed as well. Dang, she had redone her bronze highlights in her hair and it popped in the sun... not that I was checking her out—well, maybe a little.

"Oh Corey," said Rachel. "There's a girl's only meeting in your bedroom before our group meeting." Rachel grabbed a towel and dried off. She yelled to the others. "I told him."

It was hard not to laugh with Rachel laughing so hard. "If you four are taking over my bedroom, I'm calling it the hot girl's club!" I joked.

"Everyone says you're too big for your britches and you prove it every time I see you," said Madison.

It's a good thing she became generic looking because her Appalachian accent was enticing, and the other two women had it so I couldn't find my rear end with my hands in my back pockets.

My next-door neighbors called for their dog, Pigskin, and I used my Animal Domain to tell the dogs and cats it was time to go home so we didn't get into trouble. All the dogs barked and took off for home. Many of them jumped fences to come visit me when I was outside. Some of my minor powers included healing animals, so some of them came for more than just a talk with me.

The four women walked into my house, and I moved the motorcycles and my car into my carport. My driveway was going to become full shortly. Rebecca's red Audi looked positively dirty next to my competition orange GT Mustang.

I pulled the hose toward her car, but Miles and Trish drove up. I was out of time to wash her car. Miles drove his red GT mustang. He finally won the battle to keep his car instead of both of them buying an SUV. They'd had a difficult time a few months after Trish became pregnant. I knew I wasn't ready to be a father, and I was proud of them for working through the issues. They weren't done yet, but they kept at it.

It must be getting close to the time for our team meeting. His parents watched their store, <u>Miles Away From Town</u>, since it was business hours.

I waved. "Hi Trish. You're late for the hot girl's club meeting in my bedroom."

She grabbed her baby bump and laughed. "Do I still count with this tummy?

"You're hot enough for two!"

She laughed and waddled towards the front door.

"Dude, that's my wife!" He laughed. Miles stood six-eight and was a foot taller than his blonde pregnant wife. He was over three hundred pounds of solid muscle. If you didn't understand fighting, you might have thought he could take my six-one, one-eighty butt—especially when you saw my long hair.

You'd be wrong. Miles was a bit out of fighting shape. Even if he was in fighting shape, I was a druid standing barefoot on Earth.

Still, he had the spark and the class of hunter. He and I had been friends since ninth grade. I jumped up and hugged him. "Good to see you, man."

Nathan and Wesley drove up in Nathan's new white Beemer. I don't know why Preacher Jon insisted we change out our old cars for new ones, but none of us complained.

Wesley still had a shell-shocked appearance, so I kept a smile on. I brought him to a gargoyle banishing yesterday and didn't realize he was terrified until it was over. Not a pleasant introduction to my primary job.

The four of us ambled back to my patio in the back yard. "Sausage party on the patio!" I joked.

"We don't get a lot of these," said Nathan.

Miles looked around at the landscaping I'd done this past week. "Dude, you've done work this week. The rocks and grass look great."

I had a patio and a moon shaped strip of yard fifteen feet wide around the patio and the side of the house. The rest of the backyard was traditional woodland for the Southeast.

"It's the first time I've had since Spring." The last three months were brutal—the kind people our age should not need to endure, but there was no sense in belaboring the point. It sucked for all of us and was going to keep sucking until New Year's Day.

More to the point, I was still lying to myself—well, trying to. I could see through myself easily, so I'd kept as busy as possible. We started bulking, so I worked out every day and recovered with Earth power. I'd study my druid spells and then found yard work to fill in the free time.

There was a lot of stuff I was supposed to deal with, and I preferred to ignore everything.

I jumped over the new rock wall next to my patio. The stack of wood next to the firepit ran low, and I added more wood. The black metal screen kept the sparks contained. With the ladies inside, I sat in one of my favorite Adirondack chairs and faced the natural woodland area. I added Don Juan climbing roses to hide the fence behind it. I kept them blooming year-round, since you'd need to be in my backyard to see them.

With the sun out, the temperature was barely above forty degrees. Earth Power could sustain me in the lower temperature, but if I wanted people over, I needed the firepit warming up the patio stones. The thermometer said the patio temperature was sixty-five.

Wesley sat and held himself by the firepit, while Nathan prepared my grill. They were Matheletes back in high school and had successful brain degrees and stuff. I didn't have those kinds of brains. I had the brains that could love and could fight.

"Oh Corey," said Nathan. He walked over and handed me a fistful of stuff. "Here is a new phone for you. I put your music on it and bought you some wireless headphones."

Nathan controlled the budget for the Southeast Territory of the Realized. He took care of the technological stuff and knew mechanical and technological stuff made little sense to me. Plants, animals, druid magic, and fighting... those things made sense.

"Thanks, man!" I gave him a high-five and tried out the music. This was some crazy computer stuff. I put unwired doodads in my ears and would have thought it was witchcraft, but when I heard the Georgia Thunderbolts, <u>Lend a Hand</u>, it must've been some ancient Earth Power because it was perfect. Despite my happiness, I stowed it away for later.

Miles sat next to Wesley. He must have noticed Wesley's glum face and Miles was the guy who wanted to help everyone. "Hey Wesley, Corey brought you to your first gargoyle banishing. How did you like it?"

"Fine." He sat pale and silent. At least he stopped shaking.

The banishing had been normal. I made a circle, used the information from the <u>Abernathy Book of Gargoyles</u>, and summoned the gargoyle from the Realm of Darkness. Like normal, my torc lit up red, the world changed to black and white, and I banished the creature with a normal spell. The supernatural creatures thrashed, howled, and screamed at my bindings for the full ten minutes of the spell, but it was easy to get rid of.

Apparently, an eight-foot-tall gargoyle with razors for teeth, skin made of granite, and three arms with foot long claws lunging for us and threatening to escape in order to rend him to pieces disturbed Wesley. I had been bored and didn't notice he cowered and shook until I asked him if he enjoyed the show.

Miles put his arm around him. "Don't sweat it. I wet my pants on the first one I saw, and I won't let Trish see one yet."

"Hey Wesley. Rachel is in my bedroom with the hot girl's club. She's been looking forward to seeing you." They recently started dating, and neither had much experience. I hoped he'd smile.

"If you're out here, you get no credit for saying there are a bunch of hot girls in your bedroom," joked Nathan. He started scrubbing my grill in order to cook the food I prepped earlier. Ever since he and Madison hooked up his confidence had grown a thousand-fold.

My grill was as well-used as a grill could be since I cooked every meal on it. Nathan never got to grill, had a weird color fixation with foods, and asked if he could cook for these events. I was happy to let him.

Wesley finally spoke a full sentence. "I—I know when everyone dies."

That was a bummer of a power, because I remembered one of Old Donnie's stories. I tried to make him happy. "Dude. You're part of the Realized now!"

He didn't look ready to celebrate. "You have two dates oscillating—December nineteenth and over ten years out. If it's over ten years out, I get no more details." He shook. "Everyone else except Rebecca is over ten years out and she is December nineteenth too. Priests blast you with blue magic, while a man in a red shirt holds Rebecca, and another in a suit slashes her throat."

"Nice. Do you want your burger medium?" asked Nathan. He pulled out a five-pound package of ground bison.

"Corey, you're screaming trying to get to Rebecca until your skin melts." He started shaking again.

This was disturbing. Church magicians used blue lightning magic. When it hit you, it was like your skin caught fire and someone tried to put it out with a hammer. We appreciated Nathan being on the ball and making Wesley comfortable with his new power.

I kept it lighthearted too. "No worries, it's oscillating, right?"

"If you walk back to the bedroom, you and Rebecca change dates to over a dozen choices," he said. Then he put his head in his knees.

"Corey," called Rachel through the sliding glass door. "Come join us, please."

I swaggered and added, "looks like Rachel saved my life."

"I'd still be scared to go back amid the ladies," joked Nathan. He would know since Rachel and Nicole were his sisters.

Chapter 2—The Ladies

I jumped through the sliding door where Rachel took my hand and skipped. When we touched, I felt complete. Her bodybuilder muscles looked out of sorts skipping, but her joy was infectious. I skipped with her and she giggled.

We entered the bedroom, and the ladies were sitting all over my bed. Rebecca sat in her spot when we dated. She tucked her tan skirt neatly under her legs and she looked incredible. Rachel jumped up and sat next to her sister, Nicole. Technically, they were cousins but grew up as sisters since birth.

Rachel had put on jeans and a t-shirt. Nicole had on a Christmassy outfit. Few of us had good childhood memories, but she tried to be more festive than the rest of us.

I ruined my relationship with Nicole by jumping to conclusions and wanted a fresh chance. However, the ladies had a good point. I didn't know what I wanted in a relationship, and they told me none of them should date me until I got my act together.

Good thing I avoided dealing with that this past week.

My king size bed had the green wool blanket pulled back, and they pulled the comforter over the sheets and pillows. The comforter was a reminder of Old Donnie. His last lady, Nosey Kim, had taken a bunch of his pictures from when he was a roadie for Grinderswitch, plus a bunch of southern rock album art and put it on cloth patches. She sewed these all together and made a comforter for me. I started calling her Miss Kim after that and now I keep her up on the gossip. She's a good woman.

Trish sat in the only chair in the room, held her baby bump, and grinned. The new lady, Madison, sat next to Rebecca—where I used to sit to kiss Rebecca. Yep, I was a mess.

"We are going to make your life easier if you can help us out," said Rebecca. She smiled like she read my mind about us kissing.

It was strange to see Rebecca take the lead here. Trish and Nicole had more dominant personalities. Rebecca wasn't a pushover, but she chose her places.

"You don't need to promise anything. I'm alive because of multiple members of the hot girl's club. I would do anything for any of you." Rebecca, Rachel, and Nicole stood out most recently at the battle of Chattanooga.

"Stop calling us that," said Rebecca. "We are teammates." She laughed. I bet I was the only one who would get away with calling them that name.

"Okay, sexy blonde team member," I teased. I was glad I was over her breaking my heart. She was so much fun to be around.

"We'll call you Sexy Pecs Norwood," teased Rachel.

I flexed. "Do I have to pay you to call me that in public? How much?" I was winning the teasing, and it felt good.

"Don't get him started or he'll be riding a donkey to kiss a girl," said Rebecca.

I don't know why she made fun of me for that. That's how she taught me how to shoot.

"We should console Wesley. He had a rough go of it yesterday and his Realized power is rough."

"Not yet," said Nicole.

"Wesley's upset?" asked Rachel.

"Yeah, I tried to help—"

Rebecca cut me off dead. "Corey. Pay attention. We will help Wesley after this."

She used my first name and the time we dated taught me I knew I needed to straighten up if she called me Corey instead of honey.

She smiled at my attention and continued. "It's almost time for the meeting, so we'll skip the playing. We need you and Nicole to get over your dustup, announce you're back together and officially dating."

Rachel grinned. She almost jumped up and down, waiting for me to say yes.

I wasn't quite ready. "Whoa, slow your roll. Just last week, you said I needed to get my act together. You even said I couldn't date either you or Nicole until it was. I promise, my act is still not together."

All five women laughed. That made me feel no better.

"Geez, Corey," said Trish. "Take the gift. You get a free do-over with a woman you adore."

"Slow down, I need to think." I had just had contact with the Earth. I scooped up the biggest of the ladies, my codependent friend Rachel, and sat next to my closet door to think while we hugged.

"What's the problem, you goof?" asked Rachel.

"It sucks hurting people. I don't even know if I love myself yet." That was the truth. Nicole was so much like me. I yelled at her about the stuff I hated about myself. You know, like an idiot. "Plus," I looked up. "I seal all of you to the cross for this piece of information."

"Whoa," said Rebecca. She scooched over to Rachel's old spot to get a closer look at me. I'd used this line twice before with her.

"Old Donnie told me to never murder if we could help it, and even though I've been a killer, —" I paused to say this slowly. "Killing Bishop Pedrotti was the first human I've killed."

"That explains why you've been working nonstop since the battle," said Rachel. She pulled her head back and looked at me while she grasped me with her left hand. Then she hugged me.

"Look, Old Donnie taught me how to kill, and when. I knew I'd have to do it someday, but Old Donnie said it would change me and if it didn't, well, something was wrong. I've been dealing by pretending nothing happened the past couple of months." Shrugging was impossible because Rachel held me so tight and she was nearly as strong as me.

"Shit." Rebecca never swore. "Corey, we are going to have to help you deal with both items, but we need you to do your man-up thing."

Twice she used my name. This was big. "Tell me why. I need something to help me think."

Rebecca was ready. They had practiced this. "Preacher Jon has been fighting off the other areas to marry one of his kids off and the Delta Territory is making a big push for Nicole," continued Rebecca. "We want to end this, and having a lover's dust up should not mean Nicole becoming property."

Whoa. That was a good reason. I looked at Nicole and thought of the earring that blocked thoughts off to empaths. I still wore the earring because the church had empaths looking for me. The earring blocked very little right now. I blocked off all thoughts about Rebecca. With Nicole being such a strong empath, I could communicate with her with a strong thought. *Be honest with me, without them hearing. If you want to pretend to date to stay safe, I would do anything for you.*

She nodded with a slight tear in her eye and slipped off my bed and kneeled next to Rachel and I. She leaned over her sister and kissed me softly. She whispered, "if you'd do anything, then let's give dating another chance."

I made the mistake of looking into Nicole's eyes and fell into the gray mist.

"Two more pieces of information," said Rebecca. "I am giving up my chance to get back with you because while I can partially lose you, I cannot stand to lose a friend. Having friends is new to me, and getting you back, but losing Nicole would devastate me. Corey, are you listening to me?"

The third time, but I guess this was a big meeting. I tore myself from Nicole's eyes. My heart cracked when I heard Rebecca's voice. We had been close to getting back together. We also still loved each other, and my heart ached for her when I lay in bed alone at night.

"Hold on. One more thing, the hot girl's club is going to have to help with. Nicole spent her energy the past two years finding her parents' killer. Bishop Pedrotti is dead. She is primed to fill herself up with me and to quote Old Donnie, 'that ain't healthy.'"

"Corey, that's sweet," said Trish. "You say you haven't thought about it, but you know all the problems you can't solve on your own."

"He's right too," agreed Madison.

"Dammit, Corey, why do you make this so hard?" Rebecca wiped a tear from her eye. "The six in this room will help you realize killing in warfare differs from murder, help you with your abandonment issue, and help Nicole fill the huge hole in her life she has from succeeding in her parent's killer facing justice."

"That should be enough for you," said Rachel. She gave me a solid punch in the right arm.

I rubbed my arm. "Yes. I am down with rekindling the relationship with Nicole."

Rachel stood and pulled me up. She pulled Nicole off my bed. "You two give an actual kiss and let's see if the spark is back."

I stepped forward, and she took my left hand and pulled it around her waist and stepped into me. My right hand slipped up her back and played with her hair as we both leaned in. I pulled her bottom lip with my lips. We pressed in and our tongues tentatively reached into each other's mouth. The vision of our first kiss in Chattanooga mixed with a vision of us swinging on the cabin porch.

Miles knocked on the wall and poked his head in. "You're already kissing someone? You told me you'd take it slow for a few months."

He had me there. Nicole and I pulled back from each other. I remember she was an empath, and she had shared the visions with me.

"Chill out Miles," said Rachel. "These other women call him Sexy Pecs Norwood behind his back. He doesn't have any control."

Madison giggled at Rachel's joke. "Miles may have been the only one who could break up that kiss."

Miles teased back. "Why do you guys look at Corey first? I'm stable and sensible. He's an emotional disaster."

"Really, Miles?" Asked Madison. "Are you asking why a tough bad boy who rebels against authority, plays by his own rules, but is a softie with a heart of gold—makes a woman's heart melt?"

"Yes," he said.

"Honey, you already have me as your prize. You don't need to figure out attraction anymore," said Trish. She held up her hand for him to help her stand.

He stepped between Nicole and me with a grin and grabbed his wife's hand. "Oh well. Preacher Jon showed up, and it's meeting time."

Nicole stepped past me, but I took her hand. Nicole and I were both passionate, and we needed to prepare the world. "Hold your horses. Where's your sense of theatrics? Let's announce this with flare! Love with the most powerful force in the universe and we needed to celebrate it."

She put her arms around my shoulders and kicked up her leg with a tan kitten heel shoe on. "The most powerful force?"

The other three women walked out, and I lifted Nicole and carried her. She giggled and wrapped her arms around my neck and kissed me. I turned my head to navigate the hallway and into the dining room, where I could only see the dark hardwood floors. We stumbled to the doors and she grabbed my head and locked me in a passionate kiss and I tripped, stepping through the patio doors.

Rachel caught us as we fell, laughing. It was a lucky fall. Only she or Miles could have caught us safely. I scooted over near the fire pit and Nicole resumed her place on my lap. "You're right," she whispered. "That was a lot more fun."

She crushed on me since middle school and dated no one after high school waiting for me, while she carried out a loner mission to track her parent's killer. She even weaponized empathy.

I'd trained and fought gargoyles alone and had trained to where CJ of The Tribe, the toughest guy anyone of us ever met, called me a killer. Our flame was going to burn bright, and I looked forward to this much passion in my life again.

THE PATIO WAS FULL, with Preacher Jon standing next to Nathan, who already cooked on my grill. Nicole sat on my lap and announced to the group. "Guys, you better all look out. I prepared to go passionate with Corey and his thoughts are all about enjoying a ton of passion in his life. We may be the crazy couple!"

"May..." teased Miles as he rolled his eyes.

"Let's go back to discussing Corey's backyard," said Nathan. I heard the exasperation in his voice. Nicole was his baby sister... twenty-one-year-old baby sister, but still. He wasn't as down with public displays of affection as we were.

Tiberius flew and landed next to the railing. "Nathan, could you place a piece of meat on the railing for Tiberius? Don't feed him with fingers you want to keep."

Nathan gave the hawk, Tiberius, a big hunk of meat. "Corey, did you know exactly two thousand years ago druids raided Rome and killed Emperor Tiberius' son? Emperor Tiberius stopped governing after that because of his sorrow."

"History is Rachel's thing, but it's an amazing coincidence." She was new to being a bard, but she had some history type of power.

"Speaking of coincidences, exactly one thousand years ago, Druids burned the only Catholic church in the Netherlands, Dom church," added Rachel. "It was the last offensive of any druid against the church." She sat next to Wesley and rubbed his back. He was pulling it together next to her.

"Neat. Dom is the name of a coyote who hunts around here when Tiberius is busy elsewhere," I added.

"Holy crap Corey. Any more historical coincidences?" asked Rebecca. Coincidences and dreams carried more weight when everyone involved were Realized.

"The church would consider this year important to finish the druids forever," said Rachel, using the knowledge from her bard History Domain.

Our team could suck the joy out of anything with basic facts about our day-to-day lives. It didn't bother us anymore. We accepted it and moved on with our lives.

"I don't need to take heart medicine. Let's start the meeting," said Preacher Jon. "First order of business, I'd like to welcome Madison to the team. Although she comes from a lineage of witches, her spark became Realized when Corey led the team and rescued her with enough Fey and Earth Power, that magical sensors around the country broke. To her family's dismay, she has the class of a hunter. She will work at <u>Miles Away from Town</u> and train with Miles."

"Woo. Welcome Madison," I yelled and applauded with the rest. We needed to make her feel welcome. Hunters had a natural inclination to hunt witches, vampires, and werewolves. Hunters overcame the tendency, but it was hard. Modern civilization brought different Realized together and people mixed based on beliefs instead of by species a lot more than they used to.

Preacher Jon continued. "Miles has agreed to become our lead hunter, which is well deserved, especially since he has taken the request to procreate to heart."

While Preacher Jon glared at those of us who were supposed to produce the next generation of druids, we congratulated Miles.

"As a reminder, we are not prudish here and if any of you wish to be intimate with each other, enjoy. Offspring will get the best of everything." He laid it on thicker than usual. He must be getting some heat.

Rachel, Nicole, Nathan, and I stared at the sky because he directed that statement to us. We were the four people left on Earth who could produce a baby that could become a druid. Me being the last druid alive made some people antsy.

Old Donnie prepared me for how I would raise and train the next generation of druids—God rest his soul. I don't know if I was quite ready for a baby yet—you know, being a dead ass killer and all.

"Moving on," he said. "Nathan is being promoted to Strategic Leader and has responsibility for coordination with the other territories."

This was good. The Realized had its own self-governing bodies, where they divided the world into semi-autonomous territories. The territory leaders were the ones who hated me, well, except for Preacher Jon and Leander of the Chicago coven. We needed Nathan's attention to detail and communication in that role.

"Woo. Well deserved, Nathan." I applauded with everyone else.

"Some other pieces of business. We are in official negotiations with The Tribe. We changed nothing yet and won't until January or February since there are a lot of moving pieces."

I hoped we could connect with The Tribe again. Old Donnie, my deceased mentor, was good friends with them. They did not recognize the authority of the leaders of the Realized and bristled at the breakup of the world into territories.

"Corey, the patio you put in here with Grandpa Don and Rachel is remarkable. With your permission, I'd like to hold future group meetings here," said Preacher Jon.

"I'd love it," I replied. Everyone had a code for my house, and I got lonely without people near me.

"Excellent. Last order of business is one more promotion. Corey is now the team's Tactical Leader, or less formally, the battle leader and handles all combat, training, and tactics."

"Whoa!" I couldn't believe he tried to sneak this in. "That isn't right."

"Team vote," said Preacher Jon. "Raise your hand if you weren't happy when Corey overrode my plan, gave his plan in the Battle of Chattanooga?"

The others looked around. Nathan raised his hand. "Mainly because when Corey ordered me to let the other car know of the new plan, Miles towered over me and said, 'type that shit out.'" He emphasized, pointing his finger pointing down, emulating Miles.

"Hey I was excited," explained Miles. Miles had a good foot of height and over one hundred pounds of muscle over Nathan.

"Is anyone concerned about Corey being our Battle Leader?" asked Preacher Jon.

I raised my hand high. "Did you check with CJ?" CJ was with The Tribe and pointed out my training was not complete, which is one reason negotiations started with Preacher Jon.

"Yes. Thanks to you, we are negotiating with The Tribe. I asked him about this idea specifically. He said it's good for you to take responsibility and ownership instead of being the one to ride in the last minute to be a hero."

Rebecca spoke up. "Originally, I only agreed because Corey expects his orders to be followed, regardless. However, Corey's hero complex is so large this is good for him and the team."

"Motion carried. Now let's have some fun." Preacher Jon looked at me like he squared up and got me to step back.

This was something for me to address later. I was not a leader. I barely accepted becoming a team member and now they wanted me to have responsibility for people's lives.

It wasn't the time to fight, though. I was a fighter and measured every conflict the way a fighter would. I had been sucker punched and had no allies. It was time to fall back into a defensive stance. I would shut up and pretend all was fine and interact with my friends.

Chapter 3—Calming people

A wind came through and whipped the fire around, and a log fell. The crackling sent up sparks that caught in the pit's cover. I grabbed another piece of wood and threw it on. I replaced the black cover to keep the sparks suppressed.

Everyone ate and kept topics light. I kept sneaking glances at Nicole's legs in her split dress. She sensed my thoughts and winked at me. Then she slid her dress higher and showed me more of her leg.

Oh no, Rachel and Wesley weren't comfortable next to each other. I wanted to help Rachel be happy, and she needed a boyfriend, especially when I dated and spent less time with her. She liked Wesley, but neither had dated enough. They were going to have issues growing their relationship without help. "Hey, Wesley. Don't get upset at our drama here. It's common."

"I'm still upset," he stopped and cried out. "You and Rebecca die December second. In two days. You die on the road with a priest blasting blue magic and then Rebecca bleeds out in the back of an SUV."

Nicole placed some of her food on Rachel's plate and snickered. "That ain't nothing, right sis?"

Rachel grinned. Rachel and Nicole would alternate between loving and competitive sisters, but Nicole was sharp about things like this and jumped right in to help me. Which was good, since we were new lovers, again.

He looked around, and none of us looked concerned.

"Wesley, would you like to know why people aren't up in arms?" It was time for me to tell one of Old Donnie's stories.

"Yes."

Rachel pulled him close and gave him a quick kiss on his lips. They both blushed. That was a sound move, and I was proud of her.

I started telling the story calmly. "Old Donnie was my mentor and he and I would drink beer on days off. He's the one who taught me to brew beer." I paused and added, "By the way, the current batch in the basement is a pre-prohibition lager."

"This story is an excellent bit of history for Rebecca and Madison too," said Preacher Jon.

"I pieced this story together over a dozen drunken tellings. Old Donnie wasn't the easiest to understand when he drank. During the Roaring twenties, Old Donnie was rooting out a huge vampire den around the panhandle of Florida and the southern area of Alabama and Georgia. One vampire family had an older woman who was Realized and cast curses. She cursed Old Donnie that he would know the day of his death and would dream how he died every night."

"Ripped to shreds by a gargoyle on Stone Mountain," said Rachel. When Wesley winced, she grimaced and added, "Oh sorry, you just saw your first banishing."

Nicole rolled her eyes and face palmed behind them. She and Wesley had been best friends since second grade, and Nicole ran a tricky line in helping both of them.

I'd help her with them soon. "Fast forward fifty years and Old Donnie is cracking. He even took a year off from being a druid and was a roadie for Grinderswitch in nineteen-seventy-five. That ended up causing him so much pain, he wanted to end it." I knew not to give much detail here. There were some dark stories among us that were best to leave buried.

I continued. "October first, nineteen-eighty-one, someone cast a spell powerful enough to break every magical sensor in North America and shake Old Donnie awake from a drunken stupor."

"That's why we have modern sensors in North America compared to the rest of the world," added Nathan.

I kept telling the story. "That night in Old Donnie's dream, he didn't die. A faceless kid saved him."

"What? The prediction was wrong?" Asked Wesley.

"No," said Preacher Jon. "Future predictions rely upon things that have to happen. That spell was a variable the curse could not predict. Variables change all the time and magic cannot predict magic and nothing predicts love." He shifted his eyes between Nicole and me. He had reason to be leery of our relationship status.

"So, you and Rebecca dying in three weeks if you didn't walk to the back bedroom means something big happened back there," said Wesley.

Rebecca dropped her glass, and it shattered on the patio. *That wouldn't calm Wesley.*

I ignored the implications that Rebecca's plan for me to date Nicole changed the day we die. "Well, Old Donnie ran a request on an early IBM mainframe version of the Shared Supernatural System. He discovered an emotionally damaged young man would save him and how he trained this young man would determine the fate of the world."

"And that's enough of that story," said Preacher Jon. "Thank you Corey. Wesley, your power is going to be very helpful, but do not run your life with it. Let it guide you."

"Corey, is your basement fine for me to make a call?" Asked Rebecca.

"Yes. Stay close to the side of the front yard for the best signal down there and it'll keep you away from the warm fermenting."

She ran to the basement and Madison picked up the broken glass.

I pretended Rebecca did not act weird just now. "Wesley, we are all friends and have seen too much go down to be worried about little things. I want you to feel comfortable and use any place I stay at whenever you want. The cabin and my house have the same code and people come and go all the time. Use either place. The code is eight-zero-zero-eight-one-three-fi..."

"Geez, Corey, the code is boobies. If Corey has a number lock, his code is boobies," said Rachel.

That finally got Wesley to laugh and relax. First crisis averted.

The others left after lunch for other plans, and I got to finish waxing my car and motorcycle. Rachel convinced Wesley to sit in my living room to hang out together. With only one faux pas, she was knocking today out of the park. I put two coats of wax on our motorcycles to give them extra alone time.

THE GSXR SHINED WITH the second coat and I sat back before I did the second coat on my BMW F800GT. The ladies opened up a couple of painful spots and my mind put things together they should have. A killer from the Fey Spring Court who dated someone with a hole to fill meant the kid would hate me.

It made so much sense I thought through how I'd explain it to the ladies who couldn't see these connections. I could imagine Rebecca's eye roll and Rachel spinning off to think about something else. I'd have to say, hear me out, and they would.

Then I'd need to bring up the Fey Spring Court and how Nicole and I would have lots of sex around fertility faeries because of our passion and her need to fill up her life. With the agreement we all made with Preacher Jon, it'd be unprotected sex, and that meant Nicole would be pregnant soon.

But I'm a killer with abandonment issues, and Nicole is a loner with nothing else going on. I don't think that's how you get to be parents of the year.

I'd babysit and be like, here—this is a tonfa and this is how you block with it. After you block, you can counter with a quick jab. Nicole would tell me to teach them something nice, but the only other thing I knew was knives. He'd be an adult before I'd get to train druid powers, but by then, he'd hate me.

Then, I'd ask them to consider how Miles and Trish only fixed their relationship after she got pregnant by using the faeries in my house. The problem was Nicole and I would be used to the faeries and they couldn't fix us.

Then people will tell us to get married for the baby and I was barely okay dating to keep her from an arranged marriage of the Realized. I adored Nicole, but if I had my druthers, I'd want Rebecca back. Not exactly the best start to a marriage.

My mind was all over the place.

I adored Nicole and it could grow into something more. We were going to do great dating. Eventually, I'd move on from Rebecca, fall in love and we could get married, but not in nine months.

Nicole was fun and we wouldn't have any problems until we had to be serious adults. Then I'd be pining for Rebecca all over again. She was the adult I needed.

How did I get into this mess? Now that kid hates me. I mean sure, he ain't born yet and all—but he hates me and it's my fault. I'd be like Preacher Jon's father, and all my kids would run away from home.

Sadness washed over me. I sealed up the wax container and threw the rags into a bucket to clean up later. This is why I shouldn't think. I jumped up and jogged to the backyard and walked into Woodrow's tree.

Woodrow was a woodpecker who stained the bark of the red maple black. He was on vacation in warmer places for winter. More importantly, this tree led to the Tree Foyer in the Fey Spring Court. Ten feet away in this mish-mash collection of trees in the lush Fey Realm, I went into the large Red Maple that led to my cabin.

It was colder up here and the sprinkling of snow hadn't lasted, but I kicked off my shoes next to the pile of wood and sharpened the ax on the spinning grindstone. I'd found a seven-pound forest ax at the hardware store and I could split logs with this in one swing. My large canvas wood carrier could load fifty pounds of wood.

With the remaining light, I could split half a cord of wood and carry it back to my house in a bunch of carries. That should keep my brain from being a thinking machine.

Once I had physically exhausted myself, I needed to exhaust myself intellectually—that meant the Fey Realm. That was the one place I was smart. I grabbed my book bag with my spell books and entered the tree in the Fey Realm Tree Foyer. Thinking of my shelter in Verdant Woods, I skipped the other sections, and sat on my moss floor, surrounded by the plants that formed my walls and ceiling. I pulled out my books and studied until I passed out and slept.

Chapter 4—Rebecca's Afternoon

Rebecca adjusted her yellow tinted glasses and put in her hearing protection. The three-oh-eight produced sounds at a high enough decibel level to cause permanent hearing loss, and young women needed their senses. A loss of hearing compromised one's safety.

The underground range attached to the command center was remarkable. She could push targets to five hundred yards. It certainly would not work for anyone training for a three-gun competition, but for marksmanship training, it contained two booths and targets. She had the lighting set to dawn for limited visibility shooting.

She talked with Clive. The vampire, who helped keep the site operational, and he agreed an area for three-gun training might be good. Since he also owned a gun store, time was the limiting factor. He needed to find reliable help for his shop.

Rebecca recognized Clive as the young man who backed down from Corey that one night in the honkytonk bar Corey dragged her to. Sometimes she wanted the complete story, but it was too much pain now. The confrontation made her upset and she used the frustration at Corey to break up with him.

Rebecca was alone in the range this afternoon, which was fine. Proper women had so few places where they could be alone, but as the only entrance to the range was through the command center, this qualified. She needed to be alone. This morning's cookout meeting still stung. She was happy to help Nicole, but giving up on Corey, hurt.

She clipped the target to the wire and pushed the button for two hundred yards. The Lady Hunter Eleven had a bothersome name, but it fit her arm's length and was her go-to-choice for three-oh-eight shooting. Deft hands moved the safeties to a firing position, and then she kneeled in a supported kneeling firing position. Her breathing slowed. With her finger placed on her trigger, at the proper time, she pulled it back without squeezing and fired. She secured her weapon and hit the button to pull the target back.

"Excuse me. Rebecca?" Preacher Jon called her name.

She moved all safeties to the locked position. Placed the weapon down, facing the target, removed her hearing protection, and then turned around. "Yes?"

The target returned, and she unclipped it and looked at the high-powered rifle target. She obliterated the 'X' in that used to mark the inner circle. She placed it in the stack and walked over to the older man.

Preacher Jon waved in Nathan and Nicole. Rachel often stayed with Corey, so the entire command center was in the shooting range.

This morning's meeting had gone dreadfully for her personally, and she had taken immediate steps.

Her family took pride that they traced their genealogy to Ann Owen Constable and had been leaders in Virginia since the original land grant. Grace Addkinson, her grandmother, was a powerful woman who parleyed generational wealth to become head of the Realized in the Chesapeake Bay Territory. Rebecca hated using the connection, but she needed answers.

With the help of a Shared Supernatural System technician named Kim, she put in a request with a one-use password to protect the report. The report should be mundane since it only needed to report about her dating Corey, Nicole dating Corey, and neither of them dating Corey. It would take days to get the report.

Preacher Jon stepped forward, holding smaller head-only targets with circles in the center. "Could you shoot a few of these targets while they move to show something, please?"

She didn't mind. It was something new and a fresh challenge. "Which position?"

"Any position is fine."

"Range?" Warmth filled her inside. The love of shooting had filled the hole from the neglect of her parents.

"Variable twenty-five yards to two hundred by built in algorithm."

She nodded and added, "hearing protection. These are three-oh-eight rounds."

She cleared the chamber, changed out her clip, then placed the safeties in firing position, kneeled to a supported kneeling position, placed her finger on the trigger guard, and checked her breathing. "Ready." She placed her finger on the trigger.

"Away," called Nathan.

First target, one hundred yards. She pulled her finger back and fired. Reset. Second target, two hundred yards. She pulled her finger back and fired.

The weapon cleanly expelled ten rounds, one per trigger pull at the ten targets, then secured her weapon. She removed her hearing protection and placed her yellow tinted glasses on the table next to her secured rifle.

Nathan showed the targets to Nicole. The shots surprised Nathan, but Nicole nodded. She had seen Rebecca fire. Rebecca knew she hit all ten and didn't need confirmation. Nicole was a gun specialist and made the ammo for many of the weapons here. She even made special Fey magic ammo to shoot supernatural creatures.

"Did the demonstration work?" She smiled because Preacher Jon waved off the targets. He believed she could hit those targets. That's two people in her life that believed in her without proving it—well, three if you counted her grandmother. Wait, Corey was four and that meant Rachel too, so five. CJ believed in her... she was going to need to get over her old insecurities about people not believing in her. Joining this team changed her life for the better, which is why she agreed with the plan of Nicole dating Corey.

"Yes, and we would like you to hear our plan before we present it to Corey." He pointed to the setup table and the chairs. The tables were plastic and cheaper than the other furniture in the command center.

She sat and did not secure her weapon because it was within three steps of her and in line of sight. It was not required here, but following rules designed to protect you made the most sense.

Brushing her lap as if she wore a skirt, she looked at Preacher Jon the way a young lady should look at an adult male proven to be a good provider. "I imagine the plan is difficult and requires a tough shot."

"That's not the troublesome part. The tough part is the target is a living creature. A supernatural creature, but still with some version of a life force. Have you ever shot at a living creature, not counting Dark Fey, of course?"

She earned her Earth granted tattoo on her right ankle. It had four colored trumpets on it now—one for each of the Dark Fey she killed at the battle to kill Bishop Pedrotti. This was a curious question.

"Have you ever heard of a Snake-Hunter?" He asked before she answered.

"Just references from Corey." Her Corey was a druid and a powerful one, despite being twenty-four. He was battle hardened but sweet. He started all his kisses off with a gentle tug on her bottom lip, and she liked to rest her fingers on his torc. *Pay attention!*

"You can identify a Snake-Hunter from a man, as it is naked and covered in tattoos but devoid of genitalia and hair. If you see its face, it has empty black orbs instead of eyes. The church created all of them over one thousand years ago. They made a deal with the demon Patrick to create these and with these abominations of church and demonic magic, wiped out the last of the druids except for the Abernathy's."

"It sounds like you will want me to kill one to protect Corey." This was a way to help..

"A bullet cannot kill these. Corey is one of three people on the Earth we know who can kill one. Heck, the only being in North America. However, a headshot can slow it long enough for Corey to kill it."

"Without the headshot, Corey dies?" Rebecca couldn't let that happen.

"Even Corey would estimate his chances at under one in five. A Snake-Hunter is what killed Grandpa Don, the man you knew as Old Donnie. He and Corey together fought off two gargoyles and the Snake-Hunter, but Grandpa Don did not survive the encounter."

"Will Corey be cautious?" Corey had a tremendous hero complex and would stop at nothing to be a hero. She should have considered that question before asking it.

Preacher Jon chuckled. "Corey came about his style honestly. He was a bar fighter trying to punch away his abandonment issues, and his mentor trained him to fight things head on. Grandpa Don went face to face with it, and Corey will do the same."

Nathan held one of his strange food concoctions. Today must be a green food day since he ate green beans wrapped in lettuce and drank a limeade. "We ran a lot of variables for this encounter through the Shared Supernatural System. It believes Corey alone has a ten percent chance of survival against it."

Rebecca had learned about the church and gargoyles the hard way. Stunned, punched, injected with drugs, kidnapped, and held as bait to capture Corey. If she had qualms about not shooting evil before, they were gone. A part of her relished the chance to shoot at evil supernatural creatures and she could not explain that, so she would keep that to herself. "If you are worried, I won't take a shot against a beast aligned with my kidnappers—you may put that to rest."

She also owed Corey. He walked into the trap. No, he charged into the trap with tonfa, magic, bravado and laid his life on the line to rescue her. He took down the priests and killed a gargoyle to save her life, all with a broken heart. A broken heart and a hero complex—and love. He never stopped loving her.

Preacher Jon continued. "This is where it gets tricky. Staying incognito is something where Corey excels. He scopes out his areas ahead of time, shows up early, and is prepared to leave the second things are done."

"I've learned that and figured out why he disappeared for days when we dated."

"Rachel has given up how he has made reservations as Mr. and Mrs. Fitzwilliam in a honeymoon cabin near where he wants to banish the gargoyle and where the Snake-Hunter is likely to attack. He planned to bring Rachel and those two would have had a splash party in the hot tub and played pool the day before." The grin on the face of Preacher Jon was genuine, and Rebecca stifled a giggle.

"I bet you are right, and I assume you want me to pretend to be Mrs. Fitzwilliam instead of Rachel. I promise, I can handle this part of the task as well."

"Are you sure?"

She had no reason to tell him of her continued love for Corey and how she cried two straight nights when she had to give him to Nicole to save her. If Corey still loved her, it was mutual. She loved him so badly she ached. But that was her secret. "Preacher Jon. I know how to talk to people and make others comfortable. This is how society works and it's one reason grandmother let me attend her parties. I can talk with Corey. I can ignore his immensely charming side and prepare to take the shot."

"Excellent. We will outfit a new vehicle for you," said Preacher Jon.

"Corey makes a habit of the impossible." She watched him and heard the fights he won and wondered what could have Preacher Jon apprehensive. "When I saw the number of men with a gargoyle guarding me, I figured I was done. But he did the impossible, along with Rachel. When I saw an honest to God demon in Corey's control, I had no doubt about Corey then. Impossible is where he thrives."

Preacher Jon leaned forward and placed his folded hands on the table. "We are being attacked by many other territories with political machinations. It's cut and dry for leaders to leave us alone. Bishop Pedrotti strong armed thirteen vampires from the Delta Territory to travel to Chattanooga to cast a spell to give him the soul of a latent witch, with the threat the demon would come to Earth. Except people fear our growing power with our young average age."

"Do we know the fallout?" Rebecca had a little insight into political machinations as her grandmother ran the Chesapeake Bay Territory.

"We can count on one hand the amount of people in North America stronger than Corey and the world is terrified of a twenty-four-year-old with libido problems holding the fate of the world in his hands."

That was an unfair characterization of Corey. He was a lover, though, and it was hard to not love him.

"We had a lot of pressure to break up all the young people before. Now that he and Rachel joined the Spring Fey Court—more are worried." Preacher Jon brow showed a worry wrinkle.

"That shouldn't worry them. They are another guide for him." The Spring Fey Court was the court of fertility, passion, intimacy, and youthfulness—so they may have some argument. But that was an internal issue, not one for strangers.

"So, we can count his list of allies on one hand. Us and the Fey Spring Court." Preacher Jon held up his left hand with two fingers.

"Do we have a plan?"

The older man shook his head. "This is my problem. However, my biggest problem is I'm sending two young people into more danger than any of us can imagine. Corey is our Tactical Leader for a reason. He has three years of experience fighting the supernatural."

"One more thing," added Nathan. "Corey listed two men who speak Italian he has dubbed Suit and Red Shirt. They have gone missing, and we are worried where they may show up."

Rebecca knew those two, but only cared for active targets. "I'll need some items to make the shot as easy as possible."

Preacher Jon nodded. "Give a list to Nathan. He can get you everything. We will bring this up to Corey at our next group meeting at his house."

"Can I ask one question about travel?" Rebecca might need to travel back and forth to Virginia soon.

"Of course." Preacher Jon relaxed in his chair like the hard questions were over.

"It seems some people, mainly witches, travel anywhere, where our team and the vampires cannot. What's the protocol?"

"Ah, it's easy. We have an agreement with Ohio Valley, New England, and Chesapeake. All we need to do is provide our current spark signature to them so they can track us and make sure we don't use our powers there. Leander, Samantha, Morgan, your grandmother, and a couple of others have done this with us."

"If we travel without an agreement or without giving a signature?"

"Don't. Your body doesn't even need to be returned." Preacher Jon's face became deadly serious.

Rebecca nodded. "If I travel to Virginia, what do I do?"

"Tell Nathan and he'll take care of everything." Preacher Jon and Nathan stood up to make more plans.

That was easy enough. It was time to focus on the immediate issue. Well, the issue more immediate than shooting a Snake-Hunter. There would be problems for Corey and Nicole if they didn't get something done tonight. Preacher Jon hinted at growing pressure for a reason. They'd need another plan for Nicole to fight off those clamoring for an arranged marriage. She'd hoped they could wait for the report to finish, but they'd have to move immediately.

Chapter 5—The Cookout

Studying all night in the Fey Spring Court left me feeling smart and powerful. I threw on my shorts and a hoodie. It had gotten chilly back home. I picked up my messenger bag with my two spell books, the <u>Abernathy Book of Gargoyles</u>, and Nicole's notebook from her spying. The notebook was ready to be put away to make room for the ritual book.

Because of Earth Power, when I had a full connection to Earth, I was pretty smart. Here, with full access to the Fey Realm and Fey Magic, I could think and learn and nothing could slow me down. There was something I couldn't figure out. I wanted to think it through before I left.

Usually, I could only focus on two topics: love or fighting. I don't know why those topics came through clearly for me and other topics confused me.

The team's makeup confused me. When Old Donnie was the druid, Preacher Jon built a druid led team and everyone was there to support him. Now that I was the druid, the team makeup had changed. Preacher Jon was still fine with me being the strongest member and even a leader, but he did not build the team to support me. It was strange. I was the fifth person officially added to the team. I think the key relied on the links between all the team members, so I'd put this in the background and thought about it.

Last, I picked up my new green book of Fey Realm rituals. The ritual Rachel and I finished required both of us. It created eleven mason jars full of prepared viscous water. The ritual comprised water from Serene Pond collected by a druid, while a bard sang a ballad of the sorrow of eternal life, and then the two used a joint ritual to prepare the containers. They were called the Jars of Bliss. If someone was terminal, they could have their heart removed right after doing something joyful, and while the heart stayed in the jar, the soul experienced that joy. I didn't use them like that. If I were to name mine, I'd call them the Jars of Shouldn't have Messed with Me.

These jars were critical, and we'd be careful with them. The remarkable thing to me was it worked on unnatural, what the learned people called preternatural—vampires, werewolves, and the like.

Everything else done, I stepped out of my Plant Domain shelter in Verdant Woods and thought of the Tree Foyer. The woods whooshed by me, then I traveled through the Fertile Fields, Cloven Hills, and Flower Mounds. I ended at the grouping of strangely matched trees. Before I left, I looked over the two areas of the Fey Spring Court I had not visited—Playful Prairie and Gnome Valley. Gnomes, Pooka's, Feogles, Leprechauns, and Churichaun dotted the areas, but I did not have time to spend any more time here.

The Spring Fey Court was beautiful and vibrant, and every area had something majestic, beautiful, or addicting—or all three. It was best to appreciate the realm and leave. The Tree Foyer was the odd exception. There were thousands of mismatched trees here. Trees from all over and from all climate zones. I imagined the trees existed on earth and this was some type of magical replica.

I chose a Red Maple, at each house. Any Spring Court member only needed to walk into the tree to transport between the Spring Court and my houses. The daoine used them frequently. Faeries had a five-hundred-foot limit because of the limited magic on Earth.

I took two steps and strode through the black stained tree and the temperature dropped forty degrees as I stood on my frost covered lawn. I walked around my patio and pulled on the sliding glass door. Someone locked my door. That was good, even though I didn't know who it was. I wasn't the best with mechanical items, or electronic items, or thinking if I didn't touch the natural Earth or the Fey Realm.

After typing in my code, I sauntered into my basement, where my first two-week process for my next batch of beer was underway. It was in the hot fermentation part and still had eleven days to go. I got this recipe and the mash products from a local store because the ground was too hard to grow without a lot of magic. I put the mason jars into the dark crawl space portion of the basement. They built my ranch house on a hill, so half of the house had a crawlspace with a vapor barrier, and a couple of stone Earth connections I put in, and the other half had an unfinished basement where I brewed beer.

The cinderblocks, cement, and being partially underground kept the temperature fairly constant. For the warm fermentation part, Clive and I wound some copper tubing and circulated fifty-seven-degree water through the tubes and kept the fermenting mash near the top of the range for lagers. When it came time for the cold fermentation, we'd drop it to forty-eight degrees.

Back in my bedroom, I tossed the messenger bag with the Fey ritual book, the most critical part of my day-to-day life, on my bed. I checked out the comforter from Miss Kim. Rebecca hated it and only let me keep it on when I told her who made it and why. Rachel loved it.

The real reason I came back was for a warm shower. However, my shower had become almost unrecognizable. I had some basic shampoo and some tea tree oil soap. Rachel placed the shampoo, conditioner, second conditioner, and body wash that she and Nicole used in here and I still had Rebecca's body wash, shampoo, conditioner, and hair mask here as well. I guess the hair mask was in case her hair went out to fight crime.

With the spongy body wash thingermerbobs, there was a glove with bumps that was to exfoliate. Of course, each of the three women had put different colored towels in each bathroom. I recognized mine as the white ones with three thin green strips on the edges. The sink had three mouthwashes, six toothbrushes, and three types of toothpaste. Once the weather warmed, I'd feel more at home in the trough at the cabin.

Despite all that, I took a long and glorious hot shower. Late November in the North Georgia Mountains meant I had to chip away ice before I bathed and the coals around the trough just made the temperature safe, not comfortable.

When I dried, I checked out my Earth given tattoos on my chest. Three gargoyle names on my chest, a Gaelic word on my right biceps, and a honeysuckle tattoo on my right ankle. I didn't choose any of these. The Earth put them on my body when I did something the Earth approved of. The only other tattoo was the Fey Spring Court Tattoo of the sun next to the little druid. They had given Rachel one, and I assumed it was in the same spot, though I wouldn't see it below her bikini line. It protected us from the strongest effects of passion and pheromones of the faeries and marked us as denizens of the Fey Spring Court.

I threw on my old jeans, an Allman Brother's shirt, and a Boys from Doraville hoodie. Miles, Rachel, Nicole, and I had a lot of southern rock items from my mentor.

Noises came from the other bathroom, and I heard Trish and Miles laughing in the shower. That was great. She was three months pregnant and they've been having intimacy issues. They came here because the Spring Fey Court faeries traveled five hundred feet from the tree and sleeping in this house boosted desire, passion, and love for couples. They didn't have protection like Rachel and me.

The two must have come over last night for today's meeting and took advantage of the magic to help their marriage. If I could help the marriage of my friends and get to spend more time with them—this was a win. More so, I noticed the women washed the sheets in the spare bedrooms, a lot.

I strolled to the freezer and pulled the last bit of deer out. Preacher Jon bought a butchered bison to fill all our meat freezers, and it'd be here today. Old Donnie used to hunt, and I didn't feel comfortable hunting. Legal hunting was fine and all, but the Animal Domain was one of my domains. I could call a deer to me from up to a mile away and ask it to jump into a stove. That just wasn't cool. I asked Preacher Jon to remove me from hunting responsibilities and he understood.

Preacher Jon was an old guy, but the more I learned about him, the more I liked him. I was on the team because I was going to make sure he would follow up and chase the love of his life after being separated for forty years. Everyone should track down true love.

He was Realized as well and powerful even though he did not have a class. He had one power and his power allowed him to circumvent any law or regulation made by anyone with the power to enforce those rules. That was awesome. I also had a power like him. Women with the spark attracted me. Woo, Preacher Jon gets to break any law he wants and I'm attracted to magic chicks. Luckily, I have a class. In the world of magic, having a class was a fancy way of saying you had a job and my job was a druid.

For thousands of years, druids had access to four of the dozens of domains. We could only access magic from our four domains. My 'minor powers' were in the Animal Domain, Plant Domain, and Earth Domain. Where I was a superstar, was in the Circle Domain. Give me time to draw a circle on the ground, initiate it, bind something to it, and then cast a spell—well, no one could match me.

I locked my messenger bag in my car to lock it away. Sometimes, paranoia ruled my decisions.

Then, I dropped the meat into the sink and pulled out the eggs and sausage and brought them outside. It felt strange cooking for myself and I was glad Trish and Miles would be here for breakfast.

Nathan did a great job cleaning my grill. I walked over to my newly large pile of split wood and pulled out a couple of pieces. I grabbed my knife and banged it through with the piece of wood to make it thinner. After I had eight thin pieces of wood, I placed four in the patio fire pit and four in the grill. I placed two large pieces in the fire pit.

My fire starter was in my waist pack. I was normally more organized, but today, things were everywhere. I ambled through the kitchen and into the carport, my competition orange Mustang GT sparkled with its two coats of wax. While there, I did a quick inventory of all my gear and supplies—especially the magnolia seed pod after last week. After grabbing my fire starter, I ambled back to my patio.

Old Donnie, Miles, Rachel and I put this patio in two years ago and this was my favorite spot in civilized lands. I shaved some starter into the grill and the fire pit and got both lit.

After sweeping my patio, I wiped down my dumbbells and bench, cleaned and oiled my pull-up bar. Each weapon got cleaned and oiled then. I didn't use them yesterday, I just wanted to keep them in good shape.

Tiberius flew by and I thought he came to say hello, but he scooped up a rabbit and flew off.

"You've already made it cozy out here," said Trish. She and her husband Miles strode out onto the patio fully dressed. They met in tenth grade and set me up with my first girlfriend since their parents made them double date. Haley and I dated throughout high school, even though Trish and Miles dated and broke up—a lot.

"If people are going to be over, I want to appear civilized. Eggs, sausage, and toast?" I loved how my friends felt comfortable coming over here and me being able to cook breakfast with them.

"When's your next banishing?" Miles helped load up the plates.

"I got a twofer coming up this weekend and the second guy is a biggun."

"Guys, You two mentioned a gargoyle banishing as if it was nothing. You've been having conversations like this for years," said Trish. She shook her head.

Miles tried to keep Trish out of this part of his life, but I broke the ice last week because Trish was making decisions that could get Miles killed because she didn't know the ramifications. Trish was a smart take charge woman. She was more surprised when she found out Coach White was a werewolf and our friend Clive was a vampire than I was a druid. She always thought I was a little weird.

"Don't feel bad, Trish. Old Donnie taught me three things. Druid magic, how to fight, and how to stay hidden. He brought in fancy AI experts from California and everything to teach us about cameras and recognition stuff." I loved Old Donnie and missed him something fierce every day.

"Could I watch you do it once?" asked Trish.

"I don't mind, but we'll want to check church activity and make sure nothing untoward is going on. There is a real chance we'll be ducking bullets from guns shot by priests."

"Once the baby is born, right?" Miles patted her baby bump.

She stuck her tongue out at him. "Priests in the Curia, not the Catholic church, right?" She wanted to verify because her parents raised her in a Catholic house.

"Mostly, I'm sure there is some crossover, but in reality, it's not even the whole Curia, just a couple of bad dudes and their lieutenants who make things happen."

She nodded. She winced when we used the word church. I understood because it wasn't like the whole Catholic Church was out to get us, not even one percent of it.

"Did you hear the rest of us are going to watch the store for you while you travel for a honeymoon in February?"

Miles secured the grill and put two pieces of wood on the fire pit. "Hand me your plate. I'll wash up."

"Corey, you don't know how much it means to me, how you asked the Fey Court for things for your friends. When you wanted Miles and I to be supported because of recent family changes so our marriage could last—shows you paid attention to us." Trish wiped a tear away.

"Trish, we've been friends since tenth grade. Your neighbor was my first actual girlfriend and Miles has been my best friend since then. I'll have your back always."

I know she smiled, but a night of studying spells and a busy morning caught the best of me as I lay in the sun next to the fire pit and rested my eyes.

"YOU BETTER HAVE A GOOD excuse for sleeping through this," said Nicole. I opened my eyes, and she straddled my prone body and put her hand on my shoulders. She wore a red skirt today with a white blouse and a green vest with reindeer on it.

Her playful voice got my sleepy mind's attention, so when she looked up, I took her distraction and performed a jiu jitsu shrimping escape. I pinned her, kissed her passionately, which she returned, and wrapped her legs around me. She had no protection from the faeries.

"All eleven of us are here and we've started the meeting, Corey," said Preacher Jon.

I lifted my head and looked around. Nathan was grilling and chuckling to himself next to Preacher Jon. Rachel sat next to Wesley and grinned, while Wesley shielded his eyes. Miles sat in one of the Adirondack chairs and Trish sat on his lap. Rebecca and Madison also had Adirondack chairs next to the house.

"Whoops," I sat up and Nicole sat in my lap. She giggled nearly uncontrollably.

"Now, Corey, we need to alter your upcoming plan for this weekend's gargoyle hunt." Preacher Jon was trying to hide his laugh and get back to being serious.

I needed to wake up fast. I was on high alert after yesterday's big surprise of tactical leader.

"Wow. The guy who will flat out tell me to 'shut the hell up,' is listening." The old man must be confident after I stood down in the last meeting. Besides, I made that statement one time. I am a respectful person... usually.

He continued with no comment from me. "Corey, Nicole's information panned out, as usual, and the crate that was delivered is a Snake-Hunter. They have released the Snake-Hunter to kill you before the arrival of the monsignor. Second, they have dispatched two empaths to look for thoughts of druids. We do not know what either looks like."

I rubbed Nicole's back while I thought this through. The empaths were no problem. I still wore the earring so that I could block out certain thoughts. However, a Snake-Hunter was what killed Old Donnie. I could take one using all my new power, but Old Donnie had the Protection Domain, which is how he prepared me to kill it. I didn't have access to those spells. Unless we brought more people, I had the best fighter, Rachel, with me.

"Moving in teams isn't safe. I think we may have to stay with the plan." I had booked a cabin with a games room in the mountains.

He handed me a stack of papers with a silhouette head and a hole. All ten papers had the hole in the same spot.

"You don't need to tell me this is Rebecca's shooting. Do you think Rebecca firing Missy can kill a Snake-Hunter?" Rebecca taught me how to shoot. It's how we met.

He looked down when he shook his head. "No, but Rebecca has pinpoint accuracy with her favorite weapon that can put a standard bullet into its lower forehead, the only spot uncovered by tattoos."

"Your plan is for Rebecca to shoot it between the eyes to give me time to kill it?" I was the killer.

"You don't think Rebecca can make the shot?" asked Preacher Jon.

"You don't have to sell me on Rebecca making the shot." I turned to Rebecca. "I booked a cabin in the mountains for Rachel and me. It has a games room with a pool table, ping-pong, darts, and one of those tv game things. Would you be okay being alone in a cabin with me and the games room?" *Would Nicole?*

"We won't be playing games, but yes. I am comfortable spending time with you and we will barely have enough time to prepare to spend any time playing games." Rebecca looked confident and serious. "It will be even colder in the mountains, so we will need extra time to set up and strategize."

"You're going to take my games weekend and then waste a games room!" exclaimed Rachel.

She was playing, but I wanted to put everyone I could at ease. "Rachel, you and I have been fighting together for a decade. If the Snake-Hunter showed up here, you, Miles and I would fall into a natural formation without a word. Rebecca needs to do what she feels is best to be confident."

I considered Preacher Jon's new plan. If he validated the shot could put the Snake-Hunter down, this strategy could work. "Nicole—"

"Corey, we've already discussed it," said Nicole. She snuggled up to my ear and whispered, "Can you sneak me with you in a backpack?"

I chuckled. "Okay. Change of plans. We waste the games room and cancel the hot tub splash fight. Rebecca and I will do the gargoyle banishing on the day the monsignor arrives. Rebecca, we'll leave tomorrow afternoon. Let me know if you need anything for the trip."

"Way ahead of you, but change the color of your lipstick before we go." Rebecca rolled her eyes at Nicole's giggles.

I wiped my mouth and red lipstick came off on the back of my hand.

"You guys owe me a fun weekend." Rachel teased us with a pout.

"Can I ask a gargoyle question?" Asked Wesley. "When you told me I viewed a young, weak gargoyle—how do we define gargoyles?"

Everyone looked at me.

There was nothing official, but I couldn't leave him hanging. "Okay, Old Donnie got mad at me for not understanding the Mohs scale and stuff, but gargoyles are hard like granite or soft like marble. People who try to define other gargoyle types confuse rocks with rock-forming minerals, crystals, and other stuff that aren't rocks. It gets confusing. Obsidian is a kind of rock, but it's not a true rock."

"Rocks like basalt, diorite, and syenite?" asked Wesley. He was in a PhD program for some math and computer bunch of fancy word stuff. He'd ask a lot of questions I'd never be able to answer.

"Okay, now you sound like Old Donnie. Marble gargoyles have the same silica thing, like marble rocks. They're soft and damaged with well-made weapons. Granite gargoyles are hard and have the same silica as granite rocks. They're the toughest since I have to spike a gargoyle, while touching Earth, and wearing my torc. The hope is to trick it into turning part of its body into stone."

"Remember," added Rachel. "We don't need to fight if it's inside of a circle. They come from the dark place, and Corey sends them back. Fighting is only for free gargoyles, which Corey can't lure."

Wesley had his phone out. "Granite is the toughest because of quartz content." Wesley looked up and I could tell he had more squirrels spinning in wheels in his head than I could count.

"Sure. I call everything else a middle grade. And treat them the same way as granite." All those fancy questions would not get them anymore information from me. "I put marble into the weak category and everything else into the hard category."

"Why are so many marble gargoyles if they're weak?" asked Rebecca.

"I asked Old Donnie the same question, and he said the marble ones have a final form that makes the first four or five thousand years of being weak worth it." I shrugged because I had no more information there.

"What about size?" Wesley asked like he could partition this information away to make it useful one day.

"Young ones are six to eight feet tall. Eight to ten feet tall are adults. Ten to twelve feet tall are major gargoyles and taller than twelve feet are called ready for molting for final form."

"What's their final form?" Wesley seemed way too excited about information that would not keep him alive.

"Old Donnie didn't know, and neither did his grandfather, so I don't. All I know is that there is some time between five hundred and a thousand years for each stage of a gargoyle. Before you ask, I know nothing of molting."

"This is exciting stuff to research."

Yep, way too excited. I did my best Old Donnie impression. "Corey, you're too excited for a student who is too lazy to research his own answers. Why don't you focus on stuff that'll keep you alive?" I chuckled. "That meant he didn't know either."

"Thank you, Corey," said Nathan. "As battle leader, I want to give you some unconfirmed information."

"I didn't know there would be benefits to being battle leader," I joked.

He continued. "Nicole discovered a bargain between the church and Dark Fey."

"If you weren't sleeping, you'd already know this," she said.

"That would explain a lot, since I'm finding Dark Fey, which I don't sense with my *Own Area* spell." I scratched her back and caused her to arch to get her left shoulder.

"Yep, they're inside of a sacrificed human shell. Many priests hunting you are Dark Fey." Nathan read off his phone.

"Let me guess, there is no way to tell them apart until they're dead." I didn't need my phone to know the knowledge wouldn't help me.

He chuckled. "The church has an obsession with the number three and we found other centers of Gargoyle activity in Cape Horn and Osaka. Also, a coven in Osaka has verified that two Kannushi with lineage to the Yayoi era are doing something that hinders the church. The Shinto don't report to anyone, and we have learned no details, but we have hope we aren't alone."

Old Donnie said that Shinto Kannushi speak Ryukyuan from the Yayoi period to make magic. I knew only that because even if I was a good student, I graduated from public school.

Chapter 6—The Ladies' Plan

The meeting had wrapped up and most people had stuff to do. I waved goodbye to everyone. Rebecca brought Nicole with her, so I could focus on getting ready while Wesley and Rachel left together in his car despite her GSXR having two coats of wax on it. Good for them. Before packing, I had time to straighten up after the visitors. I changed my bed sheets, did laundry, sterilized bottles for my next batch of beer, cleaned the floor, swept the patio, and even cleaned out the firepit.

After dinner, I was still alone, so I started another fire on the fire pit and laid out the bear and deer skins to sleep. If the firepit had fire or coals all day, the rocks stayed warm and made this area pleasant despite the below freezing temperature. I kicked up the fire and stacked wood near where I'd set up the skins so I could feed it without getting out in the cold.

Rachel popped her head through the sliding glass door. "Leave your shorts on."

This was great. I wanted a good snuggle with her. Especially since we wouldn't travel together this weekend.

"And make it wider," said Nicole.

I didn't know what was going on, but I knew how to listen. I made it wider and pulled out all the skins.

Rachel came out in the long pants and shirt of the pink pajamas I got her and Nicole came out in a skimpy nightie. I turned away. "Nicole, don't you want to wear more?"

"If you can wear shorts you swing around in, I can be comfortable, too. Now get under them covers because it's freezing." Rachel turned off my patio light, and all we had was the fire when I got inside and they got on either side of me.

We all snuggled in the deer skins, got warm, and I went right to sleep. It was almost dawn when I felt Rachel get out of the covers. She placed a couple of logs on the fire and then jogged inside. I rolled back over and felt my shorts being tugged and that's when I remembered the faeries and pixies from the Spring Court and Nicole's slinky nightie. I had the Fey Court Sun Tattoo, but she had no protection. The Fey Court wanted nothing to do with chaos, just passion, so the passion, intimacy, and fertility pheromones of the faeries affected only couples. We were most certainly a couple.

"I read your mind and knew it'd happen when I laid next to you last night. Now, make love to me with the passion Rebecca described back when you dated and used Earth Power." She panted and the pheromones from the faeries of the Fey Spring Court consumed her.

The mention of Rebecca was a timely reminder. I turned off thoughts about sex with other women in my earring and took her in my arms and kissed her. It was time to focus, and the faeries flitted around us as they sensed my craving for her.

This was the first time we'd make love. This was the trickiest part of lovemaking in a relationship. I knew nothing of her zones or what she liked, but the first time in a relationship could set the tone for the entire relationship. Since she crushed on me for so long, I'd need to pay extra attention to make sure I didn't ruin this experience.

Old Donnie gave me three rules for relationships and three rules for physical intimacy. *Until you know a lot about women, follow these three rules and you'll do fine.*

The first rule was to start slow and tender. We were already naked, so I held her and kissed her gently and let her be the aggressive one as I ran my fingers over her back, arms, and sides, looking for her sensitive zones. If I ran my nails up her thighs and up the side of her torso, her whole body shook. It wasn't too long after I started when her moans became loud.

The second rule was three circles. Before I touched anything I desired, I circled it three times. Rules that slowed a passionate couple helped the enjoyment immensely. Sometimes passion moved the acts too quickly to savor. I altered rule two with breasts when I was with Rebecca, so I tried my change with Nicole. I circled her right breast three times and then made a figure eight around her breasts and circled the left breast. Then I reached for her left breast, but brushed her right nipple with my arm. She yanked me close and her moans were as loud as I ever heard, and it was turning me on.

Old Donnie's third rule was to listen to the woman and do what she tells you to. You'll never know as much as the woman about her own body. Since this was the first time we made love, Nicole was unlikely to give me direction, so I had to go about things using experience. Rebecca was a big proponent of rule three and gave me explicit directions.

I used all the directions I learned from Rebecca for foreplay, and Nicole was all but screaming. When I finally entered her, she screamed loudly.

After a few minutes, Earth Power surged through me and gave me endurance. I used all the energy and the angst of the past few weeks and quit thinking about anything except making love to Nicole. Once I exploded, the extra pumps kept coming, and I stayed inside and laid next to her. We lay in a pile of sweat as we panted and tried to catch our breaths.

"Now that you two are done, could you tell the nice officers that you two are well and you woke up the neighborhood because you just made love for the first time?" said Rachel.

I sat up, which pulled me out of her. Sure enough, two uniformed police officers stepped out onto the patio. "One second officer," I said. I rolled out and grabbed my shorts, and pulled them on.

"Are you the owner of the property, sir?" One officer stepped forward and looked at the top of my head. He was trying not to laugh.

"Yes, Officer. I'm Corey Norwood." This was mortifying.

"We need to make sure everyone is okay. Miss, are you fine?" said the female officer.

"Oh, god yes," said Nicole. She lay there and grinned.

"We'll just be issuing a warning to keep loud noises between seven am and nine pm. Have a nice day, folks." The officer left with Rachel and we saw her filling out forms in the kitchen with them and laughing.

The patio stayed pleasant all night, but I put a couple more pieces of wood into the firepit.

"Get back under these covers," said Nicole.

I climbed back under the covers.

"Do you always think that much about pleasing me when you make love?"

"If I focus on instructions and doing things right, I last longer and you'll enjoy it more. When you're into it like that, the last part is so much bliss, it makes all the setup worthwhile."

"Out of all your strange behaviors, I like this one the most." She traced her hand down my chest and nibbled on my earlobe.

"We have a lot of strangeness to learn about each other. It's good to find one that's a pleasant surprise," I said, still breathing hard.

"What other weirdness are we dealing with?" She teased.

"Let's see. I banish gargoyles, fight the church, get injured a lot, I'm co-dependent with your sister, need to be nude to fully connect with the Earth, we have Spring Court faeries flittering around us at my house and cabin, and I only understand loving and fighting."

"Sounds normal to me," she teased, and started stroking me.

We made love again and this time we were much quieter. Afterwards, we fell asleep in each other's arms.

"HE THINKS HE'S FOOLING us," a woman's voice startled me awake. I reached out my arm and Nicole had already left our bed.

I opened my eyes. Rebecca, Rachel, Madison, and Nicole sat in the Adirondacks on my patio with me. "It's nice to wake up to the beauty of the hot girl's club," I said. I was still flush and everything seemed better this morning.

Nicole tossed my shorts to me. "You're a wanted felon. Get dressed," she joked.

"I forgot to tell Corey," said Rachel. She covered her hand with her mouth.

"Corey! You didn't know the plan and just went with it when I started yelling?" Nicole looked mortified.

"Plan? No, the yelling turned me on." I pulled my shorts on under the covers before I sat up.

"This was a plan to announce you two dating to the world. I'm the one who called the police," said Rebecca. She started laughing. "Corey's in the dark and thinks he's God's greatest sex machine."

"He can keep thinking that," said Nicole.

Madison patted Nicole on the shoulder. "Congratulations."

"Rachel sent the police report around all the social media sites to make sure everyone in the world knew you two were an item," continued Rebecca.

"Well, all the yelling and moaning was hot anyway," I teased.

"Ignore him. He relies on being charming," said Rebecca to Madison. She threw a t-shirt in my face to pull on.

As my eyes focused, Nicole was still flush from the night. She smiled at me and I could see the same adoration towards me which I felt after a night like last night.

"Rachel, come here," said Nicole. "Everyone, kick off your shoe and do this with your right ankle." They lifted it and showed off the honeysuckle tattoo.

"Hey Corey, what do you think?" asked Rebecca.

This was to taunt me. I had a habit of buying the girls I dated ankle bracelets and made the mistake of saying I thought ankle tattoos were sexy. The tattoos they showed were Earth granted. It was a honeysuckle bush around the ankle with a coral honeysuckle trumpet colored for each Dark Fey they killed.

I thought it was sexy, but they would not get me. "You three earned those, and I am proud of each of you for those kills. The Earth gives you those tattoos for killing Dark Fey because that skill and heroism need to be rewarded. You three have all saved my life and the lives of countless others, and I wish you had even larger rewards."

"Poo," said Rachel.

"No, he's sweating and looking away from your ankles. You were right," said Madison.

I stood up and picked up the fifth chair and moved next to her. "Let me show you some pictures to help put their stories in perspective."

I had three phones, the other two were for my fake identities. I had those in labeled boxes because my secret identities were for traveling and operating around places where I used magic. My identities confused me and I was careful.

I grabbed my phone from off the woodpile. Standing near Rachel, I was smart enough to get right into my pictures. "Here is the day Rebecca asked me to date her."

"Look at you lying there with sweaty muscles and half nekkid. I kindly think there should have been a line of ladies." She had a lovely Appalachian Mountain accent.

"What I like about this picture is I look small. You can see my size, but next to Old Donnie, CJ, Fitz, and a couple of other men, I am small. Then, tiny Rebecca, wearing a skirt, pushed through everyone and put her knee next to me and asked me out."

"Tiny Rebecca? She's four inches taller than me!" said Madison. Yeah, Madison was in the five-four range. I'd probably need to leave out height when talking to her.

"Where did you get that picture?" asked Rebecca.

"Rachel took it. She said she knew you were going to ask me out and wanted to get the picture."

"Send it to me, please." Rebecca had her phone out.

"Rachel, can you do it since I haven't figured out things like sending or snapping or hash-tagging?"

She handed Rebecca her phone. Rachel wasn't much better at these things without instructions. *They must have given Rachel instructions to send the police warning out. They really planned last night.*

The next picture was on my screen. "Here's Rebecca and I in front of Symphony Hall."

Madison took the phone. "Look at you two. She looks normal, but you went from guamed up to giddied up."

"Here is one of Nicole and I getting ready for our first date," I said. "We've known each other for so long we don't look nervous at all."

"There are a lot of pictures of you, Rachel, and Nicole I've seen. My favorite is the one Rebecca showed of your performance." She giggled.

The Karaoke performance was when I supported Rachel. I'm glad I made Rachel happy, but that video got too much airplay for my taste. "That's great. Did she show you this one from the mudding day?"

I didn't come off well in the mudding video, but Rebecca was a proper young woman and she did not appreciate this video. Mud covered Rachel, Rebecca, and I. We were drunk out of our minds—and happy. We blew off steam after a bad few days and bonded. Madison paused the video just after Rebecca turned her wine bottle upside down, where Rebecca gazed at me with adoration. Her jaw dropped, and she stared at Rebecca.

Rebecca and I were still in love, though we no longer dated. "That's not when I knew she still loved me. I knew by the way she held me when I rode her around the mud. I felt our connection, and we'd never leave each other's hearts even if we never dated again."

The four looked at me. Rebecca turned red while Madison and Rachel's jaws dropped. Nicole looked at Rebecca with sadness.

"I didn't mean to say that out loud, sorry." Stupid reminiscing caught me off guard, and now I looked like a fool.

"Go shower up Corey and pack up the SUV. I'm driving after lunch." Rebecca was looking to head off any more of this conversation and I was glad to help.

"I'll beat out the skins and pack up your bed," said Nicole.

I popped up and ran into the bedroom. Soon, I showered, packed, and had everything ready.

In the car, I pulled out two camping backpacks and my combat belt. My waist pack contained all banishing necessities, plus the Magnolia seed pod and my silver sickle. The weekend pack was forty pounds and packed so that I could grab and go on a week hike and camping trip at a moment's notice. I didn't weigh my packs or worry about a couple of pounds of gear. That's what the gym was for.

My weapon's belt had a set of tonfa, a couple of combat knives to go with the two knives I kept strapped to my legs. It also had a stun gun, pepper gel, compass, gps, multi-tool, and my druid items.

I got in the car just as a light sprinkle started.

Chapter 7—Cabin with Rebecca

Rebecca drove, and I sat in the passenger seat with it moved all the way back for leg room. She had a lot of gun stuff that needed hiding and that's why we needed the SUV. It was all legal, but better to have no questions.

The seats were cloth but comfortable and the dash was a light gray. The tint looked as if it came right upon the legal limit. Rebecca eased the SUV down my dead-end road toward the main road.

"Did the hot girl's club come up with the loud sex idea together?" I wanted to focus on keeping the weekend light. I would not mention we were Mr. and Mrs. Fitzwilliam if someone came to the cabin.

"Yes." She grinned. "I'm glad you're more of a lover than a fighter."

"Am I?" I wondered sometimes. I had three gargoyle names tattooed on my chest. A bicep tattoo for a dead Snake-Hunter, and my honeysuckle tattoo on my ankle for the Dark Fey I killed. If I banished a creature, I didn't get a tattoo, only if I killed it.

"Are you less confused about women now?" She looked forward and kept a blank face.

"No. I'm more lost than last year's Easter egg. Even when I was making love to Nicole, you came to my mind." I was going to have a hard time this weekend if that question could get me.

The rain came down, but it wasn't very hard. It was good because the late fall and winter had been dry.

"Oh Corey. Please try to be happy. Plus, don't tell her that. I had to tell her to stop reading crazy women's websites to help keep you."

"You might be the only one who understands me. But all this of me being a killer and Nicole having nothing else going on causes him to hate me."

"Who's the 'him'? But you'll be happy to know that Preacher Jon kept Nicole on church spy duty. He also made her Nathan's back up for tactical leader. She was going to be your assistant as well until you two started dating. That's one problem solved." She smiled at me with one of her patented 'I told you so,' smiles.

That was fast and impressive. "I'll relax a bit. If you moved that fast on Nicole, maybe you can do something about me. Is she okay after my goof up about us remaining in each other's heart?"

"Yes. She knows she is in for a long haul and I promised not to intervene. You have time to get it right."

We drove through the night, and the rain dissipated. Eventually, we made it into the mountains of Tennessee, while keeping the conversation light. It was as if we had enough heavy stuff in our lives. She played classical music softly in the background instead of what I normally listened to, but it was fitting with her driving.

Even in the dark, the light of the headlights was enough to see the leaves changing from fall to winter.

When she became tired, we parked in a hotel lobby. To avoid leaving a trace, we pulled out sleeping bags and slept in the back of the SUV. Someone designed the SUV's interior with a mattress in the back and storage underneath it. It was cozy, but there was room for two separate sleeping bags and plenty of storage for my few items and Rebecca's arsenal.

The SUV had a coating of frost when we got out. We ran to the gas station to use the restroom. Rebecca stayed to get coffee, and I jogged back, kicked off my shoes, and stepped onto the grass next to the parking lot. There was a copse of small pine trees, so I created a small circle for the small gargoyle with no preferences. I pulled out the <u>Abernathy book of Gargoyles</u> and memorized the gargoyle's magical symbol.

Rebecca showed up, and I whispered for her to come over. "This will be your second gargoyle."

"Here?"

While I stood on the cold pine needles in my bare feet, I began the binding.

> ***Bho àm immemorial, cumhachd an t-seanairginn a 'gairm thugad. A bhith ceangailte ris a 'phortal agam agus fo smachd mo thoil.***

In ten minutes, my torc turned red, and the world turned to black and white. A small gargoyle showed up and thrashed. "I didn't get to show you much last time since Nathan was with us and scared, but this is the size of the gargoyle Old Donnie had me hold for six hours to prove to me they'd never break my circle. It's young since it's only eight feet tall and it has a mix of stone types I don't recognize. Most of these guys have horns, and it don't matter much, but this one has no wings. Its teeth aren't long and its claws are barely an inch. He'd be one that'd be easier to fight than many." I began the banishment.

> ***Tha Rìoghachd dorchadas a 'gairm agus le mo chumhachd rìoghachdan ceangailte tha mi a' cuir casg ort gu dorchadas!***

With a pop, everything was gone. "One down and welcome to binding and banishing. We need to go, but do not draw attention." The world changed back to normal, and we hurried to leave.

I sat in the SUV and wrote the update on the Fey enchanted page. *Banished by Coire Norwood, thirty November 2023. Allowed to come back on thirty November 2523. Simple ten-minute binding.* I put in the location coordinates, time completed with time zone, and noted Rebecca Adams was with me, then closed the book. "It's a lot easier with someone else driving." I slipped the book into my messenger bag. One gargoyle, first banished by an Abernathy to the Realm of Darkness in 1523, is banished again for five hundred years.

Banishings are safe unless the church catches us.

"Corey, I know this is nothing for you and you've done hundreds. You say it's safe, and you made fun of the gargoyle for looking weak. But this is the second gargoyle I've seen, and I'm shaking." She put her fingers on her temple. "I get it. You lost your family, and you always counted on yourself. You got a father figure, and he passed, but you have to work with me while I am with you. When we travel together, we are a team. You are the leader, but leaders let people know what to expect and what to do. I need more preparation time."

There was a lot to unpack there, but I had to admit I should have given her more time. I had to keep her in the loop, especially if I needed her help. "You're right. The first time I saw a free gargoyle, well, the second time I guess, I was so scared I cut everyone off and broke up with Tiffany. I'm sorry, it won't happen again."

She added nothing else but acted satisfied.

Crap, I couldn't keep that promise. "That's not the truth. I'll forget, and I will tell you why." I wanted to be upfront.

"A harsh truth is better than not knowing. Go ahead."

"This spell of the church, what we learned from Bishop Pedrotti, will turn Atlanta into a portal to the Realm of Darkness. It will be one of three portals. Okinawa, Cape Horn, and Atlanta. This triangle the three cities form will kill tens of millions, but the church can then engulf the world in the Realm of Darkness."

"Why?"

"The people and buildings will disappear, but the land will remain. The church will hold the world hostage and destroy any dissent. They can rebuild cities at their whim."

"That's horrible."

"That's why we fight." It wasn't the only reason. I fought for love, but others needed less nebulous reasons. "That's what I think about and when I have an action to prevent or slow that result, I become singly focused."

"Okay. Let's change the subject. Was your high school called Trauma High?" She pulled onto smaller roads that started winding.

"No, why?" I chuckled, though.

"Bishop Pedrotti killed Nicole's parents, and she shared parents with Nathan and Rachel," said Rebecca.

"For protection and with arranged marriages, they were already like that. Nicole having a different last name, was all I knew for years. In fact, they changed Rachel's last name before she started school to keep her and Nathan separated in the computer systems."

She took a tight right turn. "Okay, but there's your family, then the murder of the Nathan and Rachel's parents and grandmother."

I lightened it up. "My fight with Dawg, Trish, and Miles' break ups, the baseball team losing in county, the football team losing by a late field goal in regionals, and the cheerleading squad not placing in the southeast invitational. We dealt with a lot."

Rebecca cackled. "Okay, maybe I just hang out with the trauma group. But tell me why you included a fight?"

"Khalil and I are friends now, but we were both suspended, and the story blew up and students still talk about it. I was just looking for more trauma things." I smiled and kept the fight's intensity out of the conversation.

I added a fun thing. "We had fun too. Rachel and I took a project our senior year to ensure we graduated. We took part in a project about a tulip bulb stock market thing."

"That sounds fun. Did you learn anything?" She smiled at my mention of the Senior year project.

"I remember the dates sixteen thirty-four and sixteen thirty-seven. Plus, I know that the best way to make money in the stock market is to lie and cheat." I remembered that and how Dawg helped me by taking some bulbs from others and replacing them with bulbs I bought. Rachel and I ended up as the top two traders.

"From what I understand, that is how the stock market works." She smiled and focused on driving.

We drove with background classical music for an hour. "I want to cast a couple of spells before we get to the cabin."

She nodded, saying nothing, and we drove another half hour until she parked. "How come you don't use Nathan's reports on your banishing? He runs them through that big AI computer thing."

"I patted the <u>Abernathy Book of Gargoyles</u>. For gargoyles, I trust nothing else. I'll use Nathan's reports for all other battles."

We both got out, and I walked over to a nearly dead bush that was hidden by our vehicle. I cast *Mature Plant* and created the druidic magic berries with *Create Berries*. The wind was biting cold up in the mountains and it tore me to choose between more Earth Power and wearing a coat.

A raccoon led a few squirrels to us. The hurt raccoon needed healing, but the squirrels wanted to say hello. Someone had kicked the raccoon, then hit it with a baseball bat. I healed the raccoon and greeted the squirrels.

"I never understood why I saw so many animals when we dated, but if you heal them and talk to them, it makes sense now." Rebecca snuggled in a thick down coat like a northern snow bunny. It wasn't that cold up here.

"Yeh, these powers can give me away, but animals help me so often it's a good relationship." Plus, animals around humans never worked out well. We could use fewer humans.

After I ate a berry, I handed one to Rebecca. "Eat this. I want to see if eating one makes us feel less hungry or just replenishes the nutrients."

She looked as if I handed her a snake, but then popped it into her mouth. "It's red but tastes like a juicy blackberry. What does it do?"

"If you're hurt, it helps you heal faster, it cures the blackness, and it feeds you for a day. It's giving you the benefit of casting druidic magic without casting it." We both looked at my arm, but it didn't need to be exposed for me to know it had healed with a small scar. I then told her, "If I had this spell when Old Donnie was alive, it would have saved his life."

"Where'd you get it?"

"The faction of gargoyles that say they want to ally with us against the church and live in peace with humanity are the ones that gave me the new spell book."

"Please go slow. I know you're partially trained, but even a couple of years of druid training are more than my two weeks of knowing magic is real. Now we have gargoyle factions?"

"This is why I'm an awful choice for a leader. I can't think through things like that." I knew this whole leader thing was a bad idea.

"Good leaders rely on others. When I point out something, correct it and you'll be an outstanding leader."

I doubted it, but said nothing.

We got back in and drove through the state park until we reached a secluded cabin. While we moved into the cabin, we inventoried everything in the back of the SUV as we brought it into the large cabin. I noted where six hundred in cash was in one box. The guns and bullets meant nothing, but cash, food, water, and medical supplies were important.

"I am full. That berry worked." She placed her bags and equipment in the main bedroom, and I took the bed in the loft. There wasn't much more than wood decorating this house. Wooden floors, wooden walls, wooded beams and smooth circular wooden braces made up the building. Brown leather furniture, a wagon wheel chandelier, and wood tables with glass tops made up the living area, while the shiny metal kitchen was modern as all get out.

The back porch had a hot tub, but it was too cold for Rebecca and probably too frivolous. She closed the door to the games room right after she looked inside. Rachel would have loved that room and we would have stayed up all night playing.

Rebecca and I each ate a half a sandwich for some calories, then turned into bed early since we only got three or four hours of sleep in the car this morning.

SATURDAY WAS A SUNNY day as the wind blew the clouds away. We walked out onto the porch while she held a scope. I helped her carry out a rifle case while she carried a bag. She wore the same jean skirt and brown top she wore the day I got up the courage and begged her to help me learn to shoot. Not that I'd remember something like that about an ex....

"I have an excellent shot, here and there." She pointed to two clearings.

The left looked good, but I wanted to verify where she pointed. "Are you pointing to the left of the Tupelo or the area between the White Pines?"

"What's a Tupelo? Never mind, it's the pines."

She pointed me to an area down a hill and past where a small stream flowed. A flat area before elevation climbed to the next peak. "If you can do your circle thing there, will you post this orange tape chin high on the middle tree there?"

I ran down, crossed the creek and scoped out the area and put the tape on the tree at my chin height. This shaded area kept it chilly.

The creek ran, but had a thin coat of ice that formed, broke off, and reformed.

She stayed on the porch with set-ups of rifles and scopes and looked at different areas while I walked inside. With the double doors to the porch open, cold air swirled through the light wood cabin. I shifted the leather couch and the heavy dark oak living room table near the fireplace to create some room.

On the cleared-out section of hardwood floor, I stretched all my muscles. She cleaned her rifles and at one point came and got my knives and sharpened them.

Once stretched, I spent a couple of hours practicing stances, blocks, and strikes. Then, since I knew a full-body workout I could do without weights, I worked out. It took an hour and left me a sweating ball of fatigue. My arms and legs shook from the strain.

"You work out like that?" Rebecca watched me peel my shirt off as I dug out my toiletry kit.

"You saw me practice weapons with Rachel the other day."

"I thought you may have been showing off for Wesley." She was smiling and I couldn't tell if she was teasing or not.

"We don't have a higher gear to show off. But didn't you notice I had muscles?" I was too tired to give a proper flex.

"I can tell you're in shape, but not big like Miles. If we had a signal up here, I'd snap a pic of you to Nicole. Wait, no it's a good thing we don't have a signal up here. She'd worry."

I couldn't believe she said I wasn't big. "I'm six-foot one and one eighty. Miles is a giant, but I am not a small druid boy. Bodies that can fight a gargoyle take effort. A lot of effort."

She giggled. "Been compared to Miles a few times, have you?"

Exhausted from the workout, I needed to concentrate to realize she was teasing. "Maybe I have," I said. I guzzled my protein and creatine shake that I made with a banana.

"Hold on." She jumped up and went to the bathroom and carried a scale back. "You've been saying that one eighty line since before we dated. Get on."

I lumbered onto the scale.

She chuckled. "I thought so. Two-oh-seven."

I collapsed into the chair. I wondered if the scale was right, but I'd gone through two bulking cycles and a cutting cycle since I last weighed myself. "You don't care about me being strong or a good fighter. What did you see in me, anyway? You're beautiful, regal, and intelligent. You could have your choice of men."

"I was into you because you didn't treat me like arm candy. I was a person in your eyes." She smiled at me and looked up when she'd imagined happy times.

"How else would someone treat you?"

She leaned into the overstuffed leather chair that I moved against the wall with the tv. "Being pretty isn't all it's cracked up to be, and guys like you are rare."

"I don't know about that."

"I've had time to do some thinking, and since you saved my life and came to terms with things, I owe you a genuine explanation." Her eyes looked down like she was trying to remember something.

"Okay."

"Have a seat." She pointed to where I moved the couch over by the porch double doors. I sunk into the brown leather couch and leaned on the armrest instead of leaning so far back I'd need to work my abs to get out. I kicked my knees and feet up on the couch too, so I could keep them stretched.

She looked at my feet on the couch and shook her head with a grin. "I told you the reason we broke up was because you'd disappear for days, had no motivation, and you had an inner violence. But since, I've learned that none of this was true. Druid work motivates you. You fight gargoyles and are predictable about where you'll be."

"No worries." I didn't need to listen to more of my mistakes when I dated her.

"Well, the problem is who I am as a person and who you are as a person. Neither of us discussed our families when we dated, but I came from a legacy of money, my parent's generation squandered everything they got their hands on. My grandparents had a college trust for me or I wouldn't even been able to go to college."

"Okay." I did not know where this was going.

"Then when we had our big post break up fight, I told you I needed stability. I need to know someone is going to be there with me to build up money and not put our kids into the same situation as me."

"Money?" I was even more confused.

"Not just that, all things a family provides. Security, stability, and yes, money. You are a great person, but you will never be stable in society. Our lives would never be secure and I couldn't think about living like that my whole life."

Well, that was a good reason. "Well, you're right. My retirement plan is to find someone who can protect my grave from a gargoyle for seventy-two hours. This could happen tomorrow, or it could happen hundreds of years from now."

"But that's not the case anymore. My life is going to be chaotic regardless and I have to rethink things, but I will not be the on and off girlfriend. I think that's another reason I'm okay with you dating Nicole. You haven't figured out what you want and if one of us does something wrong, you have someone waiting. It'd be too easy for you to get upset with one of us and jump to the other. It would be a disaster."

She was right, but I had a ready counter. "Off and on again, worked for Trish and Miles. Those two broke up a dozen times in high school and college."

She chuckled. "Trish is strong headed and Miles lets her push until he says enough and he draws a line. I hope they figure out how to solve this issue without the breakups."

"Yeah. They have a volatile relationship." I chuckled. "Haley and I had to walk a tightrope some days with those two."

Rebecca giggled. "Trish said when you got in her face last week and told her to listen to you, it was the first time she saw why other women wanted you."

"That's funny. I think Miles secretly wants a woman to take charge of things."

"Corey. Please be aware that Nicole is a lot like you and you'll need to give her the benefit of the doubt. She's been a loner for so long. She has dated no one since high school waiting for you."

"You're right about her and me—both loners, fear of losing someone, and willing to cross the line others won't. It's scary how much alike we are. But it's frustrating how everyone is so much smarter about these things." I stood up to go to the shower.

"A leader will stop need to stop saying that around people. You figured out Nicole's plan, figured out how to address it, figured out the strategy to beat Bishop Pedrotti, and how to get your way with territory leaders who have been working a certain way for hundreds of years. People will believe that you think they're stupid."

Not knowing what she meant, I closed the door to the bathroom and showered, then tried to wash all the last conversation out of me without success. This leader thing would not be easy. I was barely comfortable being part of a team.

After I dressed, we ate a dinner of soup and sandwiches out on the porch and looked over the area next to Rebecca's setup. "Will you be able to cover me before sunrise?" I asked.

"Yes. I have night vision goggles. Do you have night vision magic?"

A hawk flew in and landed on the handrail of the porch. That explained why smaller animals were scarce.

"Hey buddy, good hunting tonight?" I went back to the plan with Rebecca. "Yeh, it's druidic vision with the torc. By the way. If we go to an urgent care center, we use cash and we are Tyler and Nancy. We were camping and fell."

"I hate using the Nancy alias. Let's not get hurt."

"Only use the alias when you travel where the church is searching for you. Skip it everywhere else. However, let's be prepared because getting hurt is a normal part of this life. So, are you good?"

"I believe my setup is prepared and I am ready to make the shot." She patted her gun and mount on the wooden railing.

It was time to lighten the mood. "If you're going to keep hanging out with the likes of me, you need to say, I'm finer than frog hair split four ways."

She laughed and then collected herself. "What does that even mean? I guess that would be a pretty fine strand of hair if they quartered it."

I laughed too. "It's an Old-South saying. Mr. Wilbanks used to say it when I'd finish up a shipment in his warehouse to mean all was good with him."

"You'll be happy to know that because of you, I have added an Old-South saying into my vernacular." She grinned like Rachel.

"I left my vernacu-whatsis in my other bag." That was one of those fifty cent words she used.

"The way a person speaks. I'll fight anytime, anyplace, and anywhere is the saying I added to talk about you."

I chuckled. "If you had to pick one for me, you did a good job."

We packed up everything except what we needed. I put the battery back in the burner phone, but left the little card out, and set the alarm for three forty-five am.

Morning came, and I packed up the SUV and Rebecca was already setting up a shot with the bolt-action rifle. I cast the druidic berries and got six and made sure we both ate one. I read the book to make sure I knew this gargoyle's symbols since it was larger than others. Then I strolled out the back door.

Chapter 8—My Very Own Snake-Hunter

"What weapons are you using?" Rebecca asked me.

"What?" She stood holding a scope in her hand and had a funky binocular thing pushed up on her forehead. It was the first thing she ever wore that did not make her even prettier.

"I need to know for tracking my target." She touched a rifle with a mount on the railing.

Fair enough. I reviewed them one at a time. "I'm an up close and personal killer. Tonfa is my go-to weapon." After I put them back, I pulled out two knives. "I use combat knives. This obsidian blade is for kill shots. I keep a glass breaker and a tactical pen nearby." As I showed her the smaller items, I pulled them out of their spot on my belt. "I keep a pepper gel and a stun gun on the belt, too. This is the build out of a killer."

"How often do you replace the obsidian knife as a wartime druid? I bet it shatters every time you use it."

It's funny how she corrected the word killer with me. She watched me plunged the obsidian blade into the heart of Bishop Pedrotti when I sacrificed him to Queen Niamh. "Never, I got it from Old Donnie. I never thought about it before." I pulled the black glass weapon from its leather sheath. It was naturally sharp and never dulled. If I left it out, I'd cut myself and it would cut anything to shreds.

She put a handgun on each side of her hip and mounted her rifle on the railing. I saw Missy, Old Donnie's gun, by the railing. She moved the goggles from her forehead to her eyes and she adjusted some knobs. "Okay, ready when you are."

After removing my shoes, I used druidic vision from the torc and had no problem navigating down the steps and crossing over the stream. The soft ground gave way as I stepped, but not enough to prevent the small jump over the stream. The cool air smelled clean up here by the little creek. Earth Power flowed into me. When I stood between the white pines, I cast *Discovery of Dispatches* to verify the next month of gargoyles and enjoyed the morning for a minute.

After that, I cast a *Create Honeysuckle* twice to get a full bush, cut seven twigs from it, and finally created a large eight-foot circle. One twig for the circle and one per hand to hold weapons with. This circle used five points of honeysuckle to help focus power. Holding two twigs was my only preparation for the Snake-Hunter. Clive wasn't exaggerating when he said he saw a shoeless druid holding one focus and a pool cue let him know he wasn't the toughest guy in the bar. However, vampires were a cut below gargoyles, and gargoyles were a cut below Snake-Hunters.

Once I began casting the binding, it took little time before my torc alerted red and the world turned black and white. The twelve-foot gargoyle of granite and obsidian who talked to me on top of Loon Mountain, Strumath, appeared. I didn't start the binding. "You, you aren't supposed to be back for fifty years." This broke the first rule of banishings.

He folded in his giant wingspan and it seemed he had more obsidian in his face. "Time is short. What coordinates doth thou defend?" His features were hard to identify, but I could feel warmth in his voice tinged with worry.

I had to think, but I could remember this. I used gps while camping. "Atlanta is thirty-three-point-seventy-six and negative eighty-four-point-thirty-nine."

"Good." The beast paused. "They move the seat, to fool enemies. The new location is thirty-four-point-zero-seven-four-six-two-two and negative eighty-four-point-two-nine-two-two-nine-seven.

I dropped to one knee and wrote them exactly in my gargoyle book.

"Thine enemy shall summon me and my will support thou. Thou might not but run, the hunter comes."

A shot rang out by the house. The gargoyle disappeared of his own accord. The world stayed black and white, and no one was on the porch!

I grabbed the tonfa while holding the honeysuckle in each hand. I used the torc's vision and saw blue magic coming from my left. There wasn't time to run to the house. I reached out for any large animals in the area with my Animal Domain magic and two bears answered. This was the Great Smokies National Park, so it must be black bears. I told them that something dangerous was here. They came to defend their land.

The blue magic was gone, so I took a cautious step forward and then another. I stepped carefully to the house. I jumped over the stream, with a cross block readied. A sizzle of burning flesh hit me with the smell of cooked meat when something my size bowled me over. Mud splashed into my face. One tonfa had warmed up from contact with this creature and the other tonfa shattered. Wood shards stuck into my arm.

I scrambled up and tried to rely on the Earth Power to catch my breath. The creature in front of me was not really a man. Its face was blank except for a mouth full of sharp teeth, holes instead of a nose and dark orbs where his eyes should be. The body was nude without genitalia, but they covered his body in tattoos—a Snake-Hunter. His large tattoo on the chest caught my attention. The word differed from the hunter that killed Old Donnie. He had once told me they all had the same word.

Roars from two bears came from the right, and the Snake-Hunter never turned to the noise. It kept its focus on me. I shifted into a square stance and still had my right foot in the stream.

Its right hand swung at me and a quick mid-block with the tonfa caught it and numbed my left arm. Its hand sizzled and this time I gagged on the aroma of burning flesh. I yanked out the pepper gel and sprayed it directly into its face. It stopped long enough to scrape it off the timeless but empty face, but was otherwise unaffected. *That wasn't good.* It gave me time to cast the spell, *Animal Control,* to help power the two black bears. They were now double strength black bears. The first bear charged and swiped the Snake-Hunter, who punched the bear and sent it sprawling.

I followed up with a right elbow swing with the tonfa while focused on the honeysuckle, but it kicked me in the chest as the tonfa burned his chin and knocked me into the creek. Then the second bear came and the Snake-Hunter picked both bears up, ignored the claws, and bashed them together. I struggled to breathe. Earth Power roared through me but could not counter the pain in my chest.

"Run," I told the bears. "Save yourself. I canceled the spell." *Crap*!

They were down and scrambling away. I stood with my obsidian knife and my unbroken tonfa and stared at the Snake-Hunter. My heron stance with the knife forward and the tonfa in the mid-block position faced this thing. I might could get a lucky swing at him with the knife.

It leaped, and I prepared to tuck and roll. A shot rang out, and it fell face down next to me. The back of its head was nearly gone. Struggling to breathe, I rolled him over. The front of its head, an inch above its eyebrows, had a small clean hole.

The back of its head was missing, but both holes repaired slowly. I drew a circle and began binding. Near the end of the binding, I rolled the creature over, placed my right hand in the dirt inside the circle, my left hand on its chest, and watched the word disappear from the thing's chest. My left biceps burned, and I knew the word was now mine.

The Snake-Hunter's face contorted, and it turned to dust in front of me. I wanted to lie down and catch my breath, but every bit of Earth Power I could muster helped me to stand and check on Rebecca.

Stumbling, I splashed through the creek, unable to run. My chest screamed to stop despite Earth's power. She was prone with her rifle in front of the porch. Blood pooled from her hip and right thigh and soaked the already maroon ground. Her eyes had puffed over and blood squirted from her nose and swollen upper lip.

"I'm getting a med kit. Be right back."

Barely able to stumble to the SUV, I traced my way to the back, and fished out the medical kit. I grabbed two berries and one of the left-over prescription pain killers and stumbled back to Rebeca. "Stay with me. This will hurt." I had to hurry. She was losing blood. I had to save her life.

Time was counting down. She was bleeding, and I had created two magical signatures. One of them was large and fifteen minutes old. If priests showed up, we'd both die. It felt like I was taking my own sweet time, though I moved as fast as I could.

I moved her bottom lip with my finger and gave her the pill with water and a berry, then cut open her pants on the right side and poured saline over the wound and patted it dry with gauze. She yelled, but I couldn't blame her. She was trying to hold it in.

The remaining butterflies and then two compresses were all I had to seal this up under the rest of my medical tape. To get a tight wrap on it, I used every bit of the four-inch gauze. Then I got an ace bandage and wrapped her waist tightly to help hold everything. Her moan of pain when I pulled it tight cut through me as bad as if the wound was mine.

She could not die! She saved my life. *I loved her.*

I grazed her cheek with my finger to get her attention. "They can find us with all this magical signature. We have to move. I'm getting you to get medical care, but it won't be close. The pain reliever is all I want to give you since we need to tell them you've had nothing." With that, I carried her to the back of the SUV and laid her on the bed. I got an ice pack out and placed it on her face where she grabbed it.

"Rifle," she mumbled. "And license plate."

"Don't talk. I'll make one trip back, grab everything, clean up the area, and then we'll jet." Tears filled my eyes. She saved my life and I couldn't let her die.

I stumbled back and climbed into the house. There was a handgun, my shoes, and her night vision goggles on the deck. I gasped every time I bent and sharp pains riddled through my body when I picked everything up.

The broken tonfa, good tonfa, my weapons belt, her gun, and rifle fit into the locked part under the bed in the SUV. I closed the pine cabinet drawer stained to match the beige interior of the SUV. After tossing the medkit on the passenger seat, I stumbled back and cast a spell from the gargoyles to clean up the ground and porch.

It took way too long, but I struggled to breathe and my chest had a carving pain combined with the sharp, cutting pain of a cracked rib. I let the bears know their territory was safe. I cast *Local Nature* to clean up this area. The twinkling of Fey power wasn't enough to help the pain, but it looked pretty.

I searched the back storage to see what she meant about license plates. There were a few leaf magnets and two other license plates to change out. I put two leaf magnets on the current license plate and brought out a license plate from Alabama for later. My motorcycle mask came out for the cameras at the state park entrance. My internal clock alarmed, and we were out of time to escape cleanly.

Getting in, I asked, "How are you doing? Can you stay awake?"

"The pill is kicking in," she mumbled.

Tires squealed, and a shot rang out. "Time to go," I yelled, but the sentence caught with pain in my chest. The engine roared, and we took off toward the shot. A gray Cadillac with a priest leaning out the passenger window pointed a rifle toward us. I gunned the SUV and mentally prepped for a game of chicken. The priest with the rifle slipped back into his seat. *You priests have met a country boy who played chicken for fun in high school.* "Hot damn, you're in my redneck world now," I said to no one.

Rocks and dirt kicked up the underside and my chest caught as I slammed into the back of my seat, having given the SUV everything it had. It felt as if the speed crawled compared to my Mustang, but this thing ate up most of this mountain road.

I left the details to myself. If Rebecca thought a wheelie on a motorcycle stood out, an actual game of chicken would shake her. They swerved before me and I stayed on the road with my late turn. They hit a patch of leaves and tires squealed. I could set up an ambush!

I slammed the brakes and blocked the road with the SUV and called for any nearby hawks. Two answered and while standing on dirt, I asked them to help me with the men in the Cadillac. My memory kicked off from when I saved Rebecca.

I ran into the house to save Rebecca, and the priest raised his hand to cast a spell. His face held shock when it didn't fire.

I kept my mask on, popped the back, and grabbed the one good tonfa, parachute cord, and a knife. I tucked the cord and knife into my pants, popped a mouthpiece in, and ran back along the ground next to the road, absorbing as much Earth Power as it would give me.

A shot rang out near me as I heard two men scream. The hawks attacked the face of both men. One had a shotgun, and the other had a rifle, but they swung them like clubs at my friends.

I ran towards one with all the speed I could muster without oxygen towards the closest and hit him in the head three times before he stopped moving. Then the other priest had calmed his frenetic swings and was about to shoot my friend! I screamed as I flung a knife at him. He held a hand out, and I dived to the side as a streak of electricity tore up the road where I had stood. *That ain't good.*

Another memory came to me of Wesley on the patio.

"I'm still upset," he stopped and cried out. "You and Rebecca die December second. In two days. You die on the road with a priest blasting blue magic and then Rebecca bleeds out in the back of an SUV."

That was a bummer of a memory.

I threw a rock and hit his arm and the shotgun fired into the ground as he ducked. He aimed the gun at me. The hawk, who escaped being shot, clawed at his eyes. The shot rang out, but the standing priest ran towards me and held up his hand. I retreated, but blue magic coursed through me and jolted my flesh and my body. The pain in my chest amplified, and I screamed. Magician church magic had the pain of electricity combined with the thump of a hammer. The mouthpiece saved my teeth and even more injuries.

I crawled back in searing pain and stumbled to the SUV. My chest threatened to break apart and my skin screamed with burning pain.

The cry of a hawk caused the priest to cry out. The electricity stopped.

How can I change the vision? Was my brain trying to help me with those memories? I'd listen because I had nothing else.

I retreated more to get out of his range. He charged as he fought off the hawks for minutes and came toward me and lifted his hand to kill me. Nothing happened. He looked at his hand with confusion. *I'll be damned.*

With a painful charge, I nailed his jaw with a wicked uppercut using the tonfa and slammed his teeth into each other. His body crumpled to the pavement. *That's why you wear mouth guards when you rumble.*

Grabbing my paracord, I bound his feet and hands and then bound them to each other. I searched him, took his wallet and shotgun. Then I pulled his vestments over his face.

One hawk was fine, but the other landed and its wing lay flat on the ground and I saw blood. I healed it and thanked my two hawk friends. They saved the life of a druid—me.

At the priest with multiple head wounds, I checked for a pulse and felt a feint one in his neck. I didn't need a murder here, but they could not follow us soon. I'd already killed one man in my life.

What if these were Dark Fey?

No. No excuses. I'd be Killer Corey—not murderer Corey.

With the first priest's wallet and rifle in my hands, I bound his wrists. Then I stabbed both passenger side tires with my knife.

I searched their vehicle and took the keys. The half empty coffee stayed, but in the glove box was a paper bag. I dumped it out and saw two stacks of hundred-dollar bills. Wow! *Thank you for your donation.* I threw the Cadillac keys into the woods with all my might.

Stumbling to the SUV, I counted the steps from the second priest to the SUV where Rebecca lay. Thirteen. About twenty-five feet. I knew one of her actual powers. Magicians in the church couldn't use magic within twenty-five feet of her. *Damn, Wesley had his power for less than an hour and saved my life.*

I tossed the two guns into the storage in the back with my weapons. After closing everything up, I pulled back out. I hoped both survived, and I had enough time to get away. There was no fresh blood on the sleeping bag under Rebecca. She might live... she had to live.

"What's going on? Were those shots?" Her mumbles gave away her pain.

I put my mouthpiece back into my pocket. "We've got an hour or more head start," I panted out.

Despite wanting to get to the closest care, we'd be dead if we stopped close by. I pulled up the navigation and set a path to the same urgent care center in Durham with Dr. Kanoska. It was nearly five hours away, but that's the best idea I had.

Chapter 9—Keep Her alive

The drive was nerve-wracking while I constantly looked in the rear-view mirror. Leaf season had officially come to North Georgia, and the leaves were beautiful, but I wished to be in my Mustang instead of this SUV that sat so high. Adrenaline faded and my chest and arms hurt. Even though I struggled to breathe, I knew they couldn't compare to Rebecca's pain. She had taken a wicked punch or two to the face and a claw wound to her hip and leg.

I needed to think of her as Nancy. I can't mess up her identity. *She had to live.*

This wasn't me needing to save a person who saved my life, I was saving a person who had touched me in non-physical ways like she'd be a part of my soul forever.

On me, it hurt to breathe, so I just focused on driving and talking to her softly, so she didn't sleep. To keep her alive, we had to talk.

"Give me a second and we'll talk to keep ourselves awake." My eyes dropped, and I felt lightheaded. I felt my head fall towards the steering wheel.

"Okay," she murmured. She touched me. Gold light traveled up my arm had stopped in my heart. My alertness came back, and I straightened us on the road.

What magic was gold? Focus! You're hallucinating.

Rebecca saved my life with that rifle shot, and Wesley saved my life. Miles and Rachel had saved my life. So had Nathan. How could I be a leader if they all needed to save my life?

We drove by a few sugar maple trees, what Madison would probably call sugar trees under stress.

Blood covered my seat and door and it had soaked through my shirt. With my adrenaline subsided and no connection to the Earth, my shoulder stung. While I kept driving, I pulled my shirt off. A bullet had taken a chunk of skin from my shoulder. I balled up a shirt and grabbed the good tonfa. I pressed the balled-up shirt into the wound by leaning into the tonfa on the dash.

It was time to keep Rebecca alert. "Yesterday you mentioned we didn't talk about our families. You told me yours, so I'll tell you mine to keep us both awake."

"Okay," she mumbled.

It was a week after my eighteenth birthday. I had a cross-country meet with Lovejoy. It was the second one after the Georgia lifted the quarantine for outside events. I came back Saturday at one am and went to a party with Miles. Like normal, I slept in my van until I showed up at work at eight am. After I worked there until three and took a shower and changed in the warehouse. I had a date with Haley that night and we spent the night in the van and we showed up to church to hear how'd we burn in hell before I brought her home.

I drove home for the first time since Friday. The police tape was already around the property and Richard, Miles' dad, was there talking to Officer Tines. Richard hugged me and the officer looked sad. They told me everyone was dead, but I couldn't go in.

"Were you a suspect?" She mumbled.

They cleared me fast, but something didn't sit right with me. That night, Miles drove me out there. I broke into the house and crept around. There was no burned furniture and no burned bodies. My bedroom had a burned bed, clothes, and dresser, but someone cleared all the other rooms.

Miles convinced me to play it cool, and he helped me come up with some questions for Officer Tines. "Did they find the fire-proof safe under my mother's bed? Was there anything just water damaged?"

We figured out the officer knew they cleaned the house out first, but then he said something I still remember, "Look, son, bad things will happen to you if you keep following up here. I've been told to seal the case."

"Did you fight it?" asked Rebecca.

"Yep, I'd come out of meetings with insurance companies. I was ready."

"I already heard that I needed death certificates, so," I said. "So, even if that were true, officer, you know I can't without death certificates. The world knows they still lived. That means I'd have to go on."

He nodded and stepped out to make a call. The next day, I had all three death certificates and the reports for the insurance companies, and he made me promise to drop it.

I did.

It's funny, I had picked up Nicole from school because of a teacher's workday and she clung to me. I swallowed my shock and hurt, but still she stared at me.

Now I know it's because she became Realized because my emotions overwhelmed her and sparked her empathy.

"Is that where your money comes from?" Rebecca's voice was weak and she could hardly pronounce words correctly.

"Most of it. I sold the old property since it had two kinds of insurance and bought my house free and clear. I had already turned eighteen and got the money without crooked lawyers in the way. But I got walked through everything with Carol and Richard. I get thirteen hundred a month after taxes. I've got twenty years and 4 months left. The rest comes from the freelance job and search and rescue."

"Has anything changed since then?"

"Nope. I didn't know how to follow up and tried to forget about it."

Five hours looking for someone to pick up my trace, making sure they did not follow us, worrying about Rebecca's wounds, the pain in my chest, and keeping pressure with my balled-up shirt on my shoulder was too much for me.

Pulling out of the national park onto a road with traffic lowered my anxiety a bit. I finally pulled off my mask with the cameras past.

"I'm drifting, what was the rest of the story..." she tried to go on. I knew she meant Old Donnie's story. The one Preacher Jon cut off.

"I got you," I said. "Preacher Jon was fine with the story where it discussed me. I was the emotionally damaged young man who saved Old Donnie's life on Stone Mountain. However, the story left off seventeen years before I was born."

"I figured you were the damaged young man." Her mumbles sounded painful.

I remembered Old Donnie telling me the rest in a drunken slur. In four years, Old Donnie got drunk enough to tell parts of the story a dozen times. I wished I could talk in Old Donnie's voice, but the pain was too much.

> *"Everyone knew it was a witch spell. All their most powerful spells take decades to cast. Hell, I heard they can even make a spell to bring a person back to life, but it needs twenty years to cast the spell and has to be cast at the time of birth. Doesn't sound too useful."*

He'd always drink a while between these parts.

> *"I was an emotionally damaged man myself. That year I took off in seventy-five had forty-six gargoyles I ignored. The church took in forty-three of them. Three escaped and killed five thousand people that year."*

He always cried here. *"Why did I play roadie for a year? Were five thousand lives worth a year of vacation?"*

Sometimes he'd collect himself instead of passing out.

> *"Well, I couldn't bring a kid up and I was a horrible parent. My grandson, well, he's a piece of shit—probably because of me. He's in charge and the territory was failing. The church raided the territory, and he was on his deathbed. All of his kids had run away from home. I sifted through the records of his kids with a sharp kid from Chicago to find the most competent one."*

> *"The smart ass fourteen-year-old who said none of us understood love before he ran away had become successful and found true love."*

"Preacher Jon," she said.

"Yep."

"I convinced him to leave true love to come back and rescue the Southeast, and I promised to back him up and let him establish his area of love when he could. The fucker did it. He saved everything and set up the world for you. Damn fucker saved me and I recovered to be the person I was in eighteen-eighty-three, when I became a druid."

"Wow. You were friends with Rachel and Nicole already. How come you didn't already know Preacher Jon?"

"I met Preacher Jon the day at Mellow Mushroom. He stayed hidden from me. Nathan was twenty, Rachel was eighteen, and I guess he reeled from his wife, and two kids, and their spouses being murdered by the church. Plus, he had to save the Southeast—again." I went back to recalling Old Donnie's talk.

"The boy who saved Rachel's life. No lie, I've seen young girls kill themselves because of depression, and you saved her. Plus, you cared for Nicole. We watched you since you had the spark. But you had such a big heart. Lots of people cried when you were the Wartime Druid. Carol, Richard, Me, Preacher Jon, and others."

"That seems weird. It seems you knew everything," she murmured.

"I only recently put it all together since, when he got drunk enough to tell the story, he was incoherent."

"That makes more sense," she whispered.

My shirt didn't soak with blood, so I put it on the passenger side floor. The SUV had enough of Rebecca and my blood. Wait—don't be stupid, Nancy, and Tyler's blood.

I was quiet for too long, so I talked again. "I figured out the second of your powers." She said statements that sounded like predictions, only they came true. When she pointed me to New Hampshire and said those locations were important—it became important to us. But now I learned she also blocked magic from church magicians. *Did she heal me with a golden light?* My heart still glowed gold.

"Please don't," she whispered.

"Do you want me to keep them from others or from you?"

"Both." Another pain entered her voice—different from the strain of the physical pain.

"Okay, but when I say I need you by my side to fight priests, I'll need you by my side. Do that and no one will hear anything from me."

"Promise." Even I was smart enough to recognize a deathbed promise.

I WAS WOOZY WHEN WE pulled into the parking lot of Appalachian Hills Care. I was going to make it. Rebecca was going to make it.

My chest hurt, I couldn't breathe, and hadn't stopped bleeding, but we had made it. I pulled into the parking lot at the same time as the doctor at nine thirty. She was about to say they didn't open until ten, but when I pulled the sleeping bag and carried Nancy in the bloody bag, she let us in and pointed me to the back, where I stumbled and carried Nancy. I placed her on a table with a blue medical mattress. *She was going to live.*

I repeated my practiced line of how she and I were camping, but Dr. Kanoska held up her hand. "Corey, she needs clean up, stitches, and an x-ray. You sit on that bed, please."

Arguing would only delay care. The nurse walked in and stared at me. I tried to take a deep breath and choked. "I'm just waiting for Nancy," I whispered.

"Shut up," said the doctor. "I recognize a bullet wound and a collapsed lung." She paused, "I also recognize Rebecca from your roster, so drop the alias." She gave Rebecca a shot and my chest stopped glowing.

The nurse dropped the forms when she caught me falling off the gurney. The floor was cold and felt so good. It should have hurt when I fell, but the cold floor felt so nice on my face.

"Doctor," she called.

That's when they say my heart stopped. They also said it should have stopped when I took the kick to the chest.

I CAME TO ON A TABLE with a machine over me and Dr. Kanoska viewing an X-ray. She put an O2 sensor on me, ran oxygen to my nose, and wrapped my chest. Then they rolled me next to Rebecca.

The doctor rolled up my left sleeve and looked at my healed left arm. She touched it and said, "I'd say your bruised lung, clean shoulder wound, and cracked ribs would take months to heal, but it won't, will it?"

I came back to my senses. Rebecca breathed clearer. I shook my head no. "Is she going to live? She saved my life. She's my ex and we'd saved each other's life." I rambled and tears filled my eyes.

"Everyone is going to be fine. Now answer my question. I know you were Druid Don's apprentice. Are you the hotshot who joined the Spring Fey Court?"

"I am the Druid of the Fey Spring Court. It doesn't look like I'm a hotshot."

"I had to use a lot of magic of my people to get you two to where modern medicine could heal you. There is no explaining how the two of you made it here alive. However, this leaves the Moon-eyed people defenseless in December's new moon. Will you protect them and give time for the magic to replenish?"

Even if we didn't owe Dr. Kanoska, I'd protect them. "Yes."

"You won't mind this extra healing. It will help you more than this modern medicine. Moon-eyed people are the best healers in the world, but this will sting."

She put a horrid paste on our wounds and made us both drink something foul.

"You know how magic has colors?" I asked the doctor.

"Yes. You have green, Dark Fey is black, and church magicians are lightning blue." She looked at me curiously.

I had to know if I hallucinated. "Ever seen gold magic?"

"I wish. That's the celestial magic of the heavens. The only power that can heal without cost and can negate the church." She turned to Rebecca. "Are you telling me the Scion is reborn?"

I didn't even know what that meant. "I'm not smart enough, but I made a deathbed promise to keep anything I saw secret."

"Well, if the Scion ever is reborn, it won't be a secret. The heavens will open and the world will see the golden beam to mark the Scion." She left us with the nurse and strolled into the other room.

I touched Rebecca's hand. It was warm, and she breathed normally. They had given her an IV. I looked at my hand and it had an IV as well. Rebecca wore blue hospital scrubs, and I had green hospital scrubs on. We were quite the pair.

The doctor and nurse came back with two packets and a bag with our bloody clothes. "In this first packet are antibiotics for both of you and pain pills for Nancy." She winked at me. "This second packet has coordinates and drawings of the lands of the Moon-eyed people."

The doctor didn't charge us, finished up the care, and helped us into the car. "We have to call the priests now so they don't kill us. Drive quickly. Remember, you cannot take any pain meds because it will hinder your breathing even more. Take deep breaths to keep up your oxygen. It'll hurt more, but keep you from passing out."

"Thank you." I owed the doctor for saving Rebecca and the Moon-eyed people. I now considered the Moon-eyed people under my protection.

"The Fey lose power in the noon sun, but they'll be attacking at night when they're most powerful," called Dr. Kanoska as we left.

I winced when I tried to chuckle. "That's the way my life goes."

Chapter 10—Healing

I laid Rebecca in the back on my sleeping bag and shut the back door. As I got into the driver's seat, the nurse opened a broken door on the side of the building and pushed a wheelchair over in front of it. Saying we escaped and broke a door appeared to be a good plan, and I hoped it worked. It was time to worry about Rebecca and me, so we picked up the highway and drove west. I drove to I-40 in Winston Salem.

"Where are we?" mumbled Rebecca.

"Alternative route. I trust the cabin now, and we will head there." I gave her a berry and took one for myself.

"Tell Preacher Jon." She mumbled and fell back asleep.

That was a good idea and I am glad she slept. My chest hurt too much to talk and I'm glad she could sleep with pain pills.

I stopped after Asheville for gas at an old building with the restroom entrances outside. With a quick spell, I sent a message via squirrel to Preacher Jon. *Hurt, but alive. Hunter dead. Have info. Tyler's and Nancy's cover and SUV compromised at the Appalachian Care Center. Cabin for healing.*

The priests had two hundred more dollars in their wallets, ignoring the stacks of hundreds. I grabbed my camping trowel and dug a hole out by the restrooms to bury the wallets.

Then I caught my breath and drove toward the cabin.

Rebecca snored gently, and I had to unload on someone. I whispered to her.

"Don't wake up. I'm not confused. You're a web. The first strand is your bravery, and it catches me. Another is your beauty. It catches me, and so does your intelligence. The three strands trap me in this web. Your kind heart and willingness to help Nicole, catches me. I'm a fly and I'm caught up in you. I'm trying with Nicole, but I want you so bad it hurts." She still snored, and I finished the drive to the cabin.

This was a new vehicle, so I stopped by Bubba, got out, and waved to him. Bubba had already met Rebecca, but this was his job. He protected this road for people that I didn't know and were none of my business. Once he saw me, I drove to the cabin and carried Rebecca into the bedroom. The blood in the SUV was everywhere. This was out of commission for a while, but we lived. We faced a Snake-Hunter and lived to fight another day.

I shuffled out to the porch and checked the firewood stack. The door frame held me up and made me want to lie on the ground. If I did, it'd be impossible to stand up to help Rebecca and, like it or not, she was in worse shape. I'd take care of her because I'd be dead without her. No, I'd take care of her because she was something that was part of me.

I carried a half dozen cut pieces of wood each in two trips. The brief relief walking on the dirt was heaven. The pain hit me the second I stepped into the cabin and disconnected from Earth Power. I opened the flue on the iron stove and then put two pieces with kindling and paper, lit it, closed the door; and put the induction fan on top to blow warm air into the bedroom. Then I sat gingerly in a recliner and napped.

I woke up to Rebecca calling me. "One sec," I called back. With deep breaths to not pass out, the five steps to the bedroom were difficult for me.

"I need to go to the bathroom." Her face contorted in pain.

Gritting my teeth, I lifted and carried her to the bathroom. At the table, trying to ignore the pain, taking deep breaths, I fished out the last two berries from my jacket. I switched out her ice pack for her face when I gave her ibuprofen for the swelling.

When she finished, she asked me to put her on the couch for the warmth. I gave her a berry and heated vegetable soup for each of us. With another piece of wood in the stove, the fire roared back to life. I closed the bedroom door to conserve heat and pointed the fan towards her.

Tears filled my eyes and my chest screamed with sharp pain. It was a struggle to breathe, and I wanted to take a pain pill, but I needed the oxygen, so I toughened up.

I wanted to sleep outside, but taking care of Rebecca came first.

After I carried her from the bathroom, I sat on the couch with her to catch my breath.

"How are you doing?" she asked.

"I can't take pain medicine and my cracked rib and bruised lung are unpleasant." It took a bit for me to get that all out.

She couldn't answer from her pain, so I held up my hand.

I made and lined up soup, water, pain medicine, and antibiotic dose on the end table and she took them one at a time.

"Is he dead?" She asked.

"The priests? No. At least they weren't when we left. Old Donnie told me never to murder if we could help it." It took me four attempts to get all that out, but I did.

"No, the guy who beat me." She groaned and held her side.

"Is it dead you mean?" I gasped. "Humans don't turn to dust when you take a tattoo from them." I rolled up my scrub's top sleeves and showed her my two biceps.

"How?"

"Earth Power, but it turned to dust, and I cleaned up with my spell when we left. By the way, that was a heckuva shot, even if you were uninjured." I could tell I was hard to listen to with my pauses and gasps of pain.

"I forecast his movement as best I could." She was murmuring. But I heard her clearly through her pain.

I pointed to my forehead, where the shot hit it cleanly. "You saved my life."

"Can anyone find us?" She lay down with contortions that showed pain rippled through her body. The pain on her face caused me to feel it.

"We're in the cabin. My first job as battle leader and should be my last."

"What? How did we get here?" She sounded confused.

"It's been sixteen hours since the attack. Over half of that had been driving." Talking was becoming painful, but I couldn't leave her in the dark.

"Will they trace us?"

"Fey power is scrambling my link to the Fey Realm."

"I took a green beam to my chest when it died." She looked at me for an explanation.

That was a wow statement from her. One Snake-Hunter made her just as powerful as I was before the Deer Woman. "The Earth rewarded you with the Snake-Hunter's power."

She was asleep again before I finished my sentence. I struggled through the pain because I had no other option. I placed another piece of wood in the oven and put away the soup bowls. We both had finished, so that was good. I shuffled out to the porch and sent another squirrel to Nathan in case Preacher Jon was driving. *Settled in. I have info on a location change of coordinates. Info soon.*

Reading my book and my notes from the spell this morning, I had the next gargoyle in six days. I napped out on the chair and woke to carry Rebecca to the bathroom, and change her dressings, put wood on the fire, and make more soup. The only trip outside was to send a squirrel to Miles. *I need help to connect to Earth. Rebecca cannot travel.*

I tossed and turned in the recliner through the night, but I kept adding wood to keep the room warm. I brought Rebecca to the bathroom once in the night and again in the morning. She took two prescription pills a day and ibuprofen and ice packs, but her face swelled and filled with puffy and purple skin.

A motorcycle roared up and parked outside the cabin. Rachel ran into the cabin. "Corey, I came the second the monsignor passed by my position."

"No hug. Pain."

She placed her face on my arm. "They spread out everyone else from the airport to Alpharetta for the monsignor's arrival. It's just me. They all but had to restrain Nicole from coming. She knew the best vantage point for spying on the monsignor. They would have certainly seen her move."

It felt good, but despite my lack of sleep and pain, I needed to clean Rebecca's wounds now. "You being here is all I need. You are a lifesaver. Please do the heated water again and carry Rebecca to the trough. I'll clean her wounds."

Rachel wiped tears from her eyes.

I wanted to hug her, but I couldn't. "Your boyfriend saved our lives. He's Realized for one hour and saved mine and Rebecca's life. That's a record."

"He broke radio silence because he was so happy when the scene changed. He was the first to know you lived." She laughed. "No one corrected radio silence since we were so happy."

I chuckled but coughed out pain.

She laughed through her tears. "Nicole and I all had our deaths moved to New Year's Eve night." She frowned. "Your death is oscillating a lot over the next two weeks. So is Rebecca's death."

"How is he handling it?" It must be tough to see the death of your friends.

"He handles seeing our deaths better, but he still needs support. He sees the full gruesome scene."

"Sounds like Trish and Miles are going to throw one hell of a party." I wished I could laugh.

Once outside, I took off all my clothes except shorts, and let Earth Power into me. On Rebecca, the antibiotic appeared to be working and her major wound was healing. Maybe the berries helped her. But there was stuff that I knew could help. Rachel carried her out to the trough and put her on towels, and we gave her a sponge bath. The Moon-eyed people's stuff was hard to get off. Rachel and I removed the puss and bloody scrubs and put a long shirt on Rebecca, which Rachel brought out.

She had lots of scrapes and I put anti-biotic on everything I cleaned before giving her another berry. With the ground warm from Rachel's Circle Appropriation Domain spell, we lay Rebecca on the towel, while Rachel helped me change the dressings on the long side wound.

My arm looked like mincemeat from the exploded tonfa. The real problem I had was the collapsed lung. But Rachel helped me change the dressings on my shoulder and arm after dressing Rebecca.

Rachel carried her inside and put her on clean sheets on the couch while I helped Rebecca stand.

"Thank you for taking care of me." Rebecca spoke a little clearer after she lay down.

"Thank you for making a headshot on an otherworldly being trying to kill me," I joked, then regretted it from the pain that shot through me.

"No really. You took me to a doctor, then brought me here. But carrying me to the bathroom, cleaning my wounds, feeding me, creating magic berries, keeping up the pills, changing my dressing, keeping the room warm, washing me, changing my clothes, and everything—well, that's something else. I am not healthy, but I know I'll be fine."

"Rachel is here and is going to help. To heal, I need to be outside." Rachel rubbed my back.

"You're nearly naked," Rebecca said and giggled, but then coughed with pain.

"I just bathed your wounds. You think Nathan will be upset?" I joked, but we just survived a near death experience.

"I was there too," said Rachel. She rubbed my back as I spoke.

"Was Rachel naked too?" joked Rebecca.

"No," said Rachel. "This is sick time only behavior." She kept a serious tone. I think we still must look a fright even though we had the best of magical and modern medical care over the past few days.

Rebecca drifted off and Rachel helped me out to the bed. She had already started the fire. "I'll keep the bed prep going. You rest."

"If Preacher Jon comes by, he doesn't need to be easy on me. My first job as battle leader showed my qualifications for the job."

"Shut up Corey. You two made it back alive." Rachel helped me lie down. "He broke down and cried when he heard your voice from the squirrel confirming Wesley's report."

Yeh, but not because of me. Earth with a little Fey power filled me, but I was asleep before I felt its full effect.

MILES SHOWED UP IN the morning while Rachel fed me soup. The sunlight bothered my eyes, but clouds were moving in and that should help. Miles walked up with bags of items that I didn't bother to check out. "You're getting lazy," he joked. "You didn't clean out all the blood in the SUV."

Rachel ran out and looked, and I heard her gasp from the back of the house. She ran back in and hugged me gently. "I am so glad you're safe."

"A lot of that blood in the back was Rebecca's," I joked back while standing. My chest caught, and I dropped in pain.

Miles helped me sit in the chair.

"You need to stay with Rachel here. Tell me Rebecca's wounds," interrupted Miles. "Plus, here." He placed a metal chain on the table. "When you take off your torc, put on the gunmetal chain. It'll hide the tan lines."

"The Snake-Hunter punched Rebecca in the face multiple times. The fatal wound is a slice down her right side."

"That it?"

"Those are the major wounds. She took a fall too, and I cleaned and put ointment on all the scrapes and cuts. I've mainly focused on life-threatening stuff."

"He's done a good job," said Rachel.

"I'm taking over," said Miles. "Dude, take a pain pill while Rachel can keep you awake."

Outside, I created druidic berries off a bush and ate one. "Rebecca needs one."

Rachel ran in to give one to Rebecca, came back and helped me.

"I have important information." I had to give them the coordinates.

"We know, and Preacher Jon will come check on you soon to get it, and we'll make a plan." Rachel ran her fingers through my hair. "Tracking the monsignor is taking lots of people. The church had a lot of watchers out and our team stationed along his route cannot come here. It'd be too easy to figure out this was a meeting spot."

"Yeah dude, I was watching the store and came here before anyone showed up at the store or it'd just be you, Rachel, and Rebecca." Miles walked back in and focused on caring for Rebecca.

Earth Power was giving me strength. "The thing had hurt Rebecca. But as she bled on the ground, with puffed out eyes, she aimed at the partially wounded Snake-Hunter charging me and made a head-shot. Without that, I'm dead."

Rachel stood up and went to the awning crank. "We're going to get some snow tonight, so I'm closing the awning. Miles brought my pajamas and I'm going to join you in bed tonight."

The area became shaded, and the clouds had moved in fast. "Since you're keeping me awake while I don't have as much pain, tell me more about your powers. I got barely a rundown and when we have time, something else comes up."

She smiled. "I'm still a Specialist but I have a bard class. I have four domains like you. The three minor ones are Circle Appropriation, Courage, and History. They're like your Animal, Plants, and Earth. Circle Appropriation lets me use another person's unused circle to do things like make the surrounding environment suitable for entertaining. Warming the ground and trough water is one we use a lot. I have a servant that does chores for me within one hundred feet of your circle, and people have to listen to me there."

"I love those powers." Those were the most awesome powers ever.

"I have History Domain. It involves work. I have to record your deeds. I'm calling this story <u>The Battle with his Separated Lover</u>. But I have a lot of knowledge I can call on with the domain."

"That doesn't sound like a fun power."

"I have the Courage Domain and it makes enemies weaker, me faster in battle, and all my allies stronger."

"There you go." That was something she wanted.

"But like Circles make you strong, My Music Domain is my jam. I improve all Fey and Earth magic of allies, can give orders and cast spells without changing songs, and even control enemies."

"Wow!"

"Yeh." Her concern for me stayed in her eyes, despite my excitement.

My mind went back to the big battle with Bishop Pedrotti. "I wonder if I would have banished the demon without your song?"

"Nathan calculated possibilities and thinks it would have never escaped your circle. It killed itself because once I powered your circle up, you could banish it. Otherwise, it might have taken you forty-eight hours to banish it. Nathan says I'm in the running for the most powerful person in the group after you."

"With your pure heart, I wish you were the most powerful." Any sane person would.

"I'm glad it's you, because you get things done. I'm happy being in the running for second." She grinned, and it always made me feel better.

Things are a little hazy, but I wondered about the caves. "Do you think we could protect the South from the beasts in caves together?" I'd need to keep her power level up with mine.

"Don't think about that. I still have nightmares from Old Donnie's stories." She put her hand on my shoulder. "Corey, Rebecca, talks in her sleep on the pain pills."

"That should be no problem."

"She can't believe the man she loves figured out her powers." Rachel turned my head and looked into my eyes.

I shook my head. "She begged me not to tell her or anyone, and I made a deathbed promise."

"Okay. Only I heard her. I guess if the battle leader knows, that's all that matters." Rachel looked glum.

"Battle leader... what a joke. I can do nothing without other people. Without her shot, or her love, I would have died."

Night finally settled, and she jogged inside and came out in her pajamas. "Miles has control of caring for Rebecca."

Once I snuggled with Rachel, I went right to sleep.

Chapter 11—They're just Priests

The next morning, snow had dusted the ground around the cabin, and it was still cloudy. When I sat up to go to the restroom, I was functional as long as I dealt with the pain. Rachel had already gone inside.

I dressed, created more berries, ate one, and carried my shoes into the house. Being able to walk and perform basic tasks again made me want to get out and about. Plus, I had been here three days, and the trees were growing. I could only imagine what the bushes out front looked like.

My chest hurt like the dickens and I couldn't take too deep of a breath, but pain was my old friend, and I knew I survived. I gave Rebecca a berry and watched Rachel carry her to the restroom, while Miles slept on the chair.

By the time Rachel got Rebecca back on the couch, Miles stirred. "You can't heal this fast, can you?"

"No, but I'm functional. Moon-eyed medicine, Earth Power, and modern medical care do wonders." I smiled at Rachel, who frowned at me.

"I was trying to let everyone sleep longer." Frustration crossed her face.

"You did great." I smiled, and she grinned at me.

"If you're going out, could you check on Trish today?" Miles headed to the restroom.

I looked around the cabin and wondered how many times I nearly died but survived by coming here. "That's a good idea. It'll give me something to do."

"I'll drive," said Rachel. "You have a bunch of bloody and goopy splotches on your back."

"Grab the butter, eggs, bread, and bacon, please." I stoked the fire on the wood stove and prepared breakfast for the four of us. I was in pain, but if I couldn't do this, then I couldn't leave the cabin.

All four of us ate and I not only cooked and ate, but I also carried the dishes to the sink. I couldn't quite wash them yet, but this was a start. "Rachel, please heat the water again."

Rachel jogged outside, rinsed and refilled the trough and then cast her spell from my circle. It was weird to feel magic in my circle when I had not initialized it. Outside, I got undressed and sunk into the water.

Rachel kneeled next to me and helped me wash the goo off my back and clean the wounds.

"I'm supposed to ask you a question." Rachel washed the section of my arm that needed more healing.

"Okay." I leaned forward in the water, dirty from me and my wounds.

"The day we did the waxing, and I came out of the shower and caught Nicole and you..." She trailed off. "Well, Nicole wants to know if she forced that."

"No. She played with me first and I could have said stop. I mean, it surprised me and turned me on, but there was more than enough time between her hand until I felt her tongue to stop her."

"You didn't ask her, though."

"No. But I've replayed that in my head a few times and if I could go back, I don't see any circumstance I would have stopped her. We had already discussed dating, and I was falling for her, so when that happened, I was just as culpable."

"I thought you looked like you enjoyed it." She splashed water in my face playfully.

"Why is this a question?"

"You're not the only one who over thinks. Now, Nicole is feeling guilty." She laughed. "The only girl in history to give oral and feel guilty. She's worried now that you're dating and wants nothing to ruin this. Plus, when you didn't know the plan the first time you made love—well, she's gone a little crazy."

"Tell her not to feel guilty. Also, tell her I enjoyed it." I grinned. "Plus, if she wants to howl when we make love up here in the cabin, I am down."

"You are a pig." She splashed me again and laughed. It was great to hear her laugh.

She helped me to stand, dry off, and put dressings on the back wounds that may re-open. "You heal so fast."

We walked back inside to get to Rachel's motorcycle helmets. "Hey Miles. The outdoor bed needs to be secured, trough emptied, and refilled."

He laughed. "As long as I'm not scrubbing any more blood from plastic and leather, I'll be good."

"Here is a big bottle of water. I haven't seen you pee in two days." Rachel stood in front of me, and pointed at the restroom.

I ambled to the restroom. "Are you going to watch?" I joked.

"Yep, I'll hold it if I have to," she joked.

I peed, and it was dark. With a fresh glass, I filled it with water from the sink, and drank it. Then I carried the water bottle with me. "Thank you. I will focus on hydrating more."

She smiled and handed me my toiletry kit. I washed up, brushed my teeth and my hair laid straight.

"TAKE THE PAIN PILL." Rachel handed me one.

"Why?"

"You may need it and I will be with you and will recognize if you need more oxygen."

"One second." I created more berries and gave one to Miles. "Give this to Rebecca for dinner." I pocketed the rest even though I'd only need one, and they disappeared at midnight.

I shrugged and took the pain pill. Then I got on the back of her bike. "Take it easy now."

"Follow the same instructions you gave Rebecca to ride on the back of the bike."

I did. I planted my chest on her back and gripped her tight. She rode and kept a sedate pace for my benefit. The pain pill kicked in after a half hour and the ride was not excruciating after that. Eventually, she pulled into the parking lot and parked near the front door.

We shuffled in the store and when I looked to my right where the camping equipment section lined the walls and dominated the displays, Trish talked to two priests and she struggled.

I'm glad I had taken a pain pill because I needed to act sharp. Miles' parents were helping in the fishing area, Candy was out back, and the other four couldn't answer intense camping questions. I tried to get a deep breath, and it caught. The second one was easier.

"Corey," waved Trish. "These two men have a lot of questions, but we need Miles or you here."

"Rachel, could you take Trish to her office to rest? I can handle the floor for a while," I said.

Carol came over and hugged me. "It is so good to see you. We will catch up later."

I felt better every time I saw Carol and Richard.

Rachel jogged to help Richard in the fishing section, and Carol and Nicole folded clothes. I winked at Nicole from across the way to let her know I was fine.

Diego and Juan moved inventory and changed out the boxed stuff and displays.

I greeted the two priests. "Hi. When Carol wants a hug from me, she is getting one." *I seemed healthier than a pain pill should make me.*

"That's great to hear. Trish says you are the camping expert." The first priest was young and wore a black shirt with black jeans. I think those were even black tennis shoes.

"I am the expert. Others can help, but Miles and I were both out today and it's been hard on Trish." It was time to gather information on them as to their visit.

"She had problems catching her breath. We are looking for a large sale and have specific camping and RV questions." The second priest was also young and wore glasses. He wore traditional shoes and slacks.

"I am the person for camping gear. I test everything here. Candy will answer your RV questions. Frankly, she'll make me look like an idiot."

They both chuckled, and I thought this appearance of the priests at our store was a coincidence, but I kept my guard up. They were both young and had genuine smiles and neither carried a weapon, and they didn't have the telltale signs of weapon marks on their belts or shirts.

"We are looking for an extensive priest and parishioner camping experience and we have questions about back woods camping and the Appalachian Trail."

My chest was fine, and I talked without an issue. "I am glad I showed. I've done two stints as a trail angel and will volunteer again next year. If you are going back country, are these good campers, and are they in good shape? I ask to understand if I should show you ultralight versus sturdy gear."

Nicole walked by and asked, "Excuse me, Mr. Norwood, the distributer sent too many of these knives." She held the box open.

The priest in the tennis shoes looked at Nicole. "Nicole?"

"Priest Fuller?" Nicole looked surprised. They separated and whispered to each other.

When they finished, Priest Fuller smiled at me like he knew me. I took the box. "Nicole, could you unlock the cabinet and grab the Corey knife and meet us in the outdoor demo area?"

She looked at me weirdly but left to grab the knife. I pulled four sets of safety glasses and led the priests out to our demonstration grounds. Once everyone wore safety glasses and Nicole handed me the display combat knife, I jabbed the combat knife into the rock with all my strength. A piece of rock chipped off.

"That's the knife I recommend. Now let me show you the one I tested recently." I grabbed a knife from the box, the same one that broke on the gargoyle. With a strong jab into the rock, the blade shattered just like it had with the gargoyle.

"This is why I believe you should buy from us. Miles has me test every bit of equipment and this knife broke on me just like that when my hand slipped while making kindling." I gathered the safety glasses and saw the demonstration impressed them and I believed that this presence here was a coincidence. "Nicole, please put all this on Miles' desk"

"Yes sir," she said and carried the box to Miles' office. She could certainly act. Though I wondered how she knew the priest.

Turning to the priests. "We've hired five people in the past month and they're all great, but don't know everything. However, I promise we are going to train them all to test equipment and make sure nothing could fail while you are out. We are a local group and everyone in your group can come in for training on the gear and on my word, we will stand by everything we sell."

After the discussion, they planned to have five groups of six people camping. They'd have a combination of back country packers, people in RVs with day packs, and others going out on day trips of two or three days. I showed them everything they'd need—emergency shelters with tarps and tent poles, gps in case they got lost, collapsible water containers, correct socks, shoes, poles, tents, as well as the difference in cold weather gear and nine season gear.

"Are you sure you are going to be employed here?" asked Priest Fuller. "You giving us deals, showing us everything, telling us when the cheap gear is better, and treating us like family."

"I am definitely going to stay employed here. These are my best friends and they run a small local business that counts on word of mouth and return business. We are all about getting more people camping and being out in the wild. I think it will help with everyone's mental health and let people be in better shape without the drill of exercising in a gym."

I knew these two shopped for a group that'd be hunting me, but I wanted them to shop here, so I gave them the Black Friday discount. When Candy took them out back to show them RVs, I ambled into the office Trish worked in with Madison. I sat at Miles' desk and started filling out the whole bill of sale.

His desk was all business and had a computer screen, but I didn't know how to use that. I wrote everything on bills of sales and invoices and used a calculator. I gave it to Trish to verify.

"What is this?" asked Trish. She looked over my shoulder, and both women looked scared.

"I don't know for sure, but it looks like they're equipping teams to hunt me."

"So, are you sabotaging them?" asked Madison.

"Nope. I'm showing them the best gear, giving them good information and showing them how to use it. I promised that any of the teams can come in for training, and we're giving them the Black Friday discount." This was my training.

"What?" exclaimed Madison.

Rachel walked into the office. "Just showing off the ice water in your veins?"

I chuckled. "I'd like to do all of their sales. Not just for the business, but so I have their plans. This is great."

"My dad would say you have cajónes of brass," said Trish.

"This is what Old Donnie taught me." Old Donnie said I excelled here.

Nicole walked in and said, "I brought you a box of knives in case you needed something for self-defense, not to make a sale."

"You knew Priest Fuller? That was a surprise." I wondered where she could have met a priest.

"Yeh, we've bumped into each other by your house. He's new at Saint Andrews. Wesley was his tour guide to show him around Roswell." She looked over the list I handed to Trish.

That made sense.

My pain pill wore off, but the pain was better than this morning when a hug sent me to the floor. I tried to sit back and wavered a bit. Rachel jumped up to help me sit. "He's got a collapsed lung, a bullet wound, a tore up arm, a couple of cracked ribs, and a couple of dozen minor wounds." Rachel leaned back in the chair next to Trish and Trish's face turned pale.

Nicole nodded. They both knew what type of wounds Old Donnie and I lived with.

"Sorry, I forgot this is new to you." I took a couple of breaths and sipped some water. "This is still better than last month when Miles showed up in the nick of time and saved me. Remember, a couple of weeks ago when he was late to work and had a torn-up abdomen?"

Nicole shook her head. "Let's leave the stories of near death for another day and let Trish relax.

Trish needed to discuss something else and listening to Rachel and Nicole, and I would not help. I'm also sure seeing my injuries wouldn't be good either. "Why don't you two relax back here and

Rachel and I will handle the floor the rest of the day?" I grabbed the desk, stood myself up with my legs while I kept my torso straight.

"No, I'm not leaving you," said Nicole. She put my arm over her shoulder. "Nice try, but your legs were shaking as you tried to act healed."

She grabbed my arm, and we walked to the hunting section next to the fishing area. We got into the hallway and she stopped me, then nuzzled me against the wall. "Thank you for answering that question. It may sound silly, but I was worried I had hurt you."

This was silly. "Nicole, I'm the one who should be worried about hurting you. You taught me the lesson that I can know something in my head but not in my heart. I knew there are two sides to every story, but I judged you without talking to you first and I ended up traumatizing you. I can't forgive myself for that."

"Corey, when the church killed my parents and your parents died, I was there when the police told you to drop the questions. It was that day, at fourteen years old, I became Realized. Then for six years, while Grandpa Jon was saving our lives, you showed up every day to make sure I ate, had hugs, had lunch money, was clean and dressed. You brought your girlfriends who helped me with womanly things and then introduced me to Carol, who recognized I was Realized. You saved Rachel's life by clinging to her. Never pretend you could hurt me. Six years Corey—middle school, high school, and even the first year of college."

"I wish I would have given you a better example to emulate."

"Yeh, but now I know what it takes to get things done and can become my own woman. You're still teaching me, and some lessons are hard."

I put my hands on her waist and looked into her eyes. I was so glad we got this chance to date again. This was a gift I did not want to waste.

"I'm an empath, remember? You're good at blocking your thoughts, but that one came through strong." She leaned forward and kissed me, and all the wonderful memories rushed to me.

"Ahem," said Rachel, but she grinned.

"If you're going to keep catching us, I'm going to put a bell around your neck," teased Nicole.

We walked to the front, and I took a seat on a stool and Nicole folded some clothes. Coming here made sense. I felt significantly better.

As I sat on a stool, Clive strode in. The good thing about vampires was if they were up on their feeding, meaning they weren't anemic, they blended in with the rest of us. Clive fed, but he could control his feeding and people were none the wiser because of a memory skill he had. I didn't mind Clive's feeding as much as Miles because at the end of the day; he hurt no one.

"Hey Buddy," he said.

"What's happening?"

"What's up with you? You know my store is right next door, and I have seen little of you recently." He came close and scoped my injuries out. "Whoa, they messed you up. What happened?"

"Worlds gone crazy." It was good to see Clive.

"Definitely. You wear the same shade of lipstick as Nicole," taunted Clive.

"He looks cute in it, though," said Rachel. She handed me a paper towel.

"Corey, you said I was too young when you met Clive to find out how you became friends. Is twenty-one old enough?" asked Nicole. *I bet she kept saying her age since she was always the baby.*

"Let me tell the story," said Clive. "You can barely breathe after fighting whatever crazy thing you fought. Everyone should know why we're friends."

Nicole grabbed a stool and sat next to me at the counter. Rachel joined us, too. "I wasn't there for the incident and just have Corey's side."

Clive chuckled. "I escaped College Park and was on scholarship to Georgia Tech. One night I was out and took a wrong turn to get home. Some vampire running for his life found me and drained me. I turned well after he left. Mad at the world and on my own, I'd go to bars, beat people, and then feed from them and made them forget the entire incident. It was an ugly few months, and I headed down a dark path. I'd lost everything. I couldn't go to school because I hadn't figured out the daylight thing."

"You fought with vampire strength?" asked Nicole.

"Yep. Well, that is until one night, I showed up in a pool hall and figured I'd take the freaky looking white boy with long hair playing pool barefoot on the wooden floor. I was a ripped black guy from College Park before the vampire turned me. How could a hippie white boy stop me—especially with vampire powers at night?"

He smiled when Nicole and Rachel both laughed.

"Well, less than 30 seconds later, I stood face to face with a shoeless druid holding a pool cue and a honeysuckle focus. That's when I discovered I wasn't the toughest guy in the bar and I ran. I ran for my life with my world turned upside down. After a day a running, he tracked me down, and treated me like a friend. With his help, I got my act together. He even convinced Miles not to hunt me and partner with me with my new store."

"That is a delightful story," said Nicole. "You sit. I'll help the people with the clothes." She left to talk to customers.

"Bar fighting and vampires, seems improper for a young lady. But you know, the next day Rebecca broke up with me, saying my being a honkeytonk fighter was the last straw." It still saddened me though I was over it.

"Man, that was her loss. She won't even talk about you at the shooting range," said Clive.

"She knows, and it still hurts," answered Rachel.

Clive clasped my shoulder. "By the way, you all have been fighting a lot. Don't leave me out. You have plenty of redneck fighting men, but you could use a brother or two on your side."

He made me laugh. "I do, and I promise you will hear from me. Be prepared for the Winter Solstice."

Coach White was working today, and he strolled over as Clive left. He and the vampire acted friendly, but the whole vampire and werewolf thing kept them from being close friends. "If something's going down, blood suckers aren't the only brothers."

"Can you still take the kind of beating to put me down?" I teased him.

"Don't need to. I have experience to avoid those beatings."

"It won't be a full moon for five days after the event, though," I teased.

He rolled his eyes and walked away, mumbling about respecting elders. Werewolves hunted when the moon was full because they could see better. The legends were wrong.

"Gotcha coach. I promise when I discover how to save the world, I'll bring you."

He looked at me and shook his head. "Dang, you're serious about this being the end of the world. Yeh, count us in."

He strode out and let Candy and the priests in, who strolled right past him. She sold the priests an RV, to be delivered the first week in January. We packed up their SUV, and they paid for everything and I had my best commission ever.

He waved to Nicole and gave her a thumbs up. Before I could ask, Carol and Richard strolled out to dinner, and Carol caught her chest. She even had a fat lip. I hoped the store wasn't too much.

I ran over. "Carol, are you okay?" I caught my chest in the same place Carol did. Weird coincidence.

"Yes. I just caught a box awkwardly. I'll be right as rain soon." She looked in pain, but Richard supported her and smiled.

Trish came back from talking to Diego and Juan. She extended the contracts of the two temporary workers to a year's contract and given them a sign-on bonus.

Those two left with big smiles for the day at the normal time with Coach White, then I sat with Rachel, Nicole, Trish, Candy, and Madison in Trish's office and reviewed the long day. The pain pill was long gone and the adrenaline from working with priests all day wore off and my chest and shoulder hurt. But I felt better than I should have.

Rachel was warm and took off her jacket and wore a ladies' cut t-shirt. It had 'Play it Pretty for Atlanta' written on it. "Did Old Donnie get you that shirt?"

Rachel looked at her shirt. "Yeh, he said one day I'd want women's styles and then I'd have a new wardrobe." She handed me a manicure kit and put her left hand on my lap. I started doing her nails, and she snuggled up against me.

"I wish you were good enough to do my nails," said Nicole. "But I'll let the professionals do my fingers and toes."

"You can still snuggle against me," I offered. I knew it was one thing to understand Rachel, and I were so co-dependent we couldn't function without regular contact with each other. It was another to watch your sister snuggle with your boyfriend.

She smiled and hugged me as I did Rachel's nails.

Trish ordered a bunch of Mexican food for delivery for the evening and waited on a couple of customers while we rested. I remembered to eat my druid berry.

Candy sat across to me and said, "the priests raved about you. How you demonstrated everything. It was a lot of pressure for me to show the RVs as well. We even drove to the garage to talk to the me-chanics we have an agreement with."

"That's the effort to make big sales," I said. I didn't know if it was or not. What I wanted to be was encouraging.

After I finished with a light shade of pink on Rachel's nails, I took Nicole's hand and walked her to the clothing section. Nicole needed some basic camping clothes and camping gear. I would not screw up this relationship. She would learn what camping was like with me. I got her decent hiking boots, size nine. "Do you own jeans?"

"Jeans?"

"You won't be wearing your beautiful dresses and heels camping. What size are you?"

She picked out jeans and showed me a shirt size but looked ap-prehensive. I also picked out a sunscreen shirt with a hood, a couple of sports bras, and socks.

My day pack had gotten visibility recently, so I picked a new one out, and outfitted it with new gear so I didn't need to repack. I paid in cash from the stack of the two priests. I'd only need to move the sickle and the magnolia seed pod over to this pack.

Chapter 12—What It Is

Rachel dropped me off and needed to change and clean up at her place. I slept on my patio and felt pretty good in the morning. Someone left a package in the kitchen while I was gone and I read it while I tossed Tiberius some of the new bison sausage and cooked my breakfast. I felt a tinge of guilt for my deer friends because deer tasted better than bison.

Nathan put together all the information we had and where it came from. I cast Squirrel Messenger to tell Nathan *we need to talk about coordinates and a new priest strategy.*

Out on the patio, I sat on the ground and opened the package and pulled out the report. The fire pit had gone out, and the patio was just warming up from the freezing temperatures again. The information started basic and covered what Preacher Jon told me. It included a picture of a plain woman with straight blonde hair with the word empath written at the bottom. I folded the picture up and put it in my wallet. I'd never remember such an average person.

There was a list of my upcoming gargoyles, which meant he had another book or a copy of Old Donnie's book. He did not have December twelfth and the defense of the Moon-eyed people I obligated myself to.

I cast *Squirrel Messenger* and described Preacher Jon and said, *Add to calendar. December Twelfth, I agreed to defend the Moon-eyed people for the healing of Rebecca and me.*

My self-health test involved stretches. I was in so much better shape than I should have been and near healthy. Unable to work out,

I could practice my stances for proper form. It was good to practice proper form for stances, strikes, and blocks while injured. I threw on a set of shorts and grabbed my tonfa and practiced stances. Practicing cold with Earth Power coursing through me had helped me fight better in cold weather.

Nicole and Rachel walked into the backyard through the glass doors.

"Oh, look a guy is shorts, sweating. Have you seen Corey? We were going to work," teased Rachel.

"I'm about to get in the shower."

Rachel laughed while Nicole strolled and put the lid on the patio's firepit. I grabbed clean clothes, my toiletry kit, and took a quick shower and changed. I came out once I washed.

"Seven minutes. I guess you were planning to be on time." Rachel pretended she wore a watch.

"How much time does it take you to get ready?" I laughed. Nicole took over an hour.

I brushed my hair back and put my helmet and gloves on and joined them to walk to the motorcycles. Nicole got on the back of Rachel's GSXR. I rode my F800GT. The maroon contrasted nicely with the blue and white of Rachel's GSXR. The three of us rode into the store and helped Trish open up.

In the parking lot, I looked over and Rachel had on jeans and her boots with a leather motorcycle jacket. Her helmet and jacket matched the colors of the GSXR. Nicole had red kitten heels tucked onto the passenger pegs. She wore a beige dress with a red jacket and a spare red helmet. She rolled the dress she wore up, and she sat on the roll to keep it from falling. It exposed her legs from her ankle with the honeysuckle tattoo to most of the way up her thighs.

Rachel lifted her visor and said, "Do you want to see what happens to Nicole when I hold the bike revolutions at nineteen hundred and fifty?"

Nicole jumped off the bike. "That is not funny. When Corey is ogling my legs like that, it makes it so much worse."

Rachel lifted her visor and winked at me.

I missed the joke, but something told me I should let it go. "I think that's a pretty style dress, Nicole."

"Thank you, Corey." She collected herself and gave me a big smile.

I cast druid berries and ate one. "Rachel, this morning, could you run two berries up for Rebecca? One for the morning and one for the night?"

I took the morning to show Diego and Juan, the two contractors, along with Nicole, and Candy, how to set up emergency tents, which apparently had become popular on YouTube and a big seller. Two customers came in and watched us because that's what they were looking for. Trish asked me to find out if the contractors were interested in learning about camping because they worked hard but understood little. I taught slower, and Nicole interpreted some lines into Spanish. Languages weren't my forte. Love and fighting were my forte.

We broke up the training around lunch because the store became busy for a Friday. The store stayed busy all day. Nicole worked a register with me. Coach White came in after he finished coaching and immediately needed to help Clive next door, who sold two of our combination rifle and hunting packages.

Juan helped Coach White, while Diego retrieved items throughout the store for me. I wished I could get items myself, but Nicole explained my injuries. He smiled and nodded and got everything correctly.

I couldn't take deep breaths, and ran out of breath with the hustle around the store. "How does Trish keep up?" I asked Rachel when she returned. The two of us put tents and poles away.

"She's sweating finances with the baby coming, but I also hear that the holidays are busy and then after returns, January, and February will be slow. She's looking forward to peace before spring starts."

It got slow, so I spent time with Rachel while we relaxed. I ordered pizza for those of us working. A handful of customers wanted to see three different fire starters. I took Diego and Juan outside with them to our testing area with eight different fire starters.

After I started and put out, I let the others try each one. Diego tried as well and could make a fire in four or five strikes on a good nest. He knew how to make a fire nest. Juan picked it up quickly from Diego's instructions.

"Jeez, guy, you started eight fires in one try with each of these in under a minute. How often do you camp?" asked one customer.

I chuckled. "A lot. I also have taken every piece of camping gear and tested it in the woods."

The woman smiled. "Do you test fishing stuff, too? Like that boat out front?"

"Nope, Miles' dad is a fisherman's fisherman and gadget guy. He tests everything we have for the ability to get the latest gear."

At the end of the day, I rode home and slept on the patio alone. The fire pit went out and my animal skins became covered with frost, but I stayed comfortable.

THE NEXT MORNING, I woke up alone and wondered where Rachel was when someone knocked on the door in the carport. It was time to pull a knife because no one knocks on my doors. Everyone has my code and comes and goes as they please.

I looked out the door window, and it was Preacher Jon. After opening the door, I said, "you can just come in. We're not sticklers for privacy."

He entered and walked into the kitchen. "The fact you aren't a stickler for privacy is why I knocked. You're intimate with my grand-daughter, and while I am fine with the decisions you two make, I'd prefer not to view any of this."

"I promise the kitchen and living room will always be safe."

"That's good to know. We have two items to cover. The first is you have information to give and your updated schedule." He walked through the kitchen and placed some items on the breakfast bar.

"Okay, the first is the coordinates Strumath gave me." I listed off the coordinates. "It's the rec center about five miles from here."

"Stay away from this new site. Also, CJ's team has eyes on the Al-pharetta Administration building and The Tribe banned you with-in a mile of the building until necessary. The Curia posted your pic-ture."

"Is it a good picture?" I smiled.

"It's a security camera shot when you marched in with CJ." He sat on one of the bar stools at the breakfast bar.

"We may want to send them one of my good side," I joked, but Preacher Jon didn't laugh.

My jokes were for me, anyway. "I'll take another day to heal before I get my workout and training in. <u>Miles Away from Home</u> scheduled me some this week, and I'm doing a Couples Camping seminar in a local park on Saturday afternoon. Tuesday workout and then I defend the Moon-eyed people Tuesday night because Dr. Kanoska used their magic to save the life of Rebecca and I."

"I thought you were our lazy druid?"

"Today I need to bring more berries to Rebecca. I'm a regular grown up." That got a chuckle out of him.

"The second reason I am here is to congratulate you for being the first druid ever to defeat two Snake-Hunters." He opened one of his folders.

I pulled up the bar stool next to his. "No way. This was a disaster. Rebecca and I should have died. I realize you came to strip me of being battle leader."

He sat and swiveled the chair towards me. "Corey, are you insane? I threw up asking you and Rebecca to do this. There was a ninety percent chance one of you would not return and a fifty percent chance you both died. Both of you living made me the happiest I've been in a long time." He opened a folder on the breakfast bar containing a handful of papers, then placed his phone next to it.

"We should have died. I barely fended the thing off and my heart should have stopped when he kicked me." I pointed to my sternum, where the bruise healed fast, even for me. "My heart stopped at Dr. Kanoska's office. Rebecca should have died as well, and we barely made it."

"Let me read the report summary Nathan put together from the magical evidence, and you let me know where it is wrong."

I nodded, and he continued. "After a successful banishing, the Snake-Hunter attacked. It surprised the backup and took her out immediately and moved to ambush the druid. The Druid made a call to the most powerful animals in the area and then moved to save the backup where the ambush happened. The druid absorbed the kill shot and rolled over with the Snake-Hunter, surprised. They both recovered when two black bears approached, which the druid powered up. The Snake-Hunter released his full power and fought through the bears easily, and then moved to the druid, who absorbed a second kill shot. The backup recovered then and implemented the plan, which the druid finished."

When Preacher Jon paused, I had some input. "That is close to what happened. We should have protected Rebecca more. Rebecca should get a lot more credit for that shot. The Snake-Hunter beat her, left her with eyes puffed out, and a lethal wound. She did a lot more than implement the plan—she did the impossible."

Preacher Jon noted what I told him and continued. "I could go on with the medical, the defeat of the priests... By the way, how did you get the priests out of the vehicle and turn the ambush around?"

"They played a game of chicken with a piece of white trash who played for fun in high school. Of course, they'd lose their nerve first."

Preacher Jon's eyes got wide. "Let me tell you what I see here, and I ran the report by CJ so he can plan for more training for you. He agrees with my assessment."

"Ok, I'm listening."

"Our Tactical Leader implemented a plan. The plan needed to change at first contact with the enemy. He improvised and delayed. He stood his ground and gave time for his team member to fulfill her job. When the battle grew, he devised a new plan on the fly and secured a safe passage for the two of them for medical. The plan succeeded. He saved the team's lives by finding required medical care. He has noted lessons learned about protecting remote team members to implement for later."

"Those are a lot of fancy words to say they should have died, but he got lucky and can learn from this."

Preacher Jon laughed and laughed hard. "CJ thought you would say something similar, so he said to ask you, 'when was the last time you were in a fight where no luck was involved?'"

He had me there. "Well, this was a lot of luck."

"Let me add that you're giving out credit to the team members and taking little for yourself, the mark of a good leader."

"I'm just speaking the truth, which was glossed over in the report."

"I'll increase Rebecca's contribution to be what you've said. Still, you are the only druid in history to face two Snake-Hunters and live."

"That, you know, is wrong. Old Donnie took out the first and had me kill it, so I'd have the word. Rebecca took this one down and I killed it and got the second word."

"Second word?" Preacher Jon's face tightened in confusion.

I pulled my shirt off and showed him the second biceps sainnithe on one arm and ghlacadh on the new biceps. "I thought they all had the same word as well."

Preacher Jon picked up his phone, put on glasses and typed into it. "I'm sending this to Nathan." Preacher Jon took a few pictures of each arm as well. "We'll find out more, but let me point out what the team has seen."

"Go for it." I was confident I could argue his point.

"You have been a successful fighter for years and Miles and Rachel like your plans, even if you think they're simple. The rest of the team has their respected input. They watched you override me at the Battle of Chattanooga, and we came out victorious. Now they watched you and Rebecca come out alive from the toughest fight anyone could predict. Tell me about team confidence if anyone else takes over for you."

I sat and thought. He had me. "That makes sense, but you could add help because I'm not a talented trainer for team tactics. I'd have to take care of personal issues, coordinate through feelings, and deal with team drama. You could say I'm not suitable for all the tasks."

He grinned and shook his head again. "How much would you be willing to bet that you're the only one who listed those three things as crucial to training... the only one of our combat team? Exclude Nathan and myself."

"Combat team is Myself, Rachel, Rebecca, Nicole, Miles, and Madison? I don't know Madison, so I'll put the rest in order. Rachel, when attached to Fey power..."

"No Fey power and wearing clothes."

"Nicole First, Miles Second, Rebecca Third."

"Interesting."

"Are you questioning Nicole? She may be the strongest person in our group without Fey power allowed."

"I learned that, but you just doubled down on why you're the best choice for battle leader. No one else would say that. Once the team is comfortable, we can discuss backups."

"We have a strong team, but she weaponized empathy and has this whole gun and bullet thing."

"We have a powerful group of individuals. With your help and Nathan's help, we'll make a strong team. Let me ask you another question. How did I build this team?" He looked at me curiously.

"I've been thinking about this. Technically, I was the fourth, or fifth person added, even though you banked on me joining. This team isn't druid support like it was for old Donnie."

"Excellent."

I put my thought to this, and I decided I was too scared to say it. "My idea is too out there."

"Then you may be on the right track."

I relented and told him what I came up with the last time in the Fey Realm. "Okay, you built it on love. Family love, romantic love, desire for love, and love of friends. Everyone on the team needs at least one other connection and the more connections they have, the stronger the team is. You are betting love will succeed when all else fails."

"I'm going to ask it again; how did you fail out of college?"

"When Miles and Rachel say I only know how to love and fight, they aren't joking. The answer was one of the two things I under-stand."

Preacher Jon chuckled. "You need to stop selling yourself short. Did you know every territory needed to reprogram druids and Snake-Hunters after this encounter? Nathan could not enter that both members survived the encounter due to input fail-safes in the system."

"Truthfully, If I'm connected to Earth, I can learn. If I'm fully connected to Earth, I can learn complicated things. If I'm fully connected to the Fey Realm, it feels like I'm a genius. Take away those and I'm just a dumb bar-fighting piece of white trash looking for a woman." That was the truth.

"You're a lot more than that. But we will meet back here on Friday for a lunch thing again. That worked out well last time." Preacher John closed his folder.

Chapter 13—The Tribe

It was time to get berries to Rebecca, then ride up to the Tribe. I needed advice, and I didn't know where I could get it anymore. Old Donnie would be so helpful right now. Lots of people could give me advice, but he could break most things down to where I could understand it. The big problem I had was, I didn't have an invitation to The Tribe, but that was a risk I needed to take. There was a good chance I could skirt the rules a little with our history.

I put my motorcycle boots on with jeans. After I zipped up my motorcycle jacket, I walked to my car trunk and after a touch inventory, got my waist pack and put it on. All these clothes didn't make me feel any warmer than when I used Earth Power.

My old pricey helmet was still in good shape. I wouldn't replace it since it had a lot more air flow around my head. It may not match the bike, but that mattered more to Rachel than me. I rolled my F800GT out and took the maroon sport bike to enjoy the ride. I'd been so busy or injured that I hadn't gotten time to enjoy anything. When the bike started, I coasted down the small hill of my driveway and rolled onto the road. Quickly into second and third, I never touched the power band.

I cruised along Woodstock Road until I picked up I-575 and hit highway speeds. The power band was smooth and I could tell that Rachel picked out a more sedate bike with a more padded seat for me. I think she had judged my motorcycle skills as wanting. Still, it was comfortable and my height helped keep the weight off my wrists.

I picked out my exit and then hit the cabin. With a wave to Bubba on the dirt road, I parked out front next to Miles' Mustang. The swing reminded me of the date with Nicole.

After I removed my waist pack and helmet, I sat on the swing and looked out into the woods. It felt strange to be near the cabin without sensing Earth Power because of the boots, jacket, and helmet.

I sat here the day I figured out Nicole's plan and convinced myself Nicole wanted me dead. I never even considered she didn't understand what my magnolia seed pod was for.

That was a dumb topic to think about. Fully depressed, it was time to go in. I created druid berries and ate one. Inside, Miles cooked and Rebecca sat up on the couch, reading one of Old Donnie's westerns. "Hey, you're looking better." Both of her eyes had bruises that had gone purple and yellow, and most of the swelling was gone.

"I feel better. As much as you love this cabin, I'm ready for a little more civilization."

I handed her a druid berry, and she popped it in. "My house is a ranch and you can get to everything on one floor. Take my bedroom. I'll clean the sheets tomorrow morning and will have whatever you want ready for you."

"You know, I'd like to be in your bed again." She put the book down as I sat on the couch.

"Okay, then. What else can I get ready for you?"

"Hold on, I got this," said Miles. He put his hand out and said, "zoom" as he passed his hand over my head.

"Oh." I missed her teasing me since I only thought about her injuries.

"So, Dude, why are you up other than to make goo-goo eyes at Rebecca?" Miles handed Rebecca a plate.

I gave Miles the other berry for Rebecca tonight. "I wanted to check on her. Did she tell you what she pulled off?" Her face swelling was going down, but it saddened me to see her hurt. Knowing about the slice on her side caused me to ache.

He started devouring his dinner and shook his head. "Nope."

"She had puffy eyes where shouldn't be able to see and poured blood onto the ground after being knocked off the porch. The Snake-Hunter knocked her rifle setup to the ground and gave her a mortal wound. I absorbed the first attack, and the thing blew up my tonfa into my arm. It kicked me a good ten feet and was coming to finish me and she did the impossible and put a bullet between its eyes."

"He pointed his fork at Rebecca. You made the shot after being punched in both eye sockets? Without your setup?"

She nodded.

"Damn Corey, love guided that bullet."

"More than you know. That kick to my chest should have stopped my heart, but it kept going until she received care. Then it stopped." I rubbed my chest, but the pain had disappeared. That was strange how fast this healed.

"Damn, Corey," he said between mouthfuls.

"Corey," whispered Rebecca. "Any problems with Nicole?"

"No, should there be?"

"You're her first adult boyfriend. Finding her parents' murderers took her complete attention. I know she looks practiced, but she isn't."

"I'll be careful." I had things under control.

"No, you won't, dude. I see it in your eyes. You're already addict-ed to crazy girl sex." He shook his head at me.

"Miles, it's not crazy girl sex." I looked at Rebecca. "Is it?"

"Corey, when was the last time you talked to Nicole?" asked Rebecca, ignoring us. "Wait, never mind. Tell me something sweet about her and I'll do the text thing."

I pulled out my phone. "This is still my favorite picture of Nicole. I kneeled next to the chair Rebecca sat in and showed her the picture as Miles looked over my shoulder."

"Dude, we were in high school then."

"This was right before homecoming, and Nicole was in ninth grade. We were seniors." Nicole sat on Rachel's lap, who I cradled like a baby. The pure joy on Nicole's face makes this picture a keeper, even though Rachel and I look exhausted. "Nicole figured out we had Rachel back and wanted this picture of the three of us."

I wiped a tear from my eye.

Miles sat back down. "Dude, you never told us the story. Rachel went from wearing black and not talking to being her old self. A switch flipped, and you two kept it secret."

"We should keep it on the down-low. But once school started after that summer, Haley and I kept showing up every morning to help Nicole and Rachel. That morning, Nicole cried and pointed out the back door. I figured what might be going on, so I tore out of the back and when I saw Rachel, I made the first perfect knife throw of my life and cut the rope from the tree."

"What?" Exclaimed Rebecca.

"She tried to run from me, but I tackled her and carried her back to the house. I had to hold her like a baby to keep her from getting away." Tears were flowing from me now.

"She wasn't as strong then," said Miles.

"Well, I told Haley to bring Nicole to school, and I held Rachel and refused to let her go. I held her all day and cooked dinner holding her. I made her eat by threatening to play zoom-zoom-beep-beep." I smiled at the thought.

Rebecca giggled at the game reference.

"I held her all night and tucked Nicole in and said not to worry, Rachel would never leave my arms until I was certain everything was over. I carried her to their couch and held her all night. She fell asleep early, but I stayed awake. About five am she woke and finally spoke."

"She didn't talk all day or night with you holding her?" asked Rebecca.

"Nope. Well, she asked how long I could keep this up and I said I'd hold her forever because if I couldn't keep her alive. I couldn't keep anyone alive. I lost my family, and she lost part of hers. If she died, so would I. Something snapped and she said, 'do you promise to be there for me?' I told her I'd always be with her."

"That's when you two became co-dependent," said Rebecca.

"Yep, well, she agreed, strolled to her room and came back out, showered and dressed. She wore her acid-washed jeans and a yellow shirt—no black. I braided her hair and Nicole came out and realized Rachel was back to normal and wanted a picture."

"Wow," said Miles. "We knew something happened, but the snuggling and being together makes sense now."

"Okay." Rebecca sniffled. "I'm going to leave the trauma part of the story open and tell her you showed me your favorite picture of her from high school and say how you love her smile, full of joy."

"Thank you."

It was time for a new subject. "Anything to say to The Tribe? I'm going up to ask for help in training the team, so I don't make the same mistakes I made with the Snake-Hunter."

"Dude, they said not to come there anymore. You nearly died when you ran their gauntlet last time." Miles started washing dishes.

"If I thought I'd have to run the gauntlet, I wouldn't go. However, I don't think they'd have as many volunteers now."

"Are you sure?" Miles had genuine worry on his face.

"Corey, is this important?" asked Rebecca. She had some familiarity with The Tribe since she worked for CJ before we met. Actually, we met because she worked for CJ.

"CJ is the one who gave me the name Killer Corey last week. Yes. It's important." I was going regardless.

"CJ said that? Dude, I'm glad I didn't test you." Miles knew what the words of CJ meant.

"Not Killer Corey. Corey the Wartime Druid with a gentle heart," Rebecca admonished.

"I hope I make that ideal one day. But I'm going there for advice on being a battle leader. I need help on how to train others."

"Dude, you got a plan to save the world yet?" Miles picked up both plates to wash them.

"It's coming together. We need to find out about the new site, we need to find the monsignor. But Strumath is going to show up at the big battle and support us, and I have the support of the best team ever assembled."

He chuckled. "You could have said no."

"Fine. You drive the lovely Miss Adams to my house tomorrow and you can get back to Trish and the store."

I strolled back outside, got my waist pack and helmet and drove up the winding mountain roads to the area I was told to never return.

I MARCHED TO THE ENTRANCE of The Tribe's area, put my waist pack, helmet, and jacket on the ground. Then, I pulled out both knives and placed them on my pack. Just in case, I took off my boots and stepped forward. Earth Power filled me with a touch of Fey magic from my territory spell.

This area was officially in the foothills of the Appalachians, but it was close to the mountains and was woodsy. It was private property and prime hunting land. They cleared this front area out and there were two cabins built for people who stood watch behind a fortified Earth wall guarding the only direct path in.

"Hold it right there. I have orders to beat any trespassers." The voice was from an over enthusiastic kid.

"Let CJ or Fitz know Corey would like to talk to them. I don't want to hurt you."

"Hey Corey. CJ is still gone. I'm radioing Fitz." That voice sounded familiar.

Was that our waiter from the first date? "Derek?"

"Yep, hold on," replied Derek.

"Hell no. We've got no Corey on this list." Some big kid came out with enough piss, vinegar, and anger that I felt the need to apologize to many people from when I was nineteen. He wore camouflage pants and a white t-shirt and had on a chewing tobacco hat. After spitting out whatever he was chewing on, he strode towards me as if he could do something. He didn't look too bright and looked a heavier version of me from five years ago.

"Kid, you've got more anger than training. I don't want to hurt you, and I'd rather you not need this lesson from me." I prepared for the charge of an oversized kid.

He charged.

I sidestepped and kicked him in the ribs. "You're too large to charge until you build up your sprint speed. Want to give me your name?"

He dove for my feet.

"Now you're off balance and susceptible to a hold." I left him down and pinned him. "What you need to do is keep your center of balance centered on all three planes. When you break a plane, it needs to be for a specific reason."

"Let me up and I'll take you." He struggled, but my hold was tight and I was a lot stronger than him.

His request was so ridiculous that he needed a lesson. "Are you sure? The next lesson will involve some pain to help my words sink in." This is how The Tribe trained—trained me at least.

"Piss off, asshole. Call me Ox."

"OK, you're right, I am an asshole." I let him up and jumped away. "Now take a stance." I took the heron stance. "I've taken an offensive stance. How should you counter?"

He took two steps towards me with no stance. I feinted a kick, and a forearm smashed his jaw, knocking him back. To his credit, he stayed standing. "You're breathing hard and have slipped into anger. Listen to me and notice I can still talk clearly. What does this mean?" I wished this kid would realize how over matched he was.

"Overconfident," he panted and came at me again.

I shook my head. "Nope. Bad open stance," I said as I kicked out his inner left knee. Then smashed his rib with the palm of my hand to crack the rib.

He landed on the ground and screamed. He tried to stand and lost his breath on all fours.

"Derek, I think I broke his rib instead of cracking it. Could you get him medical care? I don't think Ox is a good name for him." I took a step back and took in my surroundings and saw a large man in camo walking towards me.

"It's on its way, Corey. What can I do for you?" All six-ten three hundred pounds of hard life muscle belonging to Fitz stood in front of me. He wore camo pants and a long, faded camouflage winter coat and a baseball cap with an eagle on the front. He had lived outside for so long and had become thick with hard work. His weathered face had a smile, though.

"Fitz, it's good to see you. I need help learning how to train. Despite my lack of knowledge, they put me as the team's battle leader, and I know nothing about training."

He looked at his man on the ground. "You did a good job with Meat there."

"If I only trained hand to hand combat, I could handle it with Rachel. We have druids, bard, hunters, gun users, weird magic, and fighters. How do I get a plan for training this?"

"Why is it so important?" He picked his teeth with a sharpened twig.

"I almost lost a woman I love. I just visited her and am barely holding it together after seeing her beaten face and her side sliced open."

He sighed and then nodded. "Okay. You still have that house where I dropped off that load of rocks for your patio?"

"Sure do." I smiled, knowing he'd help.

"I'll gather some stuff and meet you there for lunch tomorrow. Oh, and Corey?" He grinned, and I knew a request was coming.

"Yes." I grabbed my stuff to head out.

"I prefer slow cooked baked potatoes with my steak." He smiled.

"Yes, sir."

THE RIDE HOME WAS ENJOYABLE, and I took the time to enjoy it. I stopped by the store and picked up a bunch of vegetables and potatoes, along with more butter and olive oil. If Fitz and Rebecca were coming tomorrow; I had to get chores done and be prepared to cook.

Once home, I spent an hour to finish a full-body workout since I wouldn't be able to join Rachel in the gym in the morning. My workouts were more frequent than normal people and it was cheating to recover with Earth Power, but it wasn't as if I competed with anyone. Then I swept out the carport. After stripping the bed, I grabbed my laundry, changed the sheets, and began washing everything. I cleaned out the fire pit on the patio and moved the ash to the far side, where I had a small mulch pile.

After restarting the fire, I picked everything up, put away the cleaned dishes from earlier, and vacuumed. It turned midnight when I finally cleaned the bathroom and shower. I got out the skins and threw them on the patio and beefed up the fire again.

Nicole sauntered in and kissed me without saying a word. I watched her walk to the bedroom. I washed up quickly, and she came out wearing a skimpy negligee and carrying my shorts. She didn't say a word. When I opened my mouth to speak, she put her finger on my lips. She removed my clothes in the kitchen and took my hand and led me to the skins on the patio—our bed. We made love with no one to call the police and the only other creatures around us were the pixies and faeries from the Spring Court.

Chapter 14—Lunch

It was nice to wake up next to Nicole with no one else here. I bent over and kissed her.

"Come, let's shower together." She took my hand and led me to the bedroom where the luxurious warm shower washed us—well, except for the times where I shivered in the back and handed her different shampoos. If it wasn't for the intimacy of being close, people overrated showering together.

I started the grill and the potatoes in time to get them slow cooked for Fitz. Nicole put away the skins and all signs of us sleeping out here.

Rachel arrived and taunted us. "Gee, Corey, were the police called again? Nicole, did you hear anything about a noise complaint?"

"We were ultra-quiet last night," I said and stuck my tongue out at Rachel.

"Cook me extra eggs. I worked out in the gym this morning and I'm famished." Rachel drug herself to the patio and plopped into a chair. "You know the famished you get from working out alone because your work-out partner is too busy having sex with your sister."

Nicole giggled. "We're going to grow broke feeding you then."

I chuckled. "Fitz is coming over today and Rebecca is coming here to heal and I needed to clean."

"I'll give you one free pass, then. Just because I miss Fitz." Rachel punched me on the arm playfully.

I cooked the three of us breakfast when Miles and Rebecca showed up. He helped Rebecca up the stairs. "Where do you want to go first? Bedroom, Living room?"

"Can you prepare an Adirondack chair and let me sit with you?" She looked tired but smiled around friends.

I ran outside and draped one deerskin from the top of the stack onto a chair. Then I helped Miles sit her down. "Do you want breakfast? The grill is still hot since I'm slow cooking potatoes for lunch."

"No. I'll wait for lunch." She leaned back and gave room for her side not to touch the armrest.

"Oh, Miles. Fitz is coming over for lunch."

"I wish I could stay, but I haven't seen Trish in a few days." He waved and walked out the door.

"Once I rest, you're showering and waxing me," said Rebecca.

I turned to Nicole and Rachel. "Let me know what you guys need. She has a wound along her right side." I showed where it was on my side. "It will need to be kept dry, so you'll want to pat it clean."

"I'm talking to you. Corey, I am hurt badly, and I am scared. It was too much to ask Miles to do it, and you're the only person I know who takes care of me with gentle hands. Please do a sick time grooming thing like you're my nurse." She paused. "Like you bathed me at the cabin."

I looked at her and realized there wasn't a difference here except for our history.

"Please. I want to feel normal." Her eyes pleaded.

There was no way I could say no to someone who saved my life. But Nicole and Rachel would assist me. "OK." I got out the meat and the vegetables and prepared them ahead of time for lunch.

"You did a good job cleaning the house. You're going to make someone a good husband," teased Rachel.

"If you're not careful, one night we'll be drinking and I'll marry you," I teased back.

"You sleep around too much for me." She ran up and hugged me. She grabbed my arms low and I couldn't break her strength. "I got you."

I turned around in her grasp and gave her a quick, playful peck on the nose. "Take that."

"Hey!" She laughed. "What's your future wife going to think if you do things like that?"

"Hey! You, no kissing my sister!" Nicole laughed when she said that.

Rachel let me go and picked up her phone when it made a weird jingle noise. "Guys, it worked. The comments section is going berserk."

"Thank God," said Nicole. She picked up her phone. "It's viral through the territories you and I are making love and there is a police report that proves it," said Nicole. "All the BS ends and Grandpa doesn't have to fend off the idiots who think they can marry me."

"Okay, I wonder why there wasn't a line to marry me?" I put the meats and veggies in the fridge and walked outside to add a little wood to both fires and move the potatoes around.

Rachel called out from the door, "because they fear you."

"Good." That made me happier than it should.

"Okay, I'm rested and tired of being icky," said Rebecca.

"I am putting on my medic persona and I will do this professionally so that you have the best care." I carefully scooped her up and carried her into the house.

"Corey, I teased you, but I'd trust you over anyone else. Do not worry about it." Rebecca answered seriously.

The four of us ambled back and hung out while I cleaned her and cleaned around her wound. I remembered the million things I was supposed to do with her hair and her skin and her shoulders relaxed when she saw I remembered. I kept my mindset correct, and we waxed her.

"There, now I'm clean and normal again." She smiled as Nicole slipped on a loose dress that wouldn't irritate her bindings.

I HELPED REBECCA BACK out and a group of people were on the patio. Fitz, Madison, and Nathan joined Nicole and Rachel. Nathan was cooking.

I helped Rebecca sit in another Adirondack chair with the deerskin on it. Nicole was beating the deerskin blankets. There was one hanging up by the pull-up bar.

"Corey, tell me that the leader isn't sleeping with anyone in the squad," said Fitz.

"Let's skip that question and jump right into training." That hit close to home.

Fitz shook his head and handed me a folder of papers. "Rule one: don't sleep with or fall in love with the people you're leading."

"Fitz, we are part of the Spring Fey Court. Like I told Preacher Jon when he talked about not going back after Mayven, making sure the world has love in it is more important than a battle."

"Then why do you need advice on training?"

"Because they nearly killed a woman I love. I cannot let this happen again." I pointed to Rebecca, who smiled and relaxed. "Well, she looked a lot worse recently."

Fitz looked sad. "If you have to put loved ones into harm's way, you're setting yourself up for heartbreak. You are going to have love as comrades in arms. Some people avoid friends because it's too painful. With a combination of friends and lovers who will also be comrades in arms, it will devastate you."

Rachel sat beside me. "Corey, we're going into harm's way, anyway. We want you as leader because we know you're going to give us the best chance to live."

Fitz shook his head. "Is jealously going to be a problem? Like the whichever lover isn't here."

"We're all here," said Nicole. She laughed, joining us.

"None of that. Fitz, they like to exaggerate. We are pretty sedate. Nicole and I are lovers. Rachel and I are friends, as you remember. Rebecca and I are former lovers who still have love for each other deep inside. This is normal."

"Normal." He rolled his eyes. "I get the relationship with Rebecca. My ex-wife owns the bar Frenco and a lot of The Tribe work there because she and I are good friends, but I still couldn't send her into battle. Never mind a lover or a close friend like Little Rachel."

Only someone who made me look small would call Rachel, Little Rachel. Her shoulders were as broad as mine.

Rachel grinned at her nickname. She spent a lot of time with Old Donnie training as a little girl. "Ooh Corey, speaking of lover, Wesley is going to spend the night with me tonight. Then you and I will train in the yard tomorrow to see if this relationship will work out."

"OK, do not judge him. Give him a fair shake." This was a sign they were making progress. I hoped it worked out for them.

Fitz looked at Rachel. "Little Rachel?"

"La la la," said Nathan. "Fitz, do you want the grilled veggies too?"

"Yes. Let's see what Corey thinks works well with bison."

While we ate, Fitz reviewed tactics to work on with training. "First, you need to make sure everyone has time to train on their skills. Like you and Rachel tomorrow morning. You should also take time to train with each squad member even if you don't understand the weapons."

"That makes sense. I almost wet my pants when Nicole started firing a wall of bullets."

"Wall?" asked Fitz.

"I asked if it was okay and he let me use the M240L with belt-fed seven-dot-six-two rounds." Nicole grinned.

"Holy crap, Corey," said Fitz.

"When she said bigger gun, I just thought the bullets were bigger. I wasn't expecting a gazillion bullets."

"It was effective in driving the Vatican's special forces back from the frontal assault," said Rebecca. She laughed, remembering the fight.

"I don't know if anyone saw me, but I'm pretty sure I'd peed a little when that thing fired." I was startled, for sure.

Fitz chuckled, "Familiarity with the weapon will help, so now you'll know when you need that kind of firepower—you know you have a person who can bring it to bear."

"That makes sense. Nicole and Rebecca, when you're healthy, let's train together at the cabin with shooting and work together." I hoped we could shoot that up in the mountains. "Madison, what days do you and Miles train hunter skills? We'll need to go to the cabin on Mondays, since Miles is off."

She answered, stiffer than I thought she normally spoke. "We train up there on Mondays, since I'm an archer who trains distance skills. I also need to get with others since I help others more than do my thing."

"That's awesome. I think most of us didn't realize we'd be part of a team and took individual powers," I answered.

"I figured why take more bow shooting powers when I could knock bugs off palings from the porch?" That was more like her.

"What?" said Rachel.

"Palings is the sexy mountain way to say fence post. Imagine you're sitting on the swing of the cabin. Look across the road to the stunted birch and imagine seeing a bug on the tree and hitting it."

"I'm sorry," said Madison. "I didn't mean to go back to the old way of talking."

"On Monday, it might be airish enough to get a skrift." I winked at Madison. Those were mountain terms for the weather to turn cold and drop a few inches of snow.

Madison giggled. "You are too big for your britches."

"Corey, you may not commit crimes with Madison," said Nicole. There was jealousy in her eyes, so I focused back on Fitz.

Fitz interrupted us and said, "maybe make Monday your team day and other days as catch ups since Miles may be a limiting factor."

That sounds like a good plan. "This was a great start."

Fitz handed me a pamphlet. "Here is a squad tactics book for mixed squads. It doesn't contain magic, but it contains stealth, infantry, sniper, and artillery. I enjoyed the lunch. But go easier on these guys than you did on Meat."

"I didn't mean to break his rib, I just wanted to crack it." I hoped the kid was fine.

Fitz laughed. "We were wondering how we were going to get through to him that beating peers wasn't near good enough. I called CJ, and he thought it was funny you were on the other side of those lessons."

"It is. I listened to Meat for two minutes and realized I needed to apologize to many people from my later teen years."

Fitz laughed. "We all do. I'm heading out. Hopefully, in January, we will have something formalized and can spend more time together."

I shook his hand as he left us.

Once Fitz left, we had most of the team. Nathan sat with us while the grill cooled.

I heard a car pull up, and Wesley joined us on the patio. Rachel skipped to lead him by his hand and they sat by the firepit.

"Nicole, most people won't see through your plan, and I believe Corey and you are intimate, but the Delta Valley Territory is going to be persistent," said Nathan.

"Well, I won't go there and no one lets them travel anywhere after they sent the thirteen vampires to our region," answered Nicole. "Besides, I finally have my hooks on Corey and it'd take more than one dateless loser from Mississippi to break this."

Nathan sat down as well. "Just a heads up. He is going to lose his place on his committee since he has nothing else and marrying you was his sole hope to be relevant. Expect him to do something."

"If someone tied to the vampires who tried to sacrifice Madison to a demon in Chattanooga shows up anywhere in my territory, we don't have to worry about hearing from him again." I was bound and determine their bodies would be missing.

"Hopefully that plan with a noise citation for loud sex will be enough," said Nathan. He didn't want to, but he laughed.

Nathan's rare laughter gave me an idea. "Nathan, is your face known?" I had an idea to find out some information.

"Nope. I have been internal only." He looked curious about my thoughts.

This was coming together and felt safe. "I gave Preacher Jon the new location, and I'd like to scope it out, but he was right when he said I shouldn't go there."

"You want me to go there?" He stood and scrubbed the grill.

"If you take Madison there as a date and check out the area between the baseball fields at the coordinates, you could give us a layout." The idea felt safe.

"Anything in particular?" He asked.

"Be safe first. Nothing is worse than either of you getting hurt. I'd rather you not get any information than take a risk. All I want to know is open areas large enough for a twelve foot or larger circle."

"How do we do this?" He closed the grill and sat to listen more closely.

"I can help," said Madison. "We can pretend we're a young married couple and I'm recently pregnant. We talk about if we're going to have a boy or girl and if they'd play in these fields."

I thought for a second. "That's a great idea."

She smiled. "I have a little experience there."

"Remember, safety first. I want to know layouts and potential uses. Look for an area to place a large circle that's easily hidden."

Nicole patted me on the shoulder. "Hey, if you have the evening available, you want to join me on one of my excursions?"

"Duh, yes. As battle leader, I should know all your excursions. Even if the only reason is to prepare a rescue. As a boyfriend, you better freaking tell me."

She looked up to the right. "You're right. But are you going to tell me every time you go on a mission?"

"He's not sneaky very often," says Rachel. "You know all of his trips."

Nicole looked at her sister like she was kidding.

"The answer is yes. Rachel is right. It's rare I sneak since I leave large magical signatures."

"Well, go put on your nice clothes." Nicole clapped her hands together. "Everyone, we should plan a fun day, too. If everyone wants to, we can have a group trivia and dancing night."

I looked at Rebecca. "In a couple of days, do you think you'll be able to sit at a table in a restaurant?"

"I'd need to be taken care of and helped." She frowned, and I didn't know why.

"You're injured because you saved my life. If you can make it with help, I want to you to join us." How could she think I wouldn't care for her?

"I do then." Her smile was like when we first started dating.

"Do Wesley and I have a mission tonight, too?" asked Rachel.

"You have a date night. If you can help Rebecca until you leave, Nicole and I will be back." I turned to Nicole. "We will be back?"

"Tonight's date isn't romantic and, in a crowd, where I'll be called away a few times," said Wesley and he hung his head.

"Dude, those turn out to be the best dates. You get to see each other in a normal environment." I wondered when those two would gain confidence.

He smiled at Rachel. "We can hang out here, get dressed, take Rebecca for some fresh air with us, come back and put her to bed, and have a more romantic movie night."

"Now that's thinking Wesley. Good job," said Nicole.

He beamed, and Rachel grinned. We'd get them there.

"Nathan, I had trouble with the coordinates for our area when I did the territory pole. Does your fancy AI computer system have a list of adjacent areas and their coordinates so I don't mess up again?" I hoped he didn't see through me. I wanted them, because if they came after Nicole, I'd go burnt civilization on them and turn those states in that territory back to nature.

"The Shared Supernatural System has it. I'll get you a printout of the Key West, New York, Chesapeake Bay, Ohio Valley, and Delta Region Territory coordinates."

"Cool, no rush." I didn't want to act excited.

Nicole stared at me as if I scared her.

Chapter 15—Feast of Immaculate Conception

Nicole and I strode across the street to the large parking lot. It had taken a couple of hours for her to dress the two of us just right, and I was wearing clothes that were not the least bit comfortable. She was playing a game of a gazillion questions about where we were going, and I threatened to carry her there like a sack of potatoes if she didn't tell me.

"You really don't know why we'd be doing something for a church today?" Nicole asked me.

We stood in a movie theater parking lot and waited for an Amigo taxi to bring us to a church called Saint Andrews in Roswell. I insisted our cars not being used for a spy mission, even though she rolled her eyes at me.

"No. My whole religious upbringing was being yelled at how I was going to burn in hell in a Baptist Church, as the good lord intended."

She chuckled. "Good, you'll be fine. The Catholic Church has a feast to celebrate the Immaculate Conception."

"Oh, why today?"

"Papal decree for December eighth. Lots of countries have today as a national holiday." She laughed and slapped my shoulder like her answer was so obvious.

"Cool. At normal churches, we'd call these potluck dinners and come up with a random reason. We'd go there, listen to a talk, be told we were going to hell, and then we'd eat."

"That's what this is—without the burn in hell part. The topic is Mary." She held my hand.

"I'm more up to date than you could imagine. What's our cover?"

"I'm Nicole Hendrix and you're Corey Norwood."

A bit of panic passed through me that I swallowed. "Really? I guess hiding in plain sight since we're so close to home?"

"Yes. Also, Wesley let it slip that he and I couldn't date because a hunky muscle guy named Corey held my heart."

"Well, it's your plan. I'll follow your lead." It'd be nice not to think of everything.

"Thank you. If I hadn't seen you with the priests in the store, I'd be worried, but you know how to hide in plain sight."

"CJ thinks I need more training there, but are Rachel and Wesley going to be there?"

"I bet that is his date idea to bring Rachel to the meal. You and I volunteered to help set up." She looked at me when I stared at her. "Don't be surprised. I'm a volunteer at a lot of these church functions. What did CJ point out?" She looked a little concerned.

"Says my soldier march captures the attention of well-trained troops." I shrugged.

"Not an issue here. No wonder he won't let you into Alpharetta, though."

We got into the taxi, and it was only a fifteen-minute drive. It was early enough in the evening that the cab was clean and he didn't even ring the meter. We paid him ten dollars with a five-dollar tip and got out with no record of our arrival. It was time to sneak.

Nicole immediately shouted out, "Ms. Martha!" She waved and grabbed my hand.

Some older women turned around. I barely kept up running. "Ms. Martha, can you guess who I finally captured?"

The ladies looked at us and smiled. One lady with a yellow dress and broad yellow hat smiled. "Oh Nicole, if that's Corey, I see why you waited."

"I even convinced him to come volunteer with me tonight." Nicole spun and let her dress flare out. "He does search and rescue missions for the park service."

"Oooh, you got a good one, Nicole," said Ms. Martha, the one in the yellow dress.

"Are you here to lift chairs, young man?" joked a woman in a pink dress.

"I asked Nicole if I was to prove my manhood by carrying more than a dozen chairs, and she did not know what I was talking about." I explained.

"We need to go," said Nicole, and she dragged me toward the building. We strolled in through a side door. "Deacon Johnson!"

A man turned around and smiled when he saw Nicole. "You said we were short muscle, so I brought some with me."

This deacon worked out and had the bulk underneath his shirt to prove it. "You did, young lady. Who is this fine young man?"

"This is the elusive Corey." She stood coyly now. Is this the spy Nicole act?

It was freaking me out how church people knew my real name.

"Pleased to meet you, son." He shook my hand and tried to grip me too tight, but I could out grip him if I wanted. "How are you getting those shoulders?"

"Super-setting raises and presses. I got the most improvement when I threw Arnie presses into my routine. Recently, though, I've been alternating pull ups and handstand ups."

"Nice mix up to shock the muscles. Nicole, the men are setting up the canopies and could use the muscles of young Corey here. Could you bring him to the canopy setup?"

"Yep. Come on Corey." She dragged me along.

We were in the back offices and I was sure we weren't supposed to be here. "Perfect, look like the confused boyfriend of the flighty girl," she whispered. "Friendly flighty girl is my cover."

It wasn't a big stretch to move from confused boyfriend of spy girl to confused boyfriend of flighty girl. She pulled me into an office. "Stay here and pretend to tie your shoe," she whispered. "If someone comes, say, I'm using the lady's room."

She took off, and I bent over to look at my boat shoes. Luckily, they had laces. An excruciating million minutes later, Nicole ran back and tucked a few folded pieces of paper into my underwear and made my shirt smooth again. "Now we stay and contribute. Be nice to everyone!"

We walked out of a side door into the back parking lot. Immediately, I got pulled into helping with the large canopies. At least I didn't have to think about this, and I could use my muscles to be friendly by manhandling the canvas and metal into place. Nicole grabbed me to carry tables, portable heaters, and finally chairs.

We set up a large tent for a serving line with tables in the empty parking lot and then the ten canopies each gave cover for four tables that sat ten people each.

My shoes stayed on but since this was on pavement, I was deprived of Earth power regardless. I did my best to forget I was the most wanted person by the Catholic Church. Plus, Nicole had taken something from them. Wait, I held onto the evidence. Great. At least the wanted druid held the stolen information.

Nicole skipped and gave me a hug. "Lighten up, people love you. You can't look like a prisoner. Come grab some food because we're serving, too."

I laughed. "Do they have steaks or hamburgers?"

"Friday? Oh, never mind, we're having fish."

I guess that was a thing. I missed the back parking lot Baptist beer tent at potlucks. Nicole brought me a plate, and we ate with a bunch of other older couples. After we ate, a fancy priest wearing a cassock strolled up. All the others just wore the clergy shirts with black pants.

"We need some help to unload a trailer," he said.

Nicole elbowed me. "I'd love to help." Drinking the last of my water, I stood.

"I'll clean this up sweetie," said Nicole.

"Hi, I'm Corey." The priest looked flustered, and he'd been around a gargoyle. I don't know how I knew, but I could sense it.

He didn't shake my hand. "I'm sorry, I've gotten dirty. The eighteen-wheeler has boxes with blue tape on them. There are six and they are heavy. If you could bring them in and stack them by that door there, it would be a tremendous help." He had a towel wrapped around one hand and I didn't stare until he walked away. The rag soaked with his blood.

"I'd love to, father." Feeling more comfortable, I strode to the eighteen-wheeler and opened the back of the trailer. I found a release for a ramp and pulled it down. It screeched as I pulled it, but I had a twenty-foot ramp to keep myself from making a six-foot jump with the boxes.

Inside, the truck was dark, so I used my druidic vision with my torc hidden under the fancy collared shirt. I paraded through the truck looking at boxes. "Blue, blue, blue," I said to entertain myself.

"Corey?" Nathan poked his head around the corner. "We need to get out."

Part of me wanted to scream 'what the hell,' but he and Madison needed help. They had better have a good story for this. I held up one finger. There was a box with blue tape and I grabbed it. It weighed maybe fifty pounds. Who'd call this heavy? Something inside clicked, then whirred.

Ignoring that, I strolled to the back of the tractor trailer and pretended to shuffle the load.

I looked outside. Backing up I said, "get behind me. When I say go, jump out and run to the right. You'll have a hidden run to the parking lot. Also, a gargoyle is in the area."

"He's at the Rec-center," said Nathan.

Wow. I sent these two into danger. I walked back, waited until I saw nothing, and stepped down the ramp. "Go."

I heard a couple of jumps and peeked to the right. The two of them ran towards the tree cover. *How could their plan have gone wrong? How could a gargoyle be here?*

Back inside the truck, I found the box with the loosest tape and opened up the box carefully. I moved it to the edge of the trailer where sunlight entered, got my phone out, and took a picture of the contraption inside. It looked like one of Richard's gadgets. It clicked and whirred.

I picked up a second box and put it on top of the first to keep the opened one from looking opened. Once those sat by the door, I carried the last three boxes out one at a time, secured the ramp, and shut the trailer.

When all six boxes were by the door, each of them having clicked and whirred, I strolled back to the canopies. Nicole wore a hair net and waved me over. "Let's get in line to help serve. You'll have green beans and mac and cheese to scoop out."

She put a hair net on me. "You look so cute."

I put a strong thought in my head. *I was going to take her on the patio and rock her world tonight after all this.*

She turned and laughed. "It's a deal."

We walked over to the line and twelve volunteers stood in line to serve food to a line of a hundred parishioners. *Did Catholics use the term parishioners?* The first person who came through. "Mac and cheese, no green beans."

That wasn't good for her. "That'll take two hours of cardio to work off. The green beans are the healthier choice."

Nicole whacked me with the back of her left hand. But I handed the mac and cheese and suggested walking around the dirt trail in the park down the road.

Every time someone came with a plate and wanted the simple cabs instead of the vegetables, I calculated the amount of exercise for their whole plate. Every time Nicole whacked me. I gave different recommendations for cardio too. I never mentioned hiking in the mountains.

"That will take four and a half hours of cardio to work off. Are sure you don't want more vegetables?" The older man smiled at my suggestion.

Playful backhanded whack from Nicole hit my chest.

"That's a great plate. No extra exercise for you. I wish they had proper eating medals to hand out." I told a young lady.

Whack.

"What? I was complimenting her." I was getting whacked by Nicole no matter what.

Soon people came up to ask me about their calories, but Nicole stopped whacking at me and said, "be polite." Then it became a thing of people asking me about their plate. Nicole kept saying, "polite" through clenched teeth.

"Is this the line with the judgmental server?" said Rachel. She laughed. She, Wesley, and Rebecca stood next in line. "You're the hit of the serving line."

That wasn't my goal. "Young lady, you have a great plate of food and deserve a good eating medal." If I stopped now, I'd draw attention to myself.

"I'm going to help Rebecca sit," I told Nicole.

"Everyone." She called out loudly and got at least two dozen heads to turn. She pointed to me. "I finally got to date Corey and since his injured ex-girlfriend arrived, he was going to help her sit down. Make sure he looks at me and not Rebecca. Oh, don't be mean to Rebecca. She is sweet." Nicole ran around and carried Rebecca's plate and helped her sit.

"Really, those are your ex and current girlfriends?" said a voice.

"Sometimes trying hard means you get blessed," I said, and turned around and spoke to a Cardinal. "Father," I added while jumping out of my skin.

He chuckled. "That was the perfect answer."

He walked away. "How is she feeling?" I asked Nicole when she returned. "She's in a little pain, but happy to get out and even happier to see you in a hairnet."

After a couple of hours, we took the tent and serving tables down and put them away. Nicole and I relaxed in the room with the canopies, while a priest gave his talk to those at the tables.

"We're almost home," said Nicole. "You should join me Sunday for the sermon so you can get your name mentioned in congratulations."

"Nicole, you are amazing. You've built this identity up over years and are a professional. I am shaking how much in plain sight you are hiding."

"Rebecca told me the more competent you found me, the more you'd fall for me." She bent over and kissed me. There might be something to that, because I was fighting the urge to take her in my arms immediately.

We wrapped up, and we walked out to the main road and entered a coffee shop. She received a small decaf, and I had some herbal tea. We both needed to relax before calling Amigo taxi.

I talked low. "I don't want to hear any more about how I'm the one with steel cajónes. You've been here for years."

"Did I see Nathan and Madison?" She whispered after leaning forward. She rubbed her foot up my leg.

"In the trailer, yeah. I better get a good story out of that." I whispered back. "Apparently, there was a gargoyle involved, and it injured that priest."

Nicole's jaw dropped. "Did you plan for all seven of us at a church tonight?" I was having a hard time concentrating as she rubbed my leg.

"Wesley and Rachel make sense, and then we might've guessed Rebeca wanted to get out. But the other two. No way." She scanned through her phone for something.

I chuckled and sipped on the tea.

"Oh, the church chat is going wild." She read through her phone and giggled. She pulled her leg back and scrolled through her phone.

"Did they notice what you took? Are we in trouble? Did they see me snap that picture? Should we run?"

She laughed. "No. This is the congregation. The old ladies who pay attention to gossip are discussing couples. Wesley and Rachel are in second place to you and me for the mentions of couples. They're setting up a bingo pool for wedding dates." She giggled. "Your calorie counting was the hit of dinner, just like Rachel said."

"Wesley didn't seem to stand out and call around like you did. How did he get mentioned?" Nicole had gone out of her way to get noticed.

"Wesley has been coming here for years and volunteers quite a bit. Rachel fits in with you and Miles, but she stands out next to Rebecca and Wesley. When those two kissed at the table and people realized Wesley had a girlfriend all the ladies, he volunteered with wanted to find out about Rachel and her muscles." She giggled.

"Good thing we stayed under the radar," I joked.

"Flighty girls who can go anywhere do not stay under the radar." She grinned. "By the way, I found two pictures of the empaths."

I pulled out the folded picture in my wallet Nathan sent. "Are they both as plain as her?"

"She's one, but yes. They could be sisters and both have nothing extraordinary about them."

We finished our drinks and caught a cab to the coffee shop near my house and strode down the street. Inside, both spare bedrooms had shut doors.

My bedroom door was open, so we crept in and Rebecca was sitting up, reading her electronic reader. She waved us in and whispered, "Madison and Nathan are in one room, and Wesley and Rachel are in another. I'm working in a rent by hour hotel!"

"It will not get better. You wouldn't believe what Corey said he was going to do to me for making him work at a church all night." Teased Nicole.

They both giggled.

"Shut my door, please." Rebecca waved us off.

We shut the door and strolled onto the patio. Nicole put both of her hands on my shoulders and whispered. "Madison confided she gets turned on when she gets caught up in doing illegal and dangerous things."

"They were just supposed to look!" I whispered back. "Nothing dangerous and nothing illegal."

"You shouldn't send Nathan out with Madison anymore if you want them to be careful. He'll start the night off with grand theft auto!"

We both laughed.

After I warmed the patio with a new fire, we got the deer skins out and towels. "What did we get for our work tonight?"

"Something called Project Druid Trap. I figured you may want to see it."

She took the papers from my pants.

I showed her the picture I took. "Here is a picture of what is in those boxes. It looked like one of Richard's gadgets, only much bigger."

"Wait until tomorrow." She picked up my phone and the papers and put them on the patio.

Then we made love, and it was glorious and fulfilling. A realization that I was happy with Nicole washed over me. This second chance was the best thing that could have happened to me. I wondered if the faeries were busy going between the three couples, but it didn't matter. I was content and filled with Earth Power.

Chapter 16—Training

"Oh, you'll have to wake these two up if we want to eat. They'll sleep all day if we let them." Rachel prodded me with her foot.

I held onto Nicole and looked up into the morning light and saw Rachel bending over me, grinning. "Are you sure you're ready to train?" Her voice had a taunt to it.

It was a beautiful morning, and the house blocked the sun from blinding me. Still, this was a lot of light to open my eyes to. When my brain engaged, I remembered my promise to train in front of Wesley with her.

"Do Nicole and I have time to make love one more time before we get up?" I joked.

Rachel threw me a pair of shorts and rolled her eyes.

Rebecca shouted orders from the kitchen. "Wesley, you put wood in the fire. Madison, you get out the breakfast food. Nathan, you get the grill going. We don't need Corey to get stuff done."

Nicole reached over and grabbed my shirt from last night and slipped it on under the covers. "We could use a little privacy," she exclaimed loud enough for Rebecca.

"Then wake up earlier, you sex-in-public maniacs!" yelled Rebecca from the kitchen. She laughed, but grabbed her side in pain.

Once dressed under the covers, I whispered to her, "let's turn it around. Kiss me as I carry you into the house." I picked her up, and she wrapped her legs around me and started kissing. My back hit the door with a thud when we backed up. I slid it open, and we made

155

it into the dining room without falling down. "This was not a good plan," I said. "I can't see."

She started laughing, and we stumbled down the hallway.

We came back in better shape. Washed up and dressed. I still wore shorts and a muscle shirt to work out.

While we ate, I asked, "Why was the team who were just looking hiding in a eighteen wheeler?"

"They had a gargoyle on site already and we had to hide fast," explained Nathan. "They had it on a leash and they walked the perimeter with it while they unloaded gear."

I thought. "I don't have a follow up because I wasn't expecting that answer."

Nathan laughed. "I'll get you a map. But I have a question. Why were you unloading the Druid Trap boxes?" He must be having one of his yellow food days. He ate a banana, scrambled eggs, and a lemonade he must have brought with him.

"Nicole told me to." I pointed to Nicole.

"I don't have a follow up question because I wasn't expecting that answer." We both laughed.

"Did you know Nathan can make any device work?" asked Madison.

"Yeh," I said after a second. "Like computers, and he'll give them electricity."

"Maybe, but if he touches a car, it unlocks and starts for him. No hot-wiring, no nothing. He stole two cars last night to shake any pursuit."

"You were right," I said to Nicole. "Grand theft auto." We both laughed while the others stared at us.

"We only left the parking lot and parked in a different spot away from cameras. We didn't move the cars very far." Nathan tried to explain, but Nicole and I were caught up in our inside joke.

While we ate, Nicole read the papers she took from the church. "How close were you to six boxes with blue tape?"

"The six boxes you said I should carry for the priest wearing his cassock?" I teased.

"You triggered all six boxes. We going to need to do something." Her eyes got wide and she stood.

I pulled out my phone and showed her the picture I took. "Accurate picture and it matches the description. "

"We need a plan—immediately." She was ready to act, but it was way too soon.

"Slow your roll, sugar lips," I teased. "We've got too much information to parse through to have an action item. We know there was an original site and we know they've changed sites. Now we've learned that one site, or possibly a third one, is to trap druids." We needed to feel out our opponent and see what stance our opponent took before we did anything more than feint.

"Good call, Corey," said Nathan. "Let's get our options figured out and decide what to do."

"You're so smart. Move the chairs near Rebecca. Then you and Rachel train." Nicole continued standing and waited for me to move her chair.

"Are you going to go easy on me?" I asked Rachel, as I moved the chairs over.

"Yes. Put your shoes on." She grinned at me and grabbed her staff.

I frowned and ran inside to grab my shoes. That meant no. Once outside, I grabbed my tonfa, and we got far enough away to talk silently.

"Wait one." I cast druidic berries and gave Rebecca one.

"I'm glad you prepared me not to judge him." She warmed up with cross strikes for me to make mid blocks. I was strong enough to use one arm blocks, but I'd mix it up with two arm blocks to open up my counter attacks occasionally.

Wesley and Rachel worried me. I was worried about Wesley's experience. Unsatisfactory experiences in the bedroom could doom their otherwise promising relationship. "Yeh, well, we could have guessed that."

"He cried. I think he was a virgin."

"Don't judge too much. It's not the worst thing in the world if he's willing to work on it with you." I spun around and performed a low seeping kick to let her know I was ready to pick up the pace.

"You are so upbeat, its nauseating." She smiled. "What was a druid doing, volunteering at a Catholic Church?"

"My girlfriend had this crazy idea to use the most hated person of the Catholic Church as cover for her spying." I jumped then twisted sideways with a cross counter block to catch her staff.

"Did you think it was hot when she pulled it off?" She grinned.

She tried to swipe me low, but I was ready with my low blocks and a jump and pressed with four consecutive strikes, pushing her back on the defensive. "Yes. Yes, I did. Have you thought about your brother and Madison?"

"I know, right? I'm so happy for him. It may be a one-night thing or not, but he needed something." She kept pressing with her attacks, but I wanted to get her temperature on her relationship. "So, if Wesley is down, are you still good dating him?"

"Yeh, I think so. But you should give lessons."

"Don't bring that up. Get with Rebecca. She was fantastic with helping me get better." She set a fast tempo since she did not catch me off guard. She wanted me to get into a pattern she would exploit.

"Really?" She swung low and caused me to skip, but was ready with a block on my quick counter jab.

"Yeh, really. Women who help their partners will end up much happier. That's one of Old Donnie's three lessons." I countered with a stepping strike she needed to roll out of.

"Nicole isn't having to teach you much." She started a faster spinning attack.

"She will, but—whoa, we can't talk about that. Nicole can sense me."

"No, I can't," yelled Nicole from the patio.

Rachel laughed, and I took her down with a low leg sweep.

"That was not fair. You cannot count that one." She back flipped up and took a more aggressive stance.

"It counts, sugar lips." I made a kissing face and would pay for that, but it was worth it.

Rachel came after me now with everything she had and I could do nothing but retreat and block. "Come back here, you defensive weasel," she taunted.

She was giving it her all, and I couldn't follow her weapon. I could only follow her stances and predict the attack based on our two stances. She got a couple of licks in before she tricked me to block high. She kicked me to the ground and held me with her staff. Sweat dripped off her forehead in the forty-degree weather.

"You'd be toast if I took my shoes off." Earth Power let me recover faster on the ground.

"Get off my boyfriend, you meanie!" Shouted Nicole. The others on the porch laughed and apparently, they enjoyed watching us.

"I have more energy than the sex maniacs on the patio." Rachel threw even faster attacks at me.

I kicked off my shoes and kick-flipped out. We were more evenly matched now that I had better reflexes, speed, and strength. We traded blows, stances and I took a more aggressive approach.

She drove me back, and I leaped over her head in a flip that caused her to catch my strike in the nick of time. "There is no way you do that without Earth Power!"

An hour later, we wrapped up and walked over to the others. Rebecca was back in bed. Dinner wore her out. Nicole, Madison, Wesley, and Nathan sat discussing the tasks. Nicole stood up.

She took my hand. "Ooh, you're covered with sweat. Come shower with me to conserve water," said Nicole.

"Are you two using the master bathroom?" asked Rachel.

"Yep." I answered.

She offered Wesley her hand. "I've never showered with anyone. Do you want to come figure out how showering together works with me?"

That was as bold faced a lie as I ever heard Rachel tell. But I let it go.

"Uh, sure," said Wesley.

Nicole yanked my hand to drag me faster after she heard the answer.

When we got into the master room, we were quietly walking past Rebecca, who snored gently. After closing the bathroom door behind us, I turned on the shower to get it warm and whispered to Nicole. "She thinks he was a virgin, but she's still okay."

"He was a virgin and his head is swimming. He's turned on by her muscles."

We got into the shower. "Anything we can do to help them?"

"Yes. He said when he heard you and I outside, he felt so much more confident that you and Rachel weren't an item he could relax."

"So, we make videos of us and send them to him," I joked.

"Ah! You pig." She played, hitting me.

NICOLE LOOKED AT HERSELF in the bathroom mirror. She brushed her hair back and was glad Corey wanted more bronze highlights in her hair. It meant different make up colors, but it set her complexion off nicely. They'd made love once more in the shower and it was pleasant—thankfully nothing like the outdoor love making.

She was sore down there, but she would not admit it. Since she turned nineteen, she put her efforts into finding the murderers of her parents and waited for Corey. Two years of pent-up desire were nearly out of her control. But she had gone from zero to sixty and needed to slow down.

It was time to focus on this silly training class she agreed to help Corey with. Couples Camping or something equally ridiculous. Now she'd wear clothes Corey had picked out for her. Corey came up behind her and unhooked her bra. "We don't have time." Though it would be nicer than dressing in camping clothes.

"Correct, but we don't wear lace bras for hiking." He pulled her bra off and slipped a shapeless sports bra over her head. He focused his emotions on making sure she was ready.

"They look ugly now." He shifted his hand underneath the bra and moved her breasts to a perky position. If he was going to dress her, it wouldn't be so bad. His hands were so gentle and every move caressed. At first glance, his hands were rough, except he had a way of moving his hands slowly over her body. Oops, back to thinking about getting dressed. It was hard not to be flighty when she was used to absorbing everyone's emotions.

She owned one t-shirt. She had bought a pink t-shirt at a Taylor Swift concert. He pulled that over her head. It was a pretty pink, but she had not worn a t-shirt since sixth grade. She knew she was going to be a girlie girl in middle school and enjoyed her choice. Rachel, as a tomboy, was fitting, but now even she wanted to be more girlie.

He led her to the bedroom and pushed her onto the bed, where Rebecca watched with amusement. He took the jeans they picked out at the camping store and pulled them up her legs. "These don't flatter at all," she protested.

Why was she protesting? He was doing this because he adored her and wanted to spend time with her. She couldn't lose Corey again. Nicole had him and wanted to keep him. She knew he liked how she dressed and enjoyed her long hair with bronze highlights. His thoughts were how she had good taste. These were things she wanted to keep him thinking.

"Once you do the class with me and we go camping once, we'll do some more clothes shopping and we can pick out clothes more in your style." It was like he read her mind.

Still, she had to put up some type of fight so he'd realize she was making a sacrifice. "You're making me ugly, so no one else will look at me."

His thoughts weren't like that at all, but they were a little scarce. He liked her look now and was ready to take her out to camp.

"Not likely." He smiled at her and gave her the look in her eyes as he buttoned the jeans on her. He grabbed thick socks and pulled them on while she enjoyed the comment.

"I haven't worn socks since they made me in tenth grade gym class." She had earned the Earth Tattoo for killing Dark Fey and Corey thought that was sexy. Why would she ever cover it?

"Oh Nicole, it's too late," said Rebecca. "I told him not to hide anything from you and he is going to make sure you know his woodsy side." Rebecca's emotions contained sadness, but she was rooting for Nicole. She'd have to figure out how to be the same level of friend to her.

"It's sweet of him, but... ah! What are those?" She pointed to the ugliest light brown clodhoppers imaginable.

"Hiking boots." He gave an infuriating smile as he lifted her leg to put the boots on.

Rebecca giggled.

"They hide my cute feet!" The boots weren't cute at all.

"They protect your cute feet so we can rub them for fun and not because they hurt." Corey punched them on her feet.

"These reasonable comments are stacking up. I can't believe I'm doing this." Nicole looked at her jeans and boot feet and tried to remember when she walked in something without a heel. Well, these had a heel of sorts, just not a pretty one.

"Nicole, you're missing his eyes," said Rebecca. "All these ugly clothes are turning him on."

"Really? Corey is muting his emotions and thoughts and I never learned to read eyes and expressions."

Corey stood up and looked up for a second, and then she felt more of his emotions come through. He had attraction and lust in his mind. She had never encountered someone who could control his emotions and thoughts before. He placed the tacky sunscreen shirt on her and then grabbed a jacket. He pushed her back and kissed her on the bed.

"Hey, I'm right here," said Rebecca.

Rebecca's thoughts had a bit of sorrow and jealousy in her. It must be hard to give up on Corey. She also felt relief that she wasn't the one camping with him. "Let me put on makeup and we'll go."

"No makeup when you camp," said Corey and pulled her by the hand to the hallway.

Rebecca giggled behind her. Rebecca's last thought was gladness at not dressing for camping.

They walked outside to the carport. Nathan and Madison were getting into Nathan's car. Nicole sensed the relationship with Madison confused Nathan and Madison was waiting to explain to Nathan that it wasn't a relationship, but she enjoyed the night.

"Corey, I'm going to put this together and get with Richard. Hopefully, we'll have a bunch of information for Monday," called Nathan who waved the packet they gave him.

"Cool, let's meet up at the cabin," said Corey.

He opened the door for her and put her in his car. He even put the top down, though it was barely forty degrees. Corey was a strange person. He didn't keep up with any social media and was out of touch with everything. He realized he was out of touch and just accepted everything that passed by him. Sexuality, colored hair, nose rings, whatever. He wouldn't date a girl like that, but he didn't mind if they were different. He was a strange breed.

"What are you doing?" She watched him unlatch the roof.

"It's sunny and I have a black interior. We both have our hair pulled back. It's the perfect time to drive with the top down."

"It's forty degrees!" His emotions were happy with the top going down. *How weird was Corey?*

"Not in the car, it's not!" He turned on her seat heater even though the black seats were warm from the sun.

"We are getting you a dress jacket for church, then." She was going to make deals if today was this crazy.

"Is that what you want me to wear?" He started the car and wasn't nearly as loud as his old one.

"Yes! I want you to dress up like I do. No compromises." She would hold the line here.

"Fair enough. You'll have to help me find one, though." His thoughts were fine with it. If she wanted him to wear a jacket, he would. More of this infuriating reasonableness. He was bringing her out into the world with big old work boots, jeans, no make-up, and the tackiest sunscreen shirt you've even seen.

They couldn't talk much with the wind during the drive. Once they parked in the parks' parking lot, Corey came around to her side of the car and opened the door. "Are you coming?" He smiled.

His thoughts were that she looked sexy dressed like this. Strange man, this druid of hers. "If anyone laughs at me, we're wearing matching pink." She walked with him into the park and tripped over the curb into his arms because the stupid boots were so heavy.

"You'll get used to them. But you look sexy."

She stuck her tongue out at him and clomped over the dirt into the wet grass. The bottom of her pants got wet. She wouldn't worry about that in a dress or a skirt. Across the field was the group of people Corey waved to.

There was Trish. She'd understand Nicole's predicament. Trish's emotions centered round relief at seeing them and amusement at Nicole's clothing. This was not a good start.

"Corey," said Trish. "Are you available Saturday morning—the twenty-third? The priests have a group that need lessons on the gear they bought. Would you be available?"

"Sure, Trish," he answered.

"Oh Nicole, you look so cute. Everyone, here is the Couples' Camping instructor, Corey, and it looks like he brought his girl-friend decked out in everything from the store."

"Except for the pink Taylor Swift t-shirt," said Corey. His thoughts gave away that he thought the pink concert shirt was the funny part of the outfit.

Corey went through some of his charming introductions and then said, "I'm Corey and I camp too much and this is my lovely as-sistant..." he pointed at her.

"I'm Nicole and I love too much."

The ten people laughed, and maybe this wasn't so bad.

Corey found an area with a bunch of grass—a little hilly with a root sticking out. He pointed out that people should practice in less-than-ideal locations to be ready for anything.

The yells of kids playing baseball in the fields we joyful. She won-dered if one day she'd be bringing kids to a sport area like this. She tuned out and talked with Trish until Corey called her over. "Let's show them how we fit into the two tent types."

The first tent was a normal tent and way too cramped. Then he had her get into a tiny tent with a walking pole for a tent holder upper.

"Wait. This isn't working. You stay," she would entertain herself a little. "You comfy, sweetie?" She jumped on his lap and started kissing him. "Plenty of room," she said. She kissed him until they knocked the tent on top of them.

The laughter of the other couples was worth being dressed up.

Corey helped her up. "You can see the perils of the ultralight tent." His thoughts were of how cute she looked while being funny. That was nice.

The emotions from the rest of the classes were humor and relieved of some tedium.

She helped show starting fires, making kindling, and other minor tasks. She knew how to do all that and could do it wearing nice clothing. He also had her in a sleeping bag and on a quilt, showing something about pulling the bag with your shoulder when you turned. He got into the quilt with her for a few seconds and she played with him under the covers until he jumped up. His emotions were shock and embarrassment until it turned to humor.

They finished the class and drove home and she looked forward to changing. They ran into Rachel, who giggled at Nicole.

Corey stopped them. "I'm going to go study rituals in the Fey Realm for a few hours."

"Rachel, you stay here." Nicole sensed Corey had nothing but studying on his mind, but better safe than sorry.

"I need to do something too," said Rachel. Her emotions were about having fun. Running around and playing with faeries.

Nicole held her arm. "You and I are going to sit with Rebecca and she's going to tell you how you can get Wesley to be better in bed the same way she worked on Corey."

"That is a great idea, Nicole," said Corey. He kissed her and he meant it. "You three have some girl time tonight and I'll be at the cabin after studying the ritual I want to learn." He had no thoughts except of study.

She could probably wear camping clothes occasionally. *But did he only not think about Rachel in the Fey realm when she did the woodsy stuff with him?* She was going to check that website for help with a confident man again.

Chapter 17—Bright World, Church, and Vampires

I had a successful day so far. With my messenger bag and the Fey Realm ritual book, I walked into the Fey Realm and whooshed to my shelter. After taking off my clothes, I picked up the ritual book.

Fully connected to the Fey Realm, I read about the Bright Realm and the faeries that fluttered around me lost interest quickly. The book was brilliant and made for young people with short attention spans.

The book listed three realms and two transition realms. Earth, The Fey Realm, and the Realm of Darkness were the three realms. When the world turned black and white, that was what the book called the transition plane between Earth and the Realm of Darkness. On the other side, the world could turn bright. This was Bright Earth, the transitionary realm between the Fey World and Earth. There were notes calling them the Realm of Shadow and Realm of Iridescence, but those names seemed silly for transition areas.

There was the Fey Realm, and they split half of it into the four courts of the Seelie and the other half taken over by the Unseelie. The Unseelie area broke into a perversion of the four courts, Fire, Death, Barren, and Despair. Those sounded bad.

Now Bright Earth was cool because you could stay in Earth and be stronger and move around. Most humans couldn't interact with you. It's like the world of black and white, only the colors went there with the happiness. I could use a circle and prepare it and move myself and everything I desired in my vision to this realm. It was exactly like the gargoyles moved us to the world of black and white. More importantly, I could use Earth Power to move at my Earth Power speed over any terrain. There were notes that Earth Power was amplified for druids. Imagine leaving North Atlanta and beating traffic to the Atlanta Airport.

Having memorized the ritual to move to Bright Earth and back, I planned to sleep in the cabin. I packed everything up and sat to reflect on things.

Nicole had walked with a wider stance than normal and we'd been very active the past couple of days with no windup. We described the final ten minutes of the lovemaking with Earth Power as vigorous with power. Nicole might need some time to recuperate. I'd gone months without sex recently and could take days off if it helped the relationship for the long term.

Earlier, Serene Pond piqued my curiosity, and I wanted to check it out when we didn't gather water. I also didn't want to whoosh by everything so fast, so after I dressed, I focused on a slower travel to Serene Pond.

The landscape changed, and I passed over the Fertile Fields, but turned left. It melded into the lush green grass of the Cloven Hills past the Flower Mounds. Satyrs played flutes, centaurs flirted with wood nymphs, and unicorns pranced along with the beat.

The noise soon subsided except for the splashing of water. Swans floated gracefully next to Swan Maidens. I turned away from the Swan Maidens and let them swim without my prying eyes. The peacefulness of the area caught me and I rested my eyes for a minute.

Worry woke me, and I stood. I was tired and wanted to get a full night's sleep. I grabbed my books and messenger bag, and traveled to Tree Foyer. The sun was shining on a new day as I traveled to the cabin. I spent over twelve hours at Serene Pond!

Back at the Tree Foyer, I traveled to Woodrow's tree to my house. I cast some druidic berries. The three women were stirring. It was going to be a long day for me because I had not slept at all.

"You do not look rested, young man," said Rachel. She wore her pajamas. It defined her shoulder muscles in the thin strapped top and shorts.

Rebecca leaned on a bar stool next to the breakfast bar and looked healthier and wore one of my shirts like she used to when we dated. I gave her a berry, and she smiled at me like she used to. Nicole wore her sexy nightie. Holy crap, she was bending over at the fridge.

"I won the Corey leer contest," said Nicole, standing up. "Of course, he approved of everyone here."

"I'm wearing a shirt I used to love wearing when I'd stay over. It's so comfy."

"I have dreams that start out like this. I'm going to take a shower and try to wake up. Oh, safety tip. Do not rest your eyes if you sit at Serene Pond in the Fey Realm. I thought it was a minute, but I lost twelve hours."

Rachel ran over and hugged me. "From now on, you and I set up alerts and check on each other in the Fey Realm, even if your girlfriend is jealous."

"Twelve hours in a blink?" said Nicole. For the first time, I saw concern on her face.

"Yes. Plus, it didn't give me any rest. The time was just gone." I rubbed my eyes.

"You two shouldn't play with the Fey Realm," said Rebecca.

"That kind of defeats the purpose of the Spring Court," I explained. "It's not only about passion, fertility, and intimacy. Youthfulness, singing, dancing, mischief, and playfulness are also parts of the court. Rachel and I wouldn't fit so well if we were super serious old fogies."

"Shower and change young'un," said Rebecca.

I wondered what Nicole thought of the Fey Spring Court. This could be a difference to move us forward.

Rebecca shooed me away as if I didn't know they were going to talk about this and make plans around my back. I put my messenger bags down and realized my brain worked as it did in the Fey world. It was almost eight o'clock. I considered the relation to Serene Pond and my brain still working.

I showered and put on the clothes Nicole had picked out for me. With all the 'go to meeting' clothes on and those funky boat shoes, I walked out and Nicole handed me a plate for breakfast.

"When you dress up, you're allowed to leer at me when I bend over."

I laughed. "We're lucky there weren't any guys in the house with you wearing the negligee. I'd have to go ballistic on them."

"Eat up, my pretty neanderthal." She patted my shoulder and sauntered to the back rooms, knowing full well I watched.

Rachel, who was already changing, came out first.

"My brain is still working like it does in the Fey Realm," I told her.

"What? How?" She sat in my lap and snuggled with me. "We don't have too long before Wesley is here. He knows we snuggle, but I don't want to rub it in his face."

"Good thinking. I'm wondering if there is a link between Serene Pond and my being alert. It was eight am when I walked back and noticed."

She hugged me and snuggled her nose into my neck.

"Are you wearing perfume?"

"Yep. Wesley bought it for me. What do you think?" She touched the back of her neck.

"I don't know. I'm glad it's different from what Nicole wears, so I say good for you."

She pulled back to talk to me with her grin. "Can you believe you and I are going to church?"

I kept the joke going. "Yeh, but it's not a proper church where they yell at you about going to hell like the good lord intended."

"The bible isn't even King James' version." Her grin moved into laughter.

"Oh, these people are going to burn extra hot." We both laughed.

THE FOUR OF US STROLLED into the church after Nicole parked. We stopped at least a dozen times for people to say hello to us or to say how pretty Nicole and Rachel looked.

"Did you park in the spot where we would wave to and most people would see us?" This knowing people in the church still freaked me out.

"Duh. How else do you get full cover?" Nicole rolled her eyes at me.

"Kill half of the people?" I joked—okay, half joked.

"Ah!" Nicole bust out laughing. Rachel and Wesley heard me and laughed as well, with Wesley shielding his eyes.

We stepped up the stairs to the main doors, where the deacon handed the two ladies a pamphlet. "It's good to hear joyous laughter. Discussing today's sermon?"

The others blushed, but my mind worked on Fey World power. "No sir," I said. "I used to attend a Baptist church, and I told them I failed the philosophy class that covered Thomas Aquinas and asked if I'd understand what was going on this morning."

The deacon chuckled. "You'll be fine, son. When you get lost, lean on this wonderful lady that brought you."

We walked in and Rachel whispered, "You're right, your brain is working."

We started out with calisthenics, apparently. Stand up to sing, sit, kneel to pray, sit, stand again to sing. Catholics don't skip leg day. They mentioned the feast where Nicole and I got mentioned.

The priest I remembered from the store took the podium, or whatever they called it. "Oh no," I muttered.

"What?" asked Nicole.

"It's your buddy, Father Fuller." I recognized the priest from the store.

"When I heard the name Corey Norwood, I couldn't believe it. Corey, are you here? Could you stand up?" The priest scanned the area.

Nicole giggled and pinched me on the way up.

I stood and waved. Not exactly what I hoped for as a druid being hunted by them.

"I heard he was judging calories on plates and helping spread good cheer at the feast. This is in his character, because this is the man who help the church with every camping question and walked us through every step of the camping purchases. He will teach the parishioner and priest camping introduction class in two Saturdays." He smiled and waved at me.

There was polite applause, and I waved to the congregation. Rachel and Nicole snickered on either side of me.

I smiled and muttered through my teeth, "Oh good, Priest Fuller knows me on sight and introduced me and now I'm known as the guy who does woods stuff when they're looking for a druid."

"Blush when I do this." She kissed me on the cheek and I grinned to keep from laughing and looked at my lap. "Crisis averted."

The service dragged on and leg day kept going and the normal part of church happened when they sent around the collection plate. I pulled out my wallet, and I only had a dozen hundreds from the priests who shot at me. "All I have is big bills," I said.

"Take one." She grabbed a bill from my wallet, folded it and dropped it in. She covered her mouth when she passed the plate. "Did I just drop a hundred in the collection plate?"

"Don't worry, I took if off the priests that tried to kill Rebecca and I." I whispered. "Now I grinned like Rachel to keep from laughing at the ridiculous circumstance we were in."

The sermon started, and it was about leadership. Nicole pulled a bible from the pew in front of us. She opened it to James 3:1. *My brothers and sisters, not many of you should become teachers, because we know that we teachers will be judged more strictly.*

Good, that's what I needed as a killer. Preacher Jon made me leader, so I could be judged more harshly.

Nicole pinched me. That's right, empath.

After the service, I was ready to run for my life, but the deacon from the main door and his wife headed the four of us off.

This was it. I started looking for fighters and how many people I'd need to put down to get us out and on the road.

Nicole squeezed my hand twice.

"We hate to be so forward said the woman, but we can recognize couples that are serious. We will start a six-month marriage preparation class in January and we'd like you four to consider joining. It's more relaxed with couples, you already know," said the woman who must be the wife of the deacon the way they acted.

My mind may have over-reacted. But it was a good time to tease Rachel a little for the beating she gave me in practice. I put my hand on Rachel's back and gave her a tiny shove.

"I'd love one," she said, catching her balance after a step forward.

Nicole squeezed my hand as hard as she could and yanked me forward. "We are further along in our relationship and definitely need the class," said Nicole, with a glare at me. "We better sign up too."

I squeezed her hand back. "Great idea sweetie, let's get a pamphlet because we were wondering how we were going to work on our communication," I answered.

Rachel stifled a chuckle next to me.

"That is such a critical piece of the class," said the deacon. "The fact you two are discussing it means you are far along. I'm Gary Williams, a deacon here at Saint Andrews and this is my lovely wife, Beth."

"It's a pleasure, Deacon," I said and shook his hand and hugged Beth. Then the others followed suit and Nicole carried the pamphlets out with us.

By the time we weaved, hugged, and talked through the throng of people, I sat in the passenger seat of Nicole's car and stared at the ceiling. After Nicole started the car, I felt I could speak. "What a disaster." I laughed at the roof.

"We're dressed up, let's go to lunch," said Rachel. "If Corey can throw a hundred dollars into the plate, he can buy us lunch."

"As long as the bills aren't marked," I said. "I stole these from the priest's car after I beat them and tied them up. You know, the priests who were shooting at a druid who likes the mountains and woods. Also, I sure hope no one, especially Priest Fuller, identifies me as a guy who works in the woods and asks me to stand up in a Catholic Church."

Wesley laughed, and Rachel giggled.

Lunch sounded good, though. "We might beat the Baptists to lunch if we hurry," I joked.

"Lunch is a good idea, Rachel. Corey, you were perfect. Old Donnie taught you well about hiding in plain sight. No one is going to think a druid will start dating flighty Nicole and wave to the parishioners." She patted me on the leg and turned right when the officer directing traffic out of the church waved us through.

"I can disappear, but they tied you three to me," I explained.

"You can't disappear. Why do you think they gave us the mar-riage class information?" She explained it like I was dense. Unfortu-nately, my brain had slowed to its normal speed. Twelve hours lost for three hours of clarity was an expensive trade.

"Collecting the class fee?" I answered.

"Because they know we are dating seriously. Wesley can't get hap-piness due to sex off his face. You and I act too intimate in casual responses for them to think otherwise. They want our babies to be born in wedlock, and this class is a requirement to be married in the church."

Flippancy took over. The craziness had gotten absurd. "Sign us up if it takes six months to get a wedding date." I picked up the pam-phlet. "It's over two hundred per couple." I pulled six of the priest's bills out of my wallet. "Wedding classes on me." I handed the pam-phlet with six hundred dollars to Nicole.

"Oh, I will," she said as she slid it into her purse. She grinned as she drove to the restaurant.

"Man, now I really want to save the world," said Rachel.

Oops. Poor Wesley stayed quiet. I'd need to do some damage control with him later. Stupid flippant Corey.

AFTER LUNCH, WE DROVE back to the house, and I held Wes-ley back as Nicole and Rachel crept into the house, trying to listen to what I would say to him. "Shoo," I said to Rachel as we waited for them to go in.

"We should talk softly, since they'll be listening at the door," I joked.

He chuckled.

"Hey, I'm sorry I caught you up in my marriage counseling com-ments. I didn't think about you two being new and should have held back some."

"I realized they frustrated you."

"Still, I feel bad. I am the biggest benefactor if you and Rachel work out and it pains me to hurt any chance. Outside of you two, of course."

"You?" He squirreled his mouth up in a confused manner.

"Yep. You know that Rachel and I are codependent and have to hug and spend time together. Well, when I did the weeklong trip up North, I had withdrawal symptoms and got the shakes. I had to make Rachel-stand-ins to hug in order to sleep."

"Wouldn't her staying single be better?"

I shook my head. "When I'm dating, she gets less time with me and her mood drops. Since we're co-dependent, my mood drops with hers. We have to be careful. If she is happy, then my mood gets happier and its very pleasant life."

"How come you two never dated?"

"The bond we get from hugging or snuggling is as good as it gets. Anything more complicates things and raises angst and leads to bad issues. Thinking seriously about dating Rachel gives me a panic attack."

"Whoa." That caught him off guard.

"All this to say is that I am in your corner and I can get information. I'd like to make sure you two get the best chance possible."

He explained more. "My biggest fear is when the PhD program starts back up in January, I won't be able to explain to Rachel the time I need to study."

"This is exactly the type of thing I can help with. I will not pretend to understand what you study, but Rebecca broke up with me for a few reasons. One of which was time I disappeared to banish gargoyles or study spells."

"Sounds similar." He frowned.

"Keep your schedule as updated as you can, probably through Nathan and Preacher Jon's calendar. Ping me and I can keep the temperature of Rachel and help. It could be something as simple as us coming to campus and having lunch or dinner with you."

He lit up. "By the way, Haley is coming to town for the New Year's Eve Party and she'll be here after she camps with her mom."

"I'd like to know how she is doing. Plus, seeing Anne again will be nice." I wanted to hear from Haley.

"She's doing great, but I'll let her tell you."

We walked in. "Oh. Thank you for the information about my death. Rebecca lay wounded in the back of the SUV and I saw a priest. I remembered your comments, and I needed to change the conditions. You saved our lives." I would not tell him Rebecca had celestial magic from the heavens and could block the power of priests.

"Thank you for making me useful. It'll take a while to get used to the visions."

We ambled inside, and exhaustion threatened to take me down. "I may be a party pooper, but I need to get ready for bed since I haven't sept in almost two days." A large yawn kept my mouth open too long.

"I need to verify some grades and sign off on them and I should do that before the training thing tomorrow morning," said Wesley.

"You boys rock on and we'll take care of Rebecca," said Rachel. "We'll see you tomorrow morning." I grabbed my messenger bag, the extra book, my weapons belt, and my waist pack and headed through the Spring Court Tree Foyer and through the large red maple to the cabin. I sifted through the snow, maybe an inch and a half, and started a fire for the bed, then brushed off the awning.

Soon my bed was ready, and I went to sleep before the sun set.

Chapter 18—Not making the same Mistake

When I rolled over, Rachel was next to me. I wrapped her in my arms and legs.

"I can't do it," she said and looked sad.

"Do what?" I was still snoozing and confused.

"Nicole wanted me to seduce you, and it made sense until I saw you. I'm so sorry."

Crap. That was a wake-up call. "Don't be sorry. You were perfect. She tested you and you passed."

"She wanted to test you with the faeries." Rachel had tears in her eyes and stood up.

I needed to help her. "Tell you what. If you use my circle and heat the water in the trough so I can bathe, I will braid your hair after I dress."

She smiled. "Thank you. I'm sorry I said yes to Nicole."

I needed Rachel on board today, and I needed my friend to feel happy. "Rachel, as battle leader, it is my duty to inform you of team powers. Nicole can read your mind and predict the correct statement or action to get what she wants from you."

"What?!" Her sadness went away almost immediately.

"It's why she is a great spy. However, it is not cool to use it on team members. But you are done with this. Go inside. I'll bathe, then join you."

My circle became in use without me initiating it and I saw steam rise from the trough and the snow melted in a fifty-foot diameter. She jogged inside, and I got in the warm bath.

Why would Nicole do something so stupid the day of a training exercise before a deadly fight? This was crazy. We had a trust issue, but I couldn't deal with it today.

I washed up, sat, and soaked. The white wonderland of the North Georgia Mountains in the warm bath was something I could get used to. But I got out to go do some damage control with Rachel. "Hey! Ready for a hair braiding?"

"Yes. I just ripped into Nicole. She used her power on me. I'd never use my Shotokan specialist skills on her."

When I sat on the couch, Rachel sat between my legs. I braided her hair and got her focused on the fight and away from her sister with the stupid loyalty test.

"You and I have a training session this morning and a dangerous fight tomorrow night. Let's get ready to fight."

Now I used my earring against Nicole again, intentionally. I had used it accidentally and now I didn't know what to do. I would not freak out and make a snap judgment. No more disasters due to snap judgments. One thing I loved about Rebecca is how she prepared me for Nicole. It was another strand in the web that had me caught up.

Today and tomorrow needed to be about preparing to survive the defense of the Moon-eyed people. I focused on the earring and added thoughts of women, sex, the loyalty test, and thoughts of Nicole's empathy to what the earrings prevented me from sharing. All thoughts of the Moon-eyed strategy became covered, too.

We cooked breakfast and ate with smiles. After I washed up, Miles arrived, then a group arrived of Preacher Jon, Nathan, Madison, Rebecca, and Nicole.

Outside, I created druid berries. Even though I was healthy and unsure of how I healed so fast, Rebecca needed help. She got two. "One now and one for dinner."

I washed up the dishes. "Welcome to the first squad's practice." I held up the manual Fitz gave me, along with the notes from Dr. Kanoska. "We have our toughest battle tomorrow night. My report says guns scare the Moon-eyed and we'll have a strategy without firearms." It didn't, but I didn't want Nicole around because of the distraction.

Preacher Jon interrupted. "Corey, let me give out some information and we will remove non-combatants."

I agreed.

"Let's talk about the new intel because few things are adding up," said Preacher Jon. "Nathan, could you give us the breakdown?"

Nathan handed me a folder with some paper. "These are the co-ordinates you asked for." Then he addressed the room. "Nicole pulled some data the other night that ties together what we found out and ties to the information Corey got from Strumath. When we combine it with the information Corey got from The Alpharetta Administration Center, the information stolen during the rescue of Rebecca, the information Corey got from the priests and the camping equipment, and the information from The Tribe, we finally have a decent picture of what is happening."

Finally. We've been twisting in the wind for some time.

Nathan turned to read from an index card. "Corey. When you took out Bishop Pedrotti and saved the lovely Ms. Roane, it had two effects. The first is you took a powerful enemy off the board but alerted the monsignor to our capabilities. Our team scared the church."

"They're hunting us, but since they lost the ability to track me directly, they're pulling all the stops," I offered.

"Nice summary," said Nathan. "They are sending out priests and parishioners under the guise of small revival camping trips to hunt for you. They're setting up the Alpharetta Administration Center as a trap to catch you as well. Plus, they've deployed one empath there, and The Tribe has needed to pull back except for CJ and Derek, who have empath protection."

"I'm training the revival campers in two Saturdays. Saint Andrews in Roswell had me stand up in the church so everyone could recognize me as the one training the priests and parishioners." I hoped others were as freaked out as I was at that.

"I have another update," said Preacher Jon. He read off his phone. "Somewhere between the airport and Saint Andrews, a druid tripped six sensors they're using to set up their trap."

"Probably when I offloaded them from the trailer for the priest," I said. "I bet that worried them even more to our capabilities."

That caught Preacher Jon off guard, but he nodded.

"That's the next update. Corey had seven of us at Saint Andrews last night to hide in plain sight," said Nathan.

"It wasn't the plan, but only two of us were a surprise," I said.

Nathan explained to everyone. "This is what happened. Madison and I saw a gargoyle and turned around immediately but found ourselves surrounded. If Madison didn't have breaking and entering skills, they would have caught us."

That was a mental note for later. "Good job Madison. Bringing additional skills to bear is how we all survive."

Nathan smiled at Madison. "The tractor trailed moved items from the new site in case we spied on them. Corey, from your previous reports, you reported two unnamed men we've tied to Rebecca as speaking Italian. You called them Suit and Red Shirt."

"Oh, I know them. It hurt they weren't at the battle with Bishop Pedrotti." These two guys were good, well, at least Suit was.

"They were present with the gargoyle." Nathan's face looked concerned. "But I glanced at a packet they translated. They accessed old druid records concerning the Appalachian cave system."

"Crap." The cave system is how Old Donnie's grandfather made the Southeast safe from giant monsters which the local tribes had learned to live with.

"Wow," said Rachel. "He's my great, great, great," she stopped and counted. "Great, great grandfather."

I counted the greats. "Yep."

Nathan sighed and continued. "Now, the church has gotten paranoid and believe they have insiders in the system. The monsignor controls information at Sacred Heart downtown. No more computer systems connect to the systems at Sacred Heart."

"Poo," said Nicole.

"Nathan, what's the bottom line? We know there is something at Sacred Heart. We know about the Alpharetta Administration Center, and we know about the Recreation Center down from Saint Andrews." We had a lot of sites and I missed the link between them.

Nathan pulled out his folder. "I ran these on the Shared Supernatural System and we have high confidence answers." He read them off his sheet. "Alpharetta Administration Center is a trap. Specifically, a druid trap. The Rec Center is the site for the spell during the Winter's Solstice and needs a week to finish setting up. Sacred Heart is still a closed book to us."

"Okay. They've discovered us, but not enough to track us down. Unless someone has an objection, we do nothing except maintain a presence for covers until Wednesday. Probably until Friday. We focus today and tomorrow on the Moon-eyed people." I wanted to get practicing.

"One last thing Corey, I have a piece of unactionable information," said Nathan.

"Go for it."

"It may or may not mean tonight, but the Delta Territory contacted the church and believe if they kill you, they can take Nicole."

"Did they hand over pictures or signatures of us to the church?"

"Probably not. Some rules require expulsion from the Realized. That is one. Their actions are already on the border of allowed behavior. But remember, no one can research other territories using the Shared Supernatural System." He handed me two more folders. "The legal information on the Delta vampires and information we have on the Moon-eyed village."

"It they don't hit us tomorrow night, that is Wednesday's biggest issue." I had an idea to use the ritual bottles Rachel and I created. "Rachel, as we get organized, could you get the ritual bottles in my basement and bring them here?"

"Now?"

"Yes." I wanted to remove her from Nicole's influence before Nicole left.

She ran out the back door.

"Nathan, any more sightings of Suit and Red Shirt?" I worried about them and the monsters.

"One low confidence sighting in North Carolina."

Well, they weren't close. "Okay. Madison, Miles, and I. Let's get started. We need to protect the Moon-eyed people and then strategize about the Rec-center site."

"Can we wait until Rachel is back?" said Nicole.

I ignored her and moved the other three who would train today to the back door.

"No. Nicole, you are only twenty-one and inexperienced. Let's get you back," said Rebecca, loud enough for me to hear. She had shouted the word inexperienced.

Well played Rebecca. You got the information to me.

"Thank you, Rebecca. I heard you." That should be enough for Rebecca to calm Nicole while I could sort out the rest after the upcoming battle.

Rachel returned. I grabbed the bottles and put them near the trough.

"OKAY, LET'S RELAX SOME now." I wanted to get them out of the way so we can get ready and everyone's head in the game. The Moon-eyed entrance has an open area which I can block with a circle.

Our group marched out past the trough and just past the mini farm I used to grow the ingredients for beer in better weather. The four of us continued until we were on the cusp where woods became heavy. We stood next to the path we'd ride the bikes to Old Pond for mudding.

"Today's information comes mainly from previous attacks provided with the pamphlet from Dr. Kanoska. Let's start off with a rundown of primary powers. Miles?"

"I got a big honking sword and can track any of you... on Earth. Plus, squirrel communication."

A glance at Rachel got her to give her principal powers.

"I fight and I sing, which strengthens everyone," she stated.

"Madison?" I continued.

"I don't know which are primary." She looked confused.

"Dude, she has a lot of unfocused powers. You may help her more than I." Miles shrugged.

"List them," I said. Miles was good in a lot of areas but not imagination.

Madison nodded. "I can focus and turn off any electronics within five feet and I can get lost inside of a crowd. I never lose track of prey and I have a wicked jump. Magic can summon a bow or create a temporary Fey enchanted weapon for an ally. Last, I can detect relative power levels or share power with an ally."

"Did you say create a Fey weapon for an ally?" Rachel was visibly excited.

"Hold out your hands."

A green, glowing surujin appeared in Rachel's hand. She squealed with delight.

"I can only keep one up at a time. I prefer my normal bow if I had my druthers."

Rachel ran over and hugged her. "Oh my god, my whole life I've wanted this. I wanted to prove I was more than just a helped in fights with gargoyles and Dark Fey."

I don't know if I smiled more for Rachel's happiness, Madison happiness at being more valuable, or the increased readiness of our group, but I smiled so widely I felt my cheeks scrunch up. "Guys, I only have one battle plan style, and it's based on loving. We are going for the whole schmear. We will protect the Moon-eyed, drive back the Fey creatures, and no one is expendable."

"You didn't list your powers," said Madison.

"I will give them out with the strategy."

"Is it we prepare lunch and you save the world?" joked Miles.

"Nope, sorry. I will establish a large circle. Madison, you pick out multiple sites to shoot from where your jump can get you to. Miles and Rachel, pick out the best areas to protect this circle."

"High and low?" asked Madison.

I wasn't how sure how high she could get. "Don't let my plan limit your movement. I need to see you in action. Okay, we will setup as strong a position as we can and prepare for an easy test charge like the Dark Fey do."

"Don't get overconfident when this happens," said Miles.

"Right. When they recognized a potent force, they'll try to break us with a spike rush." I drew the circle on the ground and drew a wedge of attackers so they could see what I meant.

"The strongest will be in the front, and they'll back out for weaker ones to do damage before they resume the attack with us weakenned," added Miles.

"I should already sing to make Miles and Madison stronger," said Rachel.

I hadn't considered her timing. "Excellent idea Rachel. You sing from the beginning so Madison and Miles can get used to the extra power. The plan hinges on withstanding the initial onslaught, so fight defensively and withdraw into the circle."

"Into the circle?" asked Miles.

I smiled. "New strategy for my new power. As soon as I initialize my circle, I will bind it on me and I will transform into a fighting creature. The Fey Court changes the spell, so be aware, I could look freaky."

"Freakier," joked Miles.

"Then, as we fight, I will remove the life force from creatures. If I grab your wrist, let me. I will have you kill the creature so we can increase your power. Questions?"

"Why are we in the circle?" asked Madison.

"First so I can reach you easier, but, as long as I keep the circle up with Earth Power, it will help everyone inside be healthier." There was more to it than that, but that was the end result.

"Let's practice spacing," said Rachel.

My satellite pad thingy sounded an alert. I strolled over and grabbed my pad. There was an emergency search and rescue. A woman and daughter were missing, and they fell near a ravine with caves.

I handed Rachel the notes from Dr. Kanoska. "Practice today and leave tomorrow morning and meet me in Asheville. There is an emergency search and rescue."

"We should go with you," said Miles.

"It's near caverns and I need to move at Earth Power speed to save their lives. Pick me up tomorrow morning at the bar in Asheville we liked. I'll be in the woods next to the parking lot."

With my waist pack secured, I put on my daypack and took off towards North Carolina through the woods. I'd cover the eighty miles in woods in five hours.

Chapter 19—Suit and Red Shirt

I made good time with Earth Power speed through the North Georgia mountains, past the start of the Appalachian trail into North Carolina. Old Donnie and I made this trek quite a bit because it was faster than driving around.

Because of the cabin's location, the drive to Asheville was at least six hours and if the car wasn't ready or needed gas, it was longer. Once in Asheville, it was another two to three hours to the remote hiking areas. When I used Earth Power to run there, it took half the time—that could mean the difference in life and death.

Members of The Tribe would be in the search and rescue team since it was close and the local park service knew most of them. They called Old Donnie, Ghost and when I helped without Old Donnie once, Fitz told them to call me Clone since I was a clone of ghost. It didn't matter. As long as I wasn't standing up and waving in a church, saying I was a potential druid, they could call me Frieda.

This was the trickiest part of search and rescue. I could go places other humans could not and if you knew to look for a druid, this gave me away. I had to get in, do the rescue, and get out without being seen. Well-meaning people with little sense would convince the victims that there was no special man that showed up and blame phenomena like Third-Man-Syndrome. I'd been the third man a handful of times over the past few years. Old Donnie had been the third man over a hundred times in his life.

I got close to the gps coordinates. With the map, gps, and compass, I measured out the last sighting. Crap. They were down a ravine with lots of ugly ledges and seven entrances to the cave system in roughly a square mile of space. The ravine plummeted hundreds of feet and in the middle was bottomless. We couldn't rappel down because strange winds could break any rope or chain as it slammed the person against the wall. This area was bad news, and we called it Bottomless Ravine.

Old Donnie's Grandfather had gotten to know many Cherokees through his grandfather. When Georgia was officially a state in seventeen thirty, the Nephilim balance was upset. As the Abernathy clan had settled here to hide from the church, they had to endure the monster attacks to survive.

The Cherokee had lived with the giants and their beasts in an uneasy truce for generations, but the European settlers weren't very patient. As the giants died off, their beasts and creations were no longer domesticated. Nowadays, people without the spark would call them monsters. People with the spark, well, they call them monsters too, because that was the best word to describe them.

These beasts caused the Abernathy druids to nearly die off. Old Donnie's grandfather was the one who finally drove the last of them into the dark caves.

I tuned in my radio and heard dispatch getting setup. I waited for as much information as I could and a code word to let me know someone from The Tribe was on site.

Two missing. A mother and a daughter. Daughter was age two. Grandmother was on sight. Mother's name was Haley, and Corrinne was the toddler.

Then I heard the magic words. *VASAR in command center.* VASAR, Volunteer Appalachian Search And Rescue, was the part of The Tribe that showed up to search and rescues in dangerous areas. I responded. "VASAR, this is Clone. On site and heading to likely fall points."

Roger, Clone, be careful. That was Fitz, over my radio.

The woods thinned to the amount of rock in the ground that covered the cave system and it was primarily scrub. The rock surface was sheer and plates would break off and slide, so even a druid needed to be careful moving down the cliffs. Many experienced hikers had ropes cut because of a rockslide while trying to rappel down. A half hour later, I made it halfway down the cliff and landed on the widest ridge. This was the most likely spot for survivors, so I began a search while calling the victim's names, Haley, and Corrinne.

The ledge varied from four to ten feet wide and contained no plants larger than a scrub bush and had many jagged rocks. The best case to find a fallen victim was if a tree jutting from the cliff side caught them. Within an hour, I heard a response. It sounded like someone called my name.

"Cor... ee?" came a weak response.

I climbed up to the voice. A mother held a toddler, and they landed in a bush where a tree jutted out. This scrub foliage grew thick enough to catch a person with its main branch. They were lucky, except for the sharp rocks that gashed up the mother. I crawled up to assess the situation. *Oh no, it was my Haley!*

Think Corey. I pulled the immediate actions sheet from the satellite phone. I couldn't think and needed instructions. Old Donnie warned me I'd be loopy sometimes and I should always have something written to follow. Step one and two were—*Call in location. Make the victim safe.*

I tuned to the Search and Rescue channel. "VASAR, this is Clone. Victims found alive. Sending coordinates." I took off my packs and shirt.

I recognize that voice, said a distant voice over the radio.

Ma'am, this is a stressful time. Let's not jump to conclusions. Clone 10-99. That was Fitz, and he wanted my status.

How could I do this?

He dated my daughter for two years and I taught him to cook eggs! Anne was right, and she would recognize my voice. She caught Haley and me having sex in my van my senior year in high school. She wanted us in Haley's bedroom instead of the van. I'd get up and help Anne cook while Haley got ready.

I responded with the beat codes from the same sheet. "10-23, 10-52, and 10-16." I emphasize the heck out of 10-16. The codes told him I was on site, needed an ambulance, and this was a domestic problem. I hoped he picked up the meaning of domestic problem.

Police had stopped using ten codes, but The Tribe started using them in the seventies. They printed out the ones to use because people like me couldn't remember them. I never used them without the sheet.

Understood, said Fitz. *Lifeline being arranged.*

Next step was to make the two victims safe. I climbed onto the ledge and secured the toddler, who clung to me. Haley reached out. "I got her Haley."

She mumbled. "I named her after you."

Crap, crap, crap, crap, crap. She identified me and what—named her child after me? What? I placed the toddler by the wall. Her injuries were just scratches.

I nestled the toddler behind a rock against the ledge wall and scooped up Haley. I performed immediate medical care back on the ridge. Soon, her gashed forehead was bound and broken arm splinted. The rest of her wounds were minor compared to those two. I laid her on the flat ledge and slid the two of them behind the rock to prevent rolling off the ledge.

Next was a call to the Command Center. I pulled out the Tyler phone and the satellite doo-dad.

"Command Center. Clone."

Go ahead. It was Nathan.

"We have a containment issue. Victim is Haley."

Correct, he answered. *Haley and toddler named Corrinne.*

"It's my Haley. You know, my first girlfriend and the Mathelete member." He was good friends with Haley.

Crap. Are they safe?

Shots lit up the rocks behind me. I dropped the phone.

I scrambled behind a rock. Suit and Red Shirt stood there. Suit read from a scroll that glowed with the color of blue lightning and Red Shirt had a fancy gun.

Red Shirt came around the corner. "Abbiamo spinto le vittime a portarti qui." He pointed at Haley and then at me.

Those words made no sense to me. I pulled out two knives, planted my front foot, and made two throws.

He raised his weapon.

Plunk, plunk. My two knives sunk in. The second in his forehead was sufficient.

Red Shirt was dead before he screamed, falling off the cliff.

Clone Status! Screamed Fitz through the search and rescue radio.

I jumped back and hit the button. "Busy!"

I grabbed my tonfa and checked my other weapon. I only had the obsidian knife. The two knives in Red Shirt were gone.

I looked and Suit marched towards me with a smile. "Ora balliamo giovane guerriero." He took a fighting stance.

I put in my mouth piece. Man, these guys spoke prettier than any woman asking me to have sex. But too bad for him. I didn't swing that way. "Even though you have a purty mouth, I'm going to decline."

I stepped out, and he engaged with a square stance against my rooted stance. The look on his face told me he'd been waiting since I challenged him in the restaurant.

Circular-knee-kick met my crescent-kick-block and his rising-ridge-hand-strike, combined with his double-punch, met my manjouke. His elbow-strike met my forearm-block, and he pulled away since he hit the tonfa hard. I had the advantage.

Changing my stance to the half-moon-stance I closed for a jab-strike and a stepping punch combination.

He back flipped away from me, shot a chain out of his arm guard, and it secured up high. "I tonfa ti dichiarano vincitore per oggi, ma ti ho solo ritardato per lui. Un altro guerriero del giorno." He zipped straight up away from me.

I bet those pretty words weren't about sex at all.

Behind me, the toddler screamed.

A CREATURE HAD TWO of its five feet up on the ridge and its rhinoceros-head had a horn as large as the toddler. Its mottled black and gray skin cracked as it lumbered until it barely fit on the ledge. Tentacles meandered from its head and touched the ground. The creature had no eyes but aligned itself towards me. It crushed the only live bush on this part of the ledge with its third giant foot.

Its mouth opened and drool fell from a few rows of spiked teeth. The tentacles splayed to the ground and felt around.

It bellowed, and the deep wail echoed through the canyon. The world did not turn black and white. This was no Dark Fey. Suit called out a monster from the cave!

I connected to Earth as it sniffed around and ran its tentacles on the ground. Haley clung to her daughter behind the rock and the creature took tentative steps toward me.

Hi puppy? Wouldn't you feel more comfortable in your cave? I tried communicating with it my Animal Domain power.

It reared up on three of its legs and waved the other two at me. I received rage and hatred of druids. The beast lowered to the ground and charged with froth running from its open mouth. Its roar splattered me with foam and saliva.

It got close, and I jumped up high and tried to clear it. Its reflexes were too good, and it scored my right shin with its horn. Even on all fives, it stood six feet all.

That's when I got my first break. It couldn't turn around on the part of the ledge it was on. I had time to think while I punched his hind quarters with tonfa.

Circles and banishing did not work on these guys. Some combination of Earth and Celestial power made these... if you believe the Bible—they were Nephilim. I wasn't so sure until a minute ago. I believed those crazy bible stories of fallen angels now. Old Donnie said normal humans could not make babies with angels, but people with the spark created abominations. However, Shaman and a fallen angel created a giant and a druid with a fallen angel created a human looking Nephilim—the strongest evil we had records of.

The best part of striking with tonfa was I braced the punch with the strongest part of my hand and then the punch focused to a one-inch diameter circle. With my knife away, I slammed the tonfa with my most powerful punches and put the full force of my Earth enhanced body into it. Each hit would shatter a sternum and splatter a heart on a normal human being.

I hit it two dozen times with my most powerful hits and barely cracked the armored skin. It backed me to where it turned around. Then it kicked me in the right thigh with a back kick.

Earth Power did its best with my right leg. If I wasn't engaged with Earth, I'd be down. I dropped my right tonfa and grabbed my obsidian knife. I slashed at a tentacle. It fell off!

The creature reared up and howled. I charged forward and put my shoulder into it as I pressed the knife into its unarmored underbelly.

It screamed louder and toppled off the ledge. It howled when it hit the rocks fifty feet below us and rolled further until it plummeted well out of my sight and the howling became feint.

My right leg gave out and) crawled over to my radio, packs, and Haley. Clicking the radio, I said "VASAR, Clone. Area secured for 10-52."

Roger, Clone. Status?

I thought. What was my status? "Mobile. Only extract victims."

Roger. ETA is fifteen minutes.

I picked up my cell phone and called Nathan.

What's going on? Sensors are off the chart but no magic.

"Red Shirt is dead. Suit got away. Old Donnie's grandpa's cave beasts are real. Plan still on. Will need identity containment." Then it hit me what an ass I was. I could have died, and Nicole might have thought we were through. "Is Nicole near?"

Roger, do you want her?

"No, just put me on speaker."

Go.

"Nicole. No drama. Please understand, I know you're inexperienced and flaky because you're an empath. I already decided you were worth it. Please, no more crazy without talking to me first. I'm sorry for going into jeopardy without clearing this up first. Clone out." I hung up the phone because there was too much to do to get into a conversation. I needed to let her know everything was fine between us from my point of view.

My right leg was in terrible shape. The right thigh already had the sign of broken capillaries and veins. I bandaged the gore on my shin. Luckily, the area bled little. I created druidic berries and ate one. I squeezed one in the toddler's mouth—Corrinne's mouth—and squeezed another in Haley's mouth.

The helicopter sounded overhead.

I forced myself to stand and stood by Haley and Corrinne. "Life flight will be here soon. You're both going to be fine."

I placed the giant red marker on the widest part of the ledge and held it down with my pack and rocks. The helicopter would get a status, measure the distance, and then lower the required gurney.

"Is it really you, Corey?" Haley's weak voice sounded confused.

I couldn't bring myself to lie to her. "Haley, your life will be better and safer if you believe I am a hallucination."

Haley smiled and passed out, but breathed. That meant entertaining a toddler.

The safest thing I had was the tonfa, so I let her hold it.

"Monster?" She held it wrong.

"Hold it like this." I placed it on her arm, though it was too long. I showed her a high block. She copied me and did it.

"Hibock," she said and did one.

We had time to go through a high block, mid-block, low block, and jabs many times before I heard the helicopter. She said monster every time she jabbed.

The helicopter lowered the stretcher, and I strapped Haley in. I placed Corrinne on top and then secured her to her mother with more straps. Then with a third set of straps, I secured Haley's wrists to the opposite rails to also hold Corrinne.

"Going on a ride," I told the toddler. "Hold on to mommy."

"VASAR, victims secured. Cleared for extraction. Mother has a head wound, concussion, and broken arm with multiple fractures. Other injuries not as serious. Emergency medical completed. Toddler appears fine."

After the stretcher was in the helicopter and leaving for the hospital, I gathered my belongings and cast the ritual to Bright Earth. This made the strenuous climb and walk to my distant shelter close to Asheville bearable. Since I healed faster here, I stayed in my shelter within Bright Earth. I'd make the pickup.

Chapter 20—The Life of a Proper Young Woman

Rebecca held onto Nicole. "It will be fine. He was thinking and wasn't ready to talk yet."

"Why am I so stupid?" Nicole cried, and it was just an ugly a cry as when Rebecca cried over Corey. She sat back in the basic beige leather seats of the SUV with her head against the tinted windows as cars passed by on the highway.

A proper young woman didn't answer this directly, but there were no rules for guiding young women in times like these. Rebecca emulated how Corey talked to Rachel. Preacher Jon and Nathan didn't need to hear these words, but it couldn't be helped.

Rebecca had taken a pain pill for her side and was glad she did. The side ached today from the movement and today would not be a day for naps. She wore a skirt, even though it secured next to the part of the gash that had not healed. She had gone to wound care, and the doctor had burned out dead tissue to promote healing. It did not feel pleasant.

"Nicole, when you love, part of your mind goes crazy. When you combine this with your empathy, you end up creating issues. We must figure out how to address these issues."

"I may be too crazy for Corey, and you should take him." Nicole cried.

Rebecca wanted to say yes, but she also knew a breakup now and Nicole may fall into the trap of thinking she was crazy and guys would only want her for short periods of time. It was time to be a strong woman, the kind her grandmother said she would become. "Let me tell you a story and see if it sounds familiar."

"Okay," Nicole blew her nose into a napkin and put it back in her purse folded. "Ooh." Nicole grabbed her stomach. Nathan had been driving this SUV and had brown, white, yellow, red, and blue napkins inside of it.

"Cramps? When is your next period?" Rebecca had done some research when she heard no one would use birth control. It had been eleven days since Nicole and Corey had their loud night for the police, but they couldn't be so unlucky for their first time to cause pregnancy... except with the fertility faeries flying over them... *Oh no*. "Are your breasts tender?"

"Yes, but Corey and I were pretty active." She smiled. "He likes boobs a little too much sometimes."

Rebecca grinned to hide her stress. "Nathan, please pull into a drugstore."

"Good. I need to pee," said Nicole.

"Again?" asked Nathan.

"Yes, Nathan," said Preacher Jon. "There's one in two exits."

Rebecca realized Preacher Jon figured out what Rebecca suspected, but again, it couldn't be helped. "Here's my story. I was despondent over breaking up with Corey and then fighting with him after Old Donnie passed. I was barely holding it together."

"You?" Nicole looked up with teary eyes.

"One day I was at CJ's shooting range and changing back into office clothes in the ladies' dressing room. Someone mentioned Old Donnie, and I lost it. Full ugly cry with snot bubbles and everything, completely unlike anything grandmother would approve of."

"Wow. I can't imagine you crying. You're so strong."

Rebecca held her emotions together for Nicole. "Just like you are now and for a pretty similar reason. Well, the women I barely knew listened to my entire story, then became a private detective agency.

They found the grave marker Corey purchased—which is how I ended up here."

"Thank you. I guess I'm not the only one crazy with Corey."

"Stop saying bad things about yourself. I do not think I could have navigated life as an empath. You are incredibly strong and strong enough to show emotions." Rebecca admonished her just like she did with Corey.

Nicole had another bubble forming in her nose. "I correct Corey like this, too. I'll do better."

Rebecca handed her another napkin for her to blow. "Believe me when I say I understand where you and Corey are right now. So, look at the facts. Corey isn't as stupid as he says, but he is not a smart man. He can't consider more than one item at a time."

"He makes up for it by being sweet," said Nicole, who finally smiled.

"Yes. Yes, he does. The important thing to remember is he thinks through things. So, right now, he is thinking of the battle. That's exactly what we want him to do, so everyone comes back to us."

"Okay." She folded up the napkin and placed it in her purse.

"Now, remember this morning when he thanked me for the information?" Rebecca hoped Nicole kept following along.

"Uh, huh."

"Well, it meant he was thinking and not reacting. When Corey wants something, he will talk himself into it. You need to be prepared for him to come back and want to reconcile."

"Really?" The hope in her friend's eyes was encouraging.

"Here we are ladies," said Nathan.

Rebecca helped Nicole get out of the car. They walked over the curb and through the automatic door. Rebecca guided Nicole straight to the pharmacy section and ambled to the pregnancy tests. She asked a woman with a red apron to retrieve one of the early test kits. "Wait, Nicole. Are you and Rachel on the same schedule?"

"They have three tests in them," said the woman behind the counter.

The two of them were drawing a lot of attention. "You think I'm pregnant?" Nicole started crying.

"Two pregnancy kits, please." She handed one to Nathan. "Please purchase two. We're going to use one."

Nathan took the kit and Rebecca brought Nicole to the restroom while the dozen patrons watched Rebecca guide the crying Nicole to the restroom. These things happen and Rebecca looked up and smiled while pretending nothing strange had happened. If these people had better training, they would not be gawking at a young emotional lady heading to a drugstore bathroom holding a pregnancy kit.

In the restroom, Rebecca washed her hands with Nicole, helped her blow her nose again, threw away the folded napkins, and prepared the kit. Rebecca opened the door, saw the commode was acceptably clean, and ripped a protector from the stainless-steel dispenser on the wall.

Nicole stumbled into the stall. Rebecca waited by the ugly brown sink and looked at herself in the mirror. She would be strong for Nicole. Her side ached, and she leaned against the wall. The ache of her side wasn't awful, but it was constant.

Nicole used the restroom, and the room became quiet except for a small fan in the ceiling. The instructions said to wait three minutes, and these three minutes were some of the longest in a young woman's life.

Rebecca thought back to the SUV. She kept a breathing exercise to help her fall asleep, and Corey mistook her breathing exercise for sleeping. Rebecca heard his entire story of how he was caught up in her. She was caught up in him, but something told her two words were about to come from Nicole. The words that meant however much Corey and Rebecca wanted each other, it would never happen.

The loudest wail Rebecca ever heard of "I'm pregnant!" came from Nicole.

Just like that, she could never look Corey in the eye and say, 'I'm caught up in you.'

It was time to be strong. She tossed out decorum and barged into the stall to hug Nicole. Her friend sat on the commode, holding the test in her shaking hand. "This is happy, but we will patch things up with you and Corey, and then you tell him."

Nicole just nodded.

"Look, I know Corey well and can read him better than anyone else. I promise he wants to talk and reconcile." Rebecca handed her a pad. "Just in case of spotting."

She helped Nicole get dressed, washed up, and helped her into the store. She walked her sniffling friend past the eyes of a dozen people in the store, all staring at the girl who had just screamed from the bathroom. Rebecca put on the brave face of a proper young woman.

"They feel sorry for me," said Nicole.

"That's because you screamed and you're crying. If you act happy, they'll be happy." Rebecca walked her friend to the car. She placed the opened pregnancy kit with two more uses into her purse. Soon she'd need to go through this with Rachel. They plodded into the car and Nicole sobbed into Rebecca's shoulder.

"Nicole, you eat the candy in the purple wrapper when you're sad," said Nathan. He handed her a chocolate bar in a purple wrapper.

Nicole smiled and took it. "Thank you, Nathan." She unwrapped it and broke off a square.

"Rebecca, I've only seen you eat ones with a yellow wrapper. I hope I got the correct one." He handed her a chocolate bar.

Nathan and his silly fixation with the color of food paid off. "Nathan, you did great."

"Team, we'll be in the command center. VASAR contacted us for Corey's help concerning lost hikers. It's a young mother and a toddler. Corey is on the way," said Preacher Jon.

Nicole clung tighter to Rebecca. Today was going to be a long day, and they needed chocolate.

Preacher John handed back a box of tissues—necessary tissues.

THEY WERE IN THE COMMAND center, and Nicole was now sleeping in a chair in the back of the center while Nathan geared up his station.

"Right this way, Ms. Addkinson," said Preacher Jon. "Your granddaughter has been instrumental in getting some team members settled."

It couldn't be.

"That room over there is private," said Preacher Jon.

Two men carried a box over to the room. The box looked four feet by two feet by two feet and was solid white with gold trim.

It was. Rebecca stood, straightened her skirt, and pulled her hair back to meet her grandmother.

"Oh my, look at you. You've let a friend cry on your shoulder and acted properly, and she counted on you in her darkest of times." Her grandmother was a few inches shorter than Rebecca, but always wore three-inch heels and a dress. Her white hair was curled just so, and she looked up. Today's dress was white with horses adorning it. She wore a custom Italian belt with the name of her stables impressed into the leather.

"Grandmother, what a pleasant surprise," said Rebecca.

Rebecca would change on visits from her grandmother—when she knew of them. Her jean skirt and pink blouse did not mix well with her grandmother's regal attire.

"Your wounds do not diminish your regal manner. You are the pride of the family. Let me give you a kiss." Her grandmother stepped over and kissed each of Rebecca's cheeks with a hug.

"Your friend is the young Nicole who supports so many people in this territory?"

Rebecca looked over at her napping friend. "Yes. She's had a rough day."

"I see chocolate and from the recent stories... Oh my, she is pregnant and you are helping her."

Her grandmother always put information together so quickly. "Yes. Nicole is having an especially rough day."

"Well, come with me. Your day is changing as well." Her grandmother escorted her to the private conference room past the Command Center of Nathan. "Young Nathan, I won't interrupt you, but you look professional as always." Her grandmother continued to strut as if she owned the Command Center.

"It is a pleasure, Ms. Addkinson," said Nathan. He was busy and still responded appropriately to her grandmother. That was mildly surprising.

Once inside the private conference, her grandmother pulled the door shut. "Please sit. Your wounds need to heal and we don't need to keep up pretenses in this room."

Rebecca sat and did not know where this was going. "Grandmother, the magical healing has helped me and I am much farther along."

"Yes, I get daily updates from Preacher Jon. He is a good man, despite some of his dealings. However, we have something far more important to discuss, and I believe you know what it is."

Rebecca knew, and Corey knew. The guy who said he was stupid figured it out before she did. Sometimes he could take two random facts with no link, then link them together to draw a correct conclusion.

Her grandmother sat. "I hoped the legacy would reignite with you. Your mother could not handle the pressure and the gift skipped my generation, but you, they wrote your name in the book nine days ago. You are the Scion and now own the family secret. This box contains everything you will need, and you shall protect this with your life."

The matriarch put her hand upon the box of white with gold trim. "You will need a powerful husband and make an heir strong enough to carry the legacy forward. You are the last of our line and it needs to be renewed, because if the legacy fails, humanity will follow. I know you love the druid, and if I were you, I would too." She sighed. "I still think of the love I had to leave for a proper life. However, a druid and a Scion cannot sire the next generation of the true church."

Her grandmother looked genuinely sad. "It is good you support your friend during the pregnancy."

Rebecca tried to answer but knew she would cry. Instead, she nodded and tears fell down her cheek.

Her grandmother ignored the tears. "Tell me, do you know how your powers came to grow on this date?"

Rebecca didn't have to see the date. The spark came when she had almost died, but Corey had become superhuman and saved both of their lives. Again. He was a hero, and this explained every one of his shortcomings. The day before, she told him face to face why they could never be together. She left out druids and Scions, but she said enough. Now, she hoped Corey had believed her.

Love wakened the spark in her when she made the shot to save Corey's life. Her vision blurred from the tears in her eyes.

Her grandmother gave her a silk handkerchief. "Oh my. You do, and it was dramatic. Well, don't tell me. I know too many secrets and have enough to take to my grave. Wow, that is emotion. Let me tell you some details."

She waved the handkerchief away as if it were nothing. "I have rewritten my will and everything is yours. I have an army of lawyers lined up to protect it. The owner of the box must have access to everything in the legacy."

Her grandmother opened the box. The simple white wooden box of light pine wood measured four-foot by two-foot by two-foot. It held reams of papers, a robe, a sash, a scepter, and a thin bronze ring. The robe delightfully combined high-quality linen and silk, and high-quality silk made up the red and purple sash. European royalty would consider the gold scepter ostentatious with its jewels.

The ring had intrigued her enough to try on. A thin bronze ring with the circle on top that had the face of a regal woman in the ancient Greek style.

"It's amazing you tried that on first," said her grandmother. "You'll never be able to leave it off for long. It will always appear on your left index finger."

Rebecca took it off and put it back in the box. "I know everything I am supposed to do."

"I heard that's the way it would work. You now have more pressure on you than any person rightfully should. Well, except your friends. I fought to allow you to stay here and not live in the Chesapeake Bay Territory. Your friends can support and protect you until you are ready. We do not have the protection, nor the emotional support you have here. I trust you as the Scion and the savior of the true blood of the church."

Rebecca had so many thoughts in her mind she couldn't think.

"Well, one more thing. You ordered a report. A report that has information on the end of the world. The system has a built-in fail-safe to notify the territory leader of end of Earth reports. It notified me because of this."

Her grandmother had tears in her eyes. "The information is so clear I do not need to tell you what you need to do, and it appears you've already started. You were always sharp." Her grandmother pulled a folder from inside her jacket. "I cannot even fathom how you thought to research this, but it is exactly what you should have researched."

Rebecca blew her nose and put away the handkerchief and collected her emotions.

Her grandmother helped her stand. "I am an old woman and have completed most of my duty in this life. Let us walk out together regally and remember you can always call me."

They strode out together.

"Grandmother, it was so good to see you," said Rebecca, remembering her manners.

"It's on your finger, isn't it?"

Rebecca looked at her left hand. The ring had appeared on her left index finger. "Yes, it is."

"Dear. Know that I support you, believe in you, and trust you." Her grandmother kissed her cheeks and left Rebecca. Rebecca barely made it back to the chair next to Nicole.

She dreaded opening up the report. She knew the report would have another reason she couldn't ever be with Corey.

The summary of the report was on top.

> *If Rebecca and Corey dated, the chance that the world would end was one hundred percent and the timeframe was twelve to twenty years. When Nicole dated Corey, there was a ninety percent chance the world would be safe for the next twenty years. If neither Nicole nor Rebecca dated Corey, civilization—an important distinction—ceased to exist in six years because of nuclear war.*

Rebecca grabbed the rest of her chocolate bar and finished it. She leaned back next to Nicole. Perhaps they'd cry on each other's shoulders later. For now, Rebecca got the nap her wound demanded.

"MY HALEY," SAID A VOICE that sounded like Corey.

Rebecca sat up from her nap in the chair, and Nicole stirred as well. The two of them must look a fright having slept in chairs. She grabbed Nicole's hand, and they walked down the stairs to Nathan's setup.

"Is that a new ring?" asked Nicole.

The weight immediately landed back on Rebecca as the blood of the true church and the Scion to represent the church and save humanity. She grabbed grandmother's silk handkerchief, and she wept silently. "I'll be weeping on your shoulders soon."

"What's going on? Sensors are off the chart but no magic," said Nathan.

There was silence as Nathan nodded and took notes on his computer. It was silent for a long time.

"Roger, do you want her?"

There was a quick silence, and Nathan hit a button. "Go."

Corey's voice came over some nearby speakers. "Nicole. No drama. Please understand, I know you're inexperienced and flaky because you're an empath. I already decided you were worth it. Please, no more crazy without talking to me first. I'm sorry for going into jeopardy without clearing this up first. Clone out."

"You were right," said Nicole.

The two of them held each other and cried.

"Why don't we let you get back to your regular apartment? Please stay together," said Preacher Jon.

Rebecca sniffled. "Nicole, will you help me carry a box?"

She cried on the way out because she couldn't help but think twelve to twenty years of happiness with Corey might be worth the end of the world.

Chapter 21—Moon-eyed People

I woke up early and traveled to wait for Miles at the rendezvous point. My right leg barely worked. Pain ripped through me with every step, and I moved at the speed of a normal human. I made the parking lot in time and twenty minutes later, Miles showed up in the SUV with Rachel and Madison. My bloodied leg got dragged into the back with me and I slid over and laid on Rachel. "Hold me, please."

"Pull your pants off. I recognized a guamed up leg." Madison didn't wait, and she and Rachel pulled my pants off.

"Miles, Corey messed his leg up," said Rachel.

"I had two druid berries and spent the night fully engaged with Earth," I protested, but no one listened.

Madison climbed into the back seat and put my leg on top of her lap. "Let's wrap this better."

Miles pulled over at a gas station. He came back out with more medical supplies and a bag of ice. "Crap, Corey. Are you going to walk on this?"

"I made it from the ravine to my distant shelter and then from there to the rendezvous point."

"Okay. Rachel, you snuggle with him. Madison, you wrap, ice, and elevate the top of his leg. Then put the antibiotic on the lower part and wrap that for the fight." Miles got back into the driver's seat. "We have two hours to get him some rest. Corey, you better have a damn good story."

"Boy, do I." I couldn't help but laugh despite the pain.

"Give it up, druid boy," teased Miles.

"Well, first the rescue was on a woman named Haley and her toddler." I needed to hide my pain to leave confidence high with the other three.

"Doesn't sound too exciting," said Madison.

"What if I told you, it was my Haley? My first girlfriend."

"No way," said Rachel. She had exposed her abdomen, so I had some flesh and flesh contact with her and I connected with her. My nerves soothed.

"Yep, she named her daughter Corrinne and said the name was after me."

"Whoa. Dude," said Miles.

"Yeh, I called in for containment." This was as crazy a situation as I could have imagined. The happiness that Haley and her daughter were receiving care was the silver lining.

"You're almost a dad," joked Madison as she smeared ointment on my leg.

"I'm so far from being a dad. It's ridiculous. Oh Rachel. I sent a message to Nicole to tell her no drama, and we were still fine from my perspective, but we had to talk about her needing to talk before acting." Her smile made me realize I had made the right choice.

"Oh, thank you Corey." She hugged me tighter.

"Yeh, hopefully Rebecca and Nicole had a nice day yesterday with no drama."

"Tightening," said Madison as she put the lower wrap on. "Now take some of the brown pills for swelling."

I did, and guzzled water.

Miles pulled in through a drive through and got me something to eat after he saw me guzzle. "Gee, is that it? Rescue an ex-girlfriend and trip?"

"Red shirt is dead. Suit got away and the monsters Old Donnie and his grandfather fought are real. I fought one before the life flight arrived for Haley. I kind of buried the lead there, but to be fair, all parts of yesterday could have been the lead."

"Are you telling a story?" asked Madison.

"Nope. Half rhino, five legs, hates druids, tentacles for senses. By the way, did anyone bring any extra knives? Red Shirt carried mine to the bottom of the Ravine in his face." I started shoving food into my mouth without checking to see what Miles got me.

"Bottomless Ravine?" asked Miles?

"Yep."

"Shoot fire, Corey."

We were on back country roads, and Miles concentrated on maneuvering this large thing over the old roads. The last hour of the drive, we ate while Miles reviewed the strategy.

I reminded them of one part of our strategy. "Be prepared. I going to use you to banish the strongest creatures if I can."

"Why?" asked Madison.

"We'll get the difference in power level granted to us by the Earth," said Rachel. "Corey wants us to be more powerful."

"It's a team based on love and I need all the love to be strong. Rebecca got the power from the Snake-Hunter," I explained.

Miles found a parking spot near the base in a parking lot in the Great Smoky Mountain Park, and we had five hours for a three-hour climb. I could do it by myself in under an hour, when uninjured, but I needed all three. My leg hurt with every step and it bothered my hip. I wouldn't be able to kick in a fight.

ONCE WE MADE IT TO the GPS coordinates, we stood in an open area that people trod upon for decades or even centuries. Trees surrounded packed brown forest dirt on either side and formed a barrier to an entrance into an area with mounds covered by smaller trees, bushes, and ground growth.

I created a huge honeysuckle and cut eighteen twigs of honeysuckle and caught them in my wicker basket. The bag, basket, and sickle moved to the side under a bush and the clippings locked into my belt. I put a trumpet in my torc the way Richard showed me.

We prepared to fight everything that defied Old Donnie's, and now my, boundaries. The Dark Fey preyed on the defenseless and made a pact with the church. These were my enemies. As we came up on the coordinates, I put the GPS back in its holder. I considered my mouthpiece, but I'd need to cast bindings.

All four of us scoped out the area. One hundred square feet stood in the entrance and had trees on either side. Briar bushes interspersed and made the terrain difficult for everyone but me around the sides. My leg wouldn't let me take advantage of that.

I made a fourteen-foot circle to block the entrance to the hidden village, and the others scoped out fighting areas. I placed seventeen of the honeysuckle twigs in the circle. Along with owning the area, I cast *Local Nature* here. Bits of Fey Magic jumped from the ground.

The sun was nearly gone when my senses lit up, and I saw Miles' and Madison's eyes get wider.

"Rachel, it's a little shakier than we thought. There are four dozen Dark Fey here and a portal opened." My leg was stiff and it hurt. I popped four more ibuprofen with the water and took off my clothes except for shorts.

Rachel removed her clothes as well. She had on short shorts and a sports bra.

"I sense them, too, and a lot are small, but there are six significant sized," said Miles.

"Do you fight nekkid fer fun?" asked Madison. Her shaky voice had her whole mountain accent on display.

"The connection to Earth and the Fey lining is so much stronger with four body points open," explained Rachel. "But this is all I'm doing now."

"Temple, throat, solar plexus, and groin. We keep the groin covered even though we're weaker for it. For healing and studying, I will uncover if I'm somewhere private."

"It doesn't work for me," said Miles. "I tried for a month where we were the naked group, but I stay clothed now."

I moved the topic on. "This will need to be a bloody battle to convince the rest to stay out of the fight." I cast berries on a healthy plant and we each ate one.

"My leg makes me no good in a regular fight, so I'm going to cast savagery right off the bat." I stood in the middle of my circle to let the others key their positions off me.

My torc pulsed and lit up blue with every Fey I tracked. The sun set and, using my druidic vision with my torc, the entrance to the village of the Moon-Eyed people shined in green.

Fully engaged with the Earth, I followed the second half of my plan. To kick things off and make me the target, I bellowed out a challenge to anything that came near. White orbs behind me bounced gently, but they were not here to fight. They were blind and hoped we would win.

I began initializing my circle. My torc glowed red, and the world turned black and white.

Confidence was scarce, but I've been in so many fights, I knew being wounded wasn't the end of the world.

The cowards sent one creature towards me. It emerged from the ground a few feet from me and was a three-feet-tall collection of tusks, scars, ram horns, and scales. I dropped my tonfa and caught it by its neck. Its snarls got cut off by more Earth powered strength. What unnatural creature fought a druid one on one on his land?

My fist glowed green, and the beast landed on my Earth with a thud. Earth Power surged into me as the Earth felt the creatures invade its realm.

The sole creature was powerless, and I was as powered up as I could be. I pushed its neck to the ground and kneeled to get more body contact with the ground until I pushed my hand all the way through its hideous neck until I felt the spine connecting its brain snap. My right ankle burned, and I knew I had a new trumpet on my ankle tattoo.

As I kicked the corpse away from me, I screamed my binding to six of the large Dark Fey. They could run or come kill me—if they could. Instead of adding the banishment to my binding, I cast *Primal Savagery* and the animal forms took over my body. Soon, the Fey Realm took over the spell, and the alteration began.

I stood ten feet tall and was a mass of sticks, limbs, leaves, and bark. My primal nature caused my muscles to bulge and my limbs to grow. My challenge powered with Earth Power as it echoed through the mountains. Tonfa grew from my arms of the hardest cherry wood and spikes grew out of my knees.

The savage form ignored my injuries. I wished I had more health, but here I was.

Eight small Fey charged forward to test us. *Here is the test wave.* Green arrows soared, Rachel sang and flung her new, green surujin from Madison, and Miles danced with his sword. It may have only been three weeks of training, but he was no longer in decline and his confidence was coming back. None of the eight Fey made it to me.

The team had trained well without me yesterday. Madison was high in a tree and her arrows soared true. Rachel's song of power lifted us, and Miles took his normal stance in front of me. Rachel's surujin flash with green magic and joy emanated from her as more than a decade of frustration ended as she killed Dark Fey on her own.

Six-man sized creatures with fur and heads of dogs and at least a dozen of more of those hideous scaled tusks and horned creatures surrounded us. An arrow soared and a surujin strike flew by me. Ten small creatures joined the onslaught as they tried to overwhelm me. Creatures flew, charged, and leaped towards me and my savage form.

Miles swung his giant sword and cleaved at the first. Rachel's surujin took the feet out from underneath the second, and Madison's arrows were sticking into each of them. I engaged.

The first flying creature's mouth came to me with a snarl and four-inch-long spiked teeth and I ducked to the ground, placed my left wooden tonfa on the ground in my fully powered circle and changed the other tonfa to a blade and sliced through it. Its life force transferred to me and I felt a burning on my left calf. Fey power filled me and I howled to nature.

Blood fury spun up the supernatural dog creatures in a frenzy and they attacked at once with the only positive benefit the giant dogmen could only attack me four at a time and prevented the others from getting to me. A green sword slashed, and the dogmen attacked me from the other side. Rachel sang, and the surujin danced. Arrows sunk into the enemy.

A dogman charged at me before I could get a block up. Rachel's song changed and the supernatural creature T-posed in front of me. I jerked it down onto my knife and killed it with my hand and knife in its chest and the other inside my circle. Rachel's song went back to normal.

A small creature sprinted to me on the ground, dragged by a chain. On my owned ground, it was powerless, and I stomped its head and ground it into the bloodied dirt, and another trumpet filled in.

However, a dogman crushed my hurt leg and it crumpled through its attack. Then the limb snapped.

Fear washed over me. I kept it at bay, but this was not going well.

Miles split a dogman down the middle, and I grabbed Rachel's hands when she was on the ground. I put one hand in the fallen creature's wound and another in the circle. She yelled as the creature turned to dust. My team needed more power than I did.

I released Rachel and kneeled on my one good leg to keep fighting.

Blood covered Miles and many small Dark Fey surrounded him. His green sword swung through the howls, but Rachel's song rose above the din.

They surrounded a bloodied Rachel.

Ten arrows brought another dogman down and Miles was near, and I grabbed his hands. I had him absorb the life. He didn't cry out, but his body jolted. Another Dark Fey bit into his back and now he cried out. Flying Fey chased Madison from her perch in a tree to us, and blood covered Rachel's arms.

The cries of my friends pierced through me. I felt no pain, but I heard bark snap and branches break from my body. Dogmen bit through bark on me and leaves ripped from me.

Another enemy close and arrows sunk it to the ground. I used Rachel's hands again, but she didn't cry out like last time.

Sap poured from my back and arms like Woodrow's tree and my skin-stained black from my sap... my blood. "Madison," I yelled.

Another bit me in the back and I couldn't shake it when a small creature flew in with a booted kick. The dogmen flew off my back and bit Rachel in the torso. I grabbed it, snapped its spine on the ground, and ripped its snout off with my mouth. A green sword slashed, and a dogman fell next to me and I grabbed Madison's hands, and I heard her yelp when the creature disappeared.

Rachel lay next to me and my wooden hands had quit working. Earth powered through me and snarling, drool covered bites covered my arm. My magic failed with my wavering. I prevented most of their bites with Shotokan blocks, but stances did not account for these body shapes. This was bar fighting Corey time. Only bar fighting

Corey never had wooden appendages and made of bark, wood, and leaves.

Bravado filled me, and I took a kneeling stance to fight. When weak, appear strong. Rachel's singing stopped.

The creatures worked well as a pack, but they were down to two. Smaller cowards fled and closed the portal behind them. The dogmen had learned their lesson about how they were no match for us in a straight fight and fought deviously. *Bar-fighting dogmen.*

They kept me spinning with feints and dekes. Rachel was down. Madison was down. The sweat combined with the blood that flowed from multiple bites and claw wounds to drip off of me and made the ground a slippery mess that meant my claws dug in to give me footing.

One reached in and yanked a handful of sticks from inside me and broke them onto the ground.

Rachel rolled over. *She lived*! I felt nothing but Earth Power, but the sap pouring from me told an awful story. This was a battle of attrition and we were down to two. My arms moved again of sheer will. Blood covered the inside of my circle. I jumped and jabbed my paw into the dogman's mouth and rode it down with the weight of my torso on its neck and took its life force as my fist passed through it into the ground.

Miles swung his sword around and slashed the neck of a Dark Fey, lunging for me. The fifth tattoo burning on my left lower leg barely registered as I watched the Dark Fey rip down Miles' leg and his sword extinguished out as he collapsed.

Earth Power held me up, and I would die when the binding stopped. Earth Power no longer stopped the pain, but I was primal and fed off the pain.

My voice became hoarse from screaming my binding. Rachel's song had long since stopped, but the last dogman died with its life force sucked into the Earth through me when I jabbed my hand through its flesh into its gut.

My blood was in the circle and my body had become covered with bites, claw wounds, and dog drool. As my senses told me that the Fey left, I lay in my circle and repeated my binding and removed the primal savagery. The leaves melded into my face and the twigs disappeared. My bark disappeared and my wooden appendages became my hands as my body contorted to its normal size.

There was no time to dwell on myself. I picked up Rachel's shirt and bound her leg and kept her in my circle. Then, binding her arms, I packed her deepest wounds with the cleanest dirt I could find. I kept repeating the binding and knew once I stopped, I would die. She had to live, Madison had to live, and Miles had to live.

Madison was half outside the circle. I dragged her in and saw a gash on the back of her head. I used her shirt to bind her head. The rest of her wounds were small, but many.

I wavered in and out of consciousness and borrowed time from myself.

It took all my strength to drag Miles into the circle, rip the remains of his shirt off, and bind his leg.

Everything became dark, but it was just blood in my eyes. I tried to gather myself and breathe. Just one minute lying down. Blood filled my eyes again while strange hands explored my body—touching me, feeling around my body, and putting a sticky substance on me.

Cracking my eyes open while I uttered the binding with my last bit of strength, I tried to reach for Rachel or Madison or Miles, but two short hillbillies were doing something to Rachel. Three were on Miles, three more on Madison, and four tried to hold me. I used druidic vision and short people with enormous eyes containing pupils as big as a half dollar coin crawled over me.

They wore rags and carried long rifles and I swear they had a ceramic jug from which they poured foul tasting liquid down my throat, causing me to stop my binding. My last hallucination was going to be an anime hillbilly. I couldn't fight them and laid down, knowing this was it.

The area slowly turned bright green and even the browns sparkled. We moved into the Bright Earth. I watched this take place from a lush field of grass with brand new flowers growing. The hillbilly anime dudes put paste on the three of us and poured more concoctions down our throats. Before they left, they placed a book on my chest and this fever dream of hillbilly anime people ended in darkness. Four Fey queens looked me over from their court in my hallucination. Queen Niamh looked on with pride in her eyes.

I WOKE, UNSURE OF WHAT day it was or where I lay. Daylight hit my face from the east. The world was in color and I was naked. My coral honeysuckle bushes surrounded us, but my circle was gone. On my chest was a new druid book.

Rachel lay next to me covered in brown goo—much like me. Madison was on my other side and just as covered in goo. Miles was on the other side of Madison. I reached over to a honeysuckle bush and created druidic magic berries. After pulling off four, I ate one immediately. When his tongue moved, I squirted the juice and put the skin in his throat. Rachel opened her eyes after I rolled over. I squirted and placed a berry in her mouth.

Madison's eyes flittered and ate one without help.

On my back, I looked at the new druid book. It was red like the others, and the symbol on the front had a man's bearded head with antlers. Weakened, I sat up but didn't make it.

Soon, I had some strength and sat. A white robe with our weapons lay at each of the four of our feet. I ate a second berry and the robe on. Struggling to control my hands, I remembered my wooden limbs. *Was that part of me?*

I crawled over and grabbed Rachel's robe and dressed her. I gave her a second berry and she could sit up. Madison was sitting, and I helped pull a robe over her. Miles had started with a robe, and I finished helping him get dressed and gave him the last berry.

"That'd be a helluva way to wake up from a party," joked Miles. He coughed after speaking.

"Passed out, naked, and covered with goo?" asked Rachel. "Ew." Her breath caught, and she focused on breathing.

"We've all been there," joked Madison. She gasped for air as well.

"Needs more beer bottles," I joked. But no one laughed, not even me.

We helped each other stand. I collapsed—my right leg broken. Miles and Madison grabbed wood to brace it. I didn't have the strength to yell.

"It looks like they set it," said Miles. "So, half the pain is already over with."

Pain drifted distant from me and I fell in and out of consciousness, but we had to get away. The church could track us. *Did they already track us, but we were in Bright Earth?*

Miles made a temporary splint for my leg. Then the four of us began the laborious climb down the mountain to the SUV, holding hands like we were little kids. I pulled time from somewhere to move. Miles and Rachel took turns carrying me.

I felt time slipping from me and was running out of time to borrow.

The ice had melted in the cooler, but the temperature kept the water cool enough. Miles handed twenty-four-ounce bottles of water. *How did we already make it to the car?*

We plopped into the SUV and leaned against each other. I had ended up in the middle somehow and I put my arms around my friends. "We lived."

"I feel like a team member now," said Madison. "You have to be in danger to be on the team, right?" She put her face onto my shoulder and cried.

"When you took out the fifth one," I said to Miles, "I was done. Two would have finished me."

"I wanted to be more effective but the blood. All the wasted life." Madison looked sad.

I realized I was a killer. "Killing the Dark Fey didn't affect me. I guess I'm a killer." Something else didn't feel right about me.

"No Corey," said Rachel. "You are Wartime Druid." She hugged me.

"Killers don't dress friends or feed them berries," added Madison.

"They don't calm their girlfriends before fighting and don't worry about how an ex-girlfriend recognized them," added Miles.

"The death of Dark Fey didn't faze me," I explained.

"Dude. You knew we were at war. The rest of us are learning. Give us a chance, we'll get there."

Rachel sniffed and cried into my shoulders. "Your heart is still gentle. I can sense it," said Rachel.

I fought back tears, but she cried and joined Madison crying on my shoulder. There was no more time to borrow.

"Cry some for me, Rachel," said Miles. "I'll drive us to the cabin." He started the SUV and started the drive back. We left the music and radio off and drove in silence.

Surprises, tears, and snot were nothing. I put my arm around her and pulled her back in because I needed to feel her touch. I put my arm around Madison as well. It was time to appreciate each other.

"I got a sexy ankle tattoo now," said Madison. She lifted her foot.

"Hey, I do too," said Miles. "Corey will start thinking I'm hot now."

"I wanted to make the dogman do a dance, but I could only focus enough for a T-pose," said Rachel.

I laughed, and my whole body jumped somewhere where everything was blurry.

"What was that with our hands in the goo and the zapping?" asked Rachel.

I tried to answer, but my mouth was too far away. My time ran out.

AFTER SLEEPING, I WOKE up and the two witches from New Hampshire joined us in the car. The kind one with my last name, Samantha, sat next to me. Morgan sat next to Miles with her three feet of long black hair. Reality wavered and scents I'd never smelled before caressed me and drew me to the blurry place from the darkness of sleep. I could see all of the Southeast below me in my dream.

Miles pulled up to the cabin, and I snorted awake. Miles carried me in after Rachel and Madison walked in. I held my messenger bag, the new spell book, and the ritual book. I had to get a second messenger bag.

Miles put me in the chair and went back and brought in our gear. Samantha and Morgan were with us. *Did we pick them up?*

I slammed back into my body and everything made sense in a brief vision of clarity. If the church was moving the final spell casting site and they hurried to complete it, they had a problem with the old site. We needed to take out the new site before they finished building it out. "I know what our next step is," I said. I drifted off.

Chapter 22—The Command Center

I dreamed I saw Dr. Kanoska, and I rode in an ambulance. I dreamed I soared with Rebecca in the heavens, and she wore a white robe with a special bronze ring on her left index finger. She said she still loved me. Then I stood in front of a wheel with Rachel, Nicole, another girl I couldn't see, and Rebecca on it. Queen Niamh asked me if I was going to spin it. I said, "No. The wheel will remain balanced." The person on the top won and the ones on the sides were safe. Whoever landed on the bottom received lifelong pain. Lastly, I saw two circles and the one inside the building was weaker than the one next to the tennis courts. The one near the tennis courts was still being constructed and looked weak.

"Where is our wayward druid?" asked Carol.

I must have slept hard. I sat up and everything was black and shiny. Well, there was a black glass room with lights inside. I rested on a red cherry wood table with chairs around it on a platform. Miles moved the beige chairs to the side. Below this section had an area with ten half walls around computers. Screens were on the walls and doors were all over the room. I sensed no Earth.

I needed to run, but I barely rolled over.

"Calm down, Corey, we'll get you to Earth soon enough," said Preacher Jon. "Welcome to the Command Center."

There was a gurney next to me. My leg was in a cast, and I wore a blood-covered hospital gown. "I need Earth to heal, but I know what our next step is."

"Relax hero," said Dr. Kanoska. She held me with one finger. Then she removed the Gurney's covering and put a new cover on it, one sterile and clean.

Samantha stroked my hair. Both she and Morgan slumped, and their darkened eyes drooped. Morgan stood next to Preacher Jon.

"Twenty-five years. I spent twenty-five years casting the spell with the placenta and the rest of his semen and thought it would be a waste. It's a strange feeling to see a spell work so perfectly," said Morgan.

"Corey, you'll see some visions and already have. Don't let these scare you. You've crossed realms not made for the living." Samantha moved my hair to the back and pulled and braided it.

Nicole, Rebecca, Rachel, Madison, Miles, Trish, Wesley, Nathan, and Preacher Jon stood back and stared at me as Carol and Richard stepped forward.

Dr. Kanoska removed my leg cast.

"Let me give you a hug, Corey, and then you can move," said Carol.

"Carol, you can always have a hug." Heaven and Earth couldn't keep from giving Carol a hug with everything she's done for me in my life.

She chuckled and hugged me. Then she screamed and fell where Dr. Kanoska and Richard caught her and put her into the Gurney.

"Mom!" Screamed Miles.

I jumped up. "Carol!" *I was healthy.*

"Stand back and we can help her. She only takes half the damage from her hug healing," said Richard.

"What?" What were they talking about?

"Why do you think she hugs you so often, Corey? She heals when she hugs," said Richard.

Samantha hugged me and cried.

I looked around. "Am I that big of an idiot?"

"When did this start?" exclaimed Miles.

"Didn't you think it odd that you were the only football player to never miss a game or practice?" said Richard.

"Drink up," said Dr. Kanoska. She gave her a glass of something that smelled foul. "She'll take some time to heal." The doctor turned to me. "I'd have said not to do this, but you use it more effectively than others. Don't squander this large of a gift."

"What day is it?" I asked. I was healthy and had all my energy.

"Thursday," said Nathan.

I turned to my team. Nathan and Wesley stood to the side next to a collection of small desks with computers. Rachel stood in front of Nicole, who was flanked by Rebecca and Madison. Then they changed, and they were warriors. I fell backwards and when I caught myself; they rushed towards me.

I held up my hands. "Sorry, the vision was more intense than the dream."

"What was it, Dude? Me flexing?" Miles's joke almost made me laugh. A smile was still nice.

How could I tell them that Rebecca wore a gold breastplate and held a blue and gold shield with a sword of white light with ten-foot-long angel wings? Madison had curls in her hair, wore a tartan dress, and held a bow. Rachel was herself wearing a leather dress that exposed her solar plexus and held her surujin, that glowed with celestial power. Nicole wore swan's feathers over her shoulders with a leather harness connected to a skirt of leaves. She wore plant greaves on her legs, plant vambraces on her arms, and held the Okinawan spear, the nunti-bo that also glowed with celestial power.

Samantha helped me up. "The visions are only a possibility," she whispered. "The more or stronger you see them, the more you will need them."

"We've spent a lot of magic getting you to this point," said Morgan from across the way. "The last druid who received this spell finished removing the Romans from the isles, saved the Abernathy line of druids, and crowned a king."

I knew I shouldn't try to make sense of Morgan, so I nodded to her. "Guys, I know what our next step is, but we need to move. We need everyone because this will be the most dangerous step we're taking."

"Dude, are we still going for it all?" Miles sat in one of the chairs they moved from the table they had laid me on.

"It needs to be interesting," said Morgan. She yawned, and I'd never seen her so weak.

"Safety wouldn't hurt," added Samantha. She stifled a yawn and sat in a chair next to me.

"Thank you, Miles," I said. "I'm going to ask everyone once and then I will shut up. To steal a quote from a person smarter than I am, I will not be an on and off again girlfriend. If you agree with me, I am the team's battle leader, with no more changes."

"Hurry," said Rebecca. "We will stroke your ego one more time." She grasped her side.

"I will always go for it all. Love will always direct me. There are no half measures and no one is expendable. If you agree you want this as the tactical leader or battle leader, then tell me so."

"Of course, dude." Miles said it first, but the groans from the rest of the team let me know they agreed.

"Okay. Rebecca, I had a dream about us. Can I see your left index finger?" I was ready to roll.

"It's true," she said. She frowned but showed me the ring on the finger. "I need to see you in private immediately."

"Nice," said Morgan. "No explanation and mysterious. The drama is picking up."

"Before I go on, I have to take care of personal stuff. Nicole, do you want to go somewhere?"

"No, let's do this here. Everyone knows. I am so sorry I spazzed. Please forgive me," she cried. "I promise to talk to you."

It was fine that everyone knew. "Do you promise to talk to me about everything? You can be as crazy as you want, but talk to me." I held out my arms.

She charged and jumped into my arms. "Yes." She took a deep breath and wailed, "I'm pregnant."

"Ooh, Nicole, next time you do that, make popcorn," said Morgan. "What a reveal! That made the entire trip worth it. I am on board and staying until the end!" She was clapping. Drama increased her energy.

I was cool even though I freaked out. "Oh, that's cool." I kept low-key but was freaking out. This needed to stay to the side for now, because we'd be fine. I had time to digest it later.

Nicole hugged me around my neck, and I hugged her back. Samantha hugged both of us. "Congratulations."

"Well, aren't the rest of you guys going to congratulate us?" I said to the others. I wasn't sure what to think and was freaking the heck out, but it was time to move on to a battle plan and I wasn't getting rid of Nicole or her pregnancy, so everyone should be happy.

"What information do you need?" asked Nathan.

"Is Carol, okay?" That was first on my list.

"Yes," said Preacher Jon. "You never figured out her power?"

"I guess you found out how I'm a college dropout," I joked. "I am worried about Carol."

"She only took half of your injuries. The Earth takes half for her sacrifice," said Preacher Jon. But she has to heal at a normal rate, so she's done for a while. She's on the way to the hospital for surgeries.

"I know a lot of stuff has happened and we can't go through it all because we gotta move. Here's everyone's orders. Tonight, we are going out to dinner and follow Nicole's plan for a fun night out. We will not forget what we are fighting for."

There was some light cheering.

"Miles and Trish, travel to Sacred Heart tomorrow at ten am and look around. Miles, use your senses, but take no chances," I continued.

"Got it," said Miles.

"Wesley and Nicole. Go to Saint Andrews and sign us up for the marriage classes at ten am."

"Is there a reason for the time?" asked Wesley.

"Yes, but because of empaths, I'm not telling you. Nathan and Madison, you two stroll around the Alpharetta Administration Center. Do not go in." They had to stay out.

The time was part of my plan, because I didn't know where the church would place their empaths. I planned to run out at seven thirty into the woods, banish the gargoyle, run back, use the Tree Foyer in the Spring Fey Court to move to the house. Then leave with Rachel for the Rec-center. When I attacked the circle, they church would think I was at least three hours away.

"Ten am?" Asked Nathan

"Yep. Rebecca. Park on the main road of the Rec-center, point heading out at ten with your windows down."

"Corey, if I am manning the center. Will you send me a squirrel with the plan?" Asked Preacher Jon.

"Yes. It's crucial no one out in the field has the information." I would follow the vision and make sure we extracted every bit of information from the connected sites.

"Samantha, you get to choose our next vacation too," said Morgan. "I am feeling my heartbeat faster."

"This is intriguing," replied Samantha.

"Rachel, stay at my house tonight, with Wesley and Rebecca. I'll pick you up at nine thirty. Everyone leave the cabin for Nicole and I tonight."

"Why's that?" Asked Nicole.

"We're having loud sex tonight. Carol told me not to waste this health. But first," I pointed to Rebecca. "Help her to the quiet room."

THE TWO OF US SAT NEXT to the window in the soundproof room. Rebecca looked as sad as I'd ever seen her and she stared wistfully at the ring.

I slumped in the chair next to her. A vision of an angel in black stood next to her. Then the angel in black and I danced in a fancy ball room! Rebecca danced next to us with a man holding a paintbrush.

"Are you okay?" She reached out for my cheek.

"Vision again. This one was freaky." That one couldn't be true.

She handed me a piece of paper. "We don't have a lot of time. Two things. First, read the top of this report. You will be the third person to know this."

I read how I needed to date Nicole for the fate of the world. My dating anyone else guaranteed the end of the world. "Well, this is new. I guess we keep on with the current plan and need to change a few factors. You know, unless twelve more years of Earth is a good run."

She ignored me. "Corey, how do you block empath powers?"

I pointed to my earring.

"Let me copy its powers." She touched her ring to my earring. "Thank god."

"You can do that?" That was brand new.

"The ring can. But I read the complete report and I will tell you the important parts. Nicole is the most dangerous person on the planet. The only person who could control her is you. When you and I date, you and I are just are deadly after a decade."

"What?" This made little sense.

"Do you know what scorched civilization means?" She looked at me seriously.

Of course, I knew what that meant. I made up the term. If Rebecca knew what it meant, there was a possibility I would do this in the future. "I can imagine putting an entire city into a circle and banishing it. You say Nicole is more dangerous?"

"I'm just as dangerous as you." She cried.

"Wait. Nicole is the deadliest person. Hold that thought." Things were coming together.

"Nathan, could you come here?" Everyone stayed and stared at the door. "Guys, we have orders." They ignored me and stayed put. What an outstanding leader I was.

Nathan jogged over and came into the room with us.

"Nathan, I need to tell you as little as possible and have you answer the questions without trying to figure things out." I wanted to console Rebecca, but this was too important.

"Richard gave me empath protection." He pointed to his watch. It's a thin piece of metal in here.

Rebecca wiped away her tears and spoke while I sat. "I have a report I ran through the Chesapeake Bay Territory. Here is the summary."

"Holy crap." He gave it back to her. "The shredder is next to my computer."

I needed to get to the critical piece. "That's not important, depending on the answer to this question. Did the Delta region make a push for anyone but Nicole?"

He thought. He counted on his hand. "There are a lot of requests and she was the most popular. Hmmm, the delta region only ever asked about her."

"You have a leak of our information, and the Delta Region knew about Nicole before we did. Other than emergencies, Rachel or I have to be near Nicole at all times." It was so obvious.

"You think someone has hacked us?" Nathan looked concerned, and I didn't know what that word meant.

"I do not know how information moves around, but you told me teams couldn't research other teams, but the Delta Vampires have a grudge against us from Old Donnie rooting them out one hundred years ago. Their push for Nicole means they know something, and this is too big, since the information is your fancy computer thinga-majig."

"I'll go begin diagnostics. After I block this from empaths." Nathan stood.

I took the time to add it to my earring, and I saw Rebecca focus on something, too. He left and shut the door. All the others sat and watched him run to his computer.

"So, we need to decide if running off to hide and getting twelve to twenty years together is worth the end of the world." I mean, I couldn't, but I hadn't had time to collect myself.

She started crying. "Am I a bad person for thinking that for real? Corey, I heard you in the SUV and I'm caught up in you, too."

"No. You're a good person. The world is asking too much of us." I collapsed into a chair. The world was asking a lot of us.

She sniffled. "Lead me out. We need to make sure you and Nicole stay together."

"I give you my word. The relationship gets every bit of my effort. This sacrifice will result in a happy marriage." I opened the door and led her out. The others stood around and watched us.

"I'm not sure what you all are waiting for. We have a night of trivia and dancing in front of us, and none of you have changed yet. Nicole, make sure everyone is cute." Someone had to put on a brave face.

Nicole ran over with Rachel.

"Rachel. Now that Nicole is pregnant, I want to be a little pro-tective, and one of us needs to be near her at all times." I knew Rachel wouldn't question this.

Nicole looked at me strangely, but Rachel grinned. "You got it, new dad."

EVENTUALLY, EVERYONE was ready for a night out. We had two SUVs parked near <u>Frenco Tavern and Dance</u>, but we sat in the parking lot and Nathan hissed, "that's an empath."

"This is a job for a dude with a hero complex," I joked. Using my earring, I blocked everything about church empaths, knowledge of the Curia, and the ex-Italian special forces. As I blocked the knowledge of empaths, I realized I wasn't communicating like I asked Nicole to. *Oh crap.* I grabbed Nicole's shoulders gently. "Now isn't the time, but I forgot to tell you something. I promise I'll catch you up."

Walking to the empath, I put thoughts of sexual activity with this woman in my mind. "Hi. My name is Tyler and we've bumped into each other several times and it's time we exchanged phone numbers."

Her face scrunched as she read my thoughts of my imagining what her breasts looked like given the shape of her shirt.

"Move along," said a man getting out to the car she stood in front of. He was short and had short person energy to go with his fire hydrant build, high and tight haircut and flat face.

"Don't think I will, No-neck. I can tell by her face you are not her lover but an annoyance. Plus, she was just scoping me out."

I imagined a graphic sexual situation with the two of us and it caught her off guard. She grabbed her breasts.

"You're thinking what I'm thinking." I added a wink and her face turned bright red.

Derek strode over. "Sir, is there a problem here?"

I ignored Derek for now and held up one finger. "You don't go to Saint Andrews, but your cross says Catholic, but I know I've seen this car where I umpire baseball games." I was guessing. "Wait, I know. I saw you when I sang Christmas carols in Alpharetta at the tree."

Panic spread over her face when I said that. "I am sure it wasn't me."

Bingo. I chuckled. "If it wasn't you, it was your sister who looks like you and checks me out, too. So, either you guys are scoping out my sexy body." I gave a flex. "Or scoping out places or people to rob?"

"This parking lot is for customers only, and you've been here for a few hours," said Derek.

That's when No-neck punched me. I saw it coming and absorbed it and rolled on the ground.

"Dave, call the police," called out Derek as he backed away. The woman had jumped in the car with the man and I rolled to the side as they pulled out. Man, I wanted to beat the hell out of No-neck, but I ate my frustration.

The other caught up to me, and Derek jogged back over. Derek laughed. "We did not know how to get them away from here. How did you frustrate them?" asked Derek.

I imagined the graphic picture I used with the church empath with Nicole.

"You pig!" She shouted and grabbed her breasts.

"Hey, that's what the other women did," said Rachel, and started laughing.

"Let's go get a table before someone tells me what's going on," said Nathan. The four ladies were next to each other again and the vision of them in battle regalia came to my mind again. Now I could recall this picture whenever I wanted.

"Be right there." I jogged to the trees next to the parking lot and cast *Squirrel Messenger*. I described Preacher Jon. *Banishing Gargoyle in North Georgia at eight-thirty. Will destroy new site at ten before it's finished. Confuse church and gather info.*

Nicole waited for me just inside the door next to the place where they waited to sit couples and groups. "Okay. What did you need to tell me?"

"This needs to be kept secret, which will be obvious in a second." We pulled into tight and I snuggled my mouth next to her ear and whispered. *I have magical empath protection and keep it because of church empaths.*

She covered her mouth. "That explains so much." She held me tight and whispered, "Did you open it back up the day you dressed me for camping?"

"Yes," I whispered back.

"That is twice you've out thought me before I realized you figured me out. How do you do that?"

"Lucky?"

We strode over to our group at the table in a slowly filling bar area.

Derek had sat our group at two joined tables and gave us a trivia pad. I jogged back in and joined them. An older woman, thin but more muscular than a woman her age normally looked, marched up to me. "I'm Sally. I'm the owner here. Are you okay? I heard No-neck punched you."

"Sally. You must be Fitz's ex-wife. It's a pleasure to meet you." I held out my hand.

She rolled her eyes but shook my hand. "There is only one person you can be, and this is the group you have been whispering about, isn't it, Derek?"

"This is them and that's him," said the waiter and member of The Tribe.

"Well, you be careful tonight. The fact you held back to take a punch means either you're saving something up or you are a lot more mature than your years suggest." She looked me up and down and let out a heavy sigh. She touched Nicole on her shoulder. "I do not envy you." Then she trudged away.

"What'll it be, folks?" asked Derek.

I was famished and when it came time to order. "I'm going to get two dinners. If you could bring it on one platter, so I don't look like a pig, that'd be great."

"Let's see." Derek rolled his eyes.

"The steak and salmon with broccoli and a salad, but upgrade it to a house salad. Then add the grilled chicken with green beans and asparagus."

"You better not be making a doggie bag if they can get it on a platter." He joked.

"I may eat off of other people's plates." I smiled, but I was hungry and just may. My last meal was before the Moon-eyed defense.

"Wait, we can order two dinners?" said Rachel. "I'm coming hungry next time."

"Is this the second date for you all?" asked Derek.

"No way. This is the fourth," said Nicole.

"Good thing you got that third date in before you found out you were pregnant," teased Rebecca.

"Hey, we've known each other for eight years," I said.

"Oh my god, you're pregnant. That is so great," said Derek. "I'll be right back before the dad to be starts eating the table."

Dad-to-be hit me. That explained what I was looking toward.

"It finally hit you?" asked Nicole.

"I haven't had a lot of time." I drank my full glass of water and hoped for a refill soon.

"He handled it better than you," said Nathan. "The entire store got quiet after you wailed from the bathroom."

"She was surprised," said Rebecca.

Dropping Nicole the message that we were cool was a relief. If she hadn't gotten that message while I was out... Man, I needed to work on my communication, too.

"You are very sweet," said Nicole. "This could really work." She smiled sweetly.

Empaths reading my thoughts kept tripping me up if I didn't focus on it.

"It's going to be hard for me to get pregnant because of my workouts," said Rachel.

"Nicole probably wouldn't be pregnant without the effect of being near that tree," explained Rebecca. She avoided saying the word faeries out loud. "Did you account for that?"

Rachel stopped talking when her jaw dropped.

"Come on," said Rebecca, grabbing her purse. "Grab your purse and follow me to the bathroom."

I started thinking of having sex with Nicole tonight with no worries.

She leaned over and whispered. "If I bring you to the car and do you like the day I waxed you, you won't be so ready."

I whispered back. "It'll just make me last longer tonight."

"Good." She grabbed my hand and dragged me out to the SUV. She piled us into the back seat, locked the doors, and we scrambled to the third-row bench seat. She yanked on my pants.

Then it hit me. She did this when she felt guilty or had stressful news. That wasn't good for us long term. She also shouldn't feel guilty about being pregnant. I grabbed her, rolled up her dress and yanked her panties down, and tossed them.

"What are you doing?" She helped me move her legs up.

I put her legs on my shoulder and I dove in tongue first.

She moaned but said, "Corey, I came to take care of you."

I poked my head up and said, "we don't do sexual favors when we feel guilty or breaking news. We do it when we want the other person to be happy. I want you to be happy, so relax."

Rebecca had given me specific instructions about this part of foreplay. Any moisture in there already wasn't adequate. I needed to clean it off and then pull new moisture with my tongue up. From our previous sessions, I knew I had to get under a little hood to find a harder bump and then I needed to create little circles there. It wasted time if you licked anywhere else—unless I'd penetrate her with my tongue. But she didn't respond to that like Rebecca had.

Soon, Nicole moaned, and goosebumps covered her thighs, and she pushed my head away. She lay there and panted, and I pulled my pants up.

"No, you don't. We also came out here, so you'd take even more time tonight." She pushed me over with a playful push.

I couldn't argue with that reasoning.

She grabbed me and caressed my shaft to make me hard. She rolled her tongue around and placed my erection into her mouth. I laid back and enjoyed her loving touch, the thought of her and me together. A gurgling slurp grabbed my attention, and I looked to the roof of the car, but I saw nothing as my eyes rolled back.

My right hand braced me on the seat as I straightened my right leg on the console. The leather seat cracked, and I rubbed the side of her hair with my left hand. I moaned and couldn't keep it quiet, and she sucked harder.

Her silky-smooth hair ran through my fingers as her head pumped vigorously. Her hand pushed on my stomach muscles as saliva splattered around my thighs. My stomach muscles tightened as pressure built.

The first ejaculation caused me to utter a guttural moan, and the successive pump kept me pulsing. She massaged everything out. Then she licked the sensitive head, causing me to jump.

"Okay."

She giggled and caused me to jump again with another tiny lick. "Okay, okay."

She kissed up my stomach and chest. "Did you like that?"

"Oh my god, yes."

She tucked me back in and zipped up my pants. "Okay. No more feeling guilty or softening bad news sex. Just making the other person happy. Let's go back in after I fix my hair."

I tried to regain control of my muscles and breathing.

We did not know the time, but we returned to the table all smiles.

"I'm negative," said Rachel. "In case you were wondering about me." She stuck her tongue out.

I tried not to laugh and stuffed my mouth full of the salad that was waiting for me. I had not stopped grinning and Nicole blushed slightly.

The table tried to avoid the awkwardness of what the two of us just did and the trivia was about to start. Happy for another topic, I asked, "who is today's trivia star?"

Derek came back with plates of food. "You two were gone a long time and didn't have time to finish the salads. Important business?"

"Miles!" exclaimed Nicole.

"What, I said nothing?" said Miles.

Trish whacked him and asked him something.

I knew he must have told someone it was crazy girl sex, but he was wrong. It was loving girl sex. Maybe some crazy guy sex if you wanted to be more accurate.

She smiled at me. "Well, at least you know what it really was."

No faking needed. It was the action of a loving girl, but I was still going to rock her world tonight and I'd get to howl even if she tried to keep it quiet.

She slapped my arm playfully and blushed. The food beckoned me and I piled it in.

The table didn't bother commenting on Rachel or my eating habits. They've seen it before and we ate in peace while the size of our trivia team put us into first place with no help from me.

"Um, Mr. Norwood, I would like to apologize." I looked and Meat stood there looking down. In apron and restaurant clothes, he looked even wider than before. His hair was in a hairnet and he had zero anger in him.

"First, it's Corey. Second, if you're apologizing, you are well ahead of where I was at your age. No apology needed." I point to his rib. He appeared to have a thick wrap in it. "Sorry, I only meant to crack it a little."

"The camera we have showed you pulled it and I was out of position, just like you said." He tried not to wince.

"Hopefully, the powers can negotiate us to where we can train together in a couple of months." It'd be good to train with an opponent with size using a distinct style compared to Miles.

"I'd like that, sir. Well, I need to get back to work." Meat smiled and turned to go back to the kitchen.

The rest of the table looked at me. "What? I have a life outside, you guys," I joked.

"Really. Who was that?" asked Rebecca. "He reminds me of you."

"A new member of The Tribe. He was guarding the entrance, and I didn't let him move me along. But I taught him which moves were wrong."

"And you broke a rib?" asked Trish.

"It's the way young guys learn best," said Rachel. "They used to beat the hell out of Corey to get lessons through to him."

I remembered some of those. They weren't fun.

We enjoyed our night, and it was great to see my friends enjoying themselves. It didn't matter that I didn't answer a single trivia question, or that I felt like a fool on the dance floor. We had fun. Nicole even told me to slow dance with Rebecca for a dance.

She held me and lingered. "You'll need to support me a bit."

I pulled her in close and moved her arms over my shoulders and kept my arms high enough to grip above her wound.

"She looks a lot happier than most girls who do that." Rebecca whispered to me as we danced.

"I turned it around on her. I figured out she did that when she felt guilty or broke bad news and realized it could hurt the relationship," I explained.

"Thank you, Corey. If we make this big of a sacrifice, we need to go all out."

I quoted Old Donnie and spoke in his voice.

There are going to be days where you question everything. Why save people? Why fight monsters? Let me tell you, the lesson of letting bad things happen and seeing the results hurts. Knowing you could have stopped it—will break you. When these questions come—and they will—fight your way through, because this will be the hardest part of your life.

We held each other and pretended we cried at the sad song.

Despite Rebecca and me dealing with this, Nicole's idea for a fun night out was the best idea anyone had. A killer would read his new spell book to get ready, and I was partying with friends like a Druid of the Fey Spring Court.

Chapter 23—The Big Plan

Corey 0730

After a night where I kept my promise to Nicole at the cabin, I kissed Nicole in our lover's embrace, and let her drive to her mission. It hit me she was signing us up for marriage classes, but she would be at Saint Andrews when I took out a circle of the church within a few miles of her.

We had left a little early so I could test something in the Fey Spring Court with the coordinates Nathan gave me. I arrived at the big red maple, stepped through it into Tree Foyer.

I'd read more about the Tree foyer and trees weren't off limits. If I was a member of the Fey Spring Court, I could use them. Time, or death of the owner, abandoned thousands of the trees. I thought of using other trees and I got nowhere. I needed something that connected to the Fey realm. With the sheets Nathan gave me of the territories, I focused on the territory pole at the coordinates for the Delta Region. I flashed through the mish-mash of trees and found a magnolia tree.

Wow! I put this in the back of my head. If they started a war with me, I had a quick counterattack ready, and those vampires would hate me. Hate me more.

I thought about the Key West Area and got nothing. Nothing came up for the Chesapeake Bay Territory nor anything in New England. I couldn't rule out New England, since I didn't have its coordinates. A hit happened for the New York territory and I whooshed

241

to a Virginian Juniper. The tree had a sign on it that said Great Wolf. This was information for later.

I grabbed my items, popped back out by the cabin, and ran north into the woods for the next gargoyle in the <u>Abernathy Book of Gargoyles</u>. This one wanted to be a few miles away from civilization, which was harder than a gargoyle that wanted to be summoned near a city. A town of thirty thousand would be too close. I traveled well into the backwoods to banish it.

I ran over the frozen ground and the inch or two of snow that stayed frozen in the shade. This gargoyle would be no issue. I ran for an hour and was fifteen miles north of the cabin. This gargoyle had so many choices, I doubt the church bothered to have priests waiting for me.

I made the circle with three honeysuckle focuses and cut nine more for use later.

I started the banishing with the gargoyle's symbol interspersed with the focuses. Soon my torc lit up red. The world turned black and white. The gargoyle was small, maybe my height and traditional, with horns on its head and sharp teeth. One of the middle grades of rock comprised its body, and it thrashed like many others before it, which was irrelevant since in ten minutes it was gone. My torc's red gem dimmed, and the world returned to normal. I packed up and moved towards the cabin.

On the run, I thought through our team's situation. The monsignor miscalculated moving the final site at such a late date. The only reason I could think of was he thought we had more information than we did. We had information about the Alpharetta site and the Rec-center site. But it made sense that Saint Andrews was involved, since they parked a truck in their parking lot, and Sacred Heart was involved, since they took a delivery there. I couldn't explain it, but it was linked.

If I took down the circle and destroyed their preparation, so many choices opened to us. We could raid the monsignor early if we identified him, raid the original center, or wait till the day of the spell. What I thought was the best part of the plan was that they'd not expect an attack so far away. They knew I was hours away from their sites. Unless they had a spy, this would surprise them.

The Fey Spring Court change to my *Own Area* spell created the extra noise of Fey magic, which had slowed their tracking of me. Killing Bishop Pedrotti slowed the tracking of me because his special power was gone.

However, Suit and Red Shirt set me up with search and rescue. They were also ready for Nathan and Madison on their excursion. I told Nathan the Delta Territory had information, but I suspected it went deeper. One thing in common was the information leaks surrounded Nathan. I didn't suspect Nathan, but he used that fancy computer stuff. Unexplained events around Nathan would get a response from me.

I arrived at the big red maple, stepped through it into Tree Foyer. Then I stepped through Woodrow's tree into the backyard of my house to collect Rachel. The temperature was ten degrees warmer out of the mountains and the sun was out. It was a chilly but pleasant day to raid the Curia.

REBECCA 0830

This morning was fun and not at all proper. Madison, Rachel, and Rebecca had gotten ready and spent the morning gossiping. The three sat on Corey's giant bed with the comforter over the sheets. Sitting cross-legged and facing each other helped the ladies gossip.

"I was just so horny. Every time I commit a crime and someone wants me, I'm out of control," explained Madison. "How was I to know Nathan would think he was in love? I mean, he wasn't a virgin. He was pretty good."

"Let's not talk about my brother, because Wesley was a virgin and cried after three pumps and a moan." Rachel shook her head.

Poor Rachel had her work cut out for her. All the ladies giggled.

"I mean, it's great my muscles turn him on and all, but what am I supposed to do?"

Madison and Rebecca spent an hour helping Rachel understand how to tell him what to do.

They were showered and dressed. Rebecca waited for others to arrive since she'd want to be placed in the car. Rachel waited on Corey and Madison waited on Nathan. She would try to explain to him the difference between a sexual companion and a relationship.

"Well, we can't not talk about her, can we?" asked Madison.

"We should. Can you believe they did that in the middle of dinner?" asked Rachel.

"Um yes," said Madison. "If I had a man who made sure I finished, was caring, and was trying to save the world... well I'd globber him every morning so he wouldn't forget me."

"Ah!" Rachel covered her mouth and fell backward onto the floor. She landed with a thump but kept giggling.

"That's not all," said Madison. "Her panties were in the car and Nathan freaked out. I threw them in Corey's washing machine."

"Corey said he turned it around on her," said Rebecca. She left out the 'why' because the 'what' had enough of a bang."

"He calls that a reversal. He used to do with you, too." Rachel covered her mouth. "Not that Corey told me that."

"He named it?" It didn't surprise Rebecca, the shock embarrassed her. "Let's go back and discuss Nicole."

"I can't believe she did it at dinner. You know she did it in my bed the day we practiced for Karaoke and I caught them," said Rachel.

"Oh my god," said Rebecca.

"Rebecca, tell me you wouldn't," said Madison.

Rachel stood up. "Rebecca, if you got Corey back, would you?"

Rebecca knew this wasn't proper, but this was girls' talk and wouldn't leave the room. Plus, she was having fun. She could joke more since it was impossible for them to be together. "I think Corey likes the excitement and spontaneity."

"Probably some naughtiness too," added Madison.

Rebecca smiled to get a reaction. "If we'd get away with it, I'd have crawled under the table and given him one there while everyone watched his face."

"Ah!" Rachel fell on the floor again. "No way. I'd die." She rolled over and laughed.

"Come on Rachel, you'd do more for Corey than for Wesley right now," Madison teased Rachel.

"Ew!" said Rachel after she stopped laughing.

All the girls were laughing when a car drove up and the screen door slid open.

"I love laughter," said Corey.

Rachel stood up and ran to hug Corey. "Settle an argument for us," she said, but she had a twist in her voice that said something else was up. "Corey, would you enjoy oral every morning or by surprise like last night?"

Madison and Rebecca each had their hands over their mouths and looked at each other. When Rebecca turned back, Rachel had an evil grin and Corey blushed.

"Let's focus on the job," he squeaked out. "Wesley and Nathan are here. Let me help Rebecca out."

Rachel strode outside to get the bike started since Corey would ride on the back with her for his surprise thing. He held her arm and guided her out. When they were out of earshot he said, "I bet you said I wanted the surprise more than anything else and you are right." He winked evilly and opened his orange car door.

That infuriating man. She got in and felt the heat on her face. Rebecca was a proper woman and could handle a charming man, even him. She thickened her accent and did her best Scarlett O'Hara impression. "Oh Corey, would it please you to know that you are devilishly charming?"

The man pulled out his Rhett Butler impression. "Wow, I thought I was winning, but you have bested me again. Please be careful." He blushed and stumbled over to Rachel despite a decent recovery.

After Corey stumbled to the back of Rachel's bike, he held onto his friend and they took off fast, but it was strange how that druid was just befuddled by one brief comment.

The drive was short and shifting gears caused her some pain, but she was measurably healthier. When she parked and rested, she pulled out the report and read it for a seventeenth time. Surely the world wouldn't be so cruel.

It was.

She re-read how Nicole was the most dangerous person on the planet. The only situation that kept her under control was a passionate relationship with Corey. The empath was responsible for the end of civilization if neither of them dated Corey, one hundred percent of the time. If Rebecca dated Corey, Rebecca was responsible for the end of the world a quarter of the time, Corey a quarter of the time, and Nicole half the time. It never said how the world ended. It only mentioned scorched civilization and nuclear missiles when neither dated the druid.

The safest situation for the Earth was a happy and loving relationship where Nicole and Corey created a handful of new druids, and Rebecca stayed friends with them, and worked with Corey fighting Nephilim.

The ache inside her grew, and it was no longer her side that hurt. Was destroying the world worth a good twelve to twenty years with

Corey? She told Corey they couldn't, but it wasn't as easy a question as people may wish it to be. She rolled her windows down, got out of the car to get some air.

TRISH 0955

This was Trish's first proper mission. Sure, she was traveling to her church with her husband and needed to keep her eyes open and then go back to work before lunch, but she was on the team now. She and Miles had been a little early, but she needed to correct her husband's behavior.

Well, someone who didn't know the details might think she had a role to play in his behavior, but that was irrelevant. It was her husband, and she needed to help him.

The previous night, Nicole and Corey had an encounter that should have been more private, but there was nothing wrong with it. They announced nothing. They strode arm in arm to a locked and hidden location, came back, and mentioned nothing about it. Of course, everyone knew what they were doing, but that was irrelevant. They were a passionate couple.

Her husband referred to this as crazy girl sex. What a misogynist thing to say—her own husband, of all people. So, she drove and when they parked in front of the church; she reminded him how they used to make out before church. She locked the doors and rolled up the tinted windows.

He prepared to kiss, but she unzipped his pants and reminded him that certain actions were not the province of kids or crazy girls.

After she finished, Miles made a joke. "If you want me to apologize and admit I was wrong, that wasn't a punishment."

She glared at him.

"I promise I will not only apologize to Nicole; I will make a public apology in front of everyone who heard me. I was wrong, you are right, and even if I was right, I shouldn't have hurt her."

He zipped himself up after that. Just that easy. She had her husband back.

She also would give Nicole a lesson learned. Trish had believed she changed after being pregnant and her marriage had suffered because of a lack of intimacy. Corey's request to help them must have been a simple request to fix. A night in Corey's spare bedroom surrounded by passion faeries reminded Trish that she was still a woman, not only a pregnant woman.

Now, they stood in Sacred Heart to discuss the baptism of their baby. It would be uncomfortable since they had stopped coming to church because the store was open during church hours.

In his plan with no details, Corey hadn't given them a reason to come, and she wondered if he even knew they needed to prepare for a baptism, but they had a valid reason to be here.

Trish took out her phone to get a picture of Miles near the baptismal. A door opened and a person who should not exist ran out. She knew there were no nondiplomatic monsignors anymore. Yet, a man with half graying hair from black, wearing a black cassock with purple sashes and the purple ferraiolo waving behind him, looking every bit of the cape it was.

She snapped at least five pictures of the man running before she got dizzy and sat in a pew. Miles raised his hands, then faded to shadow and disappeared. She swore she saw him hold a green sword.

The monsignor had not disappeared; he left through the front door in a full sprint.

MADISON 0955

This was a lovely day. Madison was confused. She still thought like Stormy, but the other girls said she should make decisions as Madison to become Madison.

"Ms. Roane, may I carry your bag?" Nathan was clearly a book-read man, but not learned with women, though he had two lovely sisters. Somehow, he did not suffer the same affliction as his friend Wesley and was a fair lover.

"I kin' tote my poke." She had not paid attention and her real accent came out. She paused and translated into Atlanta speak. "I'm sorry. But I prefer to carry my bag, but thank you."

He smiled at her, as if she just didn't sound like a mountain hillbilly.

The decorated city circle, what they called this fancy entrance-way, was so beautiful that she felt like a jasper. *Stop thinking like a hillbilly. Jasper means outsider, think outsider.* Nicole had asked her to be more careful around Corey with her talk, but slipping around everyone else was fine. Corey seemed a strange bird if deep southern accents smoked his sausage.

They had groomed the thick grass into enormous squares that fit an entire house, and there were fifty of them. Her Aunt Becky told her to relax with this group of city folk and Aunt Becky spent ten years rescuing her, her parents, and her grandparents. Madison tried her best to relax.

They walked toward the Christmas tree with other couples. She offered her arm to Nathan like other couples had done and he took it and they fit it. Nathan had gotten manners training Madison never had. The fact he adored her a bit too much wasn't such a bad thing. She never dreamed she'd dressed up fancy like walking with a man-ner-trained man. Well, not since she was eight.

Her great grandparents were what people called evil. They locked up her parents and grandparents when she was eight years old. Two years ago, her aunts defeated them, led by Aunt Becky, and placed them into stasis by the Chicago coven. Her grandparents and parents found her living in the woods outside of Chattanooga and brought her home. The woods were better than foster care, and she was glad she had aged out.

She had been so lonely from those years of eight years old onward. That's why Stormy became Slutty Stormy. All someone had to do was tell her they wanted her and Stormy was so desperate to be wanted. Then she met him, the first guy who ever wanted her for her, and she told him she couldn't date him. Now he treated her like a proper woman.

She missed her grandparents' house, of course, but that house had its share of good and bad memories. Here, she wasn't Stormy, Slutty Stormy, or Crazy Redheaded Stormy. She was Madison, the professional woman who loved shooting the bow. She had never fit in before.

What she wanted with Nathan was to be like Rachel and Corey. Those two were as close as peas and carrots. He plaited her hair, helped her with makeup, and probably even picked out her dress. Rachel was what she called a specialist and needed help with a lot of things. But she was super good at others. It would devastate Madison to rely upon others like that. Being valuable let others want to keep her around.

Nathan guided her to the tree, and they'd join in and sing carols.

"Nathan, what do you think of a relationship like Corey and Rachel's?"

He put his arm around her so they fit in with the other couples. "They're lucky. They both have other partners ready if they want them. In truth, I'd kill for a relationship like that, but then she'd be dating someone else and I'd be alone. The only reason it works for them is they have a real co-dependent thing where they can't function if they go more than a few days without each other."

"Really?"

"Corey left for a week and I had to hold Rachel for a couple of hours and brought her to Corey's house so she could sleep in his bed and smell him." Nathan looked wistful.

Deep down, she knew Nathan was right. It was hard to date and keep a friend of that sex close to you. They pulled up to the tree and started singing. She held onto him and wondered if it became familiarity or whether she was just lonely. But she figured she couldn't keep like this too long. She'd end up in old habits, and old habits were hard to break.

Rebecca had told her it was proper to be a serial monogamist. They giggled over the fancy words, but Madison knew what she meant. If Madison would put Stormy in her past and move forward, she could date someone for an extended period and not be a sex buddy.

She wrapped her arms around Nathan as they sang. When the song stopped, she spoke into his ear so he'd hear her clearly. "Nathan, I'm settling down and thank you for being patient. If you would like to court me and take me on an actual date, just the two of us—I'm ready to try."

"Really, I'd love nothing more." He beamed and Madison got onto her toes and kissed him. His soft fingers brushed her long red hair with his hands and looked into her with adoration. He already cared for her too deeply for such a short time, but this was partially her fault. Nice guys fell in love when they made love and when the world became dangerous and she broke laws, she became incontrollable.

Nathan tackled her, and a shot rang out. Then automatic guns fired. He covered her and the manicured grass covered her face. People were screaming, but the police had already responded.

Nathan cried out in pain. She felt his body jerk.

Her leg felt as if a giant hornet stung her and the inside of her leg caught fire.

<u>COREY 1000</u>

I scoped out the circle in the area Nathan sent me to. We parked the bike in the parking lot and didn't have many trees to hide in, but we could see the fields and the tennis courts, just like my vision. The Curia planned for something magnificent. They made the circle of metal and had gargoyle heads for focuses. They used thirteen gargoyle heads. I drew a circle with four focuses, so that when they joined, it'd register a seventeen-focus circle.

They placed this circle in some woods that separated a soccer field, two baseball fields, and the tennis courts. Checking again, this time closer, the church left a bunch of equipment inside the circle. None of it was recognizable, but it could go to the Realm of Darkness.

I initiated the circle and Rachel sang a song of druidic power through the ages. I bound the items in the circle.

> *Bho àm immemorial, cumhachd an t-seanairginn a 'gairm thugad. A bhith ceangailte ris a 'phortal agam agus fo smachd mo thoil.*

The second binding was to bind the circle.

Thig na cearcallan còmhla agus cuiridh mi ri chèile iad mar aon agus bidh e leamsa.

Soon I had it, but I needed to repeat it ten times, and the power was immense. Then I took my standard banishing to send it to the Realm of Darkness.

> *Tha Rìoghachd dorchadas a 'gairm agus le mo chumhachd rìoghachdan ceangailte tha mi a' cuir casg ort gu dorchadas!*

Then, instead of a pop, there was a boom. Ground, fence, trees, and rocks flew from the ground. Pavement near the side of the parking lot cracked and threw chunks of asphalt into the air. Rachel's song stopped.

The explosion cleared the ground around us and sent us flying. After landing with a thud, I stood disoriented and looked for Rachel. There by a tree and a rock. The rock landed on her head and gashed it!

I ran over and held her. "Rachel!"

She didn't move, but we couldn't stay here. This is why I kept Rebecca parked nearby. I cradled Rachel the same as I did that one day in high school and carried her to the GSXR. Lifting the bike with my foot, I placed Rachel's rear end on the gas tank and left the helmets on the seat hooks.

After I reached around her to secure her, I rode along the grass to the main road to get her to Rebecca. The GSXR jumped from the tiniest bit of gas. She already tuned it for herself and I didn't have the skill. I did, kind of, but was way out of practice.

After jumping the curve, I wove in and around the chaos of wrecked cars and saw my car ahead. A dazed Rebecca shuffled around and tried to get in the car.

I pulled over and carried Rachel over. "Rebecca. Can you drive?"

She ambled with dazed eyes. I did the only thing I knew to wake her mind—I kissed her. "Can you drive?"

Her eyes came alert. "You kissed me."

"Get Rachel to the house. I'm going to get Nicole and Wesley." I placed Rachel in the back seat and made sure Rebecca had her seat belt fastened and drove off. "She needs care. I'll send Nicole and Wesley to help."

NICOLE 1000

"Why yes, of course. Is he going to be fine with us making a date without him here?"

Nicole did not know, but she knew how to be confident. Deacon Williams and his wife, Beth, already had the prepared forms filled in for the two couples for the course and they would leave before ten if they didn't do something. She told them of the accident, how they talked about keeping the baby, and being married. She wept and didn't need to fake it because he wanted to keep the baby.

"So, you would like to set a date?" ask Beth. Beth's emotions were excited for her.

"Yes."

So now she and Wesley looked at open dates for Nicole and Corey's wedding.

"Corey asked everyone for congratulations," said Wesley. This changed the mood of Gary, the deacon, and Beth. Wesley's emotions were full of concerned, but those two had been friends since they were little and he had been covering her crazy ideas for two decades.

Beth and Gary had the registration program on the church computer system up. July twenty-seventy was open. "I would only be seven months pregnant," she tried not to cry.

Beth put her arms around Nicole. "Dear, we are Catholic. For us, the first baby comes any time. It's the rest of the kids that take nine months. My first baby was born after five months of marriage and he is in law school."

Nicole laughed. "I am so unprepared." *Would Corey approve of a wedding date?*

"Oh, don't worry dear. We are signing you up for that special Saturday and let's go over this entire package."

She had a huge packet and Wesley sat next to her, dumbfounded. He helped her hold packets when the whole building shook. The front doors flung open and three men in black ran in. The two normal sized men were next to a little guy who couldn't be over five feet.

She recognized him. He was the one who wanted the arranged marriage to her.

She screamed. Wesley and the deacon strode forward, and the two normal sized men were vampires. The normal sized vampires punched Wesley and the deacon across the room. Beth ran to her unconscious husband.

The two vampires grabbed Nicole.

"I'm pregnant!" she screamed.

"Be careful. We will soon have a druid in the delta region," said the short vampire.

They carried her out, and she couldn't fight two vampires. Wesley charged from behind. They stopped and one flung Wesley over their heads. Her friend since elementary school rolled to the curb along the pavement and struggled to stand.

"Wesley!" She screamed.

Rebecca told these fantastical stories of how Corey was a superhero. He would storm in and enemies fell before him with his flowing hair, muscles, and good looks. He could use fists, tonfa, or would pull something mundane off his belt, like a pen. But Rebecca said that when Corey showed up, he was a hero from the movies and it bothered her to be rescued. Nicole felt a little jealous of those stories. She had secretly wished Corey would be the same superhero with her, just once.

Then she lived one of Rebecca's descriptions. Rachel's bike with Corey riding it jumped the curb, roared into a wheelie and crashed right into the vampire holding her legs. The vampire's head hit the ground, with a motorcycle wheel spinning on top of it. The sickening splat and tire squeal caused blood and white stuff came out of the vampire's mangled head.

Corey rolled to the curb near the skidding bike and threw one of his knives. It hit the five-foot vampire square in the throat. Her man charged towards the normal sized vampire holding her. Corey ripped off his helmet. His hair flew out, and the wind caught it and there he was, her man, the movie star hero.

The vampire dropped her just in time for Corey to kick it in the groin and swing up with his helmet and smash the face of the vampire. Just that fast, Corey pulled out his knife and cut out the vampire's heart.

Nicole held onto the car and stood.

"Nicole. Are you hurt?" Corey held her and looked into her eyes, "Are you hurt?"

She shook her head no. "Just shaken up and confused."

"I need you to be Hero Nicole. I know you can do that." He needed her to be a movie star hero.

Corey needed her and believed in her. "Yes."

Her man put her in one of his superhero rescues. He cut out the heart of the second vampire. He put both hearts into Rachel's helmet. The vampires smoked on the pavement in the morning sun.

Wesley staggered over and she guided him to her passenger seat. She was a hero and had to help. Wesley needed help.

Corey cut the heart of the short guy. He, too, smoked. That heart plopped into Rachel's helmet. With ripped pants and a scraped-up leg, her man jogged over to her car with a limp. The vampire bodies were disappearing.

"Wesley, I saw you slow them for me. You're officially a front-line fighter," said Corey. "Nicole. The other car has hurt and unconscious people heading to my house. I need you to do two things. First, any communication device that's contacted Nathan or the Command Center needs to be powered off and the little card removed."

She wanted to ask why, but Hero Nicole needed to do this. She would be a hero. Her phone came apart first as he continued.

"Second, treat the injuries at the house. I need you to triage everyone and make the best care decisions."

"I will do that," she had the voice from when she was a loner. That wasn't Loner Nicole, she would be Hero Nicole. She got her wish to be rescued by Hero Corey, and that was enough. She would rescue others.

He placed the helmet on Wesley's lap. Then he cast a spell three times as he held each heart.

"Don't lose this. I'm going to rescue Nathan and Madison." He put the helmet with the three hearts on Wesley's lap.

Corey kissed her and ran to Rachel's bike. The tumble did a number on the plastic engine coverings. He put a piece of the pretty engine protector in the back seat of her car. She grabbed Wesley's phone and called 911 as she backed out and got an ambulance on its way to Saint Andrew and drove to Hero Corey's house. Hero Corey and Hero Nicole had a wedding date.

COREY 1030

I parked at the parking lot CJ used when they went to lunch and ran to the side near some trees. The ride had raised my blood pressure the entire way with nervousness, and seeing the scene did nothing to calm me. The front of the administration building was a madhouse. Nothing should have happened here. My fears about something around Nathan must be correct.

I cast *Squirrel Messenger* and described Preacher Jon. *They compromised something around Nathan. Securing all electronic communication.* Next, I cast another *Squirrel Messenger* and described Trish. *They compromised something around Nathan. Remove all phones. Miles report status with squirrels.* The third cast *Squirrel Messenger* never got cast. A boot kicked me in the ribs. I landed and rolled unceremoniously.

Out of breath and aching ribs put me in awful shape. Suit stood in front of me and I barely had time to pull out tonfa and stand. "Il giovane guerriero è druido." Suit smiled as if he knew the kick had sealed this win.

I had to go defensive immediately, with the breath knocked out of me. With the root stance. I prepared to block. Suit pulled out a knife. My step caused my breath to catch. The ass had broken the same damn rib as last time.

Knife hand strike met sweep block. Rising punch met hair grab but the follow up back elbow strike sent me failing and when I struggled to pick up my tonfa, a knife embedded in my gut. Pain welled through me.

I didn't have time to pull it out as Suit came to finish me. I raised my sole tonfa to absorb his landing that never came. Meat had charged and tackled Suit. I didn't have a finishing strike in this position, but Bar Fighting Corey did. I jumped up with my one tonfa and struck down on Suit's prone head with the full force of the tonfa punch and hit the ground when it split his head. Brains and blood splattered Meat and I. Two mangled heads in one day was a record for me.

I rolled over and tried to breathe.

"He was better than you," said Meat. I didn't get to see his face, but he sounded shocked.

"There is always someone better," I panted out. The cold ground was hard, and it made the pavement chips sting my skin.

He helped me up. "Our ribs match."

I nodded. "When The Tribe allows it, I'll support your name of Ox."

"How about that, Meat? Pass the combat test and you'll be able to change your name on Corey's recommendation," said Fitz, jogging behind me.

"Fitz, they compromised something around Nathan," I got out. "He and Madison were here to watch for unusual activity."

A squirrel came to me and spoke in Miles' voice. *Fought a Dark Fey. Will be fine after patch up. Trish got a picture of the monsignor.*

"So, something went down?" Fitz was calm, but his always aware stance looked more alert.

"I destroyed the primary spell site at the Rec-center in Roswell," I said. "Then the Delta Region sent vampires to kidnap Nicole, and she's pregnant. Everyone is injured. Shit went south." I pulled the knife out of my gut. It differed from mine and was longer. Suit had good taste. I looked at the mess I made of his head. He was dead.

Meat had a med kit and stuffed my wound with gauze and then wrapped me. His medical training was decent.

"We'll get Nathan and Madison to you," said Fitz. "Go take care of the others. Meat, take the Little Rachel's bike to a hiding spot. Corey, take my truck."

I hugged Fitz and then hugged Meat. "Thank you." Then I drove Fitz's truck to my house.

Chapter 24—Hero Work

Nicole was in charge and needed to get everything done. "Wesley, don't mention the motorcycle or her helmet to Rachel. We need to be all business."

"Uh," groaned Wesley.

She knew Wesley couldn't comprehend things, but she kept talking so he wouldn't drift off.

She parked behind Corey's car and Rebecca stood with tears. Nicole sensed Rebecca was worried for Rachel and couldn't move her.

Nicole ran over. The wind picked up and she and Rebecca shivered. Rachel didn't move, but her skin got goosebumps.

"She's breathing, but unconscious." Rebecca wasn't in much better shape.

"Corey, put me in charge. That means I know how to help. Wait! I can help." Nicole ran to Corey's car and got his large med kit out to pull out an ammonia sniffer. After she ran back, she cracked it and waved it under her sister's nose.

Rachel stirred, and Nicole and Rebecca drug her to a sitting position. The tan seats were blood free, but the t-shirt on her head showed splotches of blood.

Her car door opened. "Sit down Wesley. Do not move until I get you." Her voice carried it as an order and her door shut.

Nicole sensed Rebecca's emotions. Her friend was in pain and worried.

Nicole needed to be the hero. "Corey keeps oxygen locked away for emergencies. I'll get it out. You can sit and help her breath."

"What happened?" Rebecca was confused. Nicole did not know how she drove here.

"Explosion and an ambush of the Delta Vampires. They tried to kidnap me after the explosion happened."

They got Rachel into the door and onto the couch. "Let me get the oxygen and then Wesley."

She ran back to the closet. She would not panic because she was Hero Nicole—the one who would marry a hero. Their baby needed a mother who could be a hero, like her father.

She carried the green bottle and tubing to Rebecca. "I'll be right back."

The stiff cold hit her, but she ran to the car and grabbed the helmet. It was disgusting, but the three hearts still beat. She ran and put the helmet in the sink to brace it from tipping over. Then she ran back outside and helped Wesley to stand. His torn clothes showed scrapes covering him. He could barely walk, but he was smaller than Rachel and Nicole helped him in.

She got him into the living room and removed his pants and shirts and looked for anything bleeding. Nothing severe. "Does anything hurt more than the rest?"

His eyes didn't focus. She took a deep breath and rested her hand on the red sofa. He lay on the hardwood floor and moved his head slowly. "What's your name?"

"What?" he was confused. He had clouds in his thoughts.

Nicole announced around the room. "I am in charge. If I ask you a question, you will answer it!"

She put her hand on Wesley's forehead. "What is your name?"

"Wesley." His voice was weak, but clear.

"Wesley, have you had lunch?"

"No, but I'm not hungry." He formed a picture of Rachel in his head. *That was sweet.*

"Rachel is here. Lie down. You can sleep if you want to. Your concussion is light." She covered him with a throw blanket she placed on Corey's couch for snuggling.

"All lights stay off until further notice. Rebecca, I'm removing your shirt to check your wound."

"My head is fine. I'm just sore from the accident." Her thoughts were of Corey.

Everything looked well. "We don't know about internal injuries. If you get lightheaded, you tell me. I'm worried for him too."

"Rachel," said Nicole. She had oxygen flowing through her, and the pressure was a little high. She turned it so the ball barely floated.

The extra oxygen had made her sister more alert. "Wait. I sense Corey's ritual. I need to finish it or they will come back to life wherever their hearts are." Rachel struggled to say the words.

Crap. The vampires would kill everyone and kidnap her. "What do you need?"

"Box of bottles on patio and the hearts." Her sister's thought focused only on a Fey ritual.

She heard casting magic stopped injuries temporarily. Nicole ran out back and carried in a box with eleven mason jars filled with a clear but viscous liquid. She put it next to her sister.

"Open one for each heart and bring me the hearts."

Nicole ran to the kitchen and the hearts beat faster. She grabbed the helmet and ran into the living room.

Rachel took a heart, did some magic, placed it in a jar, and sealed it with more magic. She did that for each of the three hearts. "Move the box to a safe place and throw my poor helmet away."

Nicole moved the crazy magic mason jar box to the laundry room. Then she came back and undid the t-shirt wrap Corey must have done. "Okay, this is a nasty gash. Let me get the medical kit. Lie down on the towel."

She came back in and cleaned her sister's head and bandaged it better. It wasn't too deep, but it looked ugly and her hair had dried blood.

"Rachel, what color is your bike?" She tested her sister for a concussion.

"If Corey saved me, and we look like this..." She sighed. "My bike is gone."

"Corey was riding it when I saw him last, but he ran over a vampire to rescue me." Her sister's eyes stayed focus on Nicole.

"My poor bike." Rachel leaned back on the couch.

"Wesley's first thought was of you," she said.

"Wesley, can you hear me?" Asked Rachel.

"Yes." Wesley mumbled, but it was clear enough.

"Promise me you'll work with me on getting better in bed. I really want this to work out." Rachel did not know what she just did.

"I, err, promise." Shame filled his thoughts.

"Don't be ashamed Wesley. Rebecca had to train up Corey. I'll ask Corey to give you some advice from experience and Rebecca will show Rachel how she trained Corey and it'll be fine." She turned to Rachel. "You need to time your comments." Rachel couldn't focus on thoughts, but this was for Wesley's benefit. She had been friends with him since elementary school.

"Sorry, but I think I'm falling in love with him," she answered. "That could be the only thing that stands in our way."

"Okay. That's better timing." Nicole sensed Wesley's thoughts turned back to being with Rachel. *How did the baby sister end up as the love guru?*

Two concussions, one beat up person, and vampires almost kidnapped the healthiest person. Wait, she wasn't done. "Everyone. Phones, pads, anything electronic, now."

She gathered them up, removed batteries, powered them down, and removed sim cards. Then she laid them out on the breakfast bar.

"Wesley, check in. Rebecca, check in. Rachel, check in."

"Headache." "Sad." "My poor bike."

Nicole sat in Corey's chair and felt her stomach. She knew she wouldn't feel anything yet, but she wondered... "Oh my god. I scheduled a wedding date with Corey, and he doesn't know."

"Congratulations," said Rachel.

Rebecca reclined her seat on the couch. "Was it an accident?"

"How is than an accident?" asked Rachel.

"We needed more time, and she got it," said Wesley. "He'll understand."

"I'm glad my panic can keep you all alert." Nicole couldn't believe what she had done.

A car pulled up and Preacher Jon got out and helped the two witches, Samantha and Morgan, out of the car. Nicole sat back down.

Preacher Jon escorted the two witches in. "Who's in charge?"

"We have two minor concussions. Rachel's the worst with the gash. Wesley and Rebecca are beat up. By the way, Wesley attacked three vampires head on with the deacon."

"Here you go dear," said Morgan. "All your pamphlets. Please tell me you haven't told Corey you have a wedding date."

Nicole slumped in her chair. "It seemed like a good delaying action."

Morgan chuckled. "Nicole, I am rooting for you. I really am. This has been the best few days of my life since Corey showed up in New Hampshire."

"Relax Nicole. Your wedding date is July twenty-seventh. You'll have six months of classes to get him used to the idea." Samantha put her arm around her.

"Today might be sketchy," said Morgan. "Rebecca, sweetie, your grandmother is a strong woman and says you'll become stronger. I'm seeing why."

Preacher John checked Rachel's gash. "You did a great job, Nicole. You stay in charge and I'll give you an update. EMTs are taking care of the Deacon and his wife. They also know you are safe."

"Wait. Corey said I only needed to be a hero long enough to triage and kill electronic devices." Nicole should be through.

Morgan took off her long purple coat and patted Nicole on the shoulder. "Oh honey. I like you but I was with a druid for two hundred years of a passionate love. I changed from a normal witch to the most powerful witch whoever lived—feared by everyone. Buckle up." Then she bent over and whispered. "I think you can pull this off, which is why I'm routing for you."

"Nicole. Trish and Miles lived. He soloed a Dark Fey inside of Sacred Heart and lived."

"Corey made us power up in the Moon-eyed fight," muttered Rachel. "He wanted a stronger team, not to be stronger."

Preacher Jon nodded. "That boy did that and then discovered a hack in one of Nathan's channels and stopped the bleeding today. Yet, he failed out of college." He shook his head. "An ambush almost took out Nathan and Madison. They will survive the gun-shot wounds. Corey killed the man he called Suit with the help of The Tribe. If our Druid makes it here, he will be in the worst medical shape of anyone."

A pickup truck squealed to a stop outside. Corey stumbled out of it. He wore jeans, bandages, and wounds.

Nicole didn't even remember opening the door or running outside. She was helping him. "I did everything. I was Hero Nicole."

"Need Earth," he rasped.

She guided him through the house, through the sliding door to the patio. He created berries and handed her a handful. She removed his pants and laid him down. "I'll get the medical kit."

She handed berries to everyone.

"Lay me next to him," said Rachel.

She was right. Rachel's calming influence would help Corey focus on healing. She gave Rachel a berry and laid her sister next to Corey, and they lay in an embrace.

She worked on Corey's wounds. "Corey, sweetie? Can you hear me?"

He snored. Well, she'd tell him later.

She ignored the icy wind while preacher Jon started a fire in the fire pit. Knife wound, contusions, scrapes, broken rib, and who knows what internal injuries. She got to work because she needed to stay Hero Nicole a while longer. But tonight's sleeping arrangements were going to be different.

Chapter 25—Rough Weekend

I woke up with Nicole on one side and Rachel on the other. Rachel and I wore pajamas, and Nicole wore a thick nightgown and socks. It was cold out and the fire died down. I sat up and barely kept my yelp in.

"Let me get it for you," said Nicole. She started the fire.

"Help me to the bathroom?" I asked. She gave me a sleepy smile.

Before I got back in, I created more berries, and Nicole left to hand them out. She came back, and I wanted her to kiss me. "Could you kiss me gently?"

"I was Hero Nicole, like you asked." Her smile was wonderful to see.

"I never doubted you." She'd torn through the church in plain sight, doing things she did for years. I was the nervous one that night.

She snuggled over a little closer and placed her arm on top of my chest, and started kissing me. They were pleasant, gentle, and loving kisses. It made me happy. I made it home alive and was healing with the combination of a full connection to Earth and a full connection to Rachel. My Nicole saved the team yesterday, gave me medical care, gave me the best situation for my powers to heal me, and now kissed me gently. I was so lucky to have her.

"Oh, you are so sweet. I'm going to cry. I did my best to be your hero."

"Are you two kissing? Come here Wesley." Said Rachel.

"You two cannot have sex," said Nicole. "That's too much for concussions."

"We can take an hour break, Rachel, if you want to go inside and snuggle in private." The patio was a little crowded and it may be too cold out for the others.

"No, they both have concussions. You can go inside and embrace, but no sex. I am serious." Nicole was firm.

She was right. Stupid actions like that could make the injuries terrible.

Rachel said nothing as she stood and pulled Wesley up. He had not changed and still wore jeans, socks, and a shirt. They walked inside and Nicole kissed me again.

"I need to tell you something," she said between gentle kisses.

"Okay." No news could be worse than what happened in his plan.

"Telling stressful news is recent to me. Can I relax you first?"

"No." She grabbed me and slowly kissed my chest. "I won't be able to do anything for you and we need to deal with situations healthily."

She kissed my cheek and said, "Promise to think before you answer."

"Promise," I said. With the knife wound and the rib, and the motorcycle crash, I'd have to, anyway.

"So, I needed more time in the church to get to ten am." She wrenched her hands together.

I had forgotten her part of the plan yesterday. "Okay, I gave little instructions."

"Well, after I signed up for the classes, I told them about the baby and I signed us up for a wedding date on July twenty-seventh." She halted.

I did not know what to think, so I did as she asked and thought through it. Being pregnant was a traumatic experience, and she was the one carrying the baby. She was there and following what I asked her to do. A smarter man might have figured that as a possible outcome. Luckily, this was about love. Love and fighting were all I could think through.

Her logic was fine, and she did nothing wrong. But now he was on the way, just like I thought, and he was going to hate me. I had predicted the whole scenario and now the kid would have a father who he hated. The more important question was Nicole.

So, if we were going to have a baby and raise it together, then being married made more sense. But that wasn't why one got married. There was a mystical force where we fell in love and went from the love of friendship to something different. *Right?* We were on our way. I could feel love growing and we had seven months. This was possible. The two of us couldn't be stupid and we'd have to communicate through all problems and not run away, but we could fall in love in that time. We'd need time with just the two of us, but yeah. I was down. "Okay, I've thought it through."

She was crying and smiling. "I followed your entire thought process. Why do you think he's going to hate you?"

"Let's talk about when I'm healthy. We have lots of months and everything you did was fine."

The sliding door opened. "Are you two, okay?" Rebecca stood there with her hands on her hips. "I came out because Rachel and Wesley took my bedroom."

"Those two better not be having sex with concussions." Nicole jumped up. "I told Corey about the marriage and he said the baby is going to hate him."

"Nicole calm down. Corey told us he still had the killer thing, and he hadn't come to terms with hating himself. We've fixed one of his three issues. Of course, if he hates himself and thinks he's a killer, he believes the baby will hate him." Rebecca put her arm around Nicole, who cried on her shoulder. She glared at me.

"I was fine with the marriage and said she did nothing wrong. Why am I a pariah?" This made little sense now.

"Corey, it's her hormones from being pregnant. You're fine. You warned everyone and acted just as we predicted." Rebecca patted Nicole on the back.

"We did think that, didn't we?" Nicole sniffed.

Maybe the hot girl's club was smarter than I thought. But I needed to announce an engagement in the Fey Court. "Could someone toss me my pants? Plus, my messenger bag. I have a new spell book."

"Where do you think you're going with a knife wound and a cracked rib?" asked Nicole. "No." she was firm. "No woods either. The spell book can wait." Nicole turned around and pointed at me like I left her in charge. Wait, I had left her in charge.

"I need to announce the engagement in the Fey Court."

"Stay put, Druid of the Spring Court," said Verenuala. "The news has traveled and we need to convene the court for the announcement of a Consort to the Druid of the Spring Court."

"Listen to Verenuala," said Nicole.

"I will tell the bard and check with her on her status and let her know," said Fionnestra. The daoine strode into the house and out of my sight.

Verenuala grabbed a couple of pieces of wood for the fire. When he stoked the fire up, he sat next to me and Nicole. "Future consort, if you wish to join your... what's the word humans use? Husband."

"He's not a husband yet, he's a fiancé until we are married," said Nicole. She was clearing up her sniffles.

"Oh, I like that word so much better." He rolled it on his tongue. "Fiancé."

"Druid Corey, you have done well and are the pride of the Spring Court. You and Rachel joining is more than we could have hoped for."

"Go back to sleep, Corey. You need to heal. I'll bring you breakfast later," said Nicole.

I laid back down.

REBECCA COOKED WITH Nicole and tried to get everything out of her head. Morgan and Samantha strolled in and she made their plates first. Nicole's face changed. "Oh, be calm. Corey is asleep and others are ready to eat," said Rebecca. She needed to get Nicole back to acting properly. Pregnancy was no time for a proper young woman to toss out every rule.

Nicole giggled. "Sorry, you're right."

"You are the first group I've even known brave enough to join the Spring Court. Thirteen hundred years and everyone chickened out. Now I see why." Morgan grabbed breakfast and ate with them.

"You had altercations with Winter Court and the Summer Court," said Verenuala.

Morgan laughed. "Yes, I have, and I have no intention of ever getting mixed up with a court that can bring passion and intimacy to bear."

Rebecca took a pain pill to help her put the dishes into the sink. She rested on the breakfast bar. Though she was healthier, this was a lot of effort for her. The daoine and the witch trading lighthearted barbs were almost too much.

It was time to block off thoughts about the baby and Corey's thoughts on fatherhood. Corey had handled this remarkably well. The real problem was that he'd be killing more people this week, and he didn't differentiate between enemies and everyone else. He hadn't even put self-defense or defense of his family into the mix.

They finished breakfast, and Samantha asked Rebecca to talk. She struggled to the back bedroom Preacher Jon had slept in and sat on the made bed. Samantha looked at her with sadness.

"So, witches are an inconvenient class. We have power, but we can't do anything directly. We have too much knowledge and when we can affect the world, it's by doing things anyone could do. Morgan is the most powerful witch that's ever been, and her force of will has been more important to her than her magical power."

"You kept Corey alive after the Moon-eyed battle." Rebecca heard Corey was on death's door and the two witches flagged down Miles in the SUV and cast a spell with vials they forced down Corey's throat to save his life.

Samantha chuckled. "We prepared that combination of elixirs twenty-five years ago and we could use it once. But we're not here to talk about that. You are despondent and it's a despondency that will get many people killed."

"I could have had everything. It is sinking in that Corey will never be mine, and it's all my fault. Plus, there is no way to fix Corey's hatred of himself."

Samantha did not flinch. "One at a time. Okay, how did you mess it up?"

"I broke up with Corey because he didn't fit into Grandmother's vision for me to be successful. But my new friends do not fit her ideal either. But when Nicole needed Corey, I helped her to keep her as a friend."

"I see," said Samantha. "You've let someone go to be free and there is a real chance you'll lose them. It sounds like it was self-sacrifice to save a friend."

"I thought they would have broken up by now, but they will get married and have a baby. Everything I wanted with Corey."

"You'll always be friends with both of them, and Corey will always love you."

Rebecca couldn't help it and tears ran down her face.

Samantha hugged her. "There, there. You know, never in history has the Scion of the True Church ever been friends with a druid, never mind the Protector of Earth."

"But I agree with Corey. A world without love is a world not worth saving and I'll remain loveless." Rebecca still carried her grandmother's handkerchief.

"Let me tell you a story. There was a wise, kind witch who would make a splendid mother who agreed to bring a child into the world. However, the agreement stipulated, she had to give him up after the baby turned six months old, since that was the only way, the dark forces wouldn't kill it. After carrying the baby and caring for him for six months, she gave the baby away and did not know where they took him."

Rebecca cleared her tears and finally answered. "That would be rough. Give him up forever or keep him and wait for the day your baby would die."

"Yes. The pain and loneliness every day. The feeling of sorrow and uncertainty of if I robbed myself of a few years of his presence only for him to be killed, anyway."

"How did you deal?" Rebecca observed this woman. She understood this dilemma.

"I trusted my decisions. Then one day twenty-three years later, he showed up at my church." Samantha had tears in her eyes. "He let me braid his hair and let me introduce him to my friends, even though he was trying to be incognito. All the animals came around to be with him and I got to console him when he remembered a father figure he had lost."

"You're Corey's actual mother!"

Samantha nodded. "Yes."

"What do you think I should do?" Rebecca did not know.

"I believe your second problem has the answer to your first problem."

"Corey hating himself? How is that?"

"Is Corey going to reason his way to a philosophical solution?" Samantha smiled at her.

Rebecca mopped up her tears and smiled at the thought. "No, he'd need a mentor."

"A mentor or an example of someone he respects," said Samantha. She nodded. "Like you."

"Is the Scion that powerful?" Rebecca knew the answer.

"I think you should follow the advice you give Nicole and talk with Corey." Samantha gave her a hug.

PREACHER JON HAD MANUAL printouts of the enemy forces. Since they'd release Nathan and Madison from the hospital tonight, he'd wait to disseminate the printouts until everyone was together. Except for Corey. Corey could start reading with his college dropout brain. Well, he would give them to him after he did the most important thing. He ambled outside to join the young druid lying on the patio with his connection to Earth.

"Corey, how are you doing?" Preacher Jon wished he had worn a coat. Corey looked warm in the animal skins next to the fire pit, but Preacher Jon would rather be in a casino in Las Vegas than freezing in North Georgia.

The young man winced as he rolled over. "Other than the broken rib, knife wound, the life changes, being beaten up, and having the entire team injured because of my plan, I'm great. How are Nathan and Madison?"

"Leg shots in a public shooting. Nathan saw the shooter and tackled Madison to the ground before the first shot, so they got lucky. Each wound was superficial."

"Bullet wounds hurt, regardless." Corey rubbed his shoulder.

"You'd know. Now others can vouch with you."

"Man, my plan went south." The young druid was blaming himself for things no one could have predicted.

Preacher Jon chuckled. "Even you admit that the monsignor being in Sacred Heart with a Dark Fey, the Delta Vampires attacking at the same time, and spies with the compromised account made the plan more challenging."

"There was a lot going on." Corey smiled, seeing his own understatement.

Preacher Jon laughed. "Your plan put the church in disarray, and nearly ended the threat. However, we have something more important to discuss first."

"Go ahead." Corey appeared to want to sit up, but his rib pain prevented him.

"Stay relaxed. You don't need to stand until morning." Preacher Jon grabbed a few pieces of wood and left them near the fire pit so Corey wouldn't have to move far.

"Sounds like a plan."

"Rachel and her mother were very close. I am saving her mother's engagement and wedding band for her."

"That makes perfect sense." The druid was so close with Rachel, the young man's smile lit up his face.

"That's why I want you to have Margret's engagement and wedding band. My wife's."

"That's... Those are your memories." Preacher Jon had finally shocked the young man.

"Corey, she was a good woman and a good wife, but we loved as friends and did our duty. I don't regret the marriage, but this ring would mean more to Nicole than to me. Please take them and propose to Nicole in front of everyone." The old gambler handed him the ring.

"Whoa. Wow. I don't know what to say."

"Save it for Nicole. Now onto the other item. I will go over the results with the team tomorrow morning, but you may want a head start on what we know of the church's plans and current numbers and fighting capability." He handed Corey the folder. Preacher Jon knew there was nothing but bad news inside of it. The news was so bad that he would fold while sitting on the big blind.

Corey began to read and Preacher Jon walked into the warm house.

Rachel and Wesley were cuddling and talking like future lovers. Corey was the most injured and healing on the patio. Miles and Trish were working at their store. They would release Nathan and Madison from the hospital tomorrow with the bullets removed. Rebecca was lost in thought on the couch.

Nicole was showering and would rejoin Corey in his outdoor bed. Samantha was lying down. It was time for him to do the last item. He needed to finish the containment. He prepared himself and got ready in the main bathroom. It was unusual to see Corey's house anything but immaculate, but this was the first time it received such heavy use.

Nicole strode past him. "Nicole, you are doing a wonderful job being in charge. There is no need for anyone to get anything done until tomorrow. I will visit Carol and finish the Haley containment."

Nicole looked around the house. "If it wasn't to keep an eye on those two and Corey, I'd have nothing to do."

Preacher Jon smiled. He'd come back in the morning. There were a few too many young hormones flowing around here.

THE DRIVE TO THE HOSPITAL did not take long, and he could sidestep security and procedures using his magic. No one with authority who made rules could stop him from getting what he wanted. It was how he kept Corey, Miles, and Rachel from having records or doing time until they got their life on track. It was how he rebuilt the Southeast forty years ago and how he rebuilt it again eight years ago when disaster struck. If he needed to bypass an authority or rules set up by authority, he only needed to focus on his powers and take the actions that came to him.

Carol was in orthopedics as the doctors tried to figure out how a fall broke so many bones and ripped so many tendons. Richard stood outside her room. He did not look worried.

"Hello Richard. How is Carol?"

"She is progressing nicely. They have a few nurses bathing her right now and the room is just too crowded."

Preacher Jon chuckled. "I don't mean to laugh, but I spent a night with eight hormonal young adults, and they'd have handled this much differently."

Richard chuckled. "What is the Fey situation like there? Carol and I were talking about vacationing at the cabin."

"Make sure you're healthy. If you have a partner with you, couples cannot withstand it."

"Corey and Rachel?" Richard was concerned because he knew they were friends who had never crossed that line.

"From what I gather, they can withstand it, but it's because they have protective sun tattoos." Preacher Jon couldn't conceive how those two moved around Fey so easily.

"Miles and Trish told us it's incredible and not something they'll do very often." Richard looked at the door to the hospital room that held his wife wistfully.

"That is the best way to handle the Fey pheromones."

The heavy wooden hospital door opened.

"All done," said the cheerful nurse, walking out. Four nurses in blue scrubs walked out with a cart.

Preacher Jon followed Richard in. He stayed behind in case his friend needed to pause at the entrance.

"Oh, hi Jon. It's good to see you." Carol's voice sounded tired, but she looked better. He can't imagine how Corey had double the wounds Carol was getting healed. But then again, a witch can make a healing concoction—one that could prevent death for a small time. They made it for an adult when the child is being born. It used the placenta and fresh seed from the father. Then the spell needed to sit for two decades. Corey had been on death's door, held together with magic. Moon-eyed magic, Earth Power, and Witch magic.

Those who made the plan to bring back this druid's bloodline did everything they could. They also hit the top flush with Corey. Old Donnie's dream from forty years ago and the fears and hopes were not only true, they'd guided the world toward safety.

"You are looking so much better." Preacher Jon didn't need to exaggerate.

"The initial shock with no pain medicine and no build up is always a big deal. But did it pay off?" Carol's voice was stronger than it should have been after two surgeries.

"Corey led the team and destroyed the main spell site, fought off an attempted kidnapping of Nicole by the Delta Territory Vampires, killed the Vatican operative known as Suit, Trish got a picture of the monsignor, and everyone survived. Corey has one cracked rib and knife wound, and there are a few healing concussions. Nathan and Madison are in post operations to have bullets removed, but it was another impossible job. They nearly finished the threat in that one plan."

"Without their main spell site..." Carol's eyes opened.

"Corey just about did them in. Guessing, he is going to go all in on the river and attack the only site they have left in Alpharetta. He can do it any time. He knows he has the upper hand and doesn't have to wait until the twenty-second." Preacher Jon couldn't believe Corey split up his team and pulled this off. They gathered every bit of information and scared the monsignor into overestimating the size of Corey's force.

"How did they get it done?" Richard tried to figure it out.

"Corey can travel between the cabin and his house in seconds. He also spread out his team in twos. No one would have tried anything this crazy against a more powerful foe, and they surprised them. Heck, no one would have known the places to post teams." Preacher Jon shook his head. "But that's where the good news ends."

"The church merged defenses to one site, and it's near impenetrable?" guessed Richard.

Preacher Jon nodded. "I'll give the briefing tomorrow, and Corey is reviewing it now."

"Keep us up to date," said Carol, "but this was the most effective heal of my lifetime." She drifted off to sleep.

Preacher Jon waved and shut the door quietly behind him with a wave to Richard. He took the elevator to the fourth floor.

Down the sterile hallway, he knocked on the door for Haley's new room. Anne, Haley's mother, answered. She held Corrinne.

"Monster?" asked Corrinne, the two-year-old.

"Nope, this is the Monster's friend," said Anne. She was tired, but much happier than she was a few days ago when her daughter Haley was in the intensive care unit.

"How is she?" Asked Preacher Jon.

"Come in." She waved him in. "You would not believe the change. The doctor raved about the onsite treatment and how she got the right care so much faster than reported.

"Third man syndrome." Preacher Jon smiled when he said that.

"I know you," said the young woman in the hospital bed. "You're related to Nicole." The young woman had one IV in her and looked in good spirits despite a broken arm and broken leg. "I cannot pretend it was not him," she added. "If it was important, I might, but Corrinne wants to see the man who killed the monster."

"Monster?" said the little girl.

Preacher Jon got out his new phone. He pulled up a picture of Corey and showed it to the little girl.

"Monster! Monster!" The little girl pointed to the phone. She clapped.

That seemed pretty definite.

"I need to see him too," said Anne. "He dated my only child through high school and now saved her life and my granddaughter."

"This is what we call a break in containment. Do you mind if I sit?" Preacher Jon had a hectic couple of days and his energy ran low.

"Of course, I'm sorry," said Anne.

Preacher Jon pulled Nathan's scrambler device out. Nathan verified it was still safe from his hospital room. When it was on, he said. "This is scrambling words and no one can eavesdrop on or record us."

He paused as he brought two more people into this part of the world. "There are a small percentage of people in the world with what we call the spark. It grants powers. Corey's spark is bright and is Realized, what we call people who use the spark. He is a druid. A 'stories from old' magic casting—talks with plants and animals, druid."

"I wouldn't have believed it before I saw the thing with the rhino head," said Haley.

"Momma? Monster." The toddler wanted to jump on the bed, but Anne held onto her.

"Corey killed the monster," said Haley.

"Soon, Corey is proposing to Nicole," said Preacher Jon.

"Little Nicole?" said Haley. "I held her for her first period."

"She is twenty-one now and they have a torrid relationship. They already set their wedding date for July twenty-seventh. But the important part is there is a brief period before battle plans and the enormous battle starts where Anne could bring Corrinne to meet Corey."

"Battle?" asked Anne.

"The group of kids... err, fate has tasked these young adults with saving the world, and Corey is leading the way." Preacher Jon couldn't believe how easy those incredible words came to him. "I know what it sounds like."

"When I saw the cliff, I knew no one could climb down. I was despondent and prayed for a miracle. Then I heard Corey's voice saying he was on site. No one. I mean, no one in VASAR was surprised. Then I heard bullets and then the talk of a monster. I doubt you could surprise us." Anne had seen too many unexplained things tied to Corey in two days.

"Tonight will be safe. This should help with Corrinne's insistence of saying monster over and over. After the battle, whatever day it is this week, we will talk about other meetings."

"Thank you," said Haley. "Is this why they don't know when they'll release me?"

Preacher Jon smiled. "You would be here for two more days as it is. If it's more blame safety considerations and me."

Haley chuckled and grabbed her side. "Thank you, Corrinne will be better after tomorrow."

Preacher Jon grabbed his device, turned it off, and left. He drove to his condo to relax and sleep at home tonight.

Chapter 26—The Final Plan

Rebecca came to her senses. She could reason out her solutions. Why was she melodramatic? She knew Corey would always love her and keep her in his heart. She had friends, and she had a team. Samantha was right.

It was time to act her age and perform her duty. She accepted she would keep Nicole and Corey together. It was time to accept her position in the team.

Nicole walked back to Corey. "Nicole, could you help me up?"

"Sure, what's up?" She helped Rebecca stand around the pain of the wound.

"Time for me to act my age."

Nicole laughed. "If you're not a grown up, where am I?"

Rebecca grimaced and unblocked the thoughts of her being the Scion. "I admonished Corey for not being on the team and I've only had one foot in." She placed her hand on Nicole's shoulders. "Please tell me you can forgive me. I've held back from the team."

Nicole put her hand over her mouth. "Of course, I forgive you. As much as I screw up... and Corey knows part of it?"

Nicole's face changed and Rebecca thought about her powers.

"I see. You've never thought about it. Wow, I even helped you carry the box."

"In your defense, that was a traumatic day for us." Rebecca smiled.

"Yes. I'm down with your plan and there is nothing to forgive. Even if you weren't a crack shot, your ability to navigate us throughout all this adult stuff has made you an all-in teammate."

They shuffled outside and Nicole sat next to Corey, who had a couple of pages with notes. "I'm ready Corey."

He looked up from his prone position on the animal skins. It was forty degrees, and he wore shorts out here on the sunny patio. His face contorted in pain when he tried to sit up. He took a couple of breaths while he held up his index finger. "Okay. Go for it. What are we ready for?"

"I'm ready to join the team, as you've kept secret for me. Do you have a plan?" She felt resolute.

"I have two depending on when you were going to declare. With this much time, we can be safe. Do you know your powers yet?" Corey was trying to put on his shirt and Nicole kneeled by him and helped him pull it on.

"No. I know I'm the Scion of the True Church. That's it."

"You have some type of turning predictions into truth. Priests cannot use magic within twenty-five feet of you and you have real-honest-biblical, no-cost healing. It was you who kept my heart beating on the drive to Dr. Kanoska." He winced in pain again.

"You've been sitting in pain knowing that anytime I accepted my powers, I could heal you with no cost?" Rebecca wanted to cry.

"I know more than anyone the cost you've paid. I would never ask you to pay a smidgen more."

She wanted to say he was infuriating, but this is how he thought. "So, much of the world will know when I announce this. I figured you had a plan." Rebecca turned when the sliding glass door opened.

"He fell asleep on me in mid-sentence," said Rachel.

"How boring were you?" teased Corey.

"His sentence," she exclaimed.

"He has a concussion," said Nicole. "Cut him some slack."

"Am I crazy for wanting to be pregnant with my sister?" She asked.

"Hold that thought," said Corey. "It's good you came out." He pointed her to a chair.

Rachel pouted but sat.

"The four of us are about to tie ourselves together and not just for the next couple of years. Long story short, the Delta Vampires want Nicole and not for marriage. That was a convenient excuse. I think Old Donnie rooting them out of the panhandle a long time ago caused a century long grudge."

"Uh," said Nicole. Nicole was going to be more shocked.

"I've already told Nathan that Nicole is to go nowhere without Rachel or I." He had to hold his gut for a minute.

"I knew there was more to that statement," said Nicole.

It shocked Rebecca that Corey was laying things this close to the truth.

"I wish we had more concrete information. To be honest, Rebecca and I are guessing." He pulled up short of saying everything.

Rebecca needed to chime in. "To be fair, the guessing involves a kidnapping, and a continued threat without even the pretense of an arranged marriage."

Nicole nodded. "I hadn't thought about it, but the kidnapping made little sense for an arranged marriage."

Corey continued. "Put that aside as part one. Once Rebecca takes the next step, she will have as many people trying to kill her as the rest of us."

"That's why you're saying we can never be separate," said Nicole. "There's no one who can defend us except each other."

"Yes." Added Corey. "Rebecca is jumping out to a head start. The Earth gave her the power from the Snake-Hunter. That's why I powered up you," he nodded to Rachel. "Miles and Madison. I don't know how to power up Nicole that fast."

"We'll be together forever," said Rachel. She grinned.

"Within reason. We all have defenses, but alone, they can target each of us. But yeah, double dates, scoping out new friends and love interests. Now, I have two plans around Rebecca claiming her powers and they both have plusses and minuses."

"I'm going to be the happiest," said Rachel. "I love you guys and I want to be together always."

Nicole looked at Rebecca. "The cost is going to be the highest for you. Is your whole life self-sacrifice?"

"No. Sometimes I feel sorry for myself and it feels like that, but I'm really lucky." Rebecca leaned into the chair with Nicole's help.

Corey started laughing, then the pain caused him to cough.

Rebecca glared at him when he gasped and grabbed his chest. "What's so funny?"

"I get the sacrifice part and then needing to be around Nicole and I forever. But you're right. The final part of the decision is to become one of the most powerful people in the world and be required to stay with your friends."

Rebecca laughed at the absurdity of her position until her side caught. "Okay smart butt, what's your two plans?"

"Plan one is to ride into the fight with no announcement and you declare your Scion powers at the start of the fight and we surprise them," Rebecca could tell Corey didn't want that choice.

"That sounds cool," said Rachel. "Like boom, new secret Rebecca powers."

"But Corey wants his other option," said Nicole.

"Let me give you the reasoning. The church is already overestimating us and becoming defensive, which plays into our strengths. I want to keep up that pressure. Nathan has a leak in his computer stuff, so the plan gets implemented, with no one finding out outside the patio. The plan takes on both issues. We go to a specific place and Rebecca declares. She heals me, Rachel, and herself. I go to the Fey

Realm and travel to the territory pole in Mississippi and prepare to take over the Delta Region lands with Earth Power on their Territory pole. I travel back and we act like nothing happened."

"As soon as you cross the borders, they'll identify you," said Rachel.

"I won't cross a border. Someone has a tree in the Tree Foyer next to their territory pole. I'll be there ten minutes and be back." Corey had a devious smile.

"They won't be able to prove anything since they're not allowed to keep Corey's signature unless he crosses the border," added Nicole.

"Except, they are part of Nathan's leak and will know it's me and have to assume I have their tactical information." Corey grinned.

"That is sneaky," said Nicole.

"Well, we aren't done," He smiled like he was about to be bad. "When everyone shows up tomorrow, we leave and attack the Alpharetta Administration Circle with everything we can on short notice, however at the beginning of the attack, I remove one heart from the jars of bliss. I put it on the ground so it registers as them being in our territory and stake it with wood until the sunlight disintegrates it. It will appear as if a vampire from the Delta Territory was there with the church and I killed him at the start of the battle."

"It'll give me the right to travel to their territory pole and cast *Own Area* on their lands.

"Oooh," said Nicole. "Even I wouldn't have come up with something so devious."

"Why is that devious?" Rebecca couldn't figure it out.

Nicole smiled, and she looked at Corey with admiration. "The Delta Territory has been asking where their people are since they were last in the Southeast Territory. But since there are no bodies and no death signatures... Corey has kept it quiet and Rachel's concussion kept her from remembering she finished a ritual; Nathan told them to kiss off."

"I finished the ritual? Maybe I did bump my head," said Rachel. She touched her bandage gently.

Nicole chuckled. "You were unconscious for at least fifteen minutes."

"I was wondering how I got here."

"Anyway," continued Nicole. "When the vampire shows up again... since we have his signature legally—since he never crossed the border to leave—it will look like they ambushed us and there are still two vampires who could attack us."

"You plan to attack them and make it appear to be in self-defense," said Rebecca. Corey sat there with one of his infuriating smiles.

"I can sense devious talk," said Morgan, as she slid the door open and joined us.

Rebecca looked at the timeless witch. "How does Corey figure things out when he's not dumb, but he's not the sharpest knife in the drawer?"

"He's like his father—a druid. He thinks like him and has the same requirement to fall in love as him." Morgan winked at Nicole. "Druids are infuriating."

"I don't mind being called dumb," said Rachel. "Could you explain it to me?"

Morgan laughed. "People have hated me for centuries and I end up with a soft spot for a bunch of kids. Okay then. Druid magic isn't linear. The mind of a druid works in arcs and circles. He doesn't comprehend straight lines."

"Wait, I've sensed him thinking in straight lines," said Nicole.

"Only what he truly cared about before he came a druid," said the witch, who took off her purple coat and covered Nicole. "Sense him now."

"He fears me." Nicole stepped back. Corey gathered himself, but he fought off something in his mind.

"Love and fighting were all he understood before he became a druid," said Rebecca. She finally understood.

Morgan took the coat back. "I thought so. He has an arc to his father, my coat, and fearing me the first time he saw me wear this coat."

"So, I think A, then B, then C, and end up at D. Corey will start at A, go to G, say Q makes no sense, and end up at D," said Rebecca.

"More like E, a solution we'd never come up with." Morgan put her long purple coat back on.

"This is exciting," said Rachel. "How does Nicole use that to fall in love?"

"It took me a while for this one," said Morgan. "Women with the spark attract Corey. Nothing else. It's why Rebecca, Nicole, and Madison were equally available in his eyes."

The witch looked at Rachel. "You would be too, except for how strong the love of friendship is between you two. Strange—love overriding a Realized power."

"Maybe the power of being attracted to magic chicks is overrated," said Corey.

Morgan shook her head. "Anyway, the potential lover needs to prove competence and impress him. He wants a woman better than he is."

"Why isn't he pining over Madison?" Asked Nicole.

"I can answer for myself. She couldn't handle being different. Madison is a boring, generic person where Stormy was intriguing." Corey tried to take control of the conversation, but everyone else was too involved.

"That solves that," said Morgan. "Good on you, young man. The next requirement he has is the person needs to be a little devious. You know, something along the lines of tricking everyone to believe you're dating, so you don't worry about getting hit on."

"Or being a secret super spy," said Rachel. She was almost jumping up and down.

"Yep, assuming you have the physical and emotional stuff figured out, the last thing is you need is to teach him something using the way he thinks. Like teaching him to fire a gun by equating it to kissing a person while riding a donkey." Morgan looked at Rebecca and shrugged.

Corey looked indignant. "It made perfect sense. You prepare to get on the donkey, which will take you where you want the bullet to go, but you want to squeeze soft so the target's lips are split with the tongue, which is the bullet."

Nicole, Rachel, and Morgan looked at Rebecca. "I thought he was joking and then later even thought he learned because I let him shoot barefoot. Yeah, I prepped the saddle by giving him the grease marked scope and the yellow tinted glasses. He mounted the donkey by sighting his target. He imagined the lips he wanted to kiss and pulled the trigger gently to slip his tongue in."

"Exactly," said Corey.

"Man, my life became a lot harder," said Nicole.

"You think this is hard? Wait until he loves you and you realize he melts you with a touch." Morgan sighed. "So, where are we going?"

"Do we know where the monsignor is?" asked Corey.

"Hold on," said Nicole. She dialed her phone. "Hey Nathan, Corey has one quick question as he plans. Do we know where the monsignor is?" There was a pause. "Nope, that's it. Thanks, bro. Feel better." She hung up. "He's at Saint Andrew because he thinks we'll show up there. They released him from the hospital and they're filling out Madison's paperwork."

"We're going to Sacred Heart, then to the cabin for a little fifteen-minute task, and then back here. We should pick up dinner too, since we haven't eaten out in a while."

"I'm going to declare myself the Scion of True Church near Sacred Heart?" asked Rebecca.

"Near?" Corey got out a coughing chuckle. "We're going inside to do it to show them we have no fear."

Morgan laughed and clapped her hands. "Oh, I am so going with you. Someone helps that crazy druid stand."

Chapter 27—The Scion of the True Church

I led the small group to the SUV and Rachel carried a sleeping Wesley out to join. "He's really sleepy," said Rachel. She cradled him like a baby as she sat in the back seat of the SUV.

"Did you really tell him you wanted to get pregnant after you've been on three dates?" asked Rebecca.

"Yep. Why? Am I not supposed to do that?" Rachel tried to put the seat belt around the two of them.

Nicole interceded. "Rachel, put him down and leave him some masculinity. Plus, slow with the pregnancy talk for a while unless he brings it up."

She poked her lips out and pouted.

I hugged Rachel. "Hey, it's a new person and a new type of relationship. You'll get it." She smiled and put Wesley next to her and buckled his seat belt.

With my hand around her waist, I helped Rebecca get in next to Morgan. Nicole slid into the driver's seat, so I got in the passenger seat.

"I hate to be a party pooper, but now is the time to think of combat." She looked at Rachel. "People with concussions get a pass."

"Wait," said Rachel. "I flaked out. Be right back." She ran around the house and came back holding her surujin and kama.

Sheepishly, I got out of the SUV and struggled to my car and got my weapons belt and waist pack. Every step stung through my ribs and I tried my best not to wince on the way back.

"Should we get our stuff one at a time?" teased Nicole. "Not all of us have concussions."

I got in and tried to catch my breath. She leaned over and gave me a kiss. "You were cute walking like I embarrassed you."

"I'm leaning your seat back. Try to relax," said Rebecca.

After I reclined more, Nicole drove us to GA-400 and past the perimeter, where we picked up the connector and got off to head into downtown. I barely could see out the windshield, so I watched out the passenger window at the disappearing nature until we arrived in the middle of mankind's arrogance.

In the back, Rebecca explained to Rachel how topics like marriage and pregnancy scared a lot of men and needed to be brought up slowly. Hell, I was okay with the idea, and it scared me. Nicole grinned and patted my leg. "It's okay to be scared. I am too."

"Oh dear, you have no idea what will happen to your heart with that man," said Morgan. "Nevertheless, I envy you."

After a bunch of wasted stopping and starting because of oodles of cars, Nicole pulled into the parking lot and my ribs had finally calmed in time for me to walk to the front door.

"Are we really going in?" Asked Rebecca.

"Why are we at Sacred Heart?" asked Wesley, sitting up.

"We've been here all the time," said Rachel. "All the dreams you had about your girlfriend talking crazy weren't real." She waved her fingers up and down. "You both had concussions and Rachel is not crazy."

He chuckled but couldn't contain it and broke out into a laugh. They may actually be a good match.

"Let's go into the church," I said. "We will feel better in ten minutes."

"Yes, because churches always make me feel better," grumbled Morgan.

I set my plan firmly in my mind. Tonight, I'd send out squirrels to potential allies, telling them in honor of Old Donnie—I scheduled our attack on the Alpharetta Administration Center at high noon—which coincidentally—was when the Dark Fey was weakest.

Rebecca held my right hand, which had turned cold and clammy. Nicole took my left, and she shook.

"Our death visions just changed. Corey, you have two deaths now. You either fall to your death tomorrow, fall to your death New Year's Eve. But you also either die of old age or pushed off a stone bridge in a cavern. I've never seen two deaths before."

There were worse things than multiple deaths.

"Nathan kills Madison, Trish, and I in three days... wait, he's taken over by something. Still, we all die." He became sad. "Rachel, you either die in a cavern with a hawk-spider thing along with Nicole or you're both killed by an invisible Dark Fey that turns into an old-time gangster." Wesley's trance was taking a while. "Rebecca, you have over a dozen deaths and they're all different between tomorrow and New Year's."

"All right Rebecca. You win!" I joked.

She looked at me as if I needed to shut up.

Morgan clapped. "The chain of events you two have kicked off is remarkable."

Our group, more sedate, walked to the entrance. I read the sign as we strode around the corner to the front and saw they called this place a basilica. We moved in silence up to the large open door and walked in. The five of us ambled through a partially opened door in the foyer's right into the main chapel, or whatever Catholics called the place where the preacher told you how you were going to burn in hell.

We stood in the center between the pews that lined up inside the column underneath the domed ceiling. "Unless you want a place more specific," I said. "You can declare here."

There were perhaps a dozen people in the pews, mainly gathered near the front. They milled around and no one paid us much mind.

"May we light prayer candles?" asked Wesley.

Seemed weird, but what the hell? Or wait, what the heck? Rachel followed him up and when he kneeled, Nicole and I took a step back out of Rebecca's way. "I hope you know what you're doing inside of the Oratory of the Basilica of the Archdiocese of Atlanta," whispered Nicole.

I looked at her and wondered if she was making those words up.

She smiled at me. "Normal Catholics don't use them, but they're real."

We couldn't talk any long as Rebecca flung her arms open and announced, "I am the Scion of the True Church."

Every window, stained glass or otherwise, lit up. Golden light surrounded Rebecca and shined down from the dome. She rose ten feet in the air. She wore a white robe and held a jeweled scepter. Golden wings sprouted over ten feet on each side of her white robe, and a halo appeared above her head. *Yep, I used to date an angel.*

She turned to me and the vision from the command center of her came to me. Instead of a white robe, she wore her gold breastplate and her skirt of gold plates hung to her knees where golden greaves protected her shins. A golden vambrace protected her right arm, holding a sword of white light, while she strapped her blue and gold shield on her other forearm.

I shook my head at the vision and reality returned to her wearing the white robe, the wings, the halo, and holding the scepter.

She looked at those of us who watched below. The others in the area dropped to their knees and cried. Rebecca surrounded us in the area with a golden light and it healed all wounds. It felt so good to breathe without pain. The golden light didn't touch Morgan.

The ancient witch whispered to me. "Even the heavens fear me."

"The time has come for love to rule the church," said this new floating angelic Rebecca. She floated downward and turned into our regular Rebecca.

It was time to go. I waved to Rachel to grab Wesley, who stood dumbfounded. Rachel talked to a ghost image of her mother!

There is no way we could interrupt this, but it lasted less than a minute before the apparition floated up into the heavenly light of Rebeccas.

I grabbed Rebecca to help her walk. "We gots to go," I said.

The six of us gathered and moved outside. Rachel's smile and tears of joy made it hard for her to walk, and Wesley helped her.

"I zapped the cameras and the recordings," said Rebecca. I'd like to say she seemed normal, but I put my hand around her waist and guided her by the shoulder back around the corner to the SUV and assisted her in.

When everyone was in. I leaned over the front to buckle a still dazed Rebecca. "Don't wait! Drive to the cabin!"

Nicole took off. I buckled Rebecca and Wesley buckled Rachel. I got into the seat and we were a mile up Peachtree when Wesley and I finished buckling ourselves.

"Is Rebecca...," said Wesley.

I turned around and interrupted. "Wesley, you know how we intercede when Rachel says things that freak you out. I'm interceding now on behalf of Rebecca. She needs our compassion and friendship because she just took a big step to help save the world. Rachel, you too. Take your time."

"Thank you, Corey," said Rebecca. "I felt your heart, and it's wavering between warlike and gentleness. Please stay gentle."

"I'll help," said Nicole.

"Nicole, you too," said Rebecca. "You two are so much alike it's frightening."

"Busted," I whispered to Nicole. We couldn't help ourselves and snickered together. I couldn't tell whether Rachel grinned for her mom, for us, or for everything at once.

Rebecca gazed over at Rachel and Wesley. "You two have your hearts aligned. Your mother has joined the other druids in the area of Earth Power and who knows—Corey may bump into her."

"I'm still the same Rebecca," she said, answering a few unasked questions. "To help you all understand, my powers line up like yours. My three blessing domains are Believer, Sanctuary, and Curing. Like you are big in circles and Rachel is powerful with music. I am powerful in Angelic Form."

"Thank you for explaining it," I said.

I turned around and saw Rachel grinning. "If you were to fight, Corey. Could you win?"

"I don't intend to fight, Corey."

This had been bugging me. "Rebecca, if I went rogue, what would you need to stop me?"

"No Corey," said Nicole.

"I—I don't know. Just think of happier thoughts." She looked tired.

"The happy thought of this is we may get people to leave us alone if we had our own built-in failsafe." Maybe not, but if we had plans for Nicole, it'd only be reasonable to have a plan for me, and a plan for Rebecca.

"It's a nice thought Corey, but your enemies don't negotiate based on trusting you," said Morgan. "Think of enemies as enemies."

"Let's wait until we survive New Year's Eve to discuss it. I'd like to take a little nap to let all this sink in." Rebecca leaned back. "I'm uninjured for the first time in weeks."

"Good idea," said Wesley. Rachel hugged him.

I leaned my healthy body back into the chair and thought about swinging on the cabin porch with Nicole while holding hands. She smiled as she drove, and I kept the image in my mind for her.

"STRETCH AND PEE, WE won't be here long," I said. I jumped out of the car, relieved to feel healthy again.

"Corey," called Rebecca. She ran to me. Nicole and Rachel ran to her as well. "When you and Nicole giggled in the car together, I saw what makes your hearts stay gentle. Neither one of you will ever be able to control the other. It's only an intense, passionate love that keeps you two from succumbing to becoming warlike."

I knew exactly what she meant. The truth she spoke ripped through me and I knew it as fact. I needed unconditional, passionate love. Rachel's love was unconditional. If Nicole gave me passionate love, I'd be of a gentle heart. The vision of the four women came back to me.

I held up one finger and jogged over to the spare weapon's chest. Grabbing the wooden shield, wooden sword, and a wooden nunti-bo, I said, "I'm sorry, but the vision became stronger."

I handed Rebecca the sword and shield. "Rachel, Rebecca needs to learn these and Nicole needs to learn the nunti-bo." I handed the Okinawan spear to Nicole.

Rachel grinned and barely contained her excitement. "Corey, pick up the staff to help me train them. My mom said both of your visions were correct and we'd be your front-line defense."

"I use guns," said Rebecca and Nicole at the same time.

I held Nicole and put the vision back in my head.

"You knew she'd be an angel in the command center?" Nicole shook in my hands.

"It was a vision, and I'd just become conscious. Samantha said if they came back and stayed strong the more, I'd need them."

"Well, we look cute and apparently our breasts grow," said Nicole.

"Probably not the vision, just a memory with artistic license," said Morgan. "But if he remembers it, the vision was strong."

"What do I wear?" asked Rachel.

"Your breast stayed the same, but you're wearing a leather stripper dress." Nicole looked at the weapon she held and turned it over.

"It's a dress so she can fight with all four points exposed and stay covered," I explained.

It was too late. Rachel put her hands up and started gyrating. "Wesley, I'm supposed to become a stripper! How should I dance?"

I left poor Wesley on his own for that question and jogged to the red maple in the back. Two steps through brought me to the Tree Foyer, where I thought of the Magnolia tree for the territory pole in Mississippi for the Delta Territory. I whooshed to there and took two steps through and pulled out my gps.

After I saved the coordinates, I put a circle around the territory pole. I was about to leave and remembered Morgan's comments to treat enemies as enemies and cast *Own Area* on the pole. Ten minutes later, I sensed the entire Southeast Territory and the Delta Territory. I felt the Fey magic coming up from the ground just like back home. Boy, there were a lot of vampires here. I grouped them by state and there were over seven hundred in each of the three states. Fortunately, none of them were within ten miles, but I would not push my luck. I looked at the gps map and I was in the middle of a state park.

The magnolia tree looked old, so I cast *Mature Plant* on it to give it some health and I stepped back through it, thought of my red maple, whooshed back to the large red maple, stepped through it and was back behind the cabin.

I jogged back to the SUV and saw the others milling around.

"You are all set up?" asked Nicole.

"I'm done," I said. I couldn't hide the smile on my face. This was so much easier than I thought. "Let's pick up dinner on the way back to the house."

We had been on the road for maybe fifteen minutes when my phone rang and Nicole's phone rang. Nicole answered hers on the car speaker setup and I answered mine.

There was echoing and a squelch before whoever called me hung up.

"Hello grandpa," said Nicole.

"Are you and Corey together?" Preacher Jon was over the car speaker.

"A bunch of us together. We wanted something new for dinner and we're driving around," she said.

"Can we hear Corey's voice?" asked Nathan over the car speaker.

"I know you missed me. I was voting for tacos, but I'm not getting a lot of support. Would you want tacos?" I asked.

"Is there anyone there who knows how to use a phone?" asked Nathan.

"I'm here Nathan," said Wesley.

"This is important," said Preacher Jon. "Wesley, can you do the video feature on the phone and show everyone in the car with you?"

Nicole handed the phone back to Wesley. He touched it a few times and started moving it around. "There is Morgan. Here's Rebecca, here is me, here is my beautiful girlfriend," He moved around and Rachel hugged him and kissed him on the cheek. He pointed at me. "Here is Corey, and Nicole is driving."

"Wait, wait." I leaned over and kissed Nicole on the cheek.

Preacher Jon wasn't talking to us, but we heard him say, "That's pretty conclusive."

There was another voice I picked up, but it sounded like Leander. "It does, and without proof of border crossing, we should end this call until there is proof."

Nicole kept driving, but stole a look at me.

"I understand," continued Leander. "But this is all speculation."

"We'll see you at the house. Pick up food for everyone," said Nathan.

The phone hung up.

"I wonder what that could be." I leaned back and chuckled.

Morgan chuckled as well.

"So, Corey. I'm sorry I paid little attention to you. I heard you were traveling to the territory pole. But what did you do?" Rebecca sounded concerned.

"Saying it was me is speculation." I turned and winked at her. "But if I were to guess, it sounds like a druid took control of the territory pole, which makes the whole ground light up with Earth Power with a tad of Fey magic."

"Corey!" Exclaimed Nicole. "I thought you were setting up. The vampires can't make it there during the daytime."

"Wait," said Rachel. "I want tacos."

"Was this an act of war?" asked Wesley.

"Wesley, these are the same vampires who tried to sacrifice Madison to a demon in Chattanooga, then tried to capture my pregnant fiancé—which you bravely tried to stop and took a beating for—and are still in our territory." I left a few details out, but this was correct.

"Wait, the Delta Vampires were the Chattanooga Vampires, too?" asked Wesley.

"That has been validated," said Nicole. "In fact, one of the thirteen is one vampire who tried to kidnap me and tossed you."

"Then we already were at war," he sounded glum.

"They only have a few hundred vampires," said Nicole.

"Why do you say that?" I asked.

"They have to register all Realized," said Nicole.

"There are at least two thousand vampires spread out over Louisiana, Arkansas, and Mississippi." I focused on that region. "It's hard to get a count of that many, but two thousand would be on the low end. It's at least seven hundred in each state."

Nicole's face changed. She dialed the car phone. "No one talk but me."

"Hey Nicole", answered Nathan over the car speaker.

"Take me off speaker."

Okay go.

"There are thousands of vampires in the Delta region. How many do you have registered?"

Hold on. Two hundred and fifty-one minus the three in our region. So, two hundred and forty-eight. Nathan was typing into the computer.

Nicole shook her head. "Does anyone you know have travel rights to the delta region?"

No, they canceled all travel rights before the thirteen vampires came to Chattanooga. He paused. *How sure are you there are over a thousand vampires?*

She looked at me, and I gave her the thumbs up. "One hundred percent. It's over two thousand."

Shit.

"We are getting tacos and burritos. What color food day are you on?" Her face was back to normal. We turned the information in.

Can you get me a steak and black bean bowl? Nothing else. I'll drink coffee with it.

"Sure thing, Nathan. See you soon." She shook her head and moved into the right lane to drive a bit slower.

They hung up.

"Can you guys clue us in?" Asked Rebecca.

"Yes," I repeated. "Help me out."

"Corey, how many Realized are in the Southeast now and how many do you think we could count on?" Nicole was acting like the sharpest knife in the draw and, to be fair, she probably was.

"One minute." I leaned back and closed my eyes and focused on my territory and reduced the barrier, I counted thirty of the unnatural creatures split evenly between werewolves and vampires, Thirty Realized are the mountains in The Tribe's area, our group, the Moon-eyed, and the faeries. "Seventy-five, not counting faeries or Moon-eyed. I'm guessing we could get fifty for our fight against the church tomorrow. Maybe a few less."

"Oh no," said Rebecca.

"Exactly," said Nicole.

I wasn't sure what they were talking about until I remembered Wesley used the term war with them and they had us outnumbered nearly thirty to one. "On our best day, we could take maybe one thousand."

"Our super best, blessed day," said Rachel.

"You know, a burrito sounds good," said Wesley.

PREACHER JON SAT IN the room and looked through the food the group had picked up. He finally decided on a salad with no meat. Atlanta had picked up a better quality of southwestern food with the influx of new people, and the food had an excellent flair that reminded him of eating with Mayven.

He'd already called Anne to remind her to bring Corrinne tonight. Corey had gone off script and Preacher Jon didn't know if it was good news or bad news yet. Tonight might be the last safe night.

Nathan and Madison strode in, arm in arm, through the kitchen. They each limped and supported each other. "Everyone, Madison and I are officially dating, dating," said Nathan with a. broad smile. Madison kissed him and the two sat down. They had matching legs next to each other wrapped from the bullet removals.

"I even told him I was ready before the first shot," teased Madison.

Those two were happy and holding hands. His eldest grandchild had a girlfriend, and it was an excellent choice. Preacher Jon had thought he would need to make an exception for Nathan and having a child, but these past two months had changed the fortunes of seeing a new druid born. There could be three branches and multiple babies in the next couple of years.

Corey walked over and said something to Nathan. Nathan stood with Madison's help. Samantha and Morgan sat on the couch and Miles and Trish brough in dining room chairs. Rachel and Rebecca sat against the wall under the tv, which never seemed to be used. Corey stood in the kitchen doorway next to Nicole. They left a big open area in the large room.

"Everyone, I also have an announcement," said Miles. He stood up. "I wronged Nicole and I want to apologize. Because of my frustration, I accused her and Corey of having crazy girl sex, but it was clearly loving sex and am so sorry I said such a misogynistic line to a friend."

Trish must have done a number on him.

"I accept and thank you, Miles." Nicole hugged Trish.

"Turn around," said Trish.

His youngest granddaughter turned. Corey was on one knee in the middle of the room and he held her grandmother's ring. Nathan was already in position for a picture. Nicole had her hands over her mouth.

"Nicole, things have been unconventional for us, but it should not rob us of pleasant memories. Before I bring you to be acknowledged as Consort to the Druid of the Spring Court, and before we begin marriage classes or go through all those pamphlets, I want your hand in marriage. We have known each other for eight years and grew up together. Our relationship started out torrid because of our familiarity and while things moved fast, they moved fast because of decisions we made. Nicole, will you marry me?"

She put her shaking hand out, and he placed her grandmother's engagement ring on her.

His wife who held her when Nicole's parent were dead and Rachel's were busy with Rachel. Sharing parents was good in theory, but there was only so much time and his wife picked up the slack. His wife, who died avenging Rachel's parents when she couldn't accept the church had killed both of her children. It was his wife who promised her the ring should she be married.

"Oh, Corey. Yes." She tackled him and they lay on the floor and kissed. The rest of the team applauded.

Nathan took some pictures and a video. "I'm sending this out and saying we expect a late July wedding and when we get closer, we will send out invitations."

Corey sat up and had that peculiar smile when he was about to say something untoward. "The biggest issue we have is I don't have a pet name for Nicole. I've tried honey, sugar lips, sweetie, and lover and I cannot find a pet name. It's driving me crazy."

"Nicole works," said Nicole. She smiled and added, "Sexy Pecs Norwood."

Preacher Jon didn't want to know.

There was a knock on the door. "I'll get that," said Preacher Jon. He opened the rarely used front door. He greeted Anne and Corrinne. The toddler yelled, "Monster!" and ran towards Corey and hugged him.

"Everyone, meet Anne and her granddaughter Corrinne."

"Anne," said Trish and hugged her. "It's been so long."

The room was chaos. Corey was already off balance on the floor when the two-year-old tackled him. She reached around and grabbed his tonfa. "Hibock."

"Oh my god," said Rachel and she ran to the patio. Rachel's eyes teared with pure joy.

Preacher Jon explained. "Anne is Haley's mother, and Haley named Corrinne after Corey. Corey rescued Haley and Corrinne while undercover and the operative known as Suit released one beast from the deep caves to kill Corey, hence the use of monster. This is a loss of containment, but it is under control." He added that for Nathan's sake.

Rachel ran in and slid on the hardwood floor to the toddler. "Here, these are your size." She handed the little girl a smaller pair of tonfa while Corey put his away.

"High block, mid-block, low block," said Rachel, and the little girl moved her hands. Rachel could not contain her joy.

The girl then said, "jab." She jabbed with the tonfa. Corey taught a toddler the basics of the tonfa telling no one.

"Here's a picture of me as a little girl with those tonfa," said Rachel and showed the toddler a picture.

"Baby." The toddler pointed to the picture on Rachel's phone.

"Haley was unconscious, and it was all I could think of to entertain her." Corey seemed embarrassed.

"Baby Rachel, Rachel," said his granddaughter with tears. She touched the picture, then herself. "Oh Corey, you are going to be such a good father. She remembered the moves you taught her with your favorite weapon."

Preacher Jon swallowed the bad information he wanted to give out. Tonight was a night for happiness and good news. All of his information was bad news.

"Preacher Jon, could you help me understand one thing on the report?" Asked Corey. He kissed Nicole. "I'll be right back, I promise."

Rachel and Corrinne were going over monster and tonfa moves.

Preacher Jon followed this young man who was about to be an in law in his family. He expected this years ago with the other granddaughter, but truth be told, things have worked out for the best.

Corey shut the sliding glass door behind them.

"Sorry, the night got blown up," said the young man.

"We don't have enough fun together, and we need nights like tonight."

"We gather ourselves and leave for attack at eleven am tomorrow and attack at high noon to honor Old Donnie."

"Fast timeline." It didn't shock Preacher Jon, though.

"It's a few days early, but the situation has changed and I have it on good authority that the territory that's hiding their numbers will try to thwart us tomorrow, but they won't be able to bring numbers."

Preacher Jon could read people and knew he got correct but incomplete information. "What will you need?"

"Rebecca, Rachel, Miles, and I will be out of pocket. We'll have our own vampires, werewolves, and The Tribe to coordinate. I believe all priests will disappear, other than the main one or two, and become Dark Fey at the start of the battle."

"Okay, give out more of an update on the drive over for the team and I'll start tonight. I'll walk in now, so now one suspects what we are doing. By the way, Congratulations."

The two shook hands. "Thank you."

The young druid started sending out squirrels and Preacher Jon walked in. He turned to his granddaughter. She showed off her ring to Samantha. "He'll be right back in."

Now he had to make sure lots of social media posts of a party went out tonight to provide even more cover to the team. His team headed to a fight with the strongest druid on record, a great team that included the Scion of the True Church, and they were still drawing to fill out a flush.

Chapter 28—Oh, we brought it.

The team had stayed up late and had a great night, and nearly everyone slept late. I still was able to get everyone ready to go at eleven. We piled into two large SUVs.

Preacher Jon held a clear sphere and a packet of papers. He looked tired. The noon sun reflected through the passenger window off of the sphere.

"I like you kids," said Morgan. "Adding to your angst isn't the best, but you may see your father in this large of a battle."

I struggled to get my game face on and turned to Morgan with undeserved snark. "Not my mother?"

"No, your mother is sitting next to you." She pointed to Samantha.

What an idiot I was. She had my last name. In New Hampshire, she treated me with kindness and introduced me to her friends. She saved my life, though she shouldn't have been able to find me and treated my friends like my mother would.

I groaned and my game face slipped.

"No." This witch with a normal build grabbed me by my armpits and lifted me as if I was a toddler. She got right into my face. "I saved his semen in case I wanted his child one day. Instead, we created a new line of druids. You will face your father as the man you are. Do you understand me?"

"Oh, be nicer, Morgan. He's gotten it together each time." Samantha admonished the other witch.

Dammit, she was right. My face was on. "Nathan, you type out orders to the other vehicle. Let me know who your contact there is."

"That's the Corey to meet his father. When you see him, look him in the eye and tell him one thing about yourself." Morgan leaned back.

"I will." I was ready. This was a fight for Atlanta and eventually for Earth.

"Nicole is relaying orders," said Nathan.

"Rachel and Rebecca walk up the middle with me. Miles, I want you to perform an end around from the side."

"Can I have Drisana?" Miles' eyes danced at the thought of the unicorn.

I thought for a second and it made good sense. Speed for Miles, extra attack, more Fey magic, and a bullet blocking shield. "Yes."

"I want non-combatants in the back and Madison shoots arrows from back there after granting Rachel her surujin. Nathan, you and Wesley watch the battle and direct our vampire allies, werewolf allies, and whoever has the leadership of The Tribe to take out Dark Fey with Preacher Jon. I need to take out a circle and Rebecca has to clean up the usurper clergy."

"I'm getting Battle of Camlann vibes," said Morgan.

"Pull to the back of the building and we will park along the road. I need Rachel's chops immediately. And this is important. No pregnant team members are to be around excessive loud guns."

"Got it," said Nathan.

"Now type out, I'm serious, Nicole. If I have to yank you away from something, people could die."

"Man, I wish I could hear the conversation in that car now," said Morgan.

"Me too," said Samantha. "The women have struggled to get a control of these young men."

"Unlikely controlling Corey," said Nathan. "Without him around, they'd probably have us subdued."

Nathan pulled onto the back street and the two SUVs parked next to each other.

I took out the jar with a vampire heart in it and threw it onto the grass on the other side of the road. It beat as it smoked in the sun. I took my large wooden spike and slammed it into the heart, and then beat it with my hardest tonfa strike.

"Good thing the Delta Vampires couldn't bring more than one to bear. I wonder if they're having trouble traveling," I said aloud.

Rachel, Rebecca, Miles and I came together, and I ran to the first open area in the park and began creating a large circle and I used seventeen focuses. After pulling one trumpet, I put it in my torc before securing it back around my neck.

I cast *Beast Bond*. When Drisana showed, I pointed to Miles. "Same plan, different battle."

"I love you Drisana," said Miles. Miles mounted and Drisana grew to the size to take advantage of the large man and his giant sword. They took off at a gallop.

The Administration building was barely visible through the park trees. It sparkled with blue lightning magic and the park ground in front lit up. I cast *Local Nature* to announce my presence and subdue the ground.

With a quick pat of my weapons, I strode confidently toward the park, despite feeling anything but. I contacted the small animals nearby and told them to run and hide. A fight was coming. One they could not survive.

Rachel sprinted toward us from a scouting position with her kama in her hands. "Miles is circling."

"No time for intricacies," I said. Which was good, there weren't any. "Seen our support?"

"You've got brothers," said Clive, with fifteen other vampires.

"And brothers," said Coach White with a dozen other were-wolves.

There was no time for greetings, Miles needed help. I wondered how Strumath would show up as he promised.

CJ and Fitz marched up. The Tribe is at full strength.

Corey addressed them quickly. "Okay, I'll walk up the middle and bind my circles. The monsignor will arrive. You guys, let the three of us fight him. There are dozens of Dark Fey ready to spring. That's where we need the most help and the three of us will be too busy to give direction. When Rebecca finishes the monsignor, I'll banish their circle and we'll go to the Fey world to announce my consort."

Preacher Jon handed out small maps. The old man must have stayed up all night.

Reaching out to the circles, and saw I could bind them all. I put the sickles and my magnolia seed pod in pouches on my belt. Earth's power pulsated and longed for this fight. The corruption had been here too long.

After Rachel was down to her skirt and sports bra and I wore shorts, I took Rebecca's and Rachel's hands. "Let's go. Stay within three feet." Both hands were shaking. "We need to move fast once they see this is our full attack and not like last time. They'll try to summon reinforcements."

"I must wear the robe. Scions aren't nudists like you two," said Rebecca. She was trying to keep her voice steady.

Rebecca handed the two of us hearing protection. These aren't quiet guns. She had a rifle with a strap over her shoulder and a huge handgun on her hip. I didn't know guns, but I knew enough to listen to someone who did.

Rachel put her kama on a rope around her waist and had the green surujin from Madison. She grinned.

We made a beeline for the door while the rain drizzled. The main pathway was on my right and I stayed on the grass.

"You weren't lying, right down the middle," said Rebecca, and her voice gave away her fear.

A window broke and Miles riding Drisana flew out and landed—in a cloud of purple smoke near our feet. "You, okay?" I yelled.

Miles gave me the thumbs up and charged the ex-Italian special forces with Drisana's shield up. For a brief instant I wonder how many of their forces were ready to go to standard duty when they viewed a Clydesdale sized unicorn charging them, projecting a bullet deflecting shield, carrying a giant of a man, wielding a ten-foot-long magic two-handed sword.

Refocusing on my fight, I viewed a man with red church robes trimmed in black. He wore a purple sash and a purple cape. I didn't know what any of that was, but the way he moved and the way others deferred to him meant he was in charge. But it wasn't the man from Trish's picture. *Twenty-five feet.*

To his right, in normal priest garb, was the real one. "The priest is the actual monsignor. The man to the right of the one with the purple dress!"

Roars bellowed. Howls began. Screaming came from around Alpharetta. The world turned black and white and sounds muffled.

"Do your thing, druid boy. I sense him," said Rebecca. "I call upon the power of the heavens as the Scion of the True Church!"

Nothing muffled Rebecca's voice, and the heavens opened and bathed the battlefield in golden celestial light. She became the Rebecca of my vision. Armored and holding a sword and shield of golden celestial light. Her head glowed with a halo and her golden wings flapped and sounded of glory.

I thought her sword was white in my vision.

She flapped up to the two. "Usurper," she screamed, and it bellowed over the battlefield despite the muffled sounds. "Behold true celestial power." A heavenly trumpet blared to further announce her arrival.

Church magicians shot magic at her from afar. She grabbed the blue lines of magicians and snapped them like they were string. She held the sword with her shield arm and pulled her handgun and shot the priest wearing the monsignor's robes in the head. He stayed down.

The monsignor raised his hand, and a circle appeared.

They made their biggest mistake when I recognized Strumath. He said he'd meet me here. Strumath put on a show of acting fierce and bound as I picked up the pace. I put a tonfa in my right hand and left my left hand free for the trusting part of my plan with my magnolia pod.

The monsignor pointed at me and scowled. "Be afraid or I release this monstrosity upon you and your girls." He spat out the world, girls. "Did your girl bard grow man muscles because you failed to satisfy her?"

He was funny. I had to give him that. But his misogyny would cost him. I wasn't his threat. Rebecca was.

Rebecca screamed again and priest bodies exploded and Dark Fey filled the courtyard. My senses of three dozen Dark Fey landed on the lands I owned.

An arrow whisked by me and a rifle shot rang out, and I kept moving to the monsignor. Rachel swung her weapon and stabbed a cat human hybrid-thing. From my left, I glimpsed an assassin with a knife, but Clive jumped over my head, and I heard a scream and blood spurted from that direction.

A Dark Fey leaped towards Rebecca, but Meat jumped from nowhere and tackled it in midair and they landed with Rebecca safe.

Arrows and bullets flew. As I got close to the monsignor and his circle. I dropped the Magnolia seed pod on my foot. Then next to the circle, I dropped and erased a section of the circle and hoped Strumath was ready.

"What?" screamed the monsignor. He spun backwards from a blast from Rebecca, and flung into the wall where black magic surrounded his body. It lifted the broken body, then sneered at me and glared at the golden light of the Scion. He punched Strumath with a fist of blue lightning, who fell backwards.

Strumath recovered and attacked Dark Fey from the back and the surprise caught them off guard. He fought where he was doing the best.

Rachel's voice rose to overwhelm the other sounds. She sang the saga of <u>The Battle of Chattanooga.</u>

Next to him, his distraction with Strumath allowed Rebecca to connect with her sword of celestial light.

"He's all yours Rebecca!"

The gargoyle circle in the basement had seventeen gargoyle heads for focuses. With my seventeen honeysuckle focuses, the resulting circle wouldn't be prime.

Three more for thirty-seven. I dropped and drew a new small circle and put the three new honeysuckle bindings.

I bound and initiated my two circles, then began the binding to take over all three. The power flowing through the battle called to me and threatened to rip me apart. I focused on Earth Power.

Thig na cearcallan còmhla agus cuiridh mi ri chèile iad mar aon agus bidh e leamsa.

The Spring Court appeared above my head. They watched the unfolding battle liked they watched Nicole and I make love. The screams of humans and the supernatural surrounded me, but I needed to focus.

Rachel's surujin strangled and penetrated. Clive fed upon another priest that could not cast a spell, and they kept Rebecca clear. Werewolves roared, vampires howled, and the Dark Fey scrambled.

In the back, enough guns fired to nearly overwhelm the guttural howls of the Dark Fey.

Rebecca did not know any stances and if she'd fought a weapons master, she was done. But she could protect others, heal and a sword of golden celestial light, even in untrained hands, was scary.

The Tribe numbered in dozens; we had a couple of dozen friendly vampires and werewolves, and we brought ten Realized in the SUVs. They barely outnumbered us! A gargoyle the size of Strumath made the difference, and I was glad he was on our side.

Another beast with a mandible for a head, dark as corruption, leaped for Rebecca. A green dagger from behind us came and caught it in the head. Miles charged forward, and Drisana scooped the Dark Fey with its horn as Miles chopped off the mandible head.

I bound the first circle, then absorbed the circle on the right. I saw a dozen brooms in the sky and they soared downward. With two circles, I started binding the third, and the battle had turned in our favor. Leander led a dozen witches in a wedge formation and brought a purple cloud to choke the Dark Fey.

I reached out to take over the gargoyle circle and felt its power. I lined up my three circles and got rejected. The thick blue circle whipped at me.

Rebecca turned and wailed, and the monsignor's body of corruption was falling to her onslaught.

The battle raged behind me. Rachel's beautiful singing voice rose, and I repeated the binding.

Thig na cearcallan còmhla agus cuiridh mi ri chèile iad mar aon agus bidh e leamsa.

My body tore from the power. A thirty-seven-focus circle felt beyond me, but I was out of backup plans. The strength of sacrificed gargoyle heads as a focus was obscene.

My body nearly burst from the Earth and Fey power filling me. Bright green light exploded and ripped through everything man-made near me. My sole focus was to lie as flat on the earth as I could and opened myself up to as much power as it could channel, until it overwhelmed me.

I passed through Bright Earth but didn't go to the Fey Realm. I was in a more beautiful Earth. It was not just vibrant, but I could see living power and life everywhere. I understood life, power, and love. Love coalesced with the Earth and made huge pulsing chords that a person wearing robes would come up and wrangle. Love was a physical thing, and it pulsed.

Old Donnie stood next to my prone body. "There you go Corey, don't stop."

"Old Donnie, you're alive?" Relief overwhelmed me. I so needed him.

"No, this is the place where we control Earth Power. It's part of Earth, but not really. It's like a Realm, but not really. Try not to come here because this is where dead druids come."

"I think I bit off more than I can chew." I had no energy to give more information.

"Ain't that just like you?" His voice had the partial scolding and partial pride from my training.

"Look," he continued. "I was right about a lot of things and wrong about a lot. The only thing holding you back is being true to your natural self."

Powers threatened to rip me apart as I focused on my binding. "I'm really not able to think through that right now."

"You were always impatient, but I guess now you've a good reason. Look, adults are just big kids who are still guessing. Once you find out I was a flawed individual who did his best, you'll make the next step of adulthood. But Corey, know I loved you and your heart was more than I could have hoped for in a new druid. You saved me and let me finish my life like I had been a good man. Keep to your heart."

"You mean be a Wartime Druid with a gentle heart?" So many people told me that it might be the right answer.

"See, you already explain things, so I understand them. But please do one thing for me."

"Of course, Old Donnie." I do anything for him.

"I fixed a lot of my problems with your help. You fixed some of them yourself, but there is one left undone. I was a shit parent—to kids you knew and didn't know. Please fix that screw up in my life, especially the nig one, and it will bring me peace."

"Old Donnie, I'd do anything for you." My mentor was a saint. Sure, he may have had an illegitimate legacy to track down, but how hard could that be?

"Thank you. Here, take to the next artery of love and life that pops up for the power to finish what you started." Old Donnie faded away, and another druid waved to me behind him.

"Will you be here when I need you?" I called out to him.

"Take to the Earth and you won't need me," said a faded voice.

Okay, Earth, I needed to follow everyone else's advice to keep a gentle heart.

An artery pumping life and love through it appeared. I grabbed onto it and pulled it into my body, and became part of something larger than life. The Earth wasn't black and white. I could see into all three worlds at once.

A vision of a bearded man in blue robes talked to me. *Say to Morgana her remembrance exists within me as a pleasant dalliance from the mundane.*

"I'm a confused druid trying to do his best." I tried to follow Morgana's advice and said one thing.

We all are, but you are succeeding.

The thick blue circle that kept the church power connected outside of Georgia lay before me and tried to engulf everything else. Rebecca fought it with light from the heavens. The circle pulsed blackness and fed everything. The whole of the world saw the heavens opened.

I floated above the Earth and saw a different view of Earth. Once I could focus, the Vatican caught my attention. I saw blackness taking over a city I didn't recognize. There were Japanese people fighting next to a Shinto temple.

Atlanta had a circle reaching into the Realm of Darkness and threatened to open up a portal. I focused everything I had and poured all the power into this black circle using my bound circle and banished it.

Multiple worlds exploded around me. The dead druid's place was gone and the artery of life and love ripped from me. Bright Earth exploded and the world of black and white was back. I lost control and the touch of the Earth.

Something happened to the world. It was spinning and getting smaller. Then I realized all circles were gone, and I was spinning and soaring upwards. The midday light was gone, and I saw blackness and a circle of blue and green below me.

I struggled to breathe. Gravity reclaimed me, and I plummeted.

No Earth Power existed this high up. This is why I wouldn't get on a plane. However, I could argue a plane would make me safer right now.

There was nothing I could do. No magic would save me, so I took stock of the situation and removed my hearing protection. The rushing wind ripped them from my fingers and I made a mistake because the rushing wind was all I could hear until it stopped, and I rode in the arms of a woman in a purple velvet coat.

"Druids should not be so high," said Morgan.

"I have a message from a man in blue robes and a long white beard. The one I told one fact to."

"You—you do?"

"Say to Morgana, her remembrance exists within me as a pleasant dalliance from the mundane."

I thought I saw a tear come to her eye. "Well, let's land among our friends. Druids are such trouble."

Chapter 29—The Consort to the Druid of the Spring Court

I looked around and saw most of the people in my life. Rachel, Nicole, Miles, Rebecca, and Preacher Jon. I wished Carol and Richard were here, but Coach White and Mr. Wilbanks were here. Clive and a bunch of his friends stood on the other side of me. Madison, Wesley, Nathan, and even Trish. Leander led a group of witches and Drisana kneeled next to Miles. I missed much of the mundane and celestial fight. All I saw was earth, circles, and Old Donnie. In some ways, that was enough for me.

Dozens of people lay on the manicured park grass and the stone walkways. The noon day sun and the five dozen of us in the park must have stood out. I bet this was a containment issue. Well, it was mostly normal. Vampires, werewolves, and witches looked like people, and Rebecca looked like herself. A couple of daoine and a unicorn might have stood out, but the gore of the Dark Fey stayed in the world of black and white.

A seven-year-old girl ran towards us. "You listened! You brought the other lady."

I sat on the ground and dug my feet in to connect with the Earth. Did I mix up Ellie's message? Since I was dating her and she was at the table, I assumed she meant Nicole. "I sat next to a lady, and you told me I needed both ladies by my side and the other lady wasn't with us? You meant Morgan from the gondola."

"Duh."

"Seven-year-olds who predict the future aren't as reliable as we would like," said Leander. He held his hand out and helped me stand.

"I can't wait for you to meet my mother," she said.

Leander whispered to me, "Her mother was caught in a time vortex in the eighties. It's unlikely we'll ever see her. Our best attempt to rescue her retrieved Elliana from the bubble."

I was confused until Elliana handed me a box. "Here, I told them you wanted this more than stupid magic," said Ellie. Her grin never left her face.

"You have been through a lot and I wanted to give you a gift of friendship," said Leander in a normal voice. "Elliana picked it out."

I opened the box and inside was a collection of magically preserved papers and seeds. I read the papers; they were beer recipes from the past thousand years. "Wow!"

"I told you," said Ellie and crossed her arms with the smugness only a seven-year-old proven correct could pull off.

"This is awesome! Even the seeds are here from the plant breeds they used." I couldn't believe it. After this batch was done, I'd get right into one of these batches!

Leander shook his head, but chuckled. "Was the squirrel you sent a message for help or a challenge?"

He had told me that if I was to go into a battle, I should invite others to prove I'm not a one man show. Of course, I invited him. "I'm not that smart. I just wanted help."

He shook my hand. "You saved the world with little help from those of us who should have been here from the beginning. But please slow down, because I'd like you to be around for a long time." He took Ellie and walked away for business. I covered the box and held it tight.

Mr. Wilbanks stood with another group of men who had recently turned back from werewolves. "This was the boy I told you about, men, and look at the man he grew into."

I tried not to tear up when Mr. Wilbanks said that. He was the first father figure in my life and the man I trusted in high school. I met a lot of werewolves, then through Coach White and Mr. Wilbanks, but they needed to get back to their home turf.

Clive had traveled with the two vampires from Charleston and other friends who weren't from the Delta.

Preacher Jon put his arm around me. "You did it Corey, you saved the world."

"We did it. We're a team."

Rebecca jogged over, and kissed me on the cheek. "I didn't have time to congratulate you last night." She immediately surrounded me with a glowing light.

"Rebecca, if it takes my whole life, I'll make it up to you."

Samantha strolled over.

Nicole came over and kissed me. She held up her hands. "Look, no powder burns. I performed communications and medical."

I put my arm around her. "Strumath!" I called to the gargoyle.

The gargoyle came over and his twelve-foot-tall body loomed over us all.

"I want to introduce you to my fiancé, Nicole. We will be married in July. Will you be able to join us?"

Strumath laughed like he did on top of Loon Mountain with joy.

"We might need two ceremonies," said Preacher Jon. "That way, we could invite our new ally to one." He turned to Strumath. "I can help you continue with the start you made with Corey."

"Corey," Strumath let my name roll over the rocks in his mouth. "Yes. I would like to talk more with Corey, eventually."

"Corey. We will discuss the difference between warfare and murder in a few days. Remember who took out the humans in this fight?" Rebecca kissed me on the cheek.

I realized what she was getting at and she shook her finger. "Not now. In a couple of days."

Preacher Jon got closer. "I'm going to keep my promise, but when I return, we need to discuss my sister Diedre and my niece and nephew, Tracy and Traci."

My mouth dropped. I didn't know what to say.

"I promise, you'll know everything." He let others crowd towards me.

Verenuala and Fionnestra skipped to us. Rachel hugged Wesley, who looked like he had gotten used to his girlfriend fighting with minimal clothing and not dressing before hugging him. The Spring Court changed a lot of our behaviors.

"This was so exciting," said Fionnestra. The two daoine had huge smiles and patted Drisana.

"Ready to announce your consort? We gathered the court and your battle has sparked considerable excitement," said Verenuala.

"Not yet, he isn't," said Nicole. She lugged over a suitcase. "We are going to look cute. I found a dress to match the shoes you bought me and I bought you a suit."

"Rachel and I attend as is." We didn't need special clothes for the Halls of Youth.

She annunciated every syllable and pointed at me. "We are looking cute," she ordered.

"Ok." So, Rebecca used my first name in sentences and Nicole annunciated her words when I was not allowed to argue.

Strumath laughed. "She can order the leader of the world around?"

"Corey hasn't quite taken over the world yet," said Leander. "I am the leader of forty-one-point-eight and negative eighty-seven-point-six."

"Yes, the witch." Strumath greeted Leander. "It's a pleasure to see you and not only hear your voice."

Too much was going around and I was about to face queen Niamh. I got dressed in the clothes Nicole brought. Fionnestra and

Verenuala made a curtain of leaves after Nicole asked for privacy. She wore a pink and green dress and we dressed behind the curtain. She even made Rachel wear a dress.

Rachel shuffled out and pulled the bottom of the flowered dress.

"I think you look beautiful," said Wesley. Rachel's frown changed to a grin. "Really? I've never worn a dress."

"We could pick one out together. For a date." He smiled.

They were getting it together.

SOON, NICOLE AND RACHEL looked cute. I looked like a dork in a suit, and we followed the giggling daoine with Drisana into a tree to go to the Spring Fey Court.

I hugged Drisana again and let her know she rocked and how Miles asked for her specifically. She pranced over to the hooved section of the court. It appeared she was becoming a celebrity of the unicorns, satyrs, and centaurs.

In front of the three of us, light green moss led to a path separated by a border of flowers for us to approach the throne. The path was almost ten feet wide and faeries, daoine, swan maidens, centaurs, satyrs, dryads, sylphs, pixies, and other Spring Court denizens lined up on either side of the path.

Nicole swung out her arm and stopped me from approaching. Rachel almost bumped into me.

"Could we get a different color to approach? My shoes are blending into the ground." Nicole said loudly and looked around.

I didn't recover from my shock before she continued. Who stops a procession in the Halls of Youth in the Fey Spring Court?

She answered something I did not hear. "It's important because these shoes were the first adult gift from Corey when he recognized me as a woman. It was also the day of our first kiss. He wanted to get me these shoes with the color of the first bud of Spring. I found the perfect dress to go with the shoes and it's important for the complete outfit that we see the shoes."

The middle of the moss became white stones for us to walk on.

"What am I biting off by marrying you?" I asked, still in shock.

"You and grandpa never stopped me from being in charge." She held out her arm, and I took it. Rachel strode on my other side and held my hand. She grinned at me and enjoyed this whole exchange.

Our feet clopped with our fancy go to meeting shoes along the white rock and I looked at the shoes I bought for Nicole in New Hampshire. She was right; they looked cute.

We approached Queen Niamh. She stood and said, "this was the most perfect request I can remember being made in this court." She walked around and said, "I understand why you made the request. You say the druid picked out those shoes?"

The queen wore a full-length gown of purple and blue flowers with green striping that blended into the ground. Her hair was now millions of rose petals that flowed around her head and accentuated her youthful face.

"The correct size and my favorite type, closed toe and kitten heel." She beamed.

"That is such a surprise. The Bard and Druid look so much different. Did you dress them?"

"Yes, Queen Niamh. They have many good qualities, but fashion and style are their blind spots."

The queen looked at me. "You have surprised me again. She is such a perfect addition to your life and to the Spring Court! More youthfulness, passion, intimacy, and do I detect fertility?"

I placed my hand on Nicole's stomach. "Queen Niamh, sometimes I feel like the luckiest man to ever lived. You are correct about everything."

The queen continued after the cheering. "I hereby approve of Nicole Hendrix, eventually Nicole Norwood, to be an official member of the Spring Court as Consort to the Druid of the Spring Court." Queen Niamh raised her hands and flowers rained down from the court.

I felt a burning across from the sun tattoo. Nicole jumped too and must have had a similar tattoo.

"Ooh," said Rachel. "Nicole Norwood."

"I have awarded the Consort our sun tattoo to travel, and I have given the couple a heart tattoo that will touch when they make love. When the hearts touch, the blast of their current emotions and desire will emanate out five hundred feet and touch everyone." The Queen announced and the entire court cheered, neighed, yelled and flitted around.

"This will be exciting," said Rachel. She grinned like she was looking forward to it.

PREACHER JON GATHERED his team, the team not visiting the Fey Spring Court. "The impossible has been done, and the success exceeded everyone's expectations. The first pass of the Shared Supernatural System has calculated the church cannot get the spell off in either Atlanta or Okinawa. We ended their spell three days early and they are out of back up plans."

The allies Corey pulled together, already separated out to their factions. Who could imagine vampires, witches, druids, bards, Scions, hunters, unicorns, and rebellious Realized coming together? What a pull on the river to bring this to bear.

"Have we verified it? The computer hasn't been the most reliable around Corey," asked Rebecca. Her wistful look was the only sad part of this complete victory. Corey had spun the Queen Niamh's wheel. Nicole had won, Rachel and the other girl that had not been identified, remained safe. He sacrificed Rebecca and destined her to feel the pain of losing love forever. The Fey Courts had plans for

Corey. Preacher Jon didn't say it out loud, but if the Fey Courts thought Corey would let Rebecca leave his life, they were in for a rude awakening.

"I will begin verification immediately," said Nathan.

"He means immediately in the morning," corrected Madison.

"You have worked hard, suffered, and deserve relaxation. But we have a bit of a crisis here." Preacher Jon hated slowing the celebration.

"Corey needed to address the groups," said Nathan. "I'll take Madison and make the excuse the Fey Court required him. We will try to hold the current good feelings and prepare for a longer lasting alliance."

"Excellent. Rebecca, you come with me and I will introduce you around and we'll give the same excuse."

"I still have some celestial power left and can heal a couple of people," she said. "Let me know who."

CJ pointed to Meat lying on the ground. "Since he saved you and Corey with a rib that Corey broke—could you help him out?"

Rebecca cast the young man in golden light and he stood up and touched himself in surprise.

Preacher Jon nodded. "Everyone, we'll get together before the end of the week for a full breakdown of our status, the church's status, and what everyone's plans will be." The call he promised to make this coming Saturday weighed on him. *What could he say to Mayven?*

Preacher Jon texted Richard and Carol to let them know they had won and he would visit tomorrow. He also texted Anne and said he would find out the day for Haley to connect with Corey in the next few days. Now he had work to do.

He led Rebecca over to Leander, and the other area leaders, with Samantha, Morgan, and Strumath.

Samantha hugged Rebecca. "It doesn't matter if you're not my daughter-in-law. You will be the same in my heart and please treat me as such."

"My reputation is going to suffer for finding a soft spot for a bunch of kids," lamented Morgan.

"I would not think that," said Leander. "In fact, the fear of Corey has been added to you."

Morgan smiled. "Druids are such problems."

Preacher Jon prepared to set up the next fights and discussions. Now that the threat was over, the weak territories will ask to close the Southeast again. This was Preacher Jon's fight. No one would hurt these kids. They sacrificed physically, emotionally, spiritually and changed for it. They earned the right to lead their lives.

Corey faced love, gargoyles, loss, heartbreak, uncertainty, and kept true to his vision of love. If people could not see the victory he achieved, they should not be leaders.

The immediate concerns were Corey's information on the Delta Territory. An army of vampires preparing for invasion was an immediate threat. Unless, of course, the church released the Nephilim and monsters from the caves. No one would attack the Southeast then because there would be little left.

Of course, they defeated the Vatican soundly. The Curia wouldn't put up with this type of loss, so maybe the Delta Vampires, the Nephilim, the monsters, and the Realized politicians had to wait. The church had plenty of resources and did not take losses lightly.

Don't miss out!

Visit the website below and you can sign up to receive emails whenever Shawn McGee publishes a new book. There's no charge and no obligation.

https://books2read.com/r/B-A-MTXT-HOVHC

BOOKS 2 READ

Connecting independent readers to independent writers.

Did you love *Caught up in You*? Then you should read *Wild Eyed Southern Boys*[1] by Shawn McGee!

Rebecca dumped him and then his mentor, Old Donnie, died, so Corey decided that he didn't need people and became a loner. He is nearly killed in his first encounter and his buddy from High School, Miles, and his codependent friend, Rachel, saved his life. He continued to go alone to gigs, even though injured, despite Rachel begging him not to go alone.

Gargoyles are trying to come back to Earth faster than they ever have before and Corey is the last person on Earth who can banish them. The problem is, he'd rather find a new woman in his life, brew a better batch of beer, and relax in nature.

---

1. https://books2read.com/u/b5qenl

2. https://books2read.com/u/b5qenl

If Corey can't go over his obsession with being a loner and accept the help of others, Atlanta, and the rest of the world is doomed. Read more at https://WorldofGeoe.com.

Also by Shawn McGee

The World of Geoe
The Herald
The Regnant
The Vanquisher

Wartime Druid Saga
Wild Eyed Southern Boys
Caught up in You
Fantasy Girl

Watch for more at https://WorldofGeoe.com.

About the Author

Shawn McGee writes fantasy and is an IT professional with hobbies in mathematics and gaming. Along with his current series he is writing a new gaming system.

Please this book as reviews are the life blood of independent writers.

You can join Shawn's discord channel, join his email list, and find out all the book information at https://worldofgeoe.com

Read more at https://WorldofGeoe.com.